A MATCH MADE AT MATLOCK

A SEQUEL TO PRIDE & PREJUDICE

JAN ASHTON

JULIE COOPER

AMY D'ORAZIO

JESSIE LEWIS

Quills & Quartos
PUBLISHING

Edited by Debra Anne Watson and Jo Abbott

Cover design by James T. Egan, www.bookflydesign.com

ISBN 978-1-956613-19-3 (ebook) and 978-1-956613-20-9 (paperback) "he will be spared the indignity of gossip when I steal you from him. Surely it is an act of mercy?"

She tittered and blushed, all the while trying for a severe frown at him; and in all, it was quite satisfactory. To Mrs Goddard, however, he could not be so charitable. No indeed, for such a mother as Mrs Goddard, he could offer only the most correct of bows and beat a hasty retreat to his seat.

Mrs Goddard, alas, was beautiful in the same way as her daughter was—blonde curls, large blue eyes, and a bosom that made a man wish to plant himself within it. He was not sure exactly how old she was, but she had most certainly not turned forty-five, and indeed, she looked a decade younger.

But Mrs Goddard's charms were interesting to him only insofar as they revealed to him his future. For it was her daughter, the darling, delightful, and undoubtedly delicious Miss Lillian Goddard who truly raised Saye's ardour. Miss Goddard would be, one day, Lady Saye—hopefully before she was required to become Lady Matlock—but not yet. He believed himself full young to contemplate the gravity of matrimony, and he supposed she was too.

The hens began to cackle and scratch over the *on dit* of the *ton* and Saye, well-versed in the ability to half-listen while he read the paper, found nothing of novelty or diversion in any of it. He had just begun to consider taking his leave when Mrs Goddard, with a sharp thrust of her knife into his bosom, said, "My Lilly shall receive an offer soon, I am quite certain."

Behind his newspaper, he raised one brow, suddenly alert to the conversation. It seemed as if time stood still while he held his breath, awaiting some response to what surely must have been a mistake.

"Really?" asked Aunt Fortescue. "From whom?"

"Mr Harold Balton-Sycke," said Mrs Goddard, whilst Saye

released his breath, carefully soundless. "Lord Saye, you might know the gentleman?"

He lowered the paper with a sharp twist. "What?" he asked, sounding as peevish as he possibly could.

"Mr Balton-Sycke," Aunt Fortescue prodded. "Do you know the gentleman?"

Mrs Goddard added, "I believe he mentioned he might have been at school with you."

Saye pretended to think about it before replying cheerily, "Oh yes. Carrot-haired blunderbuss from Norwich, I believe."

Mrs Goddard's brow wrinkled, no doubt uncertain whether he meant an insult or not. "Lowestoft. I daresay Lilly will be so very happy there. She has always loved the sea and—"

"The sea is nothing to the forest," Saye opined brusquely. "The problem with the sea is all the storms and the flooding. Give me a good forest any day."

The ladies paused, looking at him, and he wondered if Mrs Goddard was envisioning her precious Lilly swept away in a flood. The thought gave him a little satisfaction but was not nearly enough to calm the tempest in his breast. How dare *his* Lilly accept the attentions of another man?

At length, the ladies returned to their conversation. Lady Burlington, it turned out, once knew someone who might have been to the Balton-Sycke family seat and felt it her duty to describe every last coverlet and curtain to them all. Saye thought he bore it all with great dignity, despite the fact that he wished to box Mrs Goddard's ears and ask her what sense there was in giving such a lovely daughter over to a stupid oaf like Balton-Sycke, known among those of Saye's set as Hairy Ball-Sack.

It came to pass that his aunt wished to know when the engagement might occur. "It could be another month complete, likely more," Mrs Goddard said regretfully. "Mr Balton-Sycke will be away from town with his sister, but once he returns..."

A month, likely more. Saye's mind was instantly enlivened. But what to do? Could anything be done? Surely she did not love the idiot, did she? At once, all three ladies were looking at him. "I beg your pardon, Aunt?" he asked.

"*I asked*," said Aunt Fortescue, "if I was wrong in thinking you once had a tendre for Miss Goddard."

The three ladies awaited his answer with faint smiles and mild interest. No doubt the civil thing to do would be to answer in the affirmative, rhapsodise over her beauty, and proclaim Hairy Ball-Sack a lucky fellow. Alas, Saye was rarely civil if another choice was given to him. He yawned, his mouth wide, then spoke in a disinterested tone. "I might have danced with her once. Short girl, is she not?"

Mrs Goddard's expectant smile faded into an uncertain frown. "No, not so short. Indeed, not short at all."

"A tall girl then? Cannot think I have danced with too many of those."

"Not tall either," Mrs Goddard protested. "Really, just a very common height. A pretty height." Looking around at the other ladies, she added, "I have always thought my children were the best possible heights. Nothing notable, neither too short, nor too tall. And in any case, my lord, she has lovely blonde hair and blue eyes."

"Very handsome girl," Lady Burlington said. "Very handsome indeed."

Saye rose. Gesturing at the women with his index finger, he said, "What you all ought to do is assign them a colour. Start of the Season, get two, three gowns, all the same colour. Then when a man wants to know about this woman or that, we simply say, 'she's the rose coloured one' or 'the one who wears green' and everyone knows exactly what's what."

He strolled to his aunt, bending to kiss her cheek. She was amused by him, he could tell, giving him an indulgent grin. "Think of all the money you should save," he added before excusing himself and leaving the old birds to their clacking.

Across town, in her mother's drawing room, Miss Lilly Goddard sat amongst the ladies she had known since her girlhood. Lady Euphemia Boothe had been the first of them to marry, likely because she boasted the most determined and unyielding mother. Miss Georgette Hawridge had been the *Incomparable* of their Season; a noted beauty with a fine fortune and exceedingly good connexions, she always had a faint expression of ennui that made gentlemen and ladies alike desperate to pique her interest. Georgette was forever receiving offers—the latest from one of the de Borchgraves of Belgium, which she had infuriated her family by refusing. Then there was dear Miss Sarah Bentley, who despite her sweetness and fortune was commonly left to sit at balls—likely because when a man did ask her to dance, she would too often run his ear off speaking of her decidedly unusual interests.

Euphemia had taken poor Sarah in her sights; having introduced her to a cousin of her husband—a dreadful old fellow with yellow teeth and an unfortunate propensity to suck on them—she wholly expected Sarah to run poetic over him.

"I thought you wanted to get married," Euphemia huffed.

"I did. I do! But..."

"At a masque?" Sarah asked.

"It began there," Lilly admitted. "But I went out onto the terrace with him later, for air."

"For air," Euphemia moaned. "How often a path to doom begins by going to the terrace for air!"

Lilly could not help herself—she had to giggle at Euphemia's theatrics. "I assure you, I am not doomed."

"You will be if you do not accept Mr Balton-Sycke!" Euphemia retorted.

"In any case," said Lilly softly, then continued telling her friends the sweet remembrances of that delightful evening, the scent of roses in the air and Saye gently easing her mask from her face, then not-so gently tossing it behind him as he kissed her quite beyond anything she had ever thought possible. And then! "He made me some promises."

"Promises?" Sarah asked.

Lilly blushed hotly but managed to tell her friends what Saye had promised her. It had shocked and scandalised her at the time, and it still did, mostly—but she was more than a little intrigued by it all.

"Impossible!" Euphemia declared while Sarah pointed out that the mantid species was known to eat males after their usefulness was concluded. To Georgette, however, the acts described did not seem quite so shocking. She wore a self-conscious half smile and looked away from the group. Lilly resolved to ask her about it all later.

"When I think about doing any such thing with Balton-Sycke," she said, "I feel rather nauseated. But with Saye..."

Georgette's small smile had now grown to a full-out grin, but she still said nothing, allowing Euphemia and Sarah to express all the outrage that was expected. Well, Euphemia had married a man who was nearly fifty, who could blame her? And Sarah? For all her fortune and good family, she was nearly wholly disinterested in feminine pursuits; fashion bored her, she was useless with a needle, and she fell over her own feet when she danced.

Lilly allowed them to turn the conversation to the delights of redecorating the house in Lowestoft, but somehow she knew that wall hangings and rugs could not colour in the lines of a grey existence. While the two other ladies were entering Euphemia's carriage, Lilly touched Georgette's arm, wordlessly asking that she accompany her.

Georgette gestured towards the street, likely needing a turn in the cold air as much as Lilly herself did. Her mother was ever-fond of a good blaze, and their rooms were nearly always stifling. When they had walked a short distance, Georgette said, "Well, Lilly, I am proud of you. You are much naughtier than I ever gave you credit for."

"I have not done anything naughty *yet*, much to his lordship's dismay. But am I a fool to consider turning my back on Balton-Sycke for...for...?" Lilly gestured helplessly.

"*Délicieux jeux d'amour?*" asked Georgette frankly, and made Lilly blush.

"No! I mean, yes...more like the general enjoyment of life! I do not mean to say that I do not enjoy spending time with—"

"I know exactly what you mean," Georgette said. "And do not think I censure you for it. Indeed, I do not! We shall, all of us, grow old with these men. Once the thrill of engagements and weddings has worn off, there must be more to life!"

"I agree," Lilly replied warmly. "And that brings me to the greatest problem of all."

"That my cousin has not spoken?"

"Oh yes," said Lilly. "I do tend to forget you are related to him."

"On Lady Matlock's side. But my darling girl, you must

know Saye might have said those things merely to be shocking."

"I know," Lilly groaned. "And I have scarcely even had the opportunity to be in society with him since that masque. I do not know if it was anything of significance, or merely the words of a man who had drunk too much and wished to steal a few kisses."

"The heart wants what it wants. Sometimes all other considerations must be laid aside."

"You sound like you know something of the matter," Lilly said with a sidelong glance at her friend. "Have you some secret lover that none of us knows of?"

Georgette laughed. "Do you not know everything I do? Come now! Mr Balton-Sycke is gone for a month. Surely there must be some way to use the time to advantage?"

"I must," Lilly said determinedly. "I cannot accept Balton-Sycke, but neither can I refuse him, not with my mother all but shopping for my trousseau."

"Just think of your strategy carefully," her friend advised, "because nothing so easy will make that boy don the leg shackles."

The January air bit at Saye as he exited his aunt's house and walked swiftly towards his club, but he scarcely felt it. His mind raced with plans and schemes and horrifying visions of what would happen if he failed to stop this calamitous event.

He had just turned onto Piccadilly when a vision arrested him. *Her*—or at least he thought it was her, blast those accursed bonnets!—walking with his cousin Georgette. For a moment he thought of walking over to them, but no; they appeared deep in conversation and, in any case, he knew not

IN WANT OF A WIFE | 11

what he might say except to demand that she immediately throw aside any notions of Ball-Sack.

His swift stride became a pensive stroll as he entered his club, nearly hurling his overcoat at the waiting manservant as he espied his brother and Darcy sitting at a table. Darcy was looking rather thunderous himself, but Saye had no time for his whinging. Today *he* would have the luxury of the whinge, and they would all shut their pie holes and hear him.

"Where have you been all morning?" Fitzwilliam asked by way of greeting.

"To visit Aunt Fortescue," he replied tersely, "and it was there I learnt of a horrible disaster about to happen."

"What is it this week?" Darcy asked. "A spot on your trousers?"

"Or on Florizel?" Fitzwilliam suggested, referring to Saye's snow-white Pomeranian.

"Maybe his carriage had the cheek to get dirty," Darcy teased.

"Or perhaps—"

"Enough," Saye snapped. "Ridicule me later if you like, but this time I have a dreadfully serious problem and there is nothing in the least humorous about it."

He paused then, scowling at them both until they assumed more contrite countenances; then he announced, with no little ceremony, "My wife is contemplating matrimony to Hairy Ball-Sack."

"Who?" asked Darcy.

"Harold Balton-Sycke from Lowestoft," Fitzwilliam informed him. "Good fellow. A year behind me at school."

"Oh yes! Has that sister who sings so beautifully."

"The very one. Good family."

"Listen here!" Saye interrupted. "The relative merits of Ball-Sack's family are irrelevant! She cannot marry him, because if she does, then she cannot marry *me*! Now let us think and think hard, men. I have one month to vanquish Ball-Sack and steal his girl, and we must plan how to do it. Darcy—you have come back from the ashes with Miss Barnett, tell me how you did it."

"Bennet."

"What's that?"

"Miss Elizabeth Bennet," Darcy said patiently. "Her name, Saye, is Miss Elizabeth Bennet."

"Bennet, Barnett, Bassett... Does it really signify? She will surrender it soon enough for a better one, will she not? And then I shall call her Lizzy," Saye retorted.

"Or Elizabeth, if she permits it," Darcy replied.

"Or Liza. She seems like a Liza."

"*Elizabeth.*"

"Zabet," Saye mused. "I heard of a gypsy called Zabet once and I was rather taken with the name."

"You will not call my wife a gypsy name," Darcy said stiffly. "Why must we always have these stupid conversations?"

"You are right, you are right," Saye conceded. "What Zabet wishes to be called is her own business, and my business is winning Lilly Goddard. How to do it is the less easy matter."

"Here is an idea," Fitzwilliam said. "What if you called on her, asked her to dance, were kind to her mother et cetera, and then simply asked for her hand?" He gave a little smirk that encompassed both his relations. "You both have a penchant for making things difficult that need not be."

"Oh really?" asked Darcy. "Well, where is your wife?"

"A facer on you, Richard," Saye added gleefully. "Where is your wife indeed?"

Fitzwilliam shrugged. "The Season is not kind to a poor soldier," he said, with more candour than was his wont. "The ladies are more apt to be enchanted by the young bucks flashing their blunt, most of whom are not even seriously pursuing matrimony. Darcy got the last good woman—I am sure of it."

As it was, there was a small estate that Saye had inherited along with his viscountcy. It was in an unfashionably north-eastern part of England, and the weather there was far too cold, but it would do for a second son. Lord Matlock had forbidden him to confer it until Fitzwilliam was engaged to a lady they all approved of, fearing he might find himself tricked into some unsuitable alliance. His brother could be rather heedless when it came to female temptations.

"Until Mr Bennet yields, I cannot marry her," Darcy intoned glumly. "We have had, already, a lengthy journey to become engaged, and I begin to fear the engagement itself will be longer still."

"Well, perhaps I shall have time to win her yet," Fitzwilliam said with a grin. He leant over then and gave Darcy a little punch on the arm. "She did rather enjoy my society at Rosings."

"She had little choice as you were forever hanging about her," Darcy muttered.

Like the days in the nursery. Saye sighed heavily. He had been forever stopping fights between the pair of them back then. "Your error," he told Darcy, "is that you neglected to anticipate your vows. Fathers become remarkably agreeable to nuptial haste once their daughters are despoiled. But enough about Zabet, we need to get back to my problems."

"Will Elizabeth be coming to town soon?" Fitzwilliam asked.

"*Miss Bennet* will come to town sometime before Easter," Darcy replied with a hard stare. "When Mr and Mrs Bingley take a house."

Fitzwilliam said something, but Saye scarcely noticed. He

had been, at last, struck by inspiration. "We should have a house party at Matlock!"

That stopped their squabbling. He continued, "I shall invite Georgette and her friends—"

"Georgette?" Fitzwilliam gave him a quizzical look.

"Our cousin. I like her, and we need to spend more time with that side of the family," Saye informed him piously. "I shall ask dear Zabet, perhaps some few of her many sisters—"

"Stop calling her Zabet."

"—an assortment of lovelies for my brother...with a masquerade ball, to be sure, to give the poor sod a fighting chance with them..."

"Travel to Matlock may be difficult," Darcy opined.

"Bah!" Saye said. "The roads are as good as any in the Empire."

He felt, suddenly, as good as he had felt for some time. Yes, bringing her to Matlock was just the thing. Let her see the place which would be her own, let her feel his significance apart from the ribaldry of London. He could already imagine his attire—not the dandy of town, but a country gentleman. A country gentleman with *éclat* to be sure.

"So you get Miss Goddard to Matlock," Fitzwilliam said. "And then?"

"And then I make her love me and accept my offer of marriage, and Hairy Ball-Sack crawls back into the sea where he belongs."

"Saye," Fitzwilliam said, laying a hand on his arm. "Just tell me this. Do you love her?"

"Do I love her?" Saye gaped at his brother. Every so often, he was reminded of just how stupid his brother really was, and this was surely one of those times.

"Yes. Do you love her?"

"Or do you just want to win her?" Darcy asked.

"That is a fool's question."

"But what is the answer?" Fitzwilliam insisted. "Love? Or the need to claim victory?"

With a deep sigh, Saye shoved his face into his hands. "I should not be required to—"

Darcy said, "Saye, if you want this woman so badly, it should not be such a difficulty to—"

"Yes! Does it suit you? Yes, yes, yes, I love her, and if I cannot have her, I shall die of misery. Besting Hairy Ball-Sack is a nice side victory, but it is nothing to my need to have her for my wife."

With a curse, he rose, shoving his chair violently against the table. He cursed again for good measure, and spun on his heel, stalking through the club, glaring angrily at everyone he saw.

When he had nearly gained the door, a large hand clapped him on the shoulder, arresting his progress. He turned to see Darcy had risen and followed him and even now offered a compassionate grin.

"Come back to the table," he said. "Your brother has ordered some of the French brandy brought out for us. Let us toast another man down!"

THE RITUALS OF ROMANCE

Sarah & Fitzwilliam

S arah Bentley left her friend's house full of shock, bemusement, wonder, and another emotion—one so seldom experienced that it took her some moments to identify it.

Envy. She was envious of Lilly. Oh, she had always adored her, of course, but she had never envied her, regardless of the fact that Lilly was far prettier and wittier, more fashionable, more graceful, and infinitely more daring. Sarah had not needed to envy her in a life so full as her own.

She lived in London in a big old house called, foolishly, The Pillows, because of the twin white brick chimneys—Papa had them painted religiously every summer—perched against its topside like two fat cushions. Papa was the younger brother of the Earl of Hampton, and still his heir. Her uncle, the earl, had produced two daughters he doted upon, and was perfectly content that his title be passed along to Papa at some date well in the future.

Papa, in turn, hoped his brother retained the title as long as humanly possible. It used to worry him, once upon a time, because management of the Hampton properties took a great deal of organisation and attention, none of which could be spared from his scientific studies. But the birth of his son—Sarah's younger brother, Percival, and the apple of her eye—nine years past had eased these concerns significantly, even as it had taken her dear Mama's life.

And though the loss of Mama was tragic, and she missed her dearly, taking over the running of the household at the age of fourteen had formed her character. She could now take pride in a household expertly managed, confident her servants would never cheat her.

However, the earl had taken over Percy's education this past year, lest Papa's bent for the scholarly be allowed to bloom within his son, and the future of the earldom be neglected amidst dusty libraries and musty papers. It was wonderful for young Percy, who adored his uncle, and riding magnificent horses across huge properties, and being spoiled and made much of by his elder cousins, both of whom were now happily married and producing grandchildren, much to the earl's delight. But it left a hole in Sarah's soft heart.

She handed her wrap to Bertie, the shorter of the two footmen guarding the entryway. Sarah knew the fashionable set liked their footmen to be handsome men of great height, perfectly matched, but she firmly held with giving her home's best positions to the kindest servants, and those were seldom the tallest, handsomest ones. Bertie, more freckle than face, would never be handsome, and she had had to change the colour of their livery when she promoted him, for the plum velvet uniforms of old clashed horribly with his red hair.

"Has Papa returned safely from the British Museum?" she asked. Papa had been known to lose track of time, and once had actually been locked inside when it was shut up for the evening and no one noticed him. She had spent a horridly anxious night, while he had come home the next morning not a bit worse for wear, chuckling at the whole episode and hoping aloud it would happen again.

"Oh, yes, miss. He's in his book room. Hasn't touched his tray yet, Mrs Figg says."

Sarah sighed. "Thank you, Bertie. I shall see to it."

She found her father, as expected, poring over a thick volume while his stew had gone cold. "Papa, you must eat! You promised you would not neglect your dinner if I went to Miss Goddard's for the day."

Wendell Bentley looked up, blinking as though he had just awakened. "Princess, you are home so soon! How do all your friends do?"

Flopping down in a somewhat inelegant manner, she sighed. "They do well enough. Except Lilly has a desperate *tendre* for Lord Saye, which worries me exceedingly. He is not always polite, if you take my meaning. I know enough of the world to never take safety for granted."

Mr Bentley's brow furrowed. "Saye, hmm. Matlock's eldest? *Aglais io*, I believe. Not a predator. Matlock would not stand for him hurting females."

Sarah giggled. "I wonder if Lord Saye would appreciate his comparison to a peacock butterfly?" It was what she liked best about Papa. Having little idea how to be a father, neither did he realise the numerous subjects he was not supposed to discuss with her.

Mrs Figg tapped on the door and was admitted, carrying a new tray with a steaming bowl. Adeptly, she exchanged it for the old one.

"See that he eats his stew, mistress. Cook will have his hide if she has to make him another, and it's tired I am of hearing my own self speak as though I'm alone in the room," she complained.

"I shall, Mrs Figg," Sarah assured. The housekeeper was stick-thin with iron grey hair and a crusty disposition—and because the kindest servants were not always the pleasantest ones, Sarah paid little attention to her grumbling. Mrs Figg was also her right hand when it came to overseeing Papa, and simply because she had been too busy to compel him to eat earlier did not mean she was incapable of managing him.

When the housekeeper was gone, Sarah enjoined, "Please, eat now, Papa, if you care for me at all, while I tell you all my troubles."

Mr Bentley obligingly took a helping, smiling benignly.

"I want a mate."

He choked a little, and Sarah was obliged to pound him on the back several times before he regained his composure. "Perhaps you ought to tell this particular trouble to your aunt, Princess," he said. "I am no hand at selecting husbands. Too selfish. Would rather you stay at home, making my life comfortable."

"Oh, no," Sarah replied, settling back into her chair. "Aunt would only set about resolving the issue, and I would have a line of suitors at my door within a fortnight. They would all be respectable men, reasonably handsome, but they would expect me to tidily fit within their list of expectations—and if I do not now, I should begin to do so. At once."

"*Chrysis ruddii*," he nodded.

She smiled again. "Cuckoo wasps, taking over the nests of the rightful inhabitants for their own mating purposes," she agreed. "I fear so. Lilly is in love with Lord Saye. I hope you are correct, and she is safe with him. It would be a better match than any of the *Lymantria dispar* constantly swarming around Georgette, making pests of themselves, while she is *Hamearis Lucina*—exotic, almost. But, I fear, most of the men I have met at parties, balls, and musicales are of Euphemia's husband's ilk. *Meloe aprilina*. Bulbous abdomens from living off the hard work of bees."

"Grinding the faces of the poor?" Mr Bentley replied somewhat cryptically, but Sarah knew her Bible.

"Exactly. I did have a reasonably intelligent dinner conversation with Mr Balton-Sycke once, and I thought he might do. But he took one look at Lilly and was lost."

Mr Bentley quickly took a large spoonful, presumably so he would not have to offer advice regarding Mr Balton-Sycke's infatuation with Lilly.

"I do not mind it, I promise, and it seems a good match for both. Although I think, upon further observation, that he does not truly want Lilly. He wants the idea of Lilly—*Colias croceus*, pretty and golden—without ever considering her inner depths. And although he is such a lovely dancer, so light on his feet, I daresay a graceful manner is no more an indicator of a good husband than Lilly's desire for an amusing one. If only he was *Maniola jurtina*, because with an ability to survive and adapt anywhere, he could have potential for either of us. But if she wants *Aglais io*, his cause is hopeless, and if he wants *Colias croceus*, mine is as well."

Sarah did not really have the entire insect world memorised. But she had discovered long ago that if she wished to have more than shallow conversations with her father, she would need to learn the language he spoke most fluently.

"I am pretty enough, really. But my figure is too generous, I cannot dance well, no matter how many masters you hire, and I have been told I have a rather odd taste in acceptable topics of conversation, especially at meals. On the other hand, my fortune is substantial, my virtue unblemished, and my lineage impeccable. All the good and all the bad seem to have cancelled each other out."

Mr Bentley smiled fondly, finishing the last of his bowl. "You will find what is best for you, Princess. And your topics of conversation at dinner are superlative."

Of course he would think so; she was not unconscious

that her education had been a peculiar one. She sighed, gathering up his tray, and pecked him on the forehead before heading for the door.

She had every intention of invading Cook's kitchen tonight. What would it be, an apple tart or an almond cheese cake? Or perhaps rice-flour pancakes. There was something so satisfying about having her hands amongst the butter, sugar, flour, and eggs, of the scent of baking wafting through the back parlours, of creating something covetous from simple ingredients. It helped her think, and calm. And, since she always shared the bounty of her ovens with the entire household, no one minded her untidiness—she did not much care for cleaning up after herself.

Sarah was almost to the door when Papa's voice stopped her.

"*Pyrochroa serraticornis* larvae," he said.

She turned to face him, a quizzical expression upon her face. "What?"

"*Pyrochroa serraticornis* larvae are flat. Like Mr Balton-Sycke. He is flat, a fool."

She beamed at her father. "Thank you, Papa," she said, but his attention had already drifted back to the thick tome upon his desk, and he did not hear.

Colonel Richard Fitzwilliam left his brother and Darcy at the club, both almost too involved in schemes and plotting of this stupid house party notion to notice his departure. He had to pretend enthusiasm, of course, or be subjected to incessant teasing.

Saye falling in love had hit Fitzwilliam hard.

He was not sure exactly why; he had always known his

brother would marry—there was never any question of the title falling to Fitzwilliam. And he had revelled in his ability to choose his own path, while his brother seemed perfectly fitted for an earldom.

Saye was the consummate bored aristocrat, sailing through life and various peccadillos practically untouched. Fitzwilliam had seconded him in no less than three duels; though Saye was a deadly shot, he could discharge his weapon in the air, make a joke out of the whole affair and somehow, by the time the meeting had finished, the duellists were drinking together. It was as if strong emotion could not touch him.

And Fitzwilliam had been glad.

It was simply that...in all he lost by being the younger son, he had supposed fate gifted him an extra margin of, well, strength of emotion. Saye would retain wealth and political power, but Fitzwilliam would be allotted another type of power entirely—the power of love.

Of course, he would have to shoot *himself* were he to admit any of this aloud.

He had always felt things deeply; a sensitive child, his father had ensured his tutors were of the type to toughen a man. He did not regret it, either, for he would not like to be some poetry-spouting fool wearing his heart on his sleeve. Furthermore, he understood his financial position; from his mother, he would have a modest inheritance, but it was unexceptional. He could not marry where he liked, and it had never truly bothered him—he had supposed love to be a choice, and it would be just as easy to choose an heiress as an impoverished gentlewoman.

That was, until he had fallen in love—or *something*, at least—with an impoverished gentlewoman.

Elizabeth Bennet was everything he had ever dreamt of in a woman...except for her non-existent portion. Witty, clever, amusing, and stunningly beautiful—he had been gripped by an interest in her since the moment of making her acquaintance. Even knowing it was hopeless—and ensuring she knew, as well—he could not help spending every moment possible in her company.

The previous Easter's sojourn at Rosings Park had been the happiest he had ever known. His dreams, of course, would remain only dreams, and though it pained him, he was glad to learn of her likes and dislikes, to know her just a little. Darcy was often with them both; it had not mattered. He had been more the paper on their walls—present, but not a part of things.

And then, on the final night of their holiday at Rosings, Darcy had confessed his love for Elizabeth and her rejection of his suit.

Once he was alone again after *that* conversation, Fitzwilliam had fallen to his knees in gratitude. If there was one thing worse than falling for a woman too poor to marry, it would be having one's younger, wealthier, more handsome cousin manage the business. Thankfully, it appeared, such an awful fate was to be avoided.

Alas, fate was a cruel mistress. In the end, Darcy won the hand of the maiden fair, and it was all Fitzwilliam could do to listen to his soliloquies upon her beauty, wit, and perfections without betraying his envy.

And now there was to be a house party, and two weeks of being in company with Elizabeth and Darcy! Of witnessing the growth of their rapport, the beauty of new love. Resentment wrapped her talons around his neck, choking the life from him.

Worse, he knew his family would ensure that other highly eligible females were in attendance. He wanted to know love, he did! But it would be impossible while Elizabeth was near, a constant reminder of 'if only'. Cupid's arrow was doomed to miss its mark at this particular party.

Sarah was an unusually good cook—she truly was. But as any scientist understood—and she firmly believed cooking to be a science—there were rules to be followed. The proper ingredients in the proper measure, at the proper time and proper heat. Even then, such inconsistencies as humidity could foil even the best cook.

Sadly, tonight's fiasco had nothing whatsoever to do with sultry air, and everything to do with Lord Saye's whispered wooing words to Lilly. How, precisely, was such a thing to be accomplished? It sounded anatomically impossible, and yet...curiously intriguing. Thus, she was unsure whether she had added the correct number of eggs—had she used six or eight? Did she put in the orange flower water twice? Had she remembered to remove two of the whites? Ah, well, nothing a little more flour could not solve. And then a little more cream. Or had she already added extra?

After trying for some time to fix everything that was wrong with her efforts, she sighed.

Cook peered over at the gloopy mixture. "Looks like ye could kill a man with that one," she chuckled. "Whoever heard of the Quality drudgin' about in the kitchen, I ask ye? Ye weren't born fer it, an' here's the proof." Nothing put Cook on her high ropes more than Sarah's infrequent culinary failures.

Sarah sighed again. "I shall toss this out in the mews. No matter how awful, the cats will enjoy it," she muttered.

"It's full dark out now," Cook said, peering out of the

window, shaking her head. "Ye'll likely catch somethin' from them toms if not the chill. Leave it until tomorrow."

"No, I want to begin afresh, and the cats will appreciate my efforts—besides which, I believe it will never come out if I do not scrape it tonight. I may have hit upon the receipt for bricks. I shall return in a moment," she said, and, throwing a dark woollen shawl around her shoulders, ran out of the back door.

Fitzwilliam had been wandering the streets, paying little attention to his direction, avoiding a return to his lonely bachelor rooms. Still, the neighbourhood was a good one, well-lit and quiet, not far from Darcy House. It took him several moments, therefore, to realise he was being followed.

Once he knew it, an eagerness filled him. Combat beckoned, with real enemies at hand, and his mouth stretched wide in a malevolent grin. For soft-hearted he might be, but that heart was surrounded by a tough shell of battle-readiness honed in real war campaigns.

The villains, two of them by the sound, were sticking to the shadows, but they were clumsy and far too noisy. *Amateurs.* Unlikely he would even need to draw his weapon. His tutors had trained him in combat methods not seen at Gentleman Jackson's.

He presumed they would attack in the darkness of the mews ahead; he would be ready. *A little farther…a bit more…*

At the point of deepest shadow, he suddenly pivoted, leaping at his would-be attackers. But at that exact moment, an unholy shriek—sounding like a thousand toms in heat—screeched in his ears while a bucket-load of viscous batter swiped the side of his head. The nasty mixture hit the miscreants as well, the bowl bouncing off the taller one's head and shattering on the cobbles; the pair scrabbled away down the street like the rats they were.

Fitzwilliam wiped the mush from his eyes, turning to see what monster of the gloom had come to assault him.

It was a girl. In the lamplight, he could see she was pretty, plump, dark-haired, and little else.

"What the devil were you thinking?" he bellowed, the energy of the aborted fight still filling him.

"I was *thinking* that you were about to be attacked!" she shouted back. But there was no mistaking her cultured accents. "I brought the botched paste out for the cats, and saw two men sneaking up on you! If you hadn't jumped into the way, all of it would have landed upon them!"

"Are you daft? They were not kittens waiting to lick up a kitchen treat! They were criminals!"

"Were you leading them along? What kind of fool lures criminals into darkened mews when he is outnumbered two to one?"

"I am a medalled colonel in His Majesty's army—I needed no assistance from a–a cat-lady!"

She was quiet, and he was thankful he had quelled her. Now that he had made his point, he opened his mouth to apologise for distressing her, if indeed he had.

"If I am a cat-lady, you are the cat's paw," she muttered.

"What?" He could hardly believe his ears. Did she think her ill-timed, even dangerous interference a joke?

"Oh, now, it was hardly a cat-astrophe," she said. "You needn't caterwaul."

"'Daft' is too kind!" he accused, disavowing all ideas of apologies in favour of wiping his face with a large hand-kerchief.

"Do not be ashamed—you were within a whisker of getting your man." And suddenly, she began to laugh. And laugh, and laugh. "I–I am sorry," she gasped, when she caught her breath. "Your whiskers! With the dough dripping from your beard, you look so–so..." then snorting again in a most *un*-ladylike manner. "Im-*purr*-fect!" And off she went again into peals of laughter.

Fitzwilliam glared at her with distaste. "I am grateful to have been an object for your humour," he gritted.

With an observable effort, she regained control. "I am sorry," she apologised again, wiping her eyes with the edge of her shawl and looking somewhat rueful.

"Miss Bentley? Miss Bentley!" a voice from the back of the house called.

"Coming, Cook!" the girl—Miss Bentley—called back. "Would you care to come into the house and tidy yourself up?" she asked politely.

"No, thank you," Fitzwilliam replied coldly. "I wish you a pleasant evening." He turned on his heel.

"Good-night, Mr Cat—er, Mr Colonel." She gave another small giggle, and then a sigh. "Drat. And that was my favourite bowl, too."

THE PLEASURE
OF YOUR COMPANY

Darcy & Elizabeth

Miss *Elizabeth Bennet.*

She read her name silently, then aloud. Elizabeth had never seen her name written so exquisitely. Certainly, she had never received a proper invitation to a house party on a faraway estate. Dinners and card parties, holidays with her aunt and uncle Gardiner, and visits to see Charlotte Collins were nothing to this.

Lady Aurelia Ferb-Uxbridge requests the pleasure of your company for a House Party at Matlock Court, Derbyshire. An answer is requested.

"Oh my," she whispered.

Darcy had written to her, telling her to expect an invitation from Saye's sister and urging her, begging her to come. *It all has been planned to facilitate my cousin Saye's wooing of the lady he hopes to wed, and allows us time together in company.*

In company. How she would love to spend time with him in a small society, in a setting where she could become acquainted with his friends and relations. Conversation and companionship with ladies and gentlemen of education and experience in the world. Humour, even, if she were fortunate.

Who would be at Matlock? She was acquainted with Colonel Fitzwilliam; he was enjoyable company. Elizabeth had imagined what his brother, Lord Saye, might be like— and how he might differ from his brother—based on Darcy's comments on his cousin's dedication to fashion and disinclination to suffer those he did not like. She could only hope the latter would not apply to her. Their sister, Lady Aurelia, was somewhat older than she and had been well-married the past three years, but Darcy had never mentioned other ladies to her—good manners would preclude any such comment. When Elizabeth pressed him on how he ever came to fall in love with *her*, Darcy was adamant in his assurances—before he met her, he had never noticed another woman's eyes or figure and had never endeavoured to determine a lady's mood from a smile or expression. Elizabeth smiled just thinking of his ardency in convincing her of his devotion.

This house party provided a wonderful opportunity to convince him of *her* devotion. More so, it was an escape from the monotony of Longbourn, an opportunity to meet the sisters and future wives of those gentlemen with whom Darcy associated—creating friendships and alliances with members of the *ton* who mattered most to her future life. After all, if she could not yet be married and be mistress of Pemberley, a house party with Darcy—in his home county, at his uncle's estate—offered her the next best thing. She might even gain a bit of the town bronze that Miss Bingley thought deficient in the Bennet sisters. Darcy would laugh at such a thought.

She bowed her head. Oh how she missed him.

After finding perfect harmony with Darcy, enjoying felicity and conversation neither had enjoyed with another,

Elizabeth now found herself more alone than she had ever imagined.

She had been too long at Longbourn, in a household she had outgrown, without good company. Jane was occupied at Netherfield with her new husband; Mrs Bennet was idle and vexed that Elizabeth's wedding was delayed; Mary and Kitty were often at odds; and her father's companionship had grown wearisome. He had kept her at home, with infrequent visits from Darcy in the weeks they had been separated. Of late, Mr Bennet was in mercurial spirits, as likely to permit as to deny her request to attend Matlock.

But what was a fortnight of pleasure and society to her father when he knew he would have her returned for close to another month afterwards, bursting with stories that might amuse him?

After Lydia, how could he deny me this? I have never disappointed him.

Elizabeth rose from her chair, equal parts excitement and trepidation, and glanced into the sitting room, where her mother and Kitty were sewing. Mrs Bennet would champion her request, but Elizabeth was just as aware that her father's intransigence would only deepen if confronted by his wife's demands and histrionics.

I am not the green girl he thinks me to be, but neither should I have to plot and scheme to get his approval.

Taking a deep breath, she knocked and entered his library. Mr Bennet looked up from his book and smiled. "Come in, Lizzy. I have wished to laugh with you about Kitty's unfortunate encounter with Mrs Goulding's angry rooster."

With no desire to hear her sister mocked yet again, Elizabeth closed the door and walked over to the desk, piled high with unopened ledgers and letters. "Papa, I have something to ask you."

Mr Bennet's eyes fell to the letter in her hands. "What have you there?"

Once the words 'house party' and 'Darcy's cousin' were spoken, Elizabeth's plans for discussion, debate, and negotiation found no purchase. Her father peered closely through his spectacles at the card she had given to him.

"Lady Aurelia, or perhaps her maid, has a fine hand, but yours is nearly as fine. You will impress her when you write to her and decline the invitation." He took off his eyeglasses and began polishing them with his handkerchief. "You will be part of such society soon enough. There is no reason to rush yourself into such dreadful company."

Astonishment at his blithe dismissal coursed through her. "This 'dreadful company' includes Darcy's cousins, who will soon be my family as well."

"Soon enough."

"You must see that declining such an offer will offend Lady Aurelia and my future relations."

"Those who dwell in the *ton*'s top spheres are accustomed to the eccentricities of country folk." Mr Bennet smiled at her in a sardonic manner that Elizabeth knew all too well. "Have patience, Lizzy. A little time apart cannot dampen the ardour of true love, only strengthen it. What is another six weeks at Longbourn with your family?"

"Exactly. What is the purpose of *another six weeks* here? There is no reason in what you ask of us with this delay. We are in—"

Mr Bennet waved away her protestations. "In love, yes, yes, of course. But Mr Darcy is asking too much too soon. We have an understanding about your understanding."

"As I see it, Papa, this 'understanding' of yours feels more like an excessive imposition."

"Lizzy—"

"Not even the thought of my collecting amusing stories

about the ridiculous conceits of the rich and ridiculous can tempt your consent?"

"I anticipate years of amusing stories from you." Mr Bennet folded his hands across his stomach and tapped his thumbs together. His own earlier amusement was gone, replaced by mild irritation. "Lizzy, I will not have you be missish."

"Do not worry, sir. I shall write the reply you require."

Yes, she would write to Lady Aurelia, but that letter could wait. Surely her mother would have much to say on the beauty of the invitation, among other things.

"Devil take it!"

I am so sorry, dearest. Under the terms of our understanding with my father, I am not to join you and your family at Matlock.

How dare a man as indolent as Mr Bennet set rules and restrictions on his daughter's future with the man she loved? Where had this paternal figure been when his youngest daughter ran off with an unrepentant reprobate?

Darcy's eyes traced again the words Elizabeth had written. How could her father, whose similarity to his detestably officious cousin Mr Collins was becoming ever more apparent, deny Elizabeth this opportunity? He disdained town and society and was ensuring his favourite daughter had no chance to make the acquaintance of those who would like her and support her in her transition to becoming Mrs Darcy.

Not only did Bennet hold firm to his ridiculous belief that Darcy would lose interest in Elizabeth once he made her his wife, he now denied his daughter her rightful place at a house party of reputable single ladies and gentlemen. Did Bennet not consider that rumours might arise at this furthering distance between himself and his unknown country girl? Could he engineer a way to get her there, *out* from under her father's thumb?

"I should ride in and sweep her away on my horse."

Furious and frustrated, Darcy stalked to the window and stared outside. He had too many thoughts to sort and dreams to rearrange. As he knew from experience, much could happen at a house party composed of unmarried men and ladies, and Matlock held such promise for he and Elizabeth to have time alone to talk, to more closely acquaint their hearts and minds and—

And now—nothing would happen. Saye would gad about romancing his lady, Clarke and Withers and Fitzwilliam would flirt and charm their way through the days and nights, and he...well, perhaps he would simply not attend. Fie on them all.

Bang.

The door flew open. Fitzwilliam burst in, looked at Darcy, and grunted. "What is the matter?"

"A letter from Elizabeth. She is unable to attend the house party."

Fitzwilliam let out a slow whistle. "That is news of the worst sort. Truly, she will not be at Matlock?"

"Yes, that is what I said. Denied, refused, deprived of company but for the perversions of the selfish man in the study." Darcy sighed heavily. "If she is not at Matlock, I shall not go either."

"My brother will have your head."

"Saye is averse to violence." Of course, his cousin would likely throttle him at least as violently in words as he wished to do to Mr Bennet. He watched Fitzwilliam stalk around the rug, muttering.

"Is this the work of Mr Bennet, or has Elizabeth come to her senses and thrown you off?"

Fitzwilliam's drollery, familiar enough in any battles of wits over the years, did nothing to lighten Darcy's mood. "Do you desire I explain the inexplicable about my future wife or satisfy your wish that I am returned to the ranks of lonely bachelors and willing to suffer long evenings with you?"

"A little of each," replied Fitzwilliam, affecting a shrug. "Why is Elizabeth not coming?"

Darcy smoothed out the creases he had made to Elizabeth's letter. "My 'agreement' with Mr Bennet precludes her joining me in such a daring setting."

"The poor girl! With her beauty and charm, Elizabeth would be the belle of the ball!"

"Of course." Darcy needed no reminder of her enchantments.

"What was it you told me? Bennet fears you will tire of her because it was the chase you enjoyed."

Darcy bitterly regretted having opened himself, and his best brandy, so fully to his cousin the night after he first returned to London. Now Fitzwilliam leant back and folded his arms, looking as insufferable as Darcy had ever thought him. He nodded and looked away, irritated that he could indeed recall Bennet's exact words: *'You are a man accustomed to order and obedience. If you wish to marry my daughter, you can wait a few months' engagement. Let patience and constancy be your guide.'*

"I take it he still has doubts about your intentions?"

"Not only does he remain disinclined to think this a lasting affection, he does not trust his daughter at a house party," he grumbled, recalling Mr Bennet's officious pronouncement that one or both of the couple would come to regret their choice.

"He is an odd man, you have said."

"An obstinate man with a perverse sense of humour." Darcy swallowed the urge to ride to Longbourn and make off with his beloved. "He holds to his belief that Elizabeth and I should have some time apart to gain clarity.

"It will 'cure us'," he added in a low voice. "As if we are sick or ailing."

Fitzwilliam sank into his favourite chair. "You are lovesick, Darcy, and oddly ineffectual in claiming your prize and taking her to the altar."

"She is not a prize!" He stepped to his desk, opening a drawer to drop Elizabeth's letter inside. "She is not a prize to be won, but a woman to be cherished."

"Aye, a fact which took you far longer to recognise than it did me. But then, you have always been too reserved. Elizabeth's open nature is opposed to your own."

Darcy returned to the window and stared out at the carriages moving past slowly in the rain. "As is that of many of my friends—Bingley, yourself..."

"Exactly." Fitzwilliam lowered his voice. "Have you considered that perhaps Mr Bennet is not alone in these directives? That he may see some reluctance in the daughter he has raised for the past twenty-one years?"

Darcy reared on his cousin. "You are insinuating that it is Elizabeth who wishes to postpone our life together?"

"Perhaps. The flush of first love fades, as we have seen in many a marriage."

"You speak of your own fickleness with ladies, Fitzwilliam. Elizabeth feels as strongly for me as I do for her."

"Can she truly be as ardent and desperate as you, Cousin? You stomp about, you brood. She is a happy heart, and you are happiest when—"

"—When I am with her." Darcy stared at him, incredulous. Beyond a brief visit in December when Elizabeth had come to London, his cousin had not seen them in company since Rosings, when she was angry about his role in separating her sister from Bingley—information she knew only because of Fitzwilliam's careless gossip.

"You are treading a thin line. I am accustomed to Saye whinging on, scolding me and every man who ever loved a woman, for insipidity and ignorance. Yet you, who have never known reciprocal love and understanding, claim to know Elizabeth's heart better than I."

Darcy could see his words wounded his cousin, but he frankly did not care. He had worked to win Elizabeth's heart, while Fitzwilliam's own heart remained untouched.

"I fail to see why you are here," he added. "Rather than commiserating, you appear bent on telling me I do not deserve Elizabeth."

"You wished for my counsel?" Fitzwilliam's gaze hardened. "Here it is. Elizabeth is of age, is she not?"

Darcy nodded.

"Make off with her and marry her. Otherwise, if she is reluctant, more worried for her father than for you, then it is time to give another man a chance." He leapt up and walked to the door, keeping his back to Darcy and his expression hidden, before he turned around and flashed a grin. "Sometimes the groom is the bigger problem than the father." Chuckling to himself—for certainly his joke had fallen flat with Darcy—Fitzwilliam slipped out of the door.

"Ridiculous man!"

Elizabeth was less accustomed to her mother's anger than she was to her nerves and effusions, her silliness and her laughter. Not since Mr Collins's engagement to Charlotte had Mrs Bennet's temper risen to such furious outpourings as were inspired by Mr Bennet's refusal to allow Elizabeth to travel to the house party.

"An earl's estate! A house party at the manor house of Matlock, with a viscount! What is he thinking?"

"He is not, Sister."

Elizabeth sat with her mother and Kitty in her aunt Philips's parlour, whiling away the afternoon—away from Longbourn, away from her father, and away from the half-written note she must send to Lady Aurelia. Having already poured out her frustrations in a letter to Darcy, she wondered whether he might now think her prone to her mother's temperament.

Aunt Philips leant closer to refill her niece's cup. "Your mother tells me how many letters you receive from Mr Darcy. A letter every day. There is no greater sign of his devotion to you and his dedication to your father's rules." Sitting back in her chair, she looked at her sister and raised an eyebrow. "It is an unfortunate time for Mr Bennet to assert his authority."

"He allows Lizzy all the latitude she wants in her walking and reading, but in this—her future? He is implacable, dismissing my pleas and demands that she go! Denying her a house party at an earl's estate! Her future uncle!" Pausing her exhortations in the face of her daughter's silence, Mrs Bennet renewed her violent attentions to her handkerchief.

"A terrible insult to his favourite!"

Fearing only apoplexy or acquiescence would calm the conversation, Elizabeth tried to reassure her mother she could endure Mr Bennet's insult. "It is to be only a small party, hosted by Mr Darcy's married cousin and comprised of his cousins and friends and their intended brides and their companions."

Kitty, who had been as eager to visit her aunt for the apple tarts as she was for the wealth of promised gossip, looked up from her plate. "Is it near Mr Darcy's estate?"

"My father made me aware that only eight miles separate Matlock from Pemberley."

Aunt Philips nodded sagely. "Ah, he does not trust you or Mr Darcy."

Mrs Bennet waved her tattered handkerchief; a bit of lace flew off and fluttered slowly to the carpet. "He trusts his books, where the words never change from their places on the page."

Elizabeth was surprised at her mother's keen under-standing of a man too irascible to allow her in his library, let alone his heart.

"You should be married now, Lizzy, but Mr Bennet has denied you that privilege and now denied you the opportunity to make the acquaintance of those you must befriend and impress."

"We have spent enough of our visit discussing my troubles. All will be well in the end, once Darcy and I are wed," said Elizabeth, though she felt no such equanimity.

Aunt Philips smiled sympathetically. "Society was never going to be easy in its welcome, but this delay of your wedding could raise questions for some."

"Lizzy is not some simple country girl!"

"I am not." She smiled at her mother for her quick defence and thought of all the words Darcy had used to express his admiration for her over the past few months. 'Simple' was not among them.

"Papa dreads your marriage, Lizzy. He will be left with only Mary and me for conversation." Kitty sighed dramati-cally. "Perhaps Jane and Mr Bingley will take me to London."

"Kitty, no one cares for your troubles. It is Lizzy's we must fix!" Mrs Bennet turned towards Elizabeth and patted her knee. "If the rest of Mr Darcy's family is like his aunt, then you truly must be out in the world, in their midst, to exhibit all that Mr Darcy admires and that your father boasts of but cannot bear to part with."

"Lady Catherine is rather singular among Mr Darcy's relations," said Elizabeth.

"As is Mr Collins among yours," murmured Aunt Philips, prompting a guffaw from Kitty.

Mrs Bennet had not finished sharing her thoughts. "I do not doubt Mr Darcy's affections for you, but I suspect society has wondered at his absence from your company, and why you have not been in London."

Although her mother's well of common sense was never deep, on this point, she had a good understanding of societal expectations.

"Mr Darcy is not required to make my excuses for me. I shall write to Lady Aurelia and explain. If I cannot attend, he may choose only a brief visit for himself."

As she anticipated, Mrs Bennet would not abide such an ending.

"You shall attend this house party," she cried. "You must be seen in company with Mr Darcy. If it leads to a hastier wedding, so be it. You may be his intended, but you must secure him before another lady uses the gathering to impose herself on him."

"He would never—"

"Mr Darcy may be a paragon, but his engagement to a lady no one has met may not be taken as seriously by society's matchmakers as he means it." Aunt Philips looked well-pleased with her prediction of her niece's ruin.

"He will not be tempted. He is not a fool like other men." Mrs Bennet gave Elizabeth a maternal smile before turning to her sister. "Did you not receive a letter from Aunt Boothe, requesting a visit from her nieces?"

Aunt Philips gave her an odd look. "Yes, you recall that Mr Philips has agreed I should leave the day after tomorrow."

"I shall join you there, for perhaps a fortnight. Lizzy may not have Mr Bennet's blessing for a trip to Matlock, but she has always been good company to Aunt Boothe." She gave Elizabeth a meaningful look. "You will go with us to Bletchley."

Elizabeth's startled expression matched that of her aunt. With an uncertain expression, Mrs Philips said, "I had planned on a week's stay with our aunt."

"We shall stay on longer," Mrs Bennet announced firmly.

Elizabeth shook her head. "My father will not sanction my absence from Longbourn."

"Aunt Boothe's household is more limited than Longbourn!" cried Kitty. "She lives with only a cook and a maid, and she reads poetry to her goat."

"Her cow is fond of sonnets," replied Mrs Philips. "A stunted thing it is too."

Elizabeth smiled. "I would prefer to discuss poetry with Mr Darcy."

"Mama, I should like to go as well."

"No, Kitty. Your father cannot spare us all."

Kitty crossed her arms and sniffed. "I wish to see the stunted cow."

Mrs Bennet turned to her. "Be a good girl and run to Mr Merton's to choose new ribbons for your blue bonnet."

Kitty hid her surprise well and rushed for her coat. When the door had closed, Mrs Bennet leant forward and took Elizabeth's hand, her eyes gleaming in excitement. Her resemblance to Lydia in that moment was startling. "Kitty cannot know of our plan. You and Robbins will take the carriage to Matlock. My sister and I will stay in Bletchley until you return."

She was shocked and thrilled at her mother's words. "Papa will never allow such a thing. If he allows you use of the carriage at all."

"I may not have the talent to hasten your wedding to Mr Darcy, but never let it be said I do not understand your father's preference for peace and quiet in his own home." Mrs Bennet reached for her cup and lifted it to her lips. "He will more easily spare you for a fortnight than host my aunt and her ear trumpet for a month."

A mad aunt, a cow, and a series of small deceits in a scheme to ensure my attendance. Already I have a story that will delight my new friends.

NEGOTIATING THE NOTABLES

Georgette & Anderson

G eorgette took the seat she always took when she visited Berkeley Square and waited for Lady Penelope Frey to arrange herself on the chaise-longue opposite. Her ladyship took a long time about it, puffing up her skirts and reclining in just such a way as to ensure she could still reach the plate of biscuits on the table.

"You are looking tiresomely well today, George," she said when all her flouncing was done. "I do wish you would make more effort to look ugly when you come here. It does nothing for my sense of worth to be constantly entertaining women who are prettier than me."

"Prettier and younger," Georgette reminded her. "You must not be downhearted, though. You have the edge when it comes to height."

"Unless you intend that we should conduct the remainder of this conversation standing up, that bears little relevance to the case."

"We had better not. You might grow weary."

Penelope narrowed her eyes. "I should as soon grow

weary of you. Have you anything of note to tell me, or have you called merely to insult me?"

"The latter," Georgette replied. "And do not pretend you are disappointed."

"I shall be disappointed if you do not satisfy me." She snatched a biscuit off the plate and nibbled it. "But if you are going to insist on playing the innocent, then you will have to give me something else on which to chew."

Georgette reached for her teacup, hiding her smile behind it. She was not ready to surrender the game just yet. "Very well. I heard that Miss Ventori is to perform at Lady Carter's soiree next week."

"I already know about that," Penelope replied, impatiently waving what was left of her biscuit in the air.

"Mr Hart is said to be considering a divorce."

"And that."

"Mr Darcy is engaged."

"Everybody knows about that. Come, George, do play along. If you will not tell me what I most wish to know, then answer me this—is it true that Miss Goddard is soon to be married?"

Georgette maintained her expression of cool amusement. Penelope was a dear and exceedingly useful acquaintance, but the girls in that circle of friends were more like sisters, and she would not give up their secrets for anyone's games.

"Now, what was the gentleman's name?" Penelope continued slyly. "Was it—I believe it was—Mr Balton-Sycke. From somewhere in Suffolk, I believe. Would not that be a terrible match? She is altogether too handsome for him. She will only tire of him, and then she will make him miserable. Is that not what always happens when ill-favoured men marry handsome women?"

Georgette put her cup down without drinking any of its contents. She despised tea. "Have you any coffee?"

"Did you hear what I said?"

"I did."

"Well?"

"Loppy, if you cannot answer my one simple question, I do not know how you expect me to answer your two-dozen."

Penelope sighed peevishly. "Leyton, pour Miss Hawkridge some coffee." To Georgette, she said, "Tell me whether it is true. Is Miss Goddard to marry Mr Balton-Sycke?"

"Why are you so concerned? Have you an interest in him yourself?"

"Hardly."

Georgette gave her friend a teasing look. She had not met Lilly's latest suitor, but she did not need to be acquainted with him to be certain he was not to Penelope's taste. "Why the fascination then?"

"My fascination for your friend's admirers will thrive precisely as long as you refuse to satisfy my curiosity on more pertinent matters."

That was as Georgette had suspected. "Alas, I have nothing to tell you. Unless Miss Goddard has accepted an offer in the last four-and-twenty hours, then I am not aware that she is presently engaged to anybody."

"Why has she not encouraged him? From what I have heard, he would have proposed already had he been more confident of her answer."

"I have no idea. Perhaps she means to take a leaf from your book and remain unhindered in that regard."

Penelope scoffed derisively. "She has neither the courage nor the fortune to do so. Nor, I sincerely doubt, the inclination." She leant forward. "Unless that is what you are implying. Now those are the sorts of whispers that would brighten up the darkest corners of Almack's."

"Very well, you intolerable wretch—you win!" Georgette relented, pulling a face at her friend when she rolled back into her previous state of repose with a complacent grin. "I saw Anderson on Tuesday. He took me for a ride in his curricle—and that is not a euphemism."

"Where did he take you?"

"To his institution in Golders Green—and that is not a euphemism either."

"Did you go alone?"

"We did."

"Therefore you have certainly not told me everything that occurred."

Georgette rolled her eyes but conceded, nevertheless. "And he took me to the whispering gallery of St Paul's." That was a euphemism, and one with which she had no doubt Penelope was intimately familiar; thus, she did not elaborate.

Her friend smiled broadly. "I like him, George. I like him very well. He will do far better for you than Hairy Ball-Sack will do for your Miss Goddard."

Georgette almost spat out her coffee.

Penelope winked at her. "'Tis an unfortunate appellation —and another good reason not to let your friend marry him."

"I did not think you cared for my friends."

"I could not give a fig about them, but you are a diamond, and if Miss Goddard is dear to you, then we cannot have her marrying an inconsequential scrotum from Lowestoft. It always depresses me when a good woman gives herself over to a man, but if she must, it is imperative that he be worth the sacrifice. Now be a dear and fetch the cards. Let me thrash you at Piquet a few times before you go, so I need not hate you so violently for having such straight teeth."

Georgette usually left Berkeley Square in good humour, not least because Lady Penelope Frey, with her infamous contempt for propriety, was the only person with whom she could safely discuss her own, occasionally salacious romantic pursuits. Yet today, she left feeling troubled. Not for herself

—she was not disposed to self-doubt, and neither did she want for faith in Anderson's intentions. Nay, her concern was all for Lilly.

Mr Balton-Sycke was evidently not a tenable prospect. As Lady Penelope had rightly pointed out, a good woman ought never to surrender herself to a man who was not worthy. And his ridiculous nickname notwithstanding, if Mr Balton-Sycke could not even make Lilly laugh, then any union between them would be doomed to misery from the outset. Which was a great shame, for the only other contender seemed to be her cousin Saye, who was about as likely to take a wife as Lady Penelope was to take a husband.

"Poor Lilly," she murmured as she turned her horse into the traffic on Grosvenor Street. She preferred to ride than to go by carriage. It enabled her to take less circuitous routes about town and vexed her father tremendously.

"Beg pardon, ma'am?" enquired her accompanying footman.

"I was lamenting the decline of romance in the modern world."

"Right you are," he replied, doffing his hat and never taking his eyes off the milling crowds.

"A noble pursuit," said someone alarmingly close by as he brought his horse abreast of her own.

Georgette let out a yelp of surprise; the footman's head whipped around and both their horses skittered sideways. "Saye! You beast—you almost made me lose my seat!"

"A thousand apologies. But your man there did not look to be paying you the attention I know you crave. I felt obliged to step in."

The aged servant looked caught between apology and apoplexy; she soothed him with a wink and turned to her cousin. "What are you doing here?"

"I live here."

"No you do not."

Saye looked all about him with theatrical bewilderment. "I did the last time I checked. This is London, is it not?"

"Very droll. You do not live in this *part* of London."

"Neither do you. Have you been anywhere interesting?"

"Lady Penelope Frey's." Her cousin raised his eyebrows. "Oh, come, I did not take you for the missish type. I visit her every Wednesday."

"*Do* you? Fancy my being here on a Wednesday also, and not any other day of the week."

"Indeed. What do you want?"

Georgette expected him to feign ignorance and was taken aback when he replied, without preamble, "I want you to come to my party."

"Pardon?"

"Fitzwilliam and I are having a house party at Matlock, and there is a distinct dearth of pretty women on the guest list."

"Oh, well, I thank you for the compliment, backward as it was."

"I did not mean you—your friends. You have some, do you not?"

The unrepentantly wicked grin he gave her made her laugh instead of scolding him for his impertinence. "I can certainly make some enquiries. Did you have anyone particular in mind?"

"*Not* Lady Penelope."

Georgette snorted. "Loppy is a good sort, you know."

"I have no doubt, but I shall need some ladies left for the gentlemen."

"Well, assuming you require some men left for the women, I should advise against inviting Miss Favers. Favers by name, favours by nature."

"Noted," Saye replied with a smirk. "I trust you will find

some suitable candidates. Aurelia has agreed to host for us, so do encourage them all to leave their fusty old companions at home."

"My, my, you do mean business. Very well. Send me the details and I shall see who is available." She waited until Saye lifted his reins to turn his horse away, then added, "One thing."

He relaxed back in his saddle and raised an eyebrow in query.

"In return for my troubles, would you be so good as to extend an invitation to Mr Anderson?"

"Who?"

"Mr Samuel Anderson. Of Gilchester Hall in Somerset."

Saye screwed up his face. "*Blanderson?* Must I? 'Tis a party, not a wake."

It was not an unprecedented reaction, and it amused Georgette more every time she witnessed it. "Do not invite him, if you prefer not to," she said with a shrug. "I only hope my friends do not all turn out to have previous engagements."

Saye rolled his eyes. "Very well, I shall send him a note. I suppose he might keep Darcy occupied at least."

"Mr Darcy?" she said dubiously.

"Another of my cousins, on my father's side."

"I know who he is. I was just wondering at your questioning Mr Anderson's liveliness when all the while you were planning to bring the Great Standing Stone of Derbyshire."

Saye grinned widely. "All the more reason for you to bring some of your livelier friends."

"I shall see what I can do."

"Obliged, I am sure." He gathered up his reins again. "But, Georgette?"

"Yes?"

"Blanderson? Really?"

"Yes," she replied evenly. "And, Saye?"

"Yes?"

"No making promises on balconies that you have no intention of keeping."

There was definite potential in the slight widening of his eyes. She smiled to herself and nudged her horse forward. Lilly might not be without hope after all.

Anderson swiped his brother's feet off his desk and perched where they had been. "I said no. Perhaps next month you will take care to make your allowance stretch beyond the first week."

Randalph huffed petulantly. "I wonder that you have enough to squander on all your little freaks, yet you cannot stump up enough for me to join a harmless game of Hazard."

"If Hazard were harmless, it would be named differently, and you would not require my money to play it. Did you sit with Grandmother at all while you were at Gilchester last month?"

"Yes, for all that she knew who I was."

"It is a pitiful state in which to end such a long and eventful life," Anderson agreed with a heavy sigh. Still, he was pleased Randalph had found time for her amidst his carousing. Any sign that his younger brother had not given over all vestiges of humanity to his new friends was welcome indeed.

They were interrupted by a knock at the door and a footman delivering the post, which consisted of one solitary but exceedingly intriguing communication.

"What is it?" Randalph enquired. "Must be interesting to put that look on your face."

"It is an invitation to a house party." His brother sat up a little straighter and Anderson hastily added, "You are not included, I am afraid."

Randalph slumped back into his chair with a huff. "Who is it from?"

"Viscount Saye."

Randalph shot upright again. "Good Lord! I had no idea you were in with that set!"

"I am not."

"But you must be acquainted."

"A little, though I have not seen him for some time. But I have been invited at the particular request of his cousin."

Randalph's brow creased. "Mr Darcy? Why the devil should he want you there? It seems a rum business to me. I should not go if I were you."

Anderson only smiled. Mr Darcy was a pleasant enough gentleman, but Randalph was thinking of entirely the wrong cousin. It was not the master of Pemberley who had expressed a desire for his society, but another of Lord Saye's cousins, Miss Georgette Hawkridge. And there was nothing that lady could request of him that he would not move heaven and earth to deliver. After another quarter of an hour dissuading Randalph from gambling away his next month's allowance in the Hells of Pall Mall, Anderson spent the remainder of the afternoon rearranging his affairs and sending a note to engage himself for his attendance at Matlock.

A Dinner
Most Diverting

Saye & Lillian

Four hours into his party, and nothing was going his way.

With long, angry strides, Saye entered his splendid apartment at Matlock, startling Florizel out of a nap. His apartment was done up in a baroque way, complete with an elaborate mural on the wall painted by Fragonard himself and titled *The Lover Crowned*. He usually found it rather inspirational, but today it could only vex him further.

Picking up his pup, he sat upon the pale blue silk of his bed and sighed heavily. It had all seemed so promising! The invitations had been somewhat last minute, but everyone had accepted—everyone, that is, except Darcy's Miss Bennet, but a few letters and coins had fixed that as well. At least these Bennet people knew how to treat a viscount!

He had arranged for every servant to be on hand to greet his guests—all of them. From the butler to the lowest scullery maid, they came and stood arrayed behind him like an army of prepared comfort and indulgence. He wanted Lilly to see what she would have at her disposal. But Lilly was among the last to arrive, and he had been forced to release them to their duties after all, gritting his teeth tightly as he gave permission for his butler to do so.

And then there she was, shown into the drawing room where everyone had begun to gather before they dressed for dinner. And she was perfectly kind to him.

He flung himself back into the softness of his bed. "Blast it to hell!"

There was none of the delicious awkwardness of *amore*. She was neither too friendly, nor too unfriendly. She was pretty and sweet and thanked Saye for including her in the invitation. *Including* her? Wretched girl! Did she not realise the whole affair was for her? Overcome by his distress, he crawled towards his pillow, digging down in the blankets and covering himself for a moment of sheer, unabashed pity of himself. Oh, the pure misery of being denied that which he wanted!

He heard a gentle knock on the door. "Not ready, Mitchell," he said, his voice muffled into his pillow. "I shall ring for you."

Nevertheless, the door creaked open, and footsteps approached, and before Saye could react a large object leapt onto the bed, landing squarely atop him. For a moment, he thought his lungs were shattered. "Ahhhhhh!" Saye yelled. "What the devil? Who dares—"

Flinging himself free of the blankets, he sat up and glared at his brother, seeing Darcy had also entered but, being more civilised, had chosen to take a seat rather than attempt to break every bone in his cousin's body. He shoved his brother, and his brother shoved him; then they began a mad tussle as in their youth which resulted in Fitzwilliam being pushed off the bed and onto the floor, narrowly missing the marble top of Saye's night table.

"I nearly broke my skull!" Fitzwilliam protested.

"You nearly broke my skull, and you could have crushed

Florizel," said Saye, calmly straightening his waistcoat. He pushed back the rest of the covers, freeing his legs before he stood, nodding to Darcy. "Well, what say you both to this troubling evening? Did you see her? She was as near to indifferent as any woman could be."

"She has only just arrived—" Fitzwilliam began.

"Yes, and at least she *did* arrive," Darcy added. "So you have triumphed over me there."

But Saye was not formed for uncertainty or despair. He began to pace the room. "I need to get her alone," he said abruptly.

"Surely over the course of the days here—"

"No, no." He gave his brother a scornful glare. "I mean tonight. As soon as possible."

"Give her some time—"

"Time?" Saye threw up his hands, sending his brother a disgusted glare. "No wonder you do not have a woman. Darcy, do you hear this?"

"Walks are good," Darcy said. "One can always ask a lady to walk out. It is how I proposed to Elizabeth, you know."

"That is such a boring idea, I think I lost consciousness in the middle of it," Saye replied, somewhat absently. An idea was forming, elaborate and uncommon, just like he was. "The point of this party is to show her that life with me will never be predictable and dull, yes?"

"And also how rich you are," Fitzwilliam added helpfully. "Rich and spoilt."

"True," Saye acknowledged. A moment later, he snapped his fingers. "I have it. It is by far one of my best ideas ever, and you will both thank me for it."

The idea, as he sketched it out to the other gentleman, was that there would be no dining table at dinner. Instead, there would be many small tables, designed to fit only two, at which the couples would dine. The tables would be spread amongst the main rooms.

"Dining room—the obvious one of course—and Father's study, the library, all three drawing rooms, the main hall, and..." He thought for a moment. "Ah! Of course. The orangery. Each lady will be given a room where she should remain the evening complete. After each course, the gentlemen will change rooms—"

"How will they know where to go?" Darcy asked.

"I shall tell them," Saye replied. He should have thought that was obvious but Darcy did need to ask about everything.

"Perhaps it should be done at random?" Fitzwilliam asked. "We could pick names from a hat and then—"

"Forgive me," Saye interrupted. "Did I give the impression I was in want of ideas? Because I assure you, I am not. I know just how it should be done."

"This is not only *your* party, Saye," Fitzwilliam retorted.

"Um, except yes, it is my party, and I shall decide who gets to eat where." More soothingly, he added, "Do not fear, little brother, I shall favour you in all the arrangements. You will have every opportunity to sample the choicest wares, so to speak."

Fitzwilliam opened his mouth to say something, then closed it again, no doubt recognising that too much protest could make his brother turn vindictive. Saye nodded, pleased by his perceptiveness.

"Darcy, alas, you will be forced to speak to people, but the pain should be of short duration."

"Lady Aurelia's dinners are never of short duration," Darcy grumbled. "And I should imagine this one, even less so."

"Oh Aurelia!" Saye snapped his fingers. "I daresay I should tell her of the change, should I not?"

Minutes later, Saye and Fitzwilliam's younger sister stood

in Saye's bedchamber. She was not a woman anyone would call pretty; the same features which had rendered Lord Matlock ruggedly handsome in his youth were less appealing on the female countenance. She was enjoying her status as the married woman at this party, but Saye was determined she should remember just whose party it was.

"Where will we get so many tables?" she protested.

"Throw a cloth over a barrel," Saye replied with a shrug. "I am sure I do not care."

"But...but what about the arrangements, the flowers and...and the candles—"

"We have enough candles in this place to light up all of Derbyshire. I shall speak to Fairbanks, I only wanted you to know about it."

Lady Aurelia seemed tempted by this. She enjoyed having things done for her.

"Perhaps tomorrow would be better," Fitzwilliam offered. "Give the servants some time to procure the needed items."

"No. There is not a moment to lose. I have days, mere days, to do this, I cannot waste an evening."

"But it seems unreasonable to ask the servants to rearrange the entire dinner—"

"Have either of you ever induced a woman to break her engagement?" Saye demanded, his hands on his hips.

Fitzwilliam said, "Um, but Miss Goddard is not exactly betro—"

"No, you have not. So pray, do not question my methods, yes?" He gave his brother and cousin both a stern glare. Walking to his armoire, he opened it and withdrew a purse. It was satisfyingly full, and he turned back to the other three, wagging it at them. "See this? I shall give this to Mrs Fairbanks."

"A wager to see which servant will wish you dead first?" Darcy asked.

Saye rolled his eyes. "No, so that when I upend all the plans and make everyone work twice as hard for the sake of satisfying my whims, their pockets will be a bit fuller for their efforts. And Fairbanks and Stevens will also have a bottle of the champagne to ease them into sleep tonight."

"Champagne?" Lady Aurelia asked, a sudden gleam in her eyes.

"Where did you get champagne?" Fitzwilliam enquired.

Saye smirked at his brother. "You did not think I arranged this party without any help from Gertie?"

Darcy frowned and Saye grinned back, happily unconcerned. Darcy disapproved of the connexion his relations maintained with Gertie Birdsell, a known and notorious smuggler, but there were advantages to be had in such friendships. A carriage full of Veuve Clicquot when one was trying to impress a lady was but one of them.

"Now," Saye announced, walking over to his writing desk. "I shall beg you all to leave me. I need to orchestrate a dinner —nay, many dinners!— for tonight."

Those in service at Matlock were as diligent and well-trained as any to be had, and yet there was an undeniable clamour that arose somewhere around the time when they were all meant to be dressing. When her maid entered while Lilly sat with Sarah and Georgette, Lilly wasted no time in pressing her for the news.

"Everyone seems to be in some agitation, Marleigh, do you know anything about it?"

"Lord Saye has proposed some alteration to the scheme for dinner," said Marleigh. "I gather his demands are rather unusual."

"Unusual?" Georgette, who had been perusing Lilly's jewellery, paused. "How so?"

"Everyone is eating in pairs, and all spread out among the rooms. Little tables, or so I am told. His lordship thought nothing of upending Lady Aurelia's plans for the evening."

"Ohhh," breathed the ladies in unison, exchanging excited glances. Lilly thought it sounded quite absurd, just the sort of thing Saye would do.

"And that is not all," added Marleigh. "You will be changing after the courses."

"Changing?" asked Sarah. "Our gowns?"

"Changing your dinner partners," said Marleigh. "Different men, in and out of the rooms."

Georgette laughed. "Well, at least we shall not be forced to endure the same man all night."

"I have never heard of such a thing," said Lilly. "Why would he do this?"

"The servants must be furious," said Sarah.

"No, Miss. They are all delighted, for his lordship sent down a sum to thank them for the trouble, and at least one scullery maid fainted from the generosity of her portion. They said one of the footmen cried, for he will be sending it home to his mother, and she's sick with the gout, and it was just the amount needed for her medicine. So no, no one is distressed, they are quite happy to oblige him."

"Well then, the real question becomes, what is everyone wearing?" Georgette drawled. "Since evidently, our partners shall have ample time to scrutinise it."

"A pink gown," said Lilly.

"Oh, yes that one," said Georgette. "Delightful. Rather clings to your bottom, does it not?"

"No!"

"Oh, the pink silk gauze?" Sarah sighed. "I love that gown. The embroidery is heavenly and your bosom looks—"

"Like anyone else's bosom," Lilly protested.

"Lilly, darling, no one, but no one, has such a bosom as you," Georgette informed her seriously. "And atop such a tiny waist! Dearest, I should despise you if I did not love you so. Drape some silk gauze over that, and Saye will not know what hit him."

"We shall not be able to partner with all the gentlemen," said Lilly. "Surely it cannot be more than three courses? And there are ten gentlemen present so…"

"Ten gentlemen, but only nine ladies," Sarah observed. "Rather strange is it not? Lady Aurelia is always so careful with her numbers."

"Perhaps someone fell ill and had to decline at the last minute."

"But how odd that she would allow Saye to contrive such a scheme with an imbalance in her numbers," Sarah insisted. "Surely she would realise it meant someone—some man— would dine alone at some point."

"Mr Darcy's intended is not here," said Lilly. "A pity, for I rather wished to meet her. I hear she is lovely."

"I should very much like to meet her. The lady who has secured Mr Darcy! She must be rather a fearsome sort, do you not think?" Sarah asked.

"No, no. I hear she is kind. He is quite in love with her," Lilly said.

They were interrupted then, for Marleigh insisted it was time to be dressed, and the other ladies were called to do likewise.

When Lilly descended the stairs, she was met by Lady Aurelia who informed her, "The yellow parlour, my dear, shall be yours for the evening."

"The yellow one? Rather far off, is it not?"

"Not so very far," Lady Aurelia replied. "My mother has just redone all the furnishings in it, very prettily I might add.

We shall have five courses, and you must remain in the yellow parlour throughout. We shall not separate tonight—all will gather in the drawing room after dessert."

"But is it not scandalous for all of us to be sent off from one another in this way?" Lilly asked.

"Your maid will dine with you," said Lady Aurelia. "She is there now...at a little distance of course, but you need not fear your reputation."

"Then I am off to the yellow parlour," Lilly said with a little smile. Never let it be said she was not an agreeable guest.

She set off, conscious of the swish of her gown against her legs. Her friends were right—it did rather set off her figure. The material draped elegantly over the curve of her hips, managing to accent her bottom and her bosom. Marleigh had been particularly aggressive with her corset this night, raising her breasts to the point where Lilly thought they might hit her chin when she chewed. She hoped it was not all in vain.

She knew not what to make of Saye. He had been friendly, but not overly so when she arrived, late because there had been some confusion the last time they had changed horses. He had expressed his disappointment that Balton-Sycke could not join them, which made her laugh.

"Sir, I daresay the reason he could not join us is that you did not invite him," she said, only faintly scoldingly.

"Just so," Saye acknowledged. "But it does not follow that I cannot regret the fact that he lacks the charm sufficient to make me like him."

She wondered whether Saye would be one of her partners tonight and prayed he would. If nothing else, it was a waste of a good gown if he did not get to see it.

The yellow parlour was as charming as had been promised. It was Lady Matlock's particular room, and everything was done to a lady's tastes. Lilly liked it immensely, particularly set as it was with the very finest of the Matlock china and silver. There were coloured sash windows which could be raised in warmer weather but which tonight reflected the multitude of candles lit within. Her maid sat in one corner; and a harpist, surprisingly, was sat in another. Where had Saye managed to come up with a harpist? She could not imagine the effort required to supply ten makeshift dining rooms with their own musicians.

The harpist began to play, not too loudly, and not too softly, as Lilly awaited her partner for the soup course. She did, on occasion, find it needful to blot her palms on her gown, and she nearly jumped out of her skin when the door opened, and Mr Darcy entered. "Good evening," he said with his customary gravity.

She smiled as he took his seat, simultaneously disappointed and relieved it was he and not Saye. A footman entered with their soup, and they began to eat. "Do tell me all about your Miss Bennet," said Lilly, and it was all he needed. He smiled, in a way Lilly had never seen him smile, and spoke at length. Miss Elizabeth Bennet was, to Mr Darcy, all things wonderful and perfect, and as Lilly watched him, she recognised that Mr Darcy was a man transformed by love. *I want that,* she thought. *I want a man to feel thrilled beyond measure to have me, not merely consent to a good match.*

Their soup finished, it was time for the next course, the chief part of which was pheasant. Lilly adored pheasant, but she was less excited to see Mr Anderson arrive to serve it to her. Not that she disliked the man—he did have a kindliness in his aspect that was very pleasing, but he tended towards reticence. She resolved to do what she could to draw him out. Georgette was great friends with the man, although why, she could not say. Her friend was always so effortlessly fashionable, everyone wished to be her friend, so why she should permit anyone as unfashionable, as uninteresting as Mr Anderson to hang about her so, Lilly could not imagine. He carved for her, delivering to her plate rather choice morsels, and she thanked him, then did what she could to induce an interesting conversation from him.

It was not easy. He had a tendency to chew for an excessively long time. Lilly found herself entranced in counting the up and down motion of his jaw, realising that each mouthful was masticated no less than thirty times. Thirty times! She supposed it might aid the digestion, but it did make conversation difficult.

When the third course appeared, Lilly could only conclude that Saye must despise her for, other than Mr Darcy, he had given her no one to dine with but the least enjoyable persons in the party. This time she was partnered with Lady Aurelia's husband, Sir Phineas.

Lady Aurelia called him Phin; no one else dared to. He was an exceedingly wealthy baronet who, it was rumoured, was fifty years old. Lilly had no idea whether it was true, but she did know he had an odd habit of peering at people like they had done something naughty, and he meant to make them confess to it. Lilly fought a near-irrepressible urge to confess stealing sweets from the larder. Thankfully, they were only meant to have a salad and cheese together before the fourth course would arrive, but somehow it seemed to take longer than all the other courses combined.

When Sir Phineas wandered off, Lilly nearly followed him. Clearly her gown had been wasted, and worse, she felt like crying. Did she feel Saye had rejected her? Who was he eating with? Why had he not chosen to eat with her?

There was a lengthy pause, and no one entered the yellow parlour. Pushing back her chair, Lilly walked to the windows, staring out into the dark night and thinking of nothing.

Suddenly, a man was reflected behind her, and she jumped a little, whirling about.

As handsome as he ever was, and perhaps more so, Saye stood resplendent in all black, the colour setting off the gold of his hair, the deep blue of his eyes, and the pure white colour of his dog, who was tight against his left ankle. "My dear Miss Goddard," he said. "What are you looking for out there?"

"I..." She found herself a little weak in the knees and forced a complaisant smile to her face. "Nothing. Nothing at all, my lord. Just...just thinking."

"Oh bosh with the 'my lord' business," he scolded. He extended his arm. "Shall we sit? Or did you wish to carry on staring out of the window?"

She laughed. "I am sure whatever is out there will still be there while I await my fifth partner."

"Ah, alas, there was a bit of a muddle," he told her, leading her back to the table. "Some error whereby you shall have to endure me as both your fourth and fifth partner."

A smile breached her face as she realised what he had done. With a bit of archness in her tone, she said, "A muddle? But sir, I thought it was you who arranged the couples."

"Mm," said Saye. He helped her sit, and she felt the lightest brush of his hand against her back. A glancing touch, but it made that peculiar weakness afflict her knees once more, and she was relieved to sit.

Lilly saw a footman enter with an enormous crustacean on a silver tray. "Is that lobster?"

"Yes, I daresay it is. Do you like it?"

"I do not know that I have ever had it...not that way. I have eaten lobster patties of course."

"You will love it. We shall drench it in butter, and it is much better than a patty, I assure you. Shall we eat then?" He signalled the footman, who somehow produced an oddly shaped bottle. "Uncork it James, and carefully."

The footman did as bid and handed it to Saye who poised it over Lilly's glass. "You have to drink champagne with your lobster. The flavours are just right together, along with strawberries, of course."

"Champagne?"

"Veuve Clicquot," he said, pouring her a generous glass. "I had it smuggled in specially."

They drank three bottles complete of the champagne, and Lilly knew she was entirely too giggly, a dreadful state to be in when sitting with a rake like Saye. He sent Marleigh away, first insisting she, too, eat some lobster and strawberries; then he summoned Florizel's footman, after feeding the canine his own bit of lobster as well. Lilly did not know which she found most astonishing, that Florizel had his own footman, or that Saye fed him lobster. She had little time to consider though, for Saye also fed the lobster to her, letting butter drip on her chin and then bending over to kiss it off her.

"Thish is...shish is most scamperous behaviour," she stammered clumsily. "Where did Marleigh go? Get her back here, Saye, my reputation is in danger."

"Silly girl," he scolded. "No one is anywhere near, and in any case, they are enjoying their own dinners, though I daresay no one is having nearly as much fun as we are."

Fun. That is Saye—lots of fun. He makes having fun his life's work and would never do something so mundane as marry. The thought was frighteningly coherent amid the haze of her champagne-addled mind. Saye did like to amuse himself. Outlandish schemes and champagne and lobster dinners seasoned with kisses and scandal were all *de rigueur* for him. His greatest fear, no doubt, was boredom. It made for a delightful evening, but it was certainly nothing to make a marriage out of.

"I need to go." She rose abruptly, nearly toppling her chair.

Saye, who had pulled his own chair over to be within six inches of hers, rose and grabbed on to her to steady her. "Whoa there. Where are you going?"

"Bed," she said and then, most humiliatingly, she hiccoughed. "Thank goodness my mother is not here. She would have had my neck."

"And such a beautiful neck it is too." Saye ran one finger down the curve of it, arriving at her collarbone, which he traced with feather-light touches. She shivered, and he leant into her.

"Shall I escort you to your apartment?"

She laughed and hiccoughed again. "No."

He pouted, looking almost comical. "No? But why not? Why end here when we are having so much fun?"

"No, Saye," she said. "Fun is not all there is, you know."

"But Lilly, come now," he said. "Tell me this, at least. When you put this gown on, did you think of me just a little?"

He smiled at her then, a devastating smile combining boyish charm with a man's intentions beneath it. A pang went through her; this was not good at all. She was falling right under his spell, just when she needed clarity more than ever.

"Perhaps I did. What of it?"

"So you did! Well, it worked, my dear girl, for I have never seen anything more—"

"And now I wish I had not."

Saye wrinkled his brow. "Why?"

"Saye." She shook her head. "I need to learn to like you a lot less than I do, and I certainly need to dress without worrying whether you should approve of me."

Too much feeling had crept into that; in a moment, the mood shifted. She saw—was it hurt? surely not—in his eyes. "What do you mean by that?" he asked.

"You are...you are this." She gestured wildly at her plate and the parlour lit up with so, so very many candles. "Fun! And I...I fall right under your thrall. I have to marry Mr Balton-Sycke."

"If you marry Hairy Ball-Sack," he said, "I shall never speak to you again."

She wondered if he was in earnest; even if he was not, it stung to hear him say so. Her champagne-fuelled delight had worn off like a dash of cold water to the face, and a headache was hard on its heels.

"I am very sorry to hear that," she said with great dignity. "Pray, give my excuses to the rest. My head aches and I must find my bed."

And with that, she was off. Saye did not follow her.

SOME EXCUSE FOR INCIVILITY

Sarah & Fitzwilliam

S arah had not known what to think of Marleigh's information on the dining arrangements. She enjoyed people and conversation, but was not overly proficient at it, especially with gentlemen with whom one was to experiment with flirtation. Their arrival at Matlock had been intimidating enough, with miles of servants lined up, staring down their aristocratic noses at her. No one was prouder than servants employed by earls, as well she knew. She often told her uncle that his butler was much more earl-like than he ever could be.

And then, there was the matter of her clothing. She knew —because her friends had explained it many times—that she had the worst taste in the history of tastefulness. She would select a fabric so bright and cheerful, and the resulting dress would look as though she had been attacked by blind dressmakers. For her first day at Matlock, she had attempted to choose a subtle, simple frock, something understated and elegant.

"Sarah," Georgette had whispered, "Are you wearing an undressing gown?"

And only then had she noticed that it did, indeed, look very much like a pattern one might use for one's favourite night-wear.

"Hm. So it is. No wonder the dressmaker looked askance at my selection."

Georgette sighed. "She ought to have guided you more helpfully. 'Tis probably just as well that there was no time to procure a whole new wardrobe. You likely would have chosen an array resembling hot air balloons."

"I saw an ascension from Hyde Park once. They were lovely."

"You *would* think so," Georgette said, but Sarah had seen her smile. "I brought an extra domino you can wear for the masquerade, in the loveliest shade of pink."

"Oh, actually, I do have my costume for the masque. It is really something, I promise."

"That is what I fear."

All her friends had attempted to help her in the past, but of course, their figures were much more fashionable, and she had been stubborn about changing from her aunt's woman, who would not argue with her. Sarah had heard herself referred to as 'sturdy'—not by any who loved her, of course. But it was the sad truth. She was strong enough to walk for miles in London's worst weather, she never took chills, and tradesmen found it impossible to cheat her. These were the positives of 'sturdiness'. But her bust was too large and, garbed in most of the current styles, she appeared about ready to begin a confinement. While Lilly might wear a dress clinging to her posterior and appear appealing, Sarah would, in the same fashion, resemble her father's Brougham carriage, sticking out at both ends.

For tonight's dinner, she had chosen her most flattering dress, to which she had added a fur-trimmed pelisse. In her imagination, it had added elegance to an otherwise simple gown. In reality, it looked rather like a weasel had lost consciousness and swooned across her shoulders.

"I shall look upon this first night as a practice," she told her reflection in the looking glass. "I am unlikely to net a mate on the first fishing expedition, after all."

She could not recall seeing any other gentleman besides Lord Saye when they arrived—so magnificent was his presence in puce waistcoat and clawhammer jacket, and so impressive was his introduction—and thus she had no idea who her dining partners might be. Why was it that Saye could be dressed in anything he wished, yet only appear the height of elegance? If she had worn that many fobs, seals, and rings, she would be mistaken for a chandelier. He had gleamed, while she appeared in a faux-undressing gown and the earl's servants snickered at her behind their hands. Except they were all too high in the instep to *actually* snicker. She would have liked them better if they had.

Despite her misgivings, however, the evening began with surprising pleasantness. She was not, as she had feared, shoved out into the garden to make way for the more popular ladies, but seated at a pretty little table in the orangery, and had Lord Saye himself as her first dining partner.

"This is unexpected," she said. "I presumed you would employ your powers of hosting to avoid the lesser stars amongst this glittering assembly."

Saye laughed at her frank speech. "A woman who speaks her mind! This might be even more fun than I had hoped. Very well, let us drop the niceties and speak as we find."

"I apologise, my lord. I have a terrible habit of saying exactly what I think, whether or not I ought to think it. It is my pleasure, of course, to dine with you."

"I do not think it needful of an apology—it is an odd habit for a woman, but I daresay I may accustom myself to it."

But then abruptly, her eye was caught by something she had never seen before, and she leant forward several more inches, peering intently at his chest.

He glanced down at his front, as if to check whether his valet had not turned him out perfectly—which of course, was not in the realm of possibility. "Have I soiled myself already?" he asked mildly.

She was hastily recalled to herself, straightening as she felt her cheeks redden. Even thus mortified, she found she must know the answer to a burning question.

"I apologise yet again, my lord."

"Apologies are like my brother's purse—utterly useless." He grinned. "Did we not already agree to speak frankly? Why are you staring so at me? Not that I blame you, understand."

"Could you tell me…is your cravat some sort of variation on the Napoleon? My young brother, Percy, is fascinated with the subject, though he is only nine years, and I thought we had learnt most of the popular styles. But I have never seen that one."

"My cravat," Saye replied loftily, as the soup was brought in, "is a variation of nothing but my valet's genius and is surely nothing so crude as the Napoleon. For a price, I might just be willing to sketch it for your dear Percy."

"A price?"

Saye ordered the footman to fetch him pencil and paper, and while they waited for it, Sarah began her soup and Saye began to question her. Did Lilly actually like Balton-Sycke? Had they an understanding? Had Balton-Sycke drawn up any papers in the nature of a settlement?

Sarah answered him to the degree she could, upholding Lilly's best interests, of course, as he, in turn, sketched out the design for Percy's benefit and education.

"I see," Sarah breathed, staring at the drawing, and then

at his neck. "But how do you maintain such a defined frill on the drape's edge?"

Saye looked left and right, as if there might be valets in the bushes, attempting to eavesdrop. Low-voiced, he said, "The secret is in the precise amount of starch to be used. Only I and my man have the receipt. There are gentlemen's gentlemen who would kill for this information, so I shall swear you to secrecy, and you may only reveal it when the boy is old enough not to embarrass himself, or me, by improper application. Do you understand?"

"I do, my lord," Sarah replied quite earnestly. "I am honoured, and I promise you that if Percy grows up to be the slovenly sort of gentleman who would wear the *Horse Collar* to a subscription ball, the secret will die with me."

Saye beamed. "You know, I like you..." he paused. "... Miss Benson, is it?"

"It is Bentley," Sarah said, returning his smile, and deciding she rather liked him as well.

"Of course, of course. Eldest child of Hampton's heir. Now, why in blazes would you apologise for anything you say? Your father, or your brother at the very least, will be an earl like as not. You must learn to wait for others to do the apologising. Your words, like you, take precedence. Do you see?"

"I know that is certainly the case with the men," she said dubiously. "Having decided to marry, I note the sad truth that those who must be in want of a wife are seldom single men of good fortune, and of those, my 'precedence' such as it is, has had little effect in nudging them towards the altar. In my experience, the more *myself* I am, the more quickly such gentlemen back swiftly out of the room, out of the door, and down the street." She sighed. "I have an appalling sense of fashion, my lord. It is an unfortunate fact that I look much more appealing unclothed than clothed, no matter how much money I spend. Only my husband will ever possess that useful crumb of information, but as we are no longer in Eden, it is hardly to my credit. Now how is it, I ask you, that you are able to wear any shade of puce without apology or regret, while I cannot even pull off ivory?"

Saye preened; there was no other word for it. "Yes, well, the ability to appear magnificent under any circumstance is a gift. Believe me when I say that capturing a mate in no way requires this degree of beauty, else few would ever marry. As an earl's daughter—or nearly so—you may saunter into a ballroom, point at one of the young bucks ever circling within, and declare, 'I shall take you.'"

Sarah sighed. "*Phymatopus hecta.*"

"Pardon?"

"Gold swift moth. A female flies up to a hovering male. They dance in the air together. The male then flies over the female and hangs, fluttering, beside her. And then they mate. It seems so simple, and yet, it seldom is."

He raised his quizzing glass, stared at her, then shook his head as if to clear it. "Never mind moths. Back to my superb sense of fashion, sagacity, perception, and obvious attraction to the opposite sex. I shall reveal to you another secret. Two words—cease caring."

"Cease caring?" Sarah repeated. "Do you mean, become a heartless, self-absorbed, pompous, ostentatious dandy?"

He considered the notion with a faint grin on his countenance. "Well yes, but only heartless when the circumstance demands it."

And Sarah laughed. Her laugh was not a dainty, melodious tinkling, but a loud, full-bodied roar.

Saye winced. "Very well, you could use some polishing," he allowed. "But believe me, you must cease worrying that every little imperfection will be the blemish that drives Prince Charming off to Bedlam. Who cares if the stupid ones fail to notice your, um, fluttering? The right man, if he hasn't manure for brains, will appreciate everything you are. If he does not, he simply is not the right man." For a moment, a strange look passed across his face, as if he heard his own advice and found the flaw in it. But he quickly recovered.

"As for the wardrobe, that is the easiest matter of all. I shall send Aurelia—my sister—to you. If I am not mistaken, and I never am, you are both built upon similar lines. She has devilish good judgment in style, colour, and fabric, and can advise you in this matter. Simply pay no attention whatsoever to any advice she gives you regarding potential husbands." He shuddered, just a little.

"Thank you, my lord. This has been a most illuminating evening thus far."

"Time spent in my company usually is," he agreed modestly, and proceeded to explain to her, in minute detail, the differences between puce and *marron*, in English and French.

Sarah's next dining companion arrived before Saye had quite finished his lecture. "Darcy, meet Miss Benson. Devilish good company." He turned back to Sarah. "Darcy is practically leg-shackled, but feel free to practise on him. He won't notice. I bid you good hunting!"

The orangery seemed rather silent, suddenly, without him. "My, he is a presence, is he not?" she said.

Mr Darcy cleared his throat. "That is one way to describe it," he muttered. "What does he wish you to practise, Miss Benson?"

"Actually, he got it wrong—my name is Bentley. Although,

now that I think of it, I believe he remembered it. It may have been a joke."

"Quite likely," her solemn dining companion agreed.

"It was a conversation we were having on the breeding rituals of moths, and my ability to attract a mate," she explained.

Mr Darcy's brow furrowed. "Ahem. A bit of advice. Whatever Saye advises regarding rituals, you may wish to disregard."

"Truly? He had some interesting opinions."

"Let us just say his opinions are often not applicable to others."

A footman arrived, looking a bit out of breath—the orangery was somewhat of a distance from the kitchens—and brought the pheasant. Mr Darcy displayed exceedingly fine manners, serving her the choicest bits, but conversation was not nearly so easy as it had been with Lord Saye. *Perhaps that is what Lilly sees in him,* she thought. *One would never run out of words with such a man. But I think he is less harmless than Papa believes. He wears the skin of* Aglais io, *but I have never seen a peacock butterfly with a predator's heart.*

"You are betrothed, Mr Darcy?" she finally asked.

The difference in his countenance was almost startling. He beamed brighter than Saye's diamond stick pin. "Yes. Yes, I am. To Miss Elizabeth Bennet, of Hertfordshire."

Perhaps I could learn from him, she thought. Despite Saye's famed success with the ladies, she could not quite imagine him crooking his finger at Lilly and expecting her to come to heel.

"I wonder if you would mind very much telling me how Miss Bennet was able to bring you to the point?" she asked politely. "Was it a case of love at first sight?"

He stuttered a bit. "Oh. Well, not quite. That is, it was not long after I met her that I thought her the most beautiful woman I had ever known. But I did not, perhaps…that is, we were somewhat slower to reach an understanding…"

"Ah," Sarah said. "So, you both gradually realised that your friendship could be something more?"

He sighed. "She hated me. I made a terrible first impression. There were other…misunderstandings to overcome. It was a long while before I won her hand at last."

"Oh, that is encouraging," she said.

"It is?"

"Indeed. I usually make the most awful first impressions. I am always putting my foot in it or finding something amusing that is not meant to be, or asking a question one ought not to ask. I have not learnt to simply keep my mouth shut and say as little as possible."

"As to that…perhaps saying nothing at all is not wise. At least, to the extent possible, one should try to-to come to know a person, especially a person one wishes to court."

"But that is just it," Sarah cried, frustrated. "Once they come to know me, it is all over. Perhaps I should just allow my aunt to arrange a match, after all, and give up on the idea of a more romantic pairing. It is likely all nonsense to believe it could be any different."

Mr Darcy's usual stern aspect softened. "As to that, of course you must do as you think best. But in my opinion, true love is worth any sacrifice, any improvement you must make to your character, any change you deem necessary to please someone truly worthy of being pleased. It is also worth waiting for."

He was, she decided, probably one of the most wonderful men in the kingdom. Such a shame he was taken. Sarah sighed and applied herself to her pheasant.

Sarah had been introduced to Mr Anderson before, and she was no more impressed this time than the last. He was, truthfully, better looking than any she herself expected to attract, though nothing to equal Mr Darcy, with whom she was half in love, and of course, no one could compare with Saye. It was just that he was so...monochromatic. Brown hair, brown waistcoat, brown coat, brown boots. Could he not add a gold thread and a shiny button or two? Anything to break up the unrelieved...brownness? She glanced down fondly at her own bright half-boots of plum-coloured leather and knew she could never love a man who did not appreciate a dash of colour in his life.

She could not dismiss him completely, for Georgette did not appear to object to his society, and her friend was something of a connoisseur in that regard. Sarah would be friendly, therefore, but he was of no interest to her romantically.

She thought of giving him a hint or two regarding his attire, but this was another problem with Mr Anderson. He was socially adept, his manners flawless, but speaking to him was like talking to a wall. One might throw advice over the top of it, but one would never see it land. Thankfully, it was merely salad and cheese, so their time together was brief. Afterwards, he introduced her, politely enough, to Mr Reginald Withers.

Sarah looked at Mr Withers with a great deal of interest, as the first bachelor of the night with possibilities. She had noticed him before, but only thought of him as one of Saye's circle—a group of men who were more interested in racing and shooting than matrimony. But of course, he was from a good family. A second son, as she recalled, who would probably appreciate her substantial fortune. Not handsome, but not repulsive, either. Hair a bit on the thin side, chin a bit on the weak side, but tall, with broad shoulders that spoke well of either physique or tailor.

To her surprise, the meal went rather well. Mr Withers was no Mr Darcy, but she hit upon the topic of horses, about which he pontificated throughout the course. He had his own specially considered breeding program, and she thought of questions enough to keep him at it whenever he protested that he'd dominated the conversation long enough. It was not, precisely, what Mr Darcy recommended—at the end of it, she could safely say he did not know her at all. But it also meant he knew nothing of her flaws, either, and that was accomplishment enough for one evening. Besides, she was an excellent listener. Her friends always said so.

Her next dinner partner was late, and she saw that Mr Withers was looking a bit nervously about for him, especially after the footman arrived with the final course.

"Please, feel free to go to your next table," she smiled.

"I do hate to leave you alone," he protested. "It has been most pleasant. I cannot imagine what has delayed Fitz."

"Fitz?" she questioned.

"I beg your pardon. Fitzwilliam, I mean. I thought I heard he was to be next in the orangery. Saye and his ideas." He shrugged helplessly, smiling, and she found his smile to be quite nice.

"I am sure he will arrive shortly, and you must not disappoint your next partner. There are some plantings in here which I am only too happy to study."

Once he departed, Sarah hastened towards the foliage— she had not been prevaricating about her desire to examine the antique cinerary urns, the vines, and odiferous plants— and she eagerly strolled amongst the rows, ignoring the long-suffering sighs of Evans, her maid, lagging behind. A section of young trees in deep beds caught her attention, and she mentally catalogued the different varieties, intrigued by the ones she could not identify. And then she saw it.

It closely resembled a *Melolontha praegrandis*—a variety of cockchafer, an enormous beetle that feasted upon leaves. It was far too early for them! However, it was much warmer in the orangery all year round. They burrowed in the ground and spent most of their lives—years, even—as grubs in the soil. Perhaps the presence of this one was a fluke, but if there was an infestation, the gardeners must remove them from the soil while they were still in their larvae state. It was vital that she capture this one as proof of their existence in the hallowed territory of the orangery, lest the gardeners disbelieve her.

Richard Fitzwilliam was most severely displeased.

Finding himself sharing a meal, alone (or nearly so) with Elizabeth Bennet had promised to be the highlight of the party. He knew she was Darcy's future wife. There was nothing to be done about that. However, he could at least bask in the beauty of her presence, enjoy her scintillating company. And, if his own dazzling wit made her wish, at least briefly, that she could have made a different decision... well, was that so awful? It was, after all, the only comfort afforded a man who had ceded the field, knowing that he, unlike Darcy, could not marry where he liked.

Instead, he had made a fool of himself in front of the one woman he least wanted to appear foolish before, had angered Darcy—for no good reason, it was to be noted—and then had to hurry to change his ruined clothing, making him late for his final course of the evening. Not that he cared, particularly, for Miss Bentley—whoever she was, for he had missed seeing her arrival—but it was ill-mannered to be so tardy, and his pride had taken enough of a beating this evening.

But when he finally arrived at the orangery, there was only an empty table.

"She's in the trees, sir," a footman explained.

He strode to the far side of the orangery where rows of trees formed a pretty little forest, but he saw no one.

"Mistress, please, come down from there!" hissed a voice from within the plantings. He turned sharply towards it, and spotted a maid, wringing her hands, while her foolish mistress—precariously perched upon a stone urn—was climbing the bloody tree!

His dress boots were not designed for speed, but he ran as fast as he could to reach her—the tree she was attempting to climb was far too fragile to support her weight!

Two things happened at once. She called, "Got you!" and grabbed for something, and her feet—clad in the most ridiculous purple shoes he had ever seen—slipped, and she began toppling.

There was not time enough to catch her; he could only serve as a sort of cushion to break her fall. Down she went, knocking the breath from his body and his head to the pavers. For a moment, he could only wheeze, unable to breathe or speak, but then a weight was lifted from him, and finally, he gasped in a breath.

"I say," came her voice. It was a surprisingly pretty voice coming from the Satan's spawn it belonged to. "Are you hurt?"

He opened his eyes. It was the cat lady! He never forgot a face—especially when fastened to a body such as hers—and though it was dark the last time he had seen her, she was particularly unforgettable. His eyes narrowed. "You!" he accused.

"Oh!" she cried. "The cat colonel!"

Carefully, slowly, he picked himself up, dusting himself off. Without saying a word, he left her—so that he would say none of the words he thought of—and made for the table. He could hear her—silently, mercifully enough—following.

He signalled to the footman to pour; he was in no mood for champagne, but that was the only liquid available.

His dining companion sat across from him and reached for her glass but waved away the footman offering the bottle. Instead, she dropped something into it, turning it upside down on the tabletop.

He nearly let out a shriek. It was the largest, ugliest, most disgusting beetle he had ever seen.

"Get rid of that thing!" he cried.

"You need not fear it. It will not hurt you."

"I am not *afraid* of it," he spoke, low-voiced and dangerous. "I simply do not wish to share a meal with the repulsive pest." And then his temper, usually kept under good regulation, broke free. "Or you, for that matter."

She only looked at him, her gaze clear-eyed, showing no sign of hurt or dismay. "Well," she said contemplatively, "you are certainly no Mr Darcy, either."

Then she scooped up her glass, the disgusting creature within, and walked away.

AN IMPATIENT
COURSE OF ACTION

Darcy & Elizabeth

The flickering glare from the hundreds of blazing candles lining the mirrored corridors was almost blinding. If she had not already toured Darcy House and Pemberley, Elizabeth Bennet might have felt overwhelmed. As it was, she had seen and had admired both homes of which she would be mistress and thus the opulence of Matlock did not intimidate her. Amuse her, yes. The estate was nothing to Rosings, of course, in its total capitulation to the French baroque, and where Rosings and its servants were faded and worn, Matlock gleamed and shone, and its servants moved with purpose and precision.

Thank goodness they did, and that they had been well-trained to unpack, dress and polish a poorly prepared late arrival. Elizabeth had hardly seen the house, swept in as she was through the kitchens and up the back stairs, into a vast bedchamber outfitted in blue and cream. She was gazing longingly at the large silk-covered bed when the door swung open and a tall young woman with tall hair swept in, followed by two maids and two bewigged footmen, each holding large pails of steaming water. Elizabeth could feel poor Robbins quaking behind her.

The lady looked her up and down and announced what was already known—"Miss Elizabeth Bennet. You are quite late, and only my brother and I know of your attendance."—before informing her that she was Lady Aurelia Ferb-Uxbridge, her hostess, and the one deserving credit for the machinations employed to hasten Elizabeth's arrival at Matlock. As Lord Saye's was the sole signature appearing on the letters sent to Elizabeth and her mother, Lady Aurelia's declaration merited some amused doubt. But the lady was her hostess, and whatever role she had played to secure Elizabeth's presence at Matlock meant little now; what mattered was that Elizabeth was here under the same roof as her beloved for the next two weeks.

"You have been all that is kind, Lady—"

"Dinner begins in one hour. You will dine in the library. I shall not inform Darcy of your arrival."

And with that, Lady Aurelia disappeared. Her retinue of servants dispersed and began pouring Elizabeth's bath, unpacking her trunk, hanging her gowns, and undressing her. She had scarcely a moment to think, let alone sample from the tray of tea and cakes delivered to her rooms.

An hour later, her hair curled (if slightly damp from the steam of the tub) and dressed in her best gown—the ivory one with dark green and yellow trim around the bodice that Darcy had confided was his favourite—Elizabeth was led into Matlock's library. The room was lit by ornate candelabras, including one set on a small table laden with gold-trimmed plates and dishes. The bookshelves held a collection less impressive than Pemberley's, but what was there glittered with gold spines; squinting, she could see something like gargoyles, or perhaps cherubs, adorning the ceiling corners. Amused, she wondered why it was the Fitzwilliams who venerated the French and the Darcys who championed their English blood. A good question to pose when both Darcy and the colonel were in the room to debate it. But not until days from now, after she and Darcy had spent many hours together. Regardless of its overwrought art and artifice, the library would be his favourite room here; silently, she thanked Lady Aurelia for granting them this private sanctuary for their evening reunion.

Hearing footsteps in the corridor, Elizabeth moved quickly to her chair; Robbins found her own seat in the corner. She held her breath, waiting to see the dear face of her beloved; after nearly a month apart, she would see Darcy at any moment.

"Ah, you are that one."

Or not.

A portly man, somewhat near in age to Mr Bennet, entered and introduced himself as Sir Phineas Ferb-Uxbridge. A tureen of turtle soup was placed on the table between them; while the aroma of the thick broth piqued her interest, one taste of the overly salted dish found her reaching quickly for her wine goblet. Sir Phineas paused at her pinched expression, raised an eyebrow, and once assured she was not in the early throes of a choking spell or the vapours, returned his attention to his bowl.

Hungry though she was, Elizabeth determined instead she would enjoy the next course, and smiled as her companion made clear his pleasure in every slurp. She commented on the weather and the roads, and posed questions on the history of the house; her companion responded with a nod or a grunt.

The first course mercifully came to an end. A bow, a curtsey, and the door closed. Elizabeth looked across the room at Robbins, who looked near to falling asleep.

"Ah...under cover of darkness, the vaunted Miss Elizabeth Bennet has arrived."

She turned eagerly to see her second partner for the evening and swallowed a little sigh of disappointment that he was not Darcy. However, she was in little doubt as to his identity; Colonel Fitzwilliam and Lady Aurelia shared the same proud brow and bright blue eyes, but this man, clearly their brother Lord Saye, wore his familial lineage far more handsomely. Bless Darcy for the long conversations and letters in which he had shared his thoughts on various family members. Eager to thank him for his efforts in squiring her to Matlock, she had looked forward to her first encounter with Lord Saye, and from the amused expression he wore as he poured her a glass of champagne, he likely assumed such anticipation and a few compliments.

"I am grateful for the opportunity to see my betrothed amongst family and friends, sir. Thank you for planning with my mother to achieve such an end. She was honoured to scheme with a viscount; you provided her the means to hold court with our neighbours for years to come." Elizabeth's arch smile became more earnest. "Pray, I hope your sister has taken no offence at my belated and stealthy foray into your party."

Although she had made no attempt to play the coquette, her companion appeared charmed. Or at least more charmed than her previous dinner partner had been.

"An escape from the castle tower, more like it. Your father appears afflicted with a protective fever as regards you and my cousin."

"I am hardly a Rapunzel, sir." *To some, such as Miss Bingley, I am hardly a beauty.*

"Darcy would have no patience for a hirsute lady." Saye stepped to the platter-laden table beside them and lifted the lid on the serving dish; he glanced sceptically at its contents.

"The sauce is too heavy. You will not care for it." He set a small bowl of almonds on the table and retook his seat.

"You are one of five sisters, and you, I have heard often and in great detail, are the wittiest and most handsome of the lot." Her blush prompted more declarations. "Darcy, who does not prevaricate and rarely boasts let alone speaks, is quite clear on this topic, as is my brother. If Darcy has found none among your sisters to rival you, then I fear, the crown is yours."

Saye raised his glass to hers, his head cocked to one side, and examined her carefully. *"Est-ce que ton père a été un voleur, Zabet? Parce qu'il a volé les étoiles du ciel pour les mettre dans tes yeux."*

Elizabeth, regretting her lack of diligence in studying her languages, thought for a moment. *Is your father a thief? Because he stole the stars to put into your eyes?*

"My father is an honest man, but I cannot speak to whether his admiration of Matlock's library would lead him to borrow, and conveniently misplace, a few volumes."

Elizabeth was uncertain what the man had meant about her eyes or what 'Zabet' could mean, but her reply had impressed him, at least if the mirth in his expression and his long, thoughtful drink of champagne meant anything. It was too much to think about, especially when all she wished to think about was Darcy, somewhere in this massive house, dining with a different lady. *Soon,* she thought, redirecting her attention to Lord Saye when he finally spoke.

"Oh my. You will be great company at parties full of people mistaken in their own self-regard."

Darcy had told her that if a man such as Mr Collins never stopped speaking opinions no one cared to hear, Saye was a man who never stopped sharing thoughts and views in a provoking and amusing manner that made one sure to listen, even if only for self-preservation. Thus far, she rather liked him.

And then Saye demanded she tell him three things about herself that Darcy did not know. "First, of course, I shall reveal his secrets. Did you know he despises frogs? Even smothered in a lemon and butter sauce, he will not go near them."

"Perhaps it is the Frenchness of the dish he despises? He dislikes toads as well, as would anyone after a trusted cousin filled his bath with the creatures." She lifted her glass and presented him with a severe look.

"Ah, my stoic cousin has told you at least one embarrassing tale." He peered at her with interest. "Here is another secret you may not yet know. He has a mole on his derriere."

Champagne burned a path through Elizabeth's nose and she reached blindly for her napkin.

"Oh, you naughty thing!" He laughed with wicked mirth and leant closer to encourage her confidence. "What do you think of it—is it a heart or a teapot? Fitzwilliam insists it is a one-eared rabbit, but no one ever said my brother has an eye for art."

Elizabeth, finally able to breathe without coughing or crying, tried to settle her shock at Saye's revelation. She could not ask how he knew—of course these cousins had played and swum as boys—but neither could she ask why he thought she knew! Did he think that she—?

He was a sharper wit than Mr Bennet. It would be a challenge to keep up, let alone best him at his teasing. Before she could reply, Saye gave her some relief.

"Oh, dear girl, I shall spare you more embarrassing expressions for the moment, but I shall hold you to your own revelations."

Saye brushed what Elizabeth desperately hoped was not a droplet of her champagne from his lapel and went on. On and on and blessedly on, for she was not certain she could remain apace with a tête-à-tête; she coughed quietly and dabbed her eyes, trying, with no little difficulty, not to think about Darcy's bottom.

"Alas, be it too cold for toads and frogs, Darcy does need to be embarrassed, for he has been dull, dull, dull these past months, and all because of you, Miss Elizabeth Bennet. Do you know Darcy is practically garrulous when asked of you? Your charms, your wit, your laugh, your joy...! Only one topic can stir his interest. You. He despises parties, is only here because of you, and yet despite declining my invitation, here you are. And he does not know! Oh, I think we should play a game. 'Let's Hide Lizzy in the Closet!' Everyone but Darcy shall know you are here."

Miss Goddard laughed too much, and may have made quite a pretty picture of it had he been able to actually look at her. But the first moment she tittered, her bosom, sat nearly to her chin, began to quiver, and Darcy was too much a gentleman—and far too desperate for his own high-spirited lady—to allow his gaze anywhere near her. It was best to let his soup grow cold and tell her all she wished of his lovely Elizabeth.

His next partner, Miss Bentley, had a curious, wistful quality about her; her gown had an odd look to it, nearly as odd as some of the observations she made before they settled on the topic of love and proposals, and he recognised that he was the gentleman with the most expertise, at least the most recent, in the pursuit and winning of a lady's hand. How amused Elizabeth would be to hear that he was confessing his heart and his missteps to these ladies—ladies, he suddenly realised, who bore a strong resemblance to other Bennet ladies, Lydia and Catherine. He had not seen Miss Hawkridge for at least two years; was she more a Mary or a Jane?

One evening into this gathering, and he had spent every minute thinking of Elizabeth, and every course talking about her. *Am I a tiresome bore? Would she be amused? Would that she were here!*

Why had she not come? He ached that she had not come, and despised that her insufferable, self-righteous father had denied her pleas. Lady Aurelia had shown him the invitation, returned with a note of regret, and said no more. He had yet to receive a reply to his latest letter, a letter he was embarrassed to recall writing while holding a lock of her soft dark hair in his other hand.

He reached the library door, relieved to know he would dine in a room where he was at his most comfortable. He could hear laughter behind the closed doors and wondered briefly whether he was too early. Then the footman swung open the door, and he saw a familiar face...was it Robbins? One of the maids from Longbourn? He practically threw himself into the room, and there she was. His beautiful Elizabeth, sitting at a small table with Saye, laughing at something the ridiculous man had just said.

"Elizabeth?"

"Darcy?"

The amusement on her face, her lovely face, faded quickly into an expression of warmth and love. She began to stand, and he moved quickly across the room to take her hands in his. *She is here!* Mindless of anything but the lady in front of him—not miles away, but mere inches—he held her gaze before allowing his focus to travel down her neck and take in the fullness of her. Elizabeth shivered, and a blush of pink blossomed on her cheeks as he lifted her hands to his lips.

"Yes, yes, Darcy, Elizabeth. Elizabeth, Darcy. We all know you know one another. You have ruined all of my plans for a game."

Caught up in the wonder of the woman he adored, Darcy could scarcely register that his cousin was still prattling on and had not left his seat. He kissed Elizabeth's fingers and spared a quick glance at Saye.

"Elizabeth was just telling me about your proposal, which does seem rather underwhelming. Walking on a dirt path, in a drab field of dead wheat, neither ring in your pocket nor flowery words from your lips?"

"Yet my ring is on her finger, and it *is* my name on her lips. Take a lesson from a man who is most happily betrothed, and—"

"And most happily welcomed," Elizabeth finished his sentence and beamed at him. Something inside him grew explosive, and it appeared even Saye could see it. Pithily observing that he had much to do before the fourth and fifth courses were served, he finally left.

The moment the door closed behind Saye, Elizabeth was in Darcy's arms. As he held her tightly, Darcy gestured to Robbins that she was dismissed, for this course, at least. When the door clicked shut behind the maid, Elizabeth loosened her hold to look around the room, and thus satisfied they were alone, smiled up at her beloved. It took but a moment for his lips to touch hers, and they spent some minutes happily reacquainting themselves with the small passionate pleasures common between two people deeply in love and too long separated.

"You are here," Darcy whispered when they finally parted. He grasped her head between his hands, and gazed at her tenderly, reacquainting himself with every feature. "I thought your father would not allow you to come. My cousin–"

"He would not, and has not," Elizabeth said. "When my

mother learnt of the invitation, she immediately had my trunks packed with everything we had already purchased for my trousseau and announced that her great-aunt Boothe in Bletchley—the one who is half-deaf and reads poetry to her cow—was ailing and in need of a visit. My mother, Aunt Philips, Robbins, and I left Longbourn five days ago," she paused, yawning, and leant her head against his shoulder, "and Kitty is likely still mulish over being left behind."

Feeling her fatigue, Darcy eased her onto the settee, then went to fill their plates.

"My mother was busily exchanging letters with your cousin, and after two days sitting by the lady's bed, I was in a carriage he sent from Matlock. And here we are, as of two hours ago."

Grinning, Darcy shook his head in wonder. *Saye. What I owe him!* "I am happy my cousin is as eager to arrange my affairs as I am to arrange those of others."

"You are not angry that I refused, at first? I feared you would be as heartbroken as I, and sit in the corner of every room, cursing the fun we could not share at this party."

"I could never be angry with you, my love." Already the happiest he had been in weeks, Darcy felt as though his heart would burst. Elizabeth was here, in his company, for a fortnight. Time with her was his greatest treasure, and finally, for the first time since they had reached their understanding, there was no one looming over them, suspecting motives or actions. No chaperon to interrupt tender moments, although...

"Your mother and aunt did not accompany you? Only Robbins?" As much as he feared an answer in the affirmative, he knew he must be grateful for Mrs Bennet's assistance in getting Elizabeth to the house party. He busied himself putting cheeses, bread, and salad on a plate and returned to the settee.

Her tired eyes lit up and she seized a piece of Stilton. "No, they will remain in Bletchley until I return. I am sure my father is enjoying his peace."

He deserves to enjoy nothing, thought Darcy, *keeping us apart for spite and mistrust of my constancy.*

Why did I mention my father? Elizabeth did not wish to discuss *him*, or even think about *him*, or do anything else at this moment other than enjoy the close company of her beloved. "I am glad to have surprised you. Writing to you with the news that I would be here held an element of uncertainty. Was the direction to be written for Matlock, or were you still in London with Georgiana?"

"I left her in town five days ago. Had she the joy of knowing you to be here, with me," he gave Elizabeth a piercing look, "she would send her warmest felicitations and heartfelt regrets that her horrible older brother would not install her at Pemberley during her own cousin's house party and bring you to Pemberley for a visit."

"Such a horrible older brother," she whispered.

"Indeed." He kissed her then, and would have again, but he heard her stomach rumble.

"Have you not eaten any of the preceding courses, my dear? The pheasant? The soup?"

"Only a few bites," she confessed, not wishing to comment on Saye's aversion to the sauce covering the pheasant or his preference for serving her champagne. "The fish course is next. I shall ignore my partner and concentrate only on my plate."

"You will have no more partners. I shall bar the door and stay here with you."

Thrilled as she was with his ferocious pronouncement, Elizabeth demurred. "I am a stranger to nearly everyone here. It would be a bad beginning if I slighted two gentlemen and you left two ladies to dine alone."

"They can find one another and make a party of it," Darcy grumbled. "You are the only partner I wish to dine with, tonight and for every meal thereafter." She nodded her agreement and he pulled her closer. "I have missed you so—"

Suddenly the door swung open and Robbins entered, nervous and red-faced. "Miss?"

"Is it true?" A deep voice boomed behind her. "Miss Elizabeth Bennet is here?"

Elizabeth watched wistfully as Darcy disappeared through the door. He was so handsome, and had been so happy; the arrival of yet another Fitzwilliam cousin to spend time with her had left him cross and her impatient. Indeed, only the colonel himself seemed to be satisfied with the arrangements.

"It is good to see you again, Miss Bennet." Colonel Fitzwilliam leant towards her with a warm smile. "Your presence is a surprise to many of us, apparently, but a most welcome one."

"Thank you, sir. I am pleased to be here as well. You have a handsome family home. The gardens must be quite beautiful in season."

The colonel laughed. "Diplomacy is among your other talents. Matlock gives proof to the truth that Lady Catherine and my father are sister and brother."

He began peppering her with questions about her health, her family, her plans for the week ahead. So many questions, and so many amusing rejoinders to her answers that she soon realised more than half their time together had passed and they had yet to eat. She eyed the large bowl of strawberries and looked eagerly at the covered platter on the table. The colonel, finally taking on his role as server, lifted the cover on the fish course, even as he invited her to begin calling him Richard and requested permission to call her by her given name.

Elizabeth granted the indulgence absently even as she eyed the huge crustacean on the platter. It was as close to a monster as anything she had ever seen, and she could not conceive of how one could eat it, let alone find anything edible inside it. Why could they not have had trout or salmon? Did the colonel understand how one would slice and cut and serve such a creature? Or how one should eat it?

The thought of the lobster dwelling under water prompted thoughts of Darcy's fear of frogs. And then she recalled the mole he supposedly had in a most unmentionable place. She felt herself reddening as her imagination took flight; in an effort to stifle a most unladylike snort, Elizabeth reached for a strawberry and popped it in her mouth. She closed her eyes to savour the fruit's sweet taste.

"Dear lord almighty," she heard her companion murmur. Elizabeth's eyes opened and she found the colonel staring at her, mouth slightly open, a full glass of champagne slipping from his hand.

"Are you well?" As she reached across the table to right the glass, he startled, rearing back and spilling the entire contents of the goblet onto the front of his jacket.

"No!" He jerked back, knocking the heavy silver dome to the floor with a loud clatter.

Instinct prompted Elizabeth to pick up her napkin and dab at the liquid dampening the colonel's jacket and lapel.

"Elizabeth! What has happened?" Darcy burst into the

library and stared at the pair. His expression of concern changed to one of suspicion—all of it directed towards his cousin.

"Oh shut it, Darcy. 'Twas an accident. My apologies, Lizzy."

Darcy's expression hardened as he said, icily, "*Lizzy?*"

Elizabeth had met only a few in the party, and was rather exhausted by men. She did not know whether there would be a separation of the sexes—there had been so much separation already in this odd sort of dinner party—but she truly looked forward to meeting the ladies. After all, for as much as she had eagerly anticipated this reunion with Darcy, so too had she desired meeting other young ladies of the society to which she must become accustomed. It was a unique opportunity for her, and one of which she intended to avail herself.

The entrance of a gentleman fully dissimilar to her previous dining companions came as a relief. Mr Anderson, modest in manner and polite enough, seemed to promise that this course could be eaten—she truly was famished— and conversation would be less heated. She wondered how much Mr Anderson might have overheard of the previous, rather explosive conversation there in the library and whether he had noticed the nearly untouched platters of lobster and strawberries removed as he entered and Darcy stalked out.

While Mr Anderson was quiet and seemed content to let her eat before engaging in much conversation, Elizabeth noted the pleasure and interest he took when she mentioned outings to the park and puppet shows with her young cousins. She had cracked open a door with him, and he stepped through almost eagerly, speaking more openly, albeit formally and as a gentleman, to her. It was the easiest half an hour she had yet passed at Matlock, and the most filling; the sugarplums and candied plums were delicious. No longer peckish, she sat back and enjoyed Mr Anderson's conversation until their time together came to an end.

If he took his leave abruptly rather than escort her to wherever destiny beckoned next in this cavernous castle, well, she would thank him later. After all, the man who loved her had, apparently, been waiting, and his fearsome expression of some thirty minutes earlier had faded into one of contrition.

She eyed him expectantly. "Mr Anderson has been sent on his way?"

Darcy nodded. "Some fresh air and a chance to see the night sky, madam?" He regarded her hopefully and at her nod, offered his arm and led her from the library.

"I wish for a few minutes alone before we join the others," he said as he led her down a long corridor. Other couples were moving in the opposite direction, but he urged her on. "My uncle cannot boast of his library, but the orangery is rather magnificent."

She smiled. *The ladies can wait.*

DISCRETION AND DESIRE

Georgette & Anderson

Georgette was seated demurely at the head of the vast dining table, sipping champagne, when her cousin entered the room. It was a far more acceptable attitude than that in which the footmen had discovered her when they entered bearing platters of pheasant and vegetables a few moments before. Most of them had exhibited a commendable degree of myopia. One—a nervous, freckled thing—had flushed crimson and almost dropped his tray. She winked at him as he carted away the untouched first course, chuckling to herself when he ducked his head and broke into a shuffling sort of run.

"You did not care for the soup?" Fitzwilliam remarked, peering into the tureen as it was carried past him.

"I have never much cared for things with too little bite. I am rather partial to pheasant, though. Would you do the honours?"

He obliged and brought her a plate of food. After a moment or two staring in consternation at the seating arrangements, he sat decisively in the chair next to hers and dragged the cutlery peevishly along the table from where it had been set out two places farther away. "Blasted rum idea this," he grumbled.

"Oh, I do not know. I have rather enjoyed myself so far."

"Because you were afforded the dignity of eating in the actual dining room. I have just eaten my soup off the lid of the pianoforte."

Georgette smirked; he had always been the testier of her two male Fitzwilliam cousins. "One can only assume," she said, taking up her knife and fork, "that your dinner partner was not charming enough to compensate for the unusual dining arrangements?"

"I was allocated Miss Parker." He stopped speaking and shrugged, his expression nonplussed.

"Aye," she agreed, laughing. "She is distinctly decorative."

Fitzwilliam snorted. "It is a pleasure to see you, Georgette. It has been far too long."

"It has been almost half a year." She took a sip of champagne before continuing. "I confess, I found it rather odd that Saye should suddenly wish for my company, and that of my friends, after such an age."

"There is nothing strange about it. He wished to have a party, and you are our liveliest relation with equally delightful friends. You were an obvious choice."

"Is that so? It had nothing to do with my dear friend Lilly's imminent engagement then?"

It clearly had everything to do with it—even Fitzwilliam's excessive, army-issue side whiskers could not conceal the tinge of guilt pinking his cheeks. Nevertheless, Georgette could not be easy, for though it was evident Saye admired Lilly, she was entirely unconvinced this party was not simply his means of securing what fun he could have with her before she married someone else. And though she approved of her cousin's zest for life, she had no wish to see her friend ill-used. "He has secured himself quite the reputation as a man who enjoys liveliness," she continued. "But I wonder whether anybody could ever be truly satisfied with fun alone. Does he not seek anything more?"

Fitzwilliam would not be drawn. "Speaking of liveliness, why did you insist on inviting Blanderson? What business has he at such an event as this?"

She wondered what Fitzwilliam would have made of Anderson's liveliness had he seen him a quarter of an hour ago. "It is not business," she replied with a sly smile. "It is pleasure. You ought to try it."

Expecting that he would continue sparring, she was taken aback when instead he grew morose and shook his head. "'Tis not my hour." He sighed deeply, and Georgette thought he might elaborate until the door burst open and her maid stumbled into the room.

"Ah, Prinny! You are back. Excellent."

"Forgive me, Miss Hawkridge," she babbled, sidling into her seat in the corner. "I was not aware the second course had started."

"No matter. I think I am safe from my own cousin. This one, at any rate."

"Prinny?" Fitzwilliam enquired sceptically.

"Her real name is Regent," Georgette explained. "It was too delicious to leave it alone."

"How droll. And where has she been this evening, when she was supposed to be chaperoning you?"

"The poor dear came over faint and stepped out for some air." Georgette made a private note to congratulate Prinny later for the sterling performance she then gave, wilting in her chair and exhaling pathetically. It did not fool her cousin, who squinted suspiciously.

"Whom did you say your first dinner partner was?"

Georgette batted the question away with a wave of her fork and diverted the conversation in a far safer direction. The next ten minutes or so proved exceedingly enjoyable as she recalled what an interesting life Fitzwilliam had led and how well he told a good tale. Still, at a lull in their discussion, she could not resist goading him, just a little. "What was that about it not being your hour for pleasure?"

Fitzwilliam baulked, though he recovered well and immediately returned fire. "Why did you not call for a different companion, if your maid was indisposed?"

"Because," Georgette replied in an indifferent tone, "my previous dinner partner is, by your own account, the most insipid person in this house. You cannot think a chaperon was necessary for the few minutes Mr Anderson and I were alone. But never mind that. Tell me more about what is preventing you from having your share of entertainment. As the son of an earl, you cannot want for attention. But, if you say it is 'not your hour,' perhaps you have been pipped at the post for the lady you would choose." She stopped speaking and gasped, her eyes widening. She had been teasing him only to distract him from asking about Anderson, but her reasoning had brought her to a startling notion. "You do not hold a candle for Lilly as well, do you?"

"Of course not. Though I should have more chance of success if I did, for Saye might only wound me if I attempted to cuckold him. Darcy would definitely kill me."

"What would Mr Darcy care if you made overtures to Lilly?"

Fitzwilliam floundered over his answer, planting another idea in Georgette's mind. But then his eyes grew wide and he said, rather too emphatically for her liking, "Hold fire! You said it was not business but pleasure that you enjoyed with

Anderson. Precisely how much pleasure did the two of you just have?"

"For heaven's sake, Fitzwilliam, I am not Saye. And I resent your implication. I beg you would not take out your frustrations on me."

The door opened again, this time admitting a footman who set about clearing the table.

"I beg your pardon," her cousin said quietly. "That was abominably ill-mannered, and I apologise."

"I shall forgive you if you answer me one question."

"Go on."

"What is so special about Miss Elizabeth Bennet?"

She had hit the mark! He averted his eyes and fidgeted uncomfortably—until a footman leant around him to remove the used cutlery, whereupon he abruptly snatched the soup spoon from the servant's hand and held it aloft. "This has not been used. Did Mr Anderson dislike the soup also?"

Georgette did her best not to laugh. "I cannot recall that we discussed it."

"What did you discuss?"

"We did not have much opportunity for talking. Time passes so quickly when one is having fun. As it has done again now. Good evening, Mr Emerson." With the arrival of her next dinner partner, her cousin was forced to let the matter drop. "It has been fun sparring with you, Fitzwilliam. Perhaps we ought to try it with real swords tomorrow, as we used to when we were children."

"Do not tempt me," he replied, before giving her a cursory bow and stamping out of the room.

The dining arrangements were unusual, but Anderson had no objection. Not when they afforded such a rare opportunity to be alone with Georgette—an opportunity of which they had wasted not a moment. Now he could scarcely attend to aught but the memory of it and feared he was being awful company for his present dinner companion. To make matters worse, they were situated in a parlour that he understood was Lady Matlock's favourite, and newly decorated to boot. He sincerely doubted her ladyship would approve of it being used as a makeshift dining room, no matter her son's enthusiasm for the scheme, and he felt compelled to take exceedingly great care with his dinner lest he drop or spill anything. Regrettable enough that the dining room had been left in such disarray. He sincerely hoped the spilled wine would not stain.

"Do you have any brothers or sisters?" Miss Goddard enquired.

Anderson tore his mind away from the act that had caused his wine to be overturned, gulped down his over-chewed mouthful, and answered politely that he had one younger brother. He did not mention that Randalph was a spoilt, dissolute wastrel, or that his older brother had died at fifteen from the complications of a childhood bout of infantile paralysis. These were hardly dinner table topics, but their omission rendered the conversation stilted in the extreme.

Matters were not helped by Miss Goddard's own absence of mind. She seemed equally distracted and looked frequently at the door. He did not take offence. Apprised by Georgette of almost every other guest's present state of romantic dissatisfaction, Anderson understood her to be more impatient for Lord Saye's company than she was displeased with his. He nevertheless resolved to give a better account of himself tomorrow.

He made a concerted effort to be more gentlemanlike for

his next dinner partner, for she was another of Georgette's particular friends. Miss Bentley took the conversation on more than one unusual tangent, and he gamely followed. She had dined with Mr Darcy and Lord Saye before him, he gathered, and he soon began to suspect that it was her design to compare him to them. Feeling no compulsion to compete with either gentleman, Anderson did not elaborate his answers to any of her many questions, giving the simple truth and allowing her to do with it as she pleased.

She had a handsome frown that flitted in and out of view between her brows as she appraised him with endearing tactlessness. He did not tell her so, for he would bet a pretty penny that she would not know what to do with a compliment if it came to her wrapped in instructions. He would tell Georgette, and she would pass it on in a manner more palatable to her friend.

Mr Emerson proved disappointing; Georgette enjoyed speaking to him about as much as she enjoyed the wilted lettuce he accompanied. Both were equal in charm, though, perhaps, the lettuce had the advantage when it came to presence.

The fourth course looked as though it would be far more promising when a tray-laden footman entered, followed by her next partner. She did not expect that the conversation would improve much, but if it were presence one desired, then both the huge, livid-red lobster and Mr Darcy perfectly satisfied the brief. One glared at her sullenly; the other bowed formally and greeted her with a pleasing little turn to his mouth that inclined Georgette to be far gentler with him than she had planned to be. Not that she would have been terribly mischievous, for Anderson had urged her to be sympathetic to his situation. "After all," he had said in that particular manner that softened every bone in her body, "you and I know better than most what it is to wait."

She returned the greeting and set about eating the lobster with well-practised elegance. Mr Darcy did likewise. They exchanged a few pleasantries on the dish and the gathering, each time his small smile disposing Georgette to like him a little more.

"I believe it is your turn to say something now," he said abruptly, and rather testily, startling Georgette out of her reveries of Anderson's delectable smile.

"I beg your pardon, Mr Darcy. I was in a world of my own. Did you say something?"

"No. I was rather hoping you would."

She smiled languidly. "Really? You do not strike me as the sort who enjoys small talk, and I am far too vain to exert myself only to be found displeasing."

He laughed; it was a surprisingly beautiful sight to behold. And she did so appreciate beautiful things.

"You have the right of it, madam. My cousin could not have conceived of an evening's entertainment I would despise more, in the usual course of things. But I find myself uncommonly desirous of distraction at the present moment, and you have been surprisingly restrained."

"Surprisingly? Were you expecting me to run on like a bird-brained ninny because I am handsome and wearing an exquisite gown?"

"Not at all. I was expecting you to ask me about Miss Bennet, because that is all anybody else has talked to me about this evening."

"That is the only way anybody can get you to talk at all. But it would be better if you did not tell me anything about

Miss Bennet, for I should much rather form my own opinion of her than adopt yours."

He inclined his head, the enchanting curve of his mouth now mirrored by the expression of satisfaction in his eyes. "You will have the opportunity to do just that, now that she has come to Matlock."

"She is here? I understood she declined the invitation." She thought of Fitzwilliam and questioned whether this was such a fortuitous development.

"It is a long story, but yes, she is here. I have just dined with her in the library. And now I would very much appreciate some conversation to distract me from the fact that I am no longer doing so."

Georgette shook her head and laughed to see such impatience in a grown man. "Very well. Shall we discuss our cousins, since we have them in common? Tell me your opinion—is it the army or age that has made Fitzwilliam such a cantankerous old goat?"

Mr Darcy pulled a face. "He is the last person I would talk about. He is presently dining with Elizabeth and has absolutely no cause to be cantankerous."

Au contraire, Mr Darcy, she thought as she attempted to imagine what Fitzwilliam's reaction to Miss Bennet's arrival must have been, for she was certain that he esteemed her. And though he was cantankerous, she hoped he would not do anything that would actually result in Mr Darcy killing him.

"Pray what is it?" her companion enquired. His mouth was a hard line now, the pleasing lilt banished.

"What is what, sir?"

"Why did you look so concerned just then, when I said Fitzwilliam was with Miss Bennet?"

"You ought not to impose your own feelings onto other people's actions, Mr Darcy. If you are concerned that Miss

Bennet is dining with somebody other than you, perhaps you ought to do something about it. After all, you cannot think Saye means to stick to his own ludicrous dining arrangements."

Several emotions flickered across Mr Darcy's countenance as he fought a visible battle with his conscience. Georgette took pity on him. "It is well, sir, I shall not be offended if you go."

She sighed to herself as he departed. Handsome he may be, but he was rather too theatrical for her liking. Anybody would think he was the only person ever obliged to wait for happiness.

Sir Phineas blustered into the dining room along with dessert. He filled two seats, ate three helpings of candied plums, and turned out to be the most entertaining partner of the evening, bar one. Once Georgette let it be known that she was a dab hand with a fowling piece, their conversation grew livelier by the moment.

When they both had finished, she threw her napkin on the table and came to her feet, forcing his overstuffed lordship to do likewise. "Come! Let us see what trouble everybody is getting up to in the drawing room. I should not like to arrive late. I do hate to miss out."

Anderson felt for Miss Bennet. There had clearly been some manner of disagreement, for he had heard raised voices as he neared the library, and Colonel Fitzwilliam had stormed past him as he approached the door, his lapels soaked. He had discovered Mr Darcy within, and there had been a moment of silence that was evidently mortifying for the young lady before that gentleman finally consented to leave and stalked away with barely less rancour than his cousin. Now Miss Bennet was subdued and discernibly embarrassed, and Anderson was struggling to think of how he might put her at ease.

"Can I help you to dessert, madam?" he enquired.

"Thank you," she replied. "That would be appreciated. I did not have the opportunity to eat much of the lobster."

"I believe Lord Saye intended that this should be a diverting way to pass the evening," he said as he returned with a plate for each of them. "But he overlooked the fact that, without the distraction of twenty people around one table, everybody's behaviour—and misbehaviour—is far more noticeable."

"Yes," she replied quietly.

"Ordinarily, for example, I might never have noticed that Lady Aurelia was three sheets to the wind, but it was really impossible not to notice when her food dropped off her fork into her wine and she began examining the ceiling, convinced the plaster was falling off."

Miss Bennet huffed a soft laugh and smiled gratefully. "I only found out recently that Colonel Fitzwilliam had a sister —and even then, it was Mr Darcy who told me. The colonel did not mention her to me himself."

"He would not be the first person with a brother or sister to whom he would rather not draw attention," he replied, thinking of Randalph—and Matthew, though it was his parents who had forbidden any mention of him.

"Very true," Miss Bennet replied. "I am one of five sisters, and though I like to think we were all charming as young children, not all of us made it into womanhood with that charm intact."

"Children are far less complicated than adults."

She agreed whole-heartedly before delighting him with an account of her young cousins, whom she explained lived in

London. Speaking of them seemed to return a measure of her composure, and though he generally shied away from mentioning his private affairs, Anderson resolved to tell her about his own experience with youngsters in the hope it would restore her equanimity completely.

"If you are fond of children, you will have to visit some of mine next time you are in town." He laughed at her expression and hastened to explain. "I own an institution for sick and disfigured children. All those dear souls whose families no longer want them. We do as much as we can for as many as we can there—which is not many, more's the pity." He proceeded to tell her, because she seemed genuinely interested, about the management of the institution and some of the children it had helped.

"That is wonderful," Miss Bennet said, sitting forward in her seat, with ingenuous approbation that made her eyes gleam prettily.

"I am glad you think so. Not everybody is as convinced of its worth."

"Who would think helping children is not a worthy cause?"

Anderson smiled ruefully. "More people than you might imagine. Most of these children are exceedingly unwell. They do not look or behave as others their age do. They would ordinarily be consigned to an asylum, put out on the streets, or worse. They are unwanted—considered unholy by some and disgusting by most. My involvement in the home is distasteful to almost all who know of it."

"I am very sorry to hear that."

"Society does not do well with whatever is different, Miss Bennet. And it is entirely too free with its scorn."

She raised her glass. "Then let us toast to differences, Mr Anderson. For I have never cared for the world's scorn."

Anderson joined Miss Bennet in her toast, heartened to

have discovered such a compassionate soul among Lord Saye's guests. He thought he heard a shuffle outside the door and paused. There was another shuffle, and then he distinctly heard someone sigh. He was fairly certain he could guess who it was, for never had he heard an exhalation imbued with such impatience. Repressing a chuckle, he said, "I thank you for your commendation, madam. Now, I find I have eaten quite enough plums for one day, and since I can hear another gentleman anticipating the pleasure of your company, I hope you will excuse me." He rose to his feet and bowed. "It has been most enjoyable, Miss Bennet."

Mr Darcy nodded his thanks as they passed each other. Anderson returned the gesture, privately hoping the man had put the last half an hour to good use and thought of some more successful ways of pleasing his betrothed. He made his way to the drawing room, expecting to be the first to arrive, since his dessert course had been curtailed. He was not particularly surprised to find Georgette already there, holding court before several of the other gentlemen, all laughing uproariously at something she had just said.

He sent a silent prayer of thanks heavenward to have won the heart of such a woman. She truly was astounding, not least for her flawless person, but for her conviviality. Her present audience comprised a motley selection of drunks and dotards, but it did not trouble her. She gave her time as willingly to them as she did to the children at his institution, or his dissolute and undeserving younger brother, or her own recalcitrant father. There was nobody Georgette considered beneath her notice, nobody from whom she would withhold her charm, and Anderson adored her for it.

She caught his eye and winked, which provoked Lord Phineas to frown between them disapprovingly. Anderson sighed to himself and walked away to request a cup of coffee from the footman serving the drinks. Moments later, Georgette arrived at his side and requested one for herself.

"Pray tell me why my winking at you should cause such obvious vexation, Mr Anderson," she enquired airily, and not at all quietly.

He gave her an expressive look and gestured for her to step away from the refreshment table with him. "Lord Phineas saw you," he said in a low voice. "We agreed we would be careful, love. Your father would hear of it in a blink if we were discovered here, in your own cousins' house."

"Oh, fie on my father," she replied in an angry whisper. "I have a good mind to tell him how thoroughly I have already allowed you to compromise me and let him choke on the shock."

"He would not choke before he put a stop to it. Georgette, we would never marry if he got wind of our plans now." She looked chastened, which made him wish to kiss her back to her usual liveliness. In a gentler tone, he added, "Besides, I have not compromised you as completely as I would like. It is only a few months until we may do as we please without his consent. I beg you would do nothing to expose us before then."

She grinned saucily at him. "No more than you exposed me in the dining room?"

"There were no witnesses there. Winking at me in front of half the guests is riskier."

"You must not concern yourself on that score. I winked at every other gentleman who came into the room as well."

Anderson smirked. *Of course she had!* "Have I told you how well you look this evening, Miss Hawkridge?"

"Not with words, but I took your meaning when you did that wonderful thing at dinner." With a look that almost rendered Anderson indecent to remain in company, Georgette returned to her seat.

With a complacent smile, he relaxed into the corner of the nearest settee, firmly of the opinion that Lord Saye's unusual notion for a dinner party had been a triumph. By the end of the evening, it seemed his lordship was of an entirely contrary opinion, and Anderson took some comfort in the fact that he was not alone in finding courtship a troublesome business.

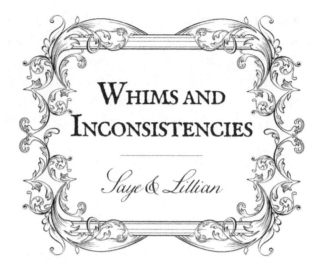

WHIMS AND INCONSISTENCIES

Saye & Lillian

I n dire need of air, Saye exited the house, coming upon Darcy and his miss as they evidently tried to sneak off for some kisses. "Miss Bennet," he said with as much disapproving hauteur as he could summon. "I assure you, madam, such goings-on are not the way at Matlock. Where is your chaperon?"

To her credit, Miss Bennet looked horrified, her eyes flying wide as she attempted to put some distance between herself and Darcy. "I...forgive me, my lord, I did not mean—"

"Ignore him, Elizabeth. He is the last person to play the puritan," Darcy said with a frown in Saye's direction. "Do not torment my beloved, Saye."

"I have to welcome her into the family, do I not?" Saye replied with a half-smile, giving Miss Bennet a courtly bow. She smiled back, looking relieved. "I antagonise them all, do not fear."

"Not now. We have not seen one another for months and—"

"Months?" Miss Bennet turned shining eyes towards Darcy.

"A twelve-month at least," Darcy said tenderly, looking down into her countenance, and Saye nearly gagged. "Or so it seems."

They had both become lost in one another's gaze, and Saye reminded them of his presence with a pointed clearing of his throat. "Much as I am loath to interrupt Darcy's love-making, I am in a crisis."

"I shall be glad to speak to you of it later, Saye," Darcy offered.

"Later will not do," Saye replied. "I need help, this very moment. Perhaps Miss Bennet will hear me and offer her thoughts as well?"

Saye could see that Darcy was about to refuse him, so he turned his attention to Miss Bennet. "Surely you would not wish to see my own romantic endeavours go so wrongly astray? A few moments of your guidance shall be just what I need."

Miss Bennet looked up at Darcy again. "A few minutes could not hurt, could it?"

Darcy acquiesced, but not without casting his blackest scowl at his cousin. "I daresay I am obliged to give him some concession for his efforts in bringing you here."

The three stepped back inside, Darcy and Miss Bennet sitting on a nearby stair which was mostly for servants' use, while Saye paced before them. For the benefit of Miss Bennet, Saye summarised quickly his dilemma and his plan to end the week engaged to Miss Goddard. "So then," he announced. "It was a simple plan for tonight. Get her drunk, feed her lobster, kiss the butter off her chin. But somehow, it all went off and next I knew—"

"That was your plan?" Miss Bennet interrupted. "Truly?"

"Yes, truly," Saye retorted. "I want her to see that life with me could not be dull, that I am in all ways different from Hairy Ball—"

On Darcy's quick but nevertheless frightening glare, he amended, "Mr Balton-Sycke."

"And this Mr Balton-Sycke is dull?"

"Frightfully so," Saye told her. "Like watching a scrim of ice melt on a pond while you pi—"

On Darcy's quick but blistering frown, he amended, "... when it gets warm."

"Hmm." Miss Bennet looked thoughtful, and Saye was immediately energised. Darcy had said she was witty... perhaps she would understand Lilly?

"What is it?" He leant over her. "What are you thinking?"

"Well...I do not know Miss Goddard, of course, so my prediction of what she is thinking cannot account for too much." She smiled up at him, very sweetly. "But I would suppose that she already knows how much fun you are, yes?"

Saye shrugged. "Possibly."

"Possibly?" Darcy scoffed. "Saye, they all know the stories. Amusement is your religion."

"So it is," Saye agreed. "I see no purpose in tedium."

"And your efforts to amuse yourself have grown increasingly outlandish," Darcy added.

"I am two-and-thirty," he owned. "I require more to divert myself now than I did as a boy at school."

"Perhaps," said Miss Bennet, "what Miss Goddard needs to see, then, is your more serious side."

"A more serious side?" Saye pondered this for a moment. "I do not think I have one."

"You do," she said, most earnestly. "You must."

"I might not."

"No," said Darcy. "He certainly does not. In truth."

Miss Bennet considered this a moment, head tilted and curls falling rather fetchingly to one side. Saye glanced at Darcy and saw that his cousin, too, had noted the appeal of his betrothed, and no doubt wanted to make short work of this confabulation. Feeling an uncommon burst of magnanimity, he said, "I daresay I shall toddle off—"

"It is evident," said Miss Bennet, "that there is, in Miss Goddard, something that longs for a serious side of things. Something in this Mr Balton-Sycke must appeal to her."

"Impossible," Saye declared. "There is nothing appealing about him in the least. Do you know, the man actually possesses enormous fluffs of hair which extrude from his nostrils? Try kissing a man whose nostril hair might assault you at any moment!"

To this, Darcy snorted with suppressed laughter, but Miss Bennet was undeterred. "But if it were impossible," she insisted gently, "then surely, it would not concern you so."

Damnation! If the witch had not neatly cut to the heart of him. Saye gave Darcy a helpless look, but at this moment, Miss Bennet, overcome by cool air in the hall and her rather useless-looking pelisse, shivered. Darcy was immediately on his feet, pulling her close. "Right then. We shall be inside, Saye, and I hope I shall see you in the drawing room shortly."

Tucking her under his arm, Darcy prepared to take his lady off, but Miss Bennet stayed him. Looking backwards, over Darcy's enormous arm encircling her shoulders, she said, "If it is true, my lord, that you lack a serious side, might I offer only this—a woman cannot help but fall in love with a man who changes for her, or who shows a side to her that no one else has seen."

She was given a kiss on the lips for this utterance, though in truth it sounded like the babblings of a madwoman to him, and then the pair of them walked off. Saye sank onto the stairs himself, feeling utterly defeated. "Women," he muttered. "Just when you think they know something, they shoot a bunch of gibberish out the lips at you."

Lilly went to her bedchamber where she refreshed herself and washed her face with cold water, trying as best she could to shake off the vestiges of too much champagne. As she regained her composure, she looked about her, wondering if all the guest apartments at Matlock were as fine as the one she was in.

She sat on the bed, kicking off her shoes while she wondered whether she ought to call her maid. Was she in for the night? She was never one to shirk a party, although she felt very little like being amused or amusing by this time. Why, oh why, did Saye always vex her so!

There was a little knock on her door and before she could utter a word, Sarah entered. "Lilly? Whatever are you doing up here?"

"Oh...resting."

"Resting?" Sarah walked across the room to peer at her. "Are you drunk?"

"Of course not!"

Sarah smiled. "Perhaps just a little?"

"A little," said Lilly with a rueful giggle. "We shall see how much mercy my head extends to me tomorrow morning for the truth of it."

"Your mother is not here to scold you, dearest, so eat, drink, and make merry to your heart's content."

"I know." With a sigh, Lilly admitted, "It was Saye."

"Saye? Was he cruel to you?"

"Lord no. He has never been cruel to me."

"Then what is it? It seems like you are hiding away in your bedchamber."

"I only meant to rest a little. What are they doing down there? Has Saye been in?"

"Lord Saye is not yet in, nor is Mr Darcy. But I hear that Miss Bennet arrived unexpectedly to surprise him, so I should imagine they are greeting one another in private somewhere." Sarah giggled and blushed, even as she said it. Lilly had no doubt her imagination was running wild, and no wonder! They all had pined after Mr Darcy at some point. Learning that he had some untold reserve of passion for this unknown country lady had only heightened his allure for them all.

"I am sure I have had quite enough of Lord Saye already tonight, so if he is absent, so much the better."

"Oh Lilly, do you really wish him gone?"

"Why should I not?" Lilly huffed. "He is so irritating! He just rattles away and thinks we should all love the very ground he deigns to walk on."

"He does rattle on a bit, it is true." Sarah nodded slowly.

"Rattles away about anything and everything...everything except marriage, that is." Lilly frowned. "I daresay everyone is right—he is not the marrying kind. He will allow Matlock to go to Colonel Fitzwilliam's son so he can be sixty and still behaving as if he is twenty." She watched with amusement as Sarah flushed scarlet at the mention of the colonel. *Interesting!*

"In any case," she continued, "I cannot dangle about, wishing for something that may never come to pass. Stolen kisses and naughty whispers will not get me out of my father's house, but Balton-Sycke will."

"Well," Sarah said, "it seems your mind is made up. Which is good! One should not enter into an engagement without certainty."

"Yes," Lilly agreed. "If spending some time here in the absence of Balton-Sycke can at least give me certainty it will be time well spent."

"Indeed, it shall." Sarah smiled. "But I hope you do not

intend to spend that time holed away. Come down, join us in the drawing room. Perhaps we can all meet Miss Bennet."

Lilly agreed and rose, patting a bit of rice powder on her face and adjusting a few of the curls around her temples. Balton-Sycke was an excellent match from a good family, and she would never want for a thing. And if he never made her laugh, neither did he make her want to pull her own hair out, so surely that was for the best?

Laughter, and the sound of someone at the pianoforte, rang out from the drawing room. Lilly smiled, smoothing her skirts before she entered. A quick glance about the place showed Saye was not there. *Better and better.*

"Lilly? Come and meet Miss Bennet," called Georgette, and Lilly crossed the room, eager to do so.

Miss Bennet sat in the middle of a settee with Mr Darcy looming behind her. She rose as Lilly came over, revealing she was a bit shorter than Lilly herself was, but very pretty. Not beautiful, perhaps, but pretty enough.

The two ladies curtseyed to one another, and then Lady Aurelia, who had been sitting next to Miss Bennet, was summoned by Mrs Ambrose, Matlock's housekeeper. She excused herself, offering Lilly her seat. Lilly settled into it. Georgette was on her other side, and leant over saying, "Miss Bennet has been telling us all about how she met Mr Darcy."

"Have I missed a good tale?"

Georgette snorted. "An unconventional tale to be sure." She looked over her shoulder, "Really, Mr Darcy, that first proposal sounded positively ghastly."

Lilly's eyes widened. In her experience, people did not

speak so to Mr Darcy, and she wondered what icily terrifying jaw-me-dead might now rain down upon them.

But Mr Darcy, shockingly, laughed. "What can I say? She had me tongue-tied from the first."

"I must admit," Miss Bennet said, "he has proven far more garrulous than I ever imagined, since our engagement." She said it with a smile over her shoulder at Mr Darcy, and Lilly noticed how much prettier she was when she smiled. *She has very sparkly eyes,* she observed. *Mr Darcy must like that.*

But her observations of Miss Bennet were halted as the door opened and Saye entered. Lilly tried not to stiffen, but she did. Determinedly, she turned her sights away from him, shifting in her seat so she would not see him.

"How do you find Derbyshire, Miss Bennet?" she asked. "I am sorry, I do not know where you are from."

"My father's estate is called Longbourn."

"You must tell me all about it," Lilly said kindly, then looked with intent interest while Miss Bennet spoke of her sisters and the numerous rivers and how the entire place had four-and-twenty families. All the while Lilly fancied that Saye's eyes were boring into her back, but when she chanced to glance over, he was talking to Sir Phineas. Arguing with him, it looked like. Ugh, why did she care?

Determinedly, she turned back to Miss Bennet and asked about her wedding arrangements. Evidently this ground had already been covered with the other ladies. Georgette rose and said she was going to get some more coffee, and was instantly engulfed by at least three gentlemen, all offering to fetch one for her. Miss Morgan, who had been sitting in silence on Georgette's opposite side, also rose, murmuring something about who knew what. Mr Darcy leant down and whispered something, then said, "Excuse me," to Lilly and left the two ladies alone.

"I understand that you surprised Mr Darcy," said Lilly. "How did you manage it? It is no easy distance, all that way."

"Lord Saye surely made it as easy as it could possibly be," said Miss Bennet. "He made certain of all the details of my travel."

"My invitation came from Lady Aurelia," Lilly protested. "Surely yours did as well?"

"The invitation did, yes, but when I informed Lady Aurelia that my father would not permit me—"

"He did not?"

Miss Bennet shook her head and with a regretful smile said, "My father has been difficult about my engagement, to say the least. My mother was required to conspire with Lord Saye, and she was quite pleased with herself to be scheming with a viscount."

"Saye?" Lilly scoffed. "I assure you, it was likely his secretary. Not Saye himself. He likely just waved his hand about and said, 'see it done'."

"I do not think so," Miss Bennet replied. "I am no expert, of course, but the notes and the directions all seemed to be in his hand."

"And so you are here against your father's wishes?" Lilly exclaimed. "*That* part of it does seem like Saye—he delights in thwarting people."

"My mother was delighted to become his ally in thwarting Papa in this instance," said Miss Bennet. "I have two yet-unmarried sisters at home, and it is a wonder my mother did not contrive to have them here too! I should not be a bit surprised if I opened my trunk and one of them popped out!"

The two ladies laughed comfortably, but Lilly was perplexed. Saye, attending to details? Saye, caring about something wholly unrelated to him? Saye, seeing to someone's comfort?

"You are not fond of Lord Saye?" Miss Bennet asked. "Forgive me—I only ask because it seemed so, from your previous comments."

"Oh, all of these young bucks about town." Lilly rolled her eyes. "I daresay you were not much in London?"

Miss Bennet shook her head.

"They gad about running up debts and trifling with hearts, and then, once they cannot avoid it any longer, they marry. Trust me, Miss Bennet," said Lilly, "you managed to secure one of the few good men around."

"Now that is a grim picture indeed," Miss Bennet exclaimed. "But surely Lord Saye is not—"

"The worst of the worst," Lilly said. "He once gambled seven thousand pounds away!"

"To my brother," Saye announced, arriving behind them. Both ladies startled guiltily. "I lost the money to Fitzwilliam, you know, and if you think I could not have trounced him soundly, you are as much a fool as he is."

"Hey!" Fitzwilliam had also arrived at the settee, but took the liberty of sliding himself in next to Miss Bennet. Lilly was surprised by his boldness, but Miss Bennet did not seem so. "It was not seven thousand in truth, only the tattle had it so."

"How much was it then?" Lilly asked, not caring if she seemed a little rude to ask so plainly.

Saye smiled at her but only said, "It was not seven thousand. Not nearly."

"It was above five thousand," Fitzwilliam interjected. "And if the truth be known, I had got myself in a bind and needed my dear brother to help me. And he did, and even afforded me the dignity of imagining I had won it, and for that I am most grateful."

It was curious, Lilly thought, how awkward and discomfited Saye looked at this tale of his kindness.

"But enough of that! Did you hear," Saye said, "how that Ackers fellow had his front teeth removed?"

A nice change of subject it was, indeed, for the ladies recoiled in horror and the men laughed, and Mr Darcy returned to hear how Mr Ackers was so fond of racing about London, fingering the ribbons like some coachman, that he wished to be able to spit like a coachman as well. Soon enough, nearly the whole room had gathered to tell extraordinary tales of the antics of the Four-in-Hand Club, persons they had reportedly run down on the street, and enormous feasts they were supposed to have eaten.

"But all that is nothing," Saye announced, "to the feast I have planned for two nights hence. Who here...?"

He let the sentence dangle, no doubt hoping to tantalise them all.

"...has ever heard of a feast of *aha'aina*?"

"What?" Mr Darcy asked.

"He is speaking gibberish," Fitzwilliam announced. "Does this have something to do with that pit I saw them digging near the orangery? You know Father will have your head if that ruins Mother's gardenias."

"It will be long gone by the time Mama's gardenias can be prevailed upon to care," Saye retorted. "But do hear me. This is a feast of a tribe in Polynesia, and we shall roast a pig in that pit and sit on the floor for our meal."

The room immediately erupted in protest and shock, which was, no doubt, Saye's first object. Evidently savages liked to dance half naked whilst they all shoved strange foods into their mouths with their hands.

"And we shall learn their dances," Saye added, only heightening the appalled protests of the room. "See here, the women at these feasts are generally half-naked as well, so at least I have not gone so far as that!"

Lilly rolled her eyes. It was a good thing Saye had

revealed this strange notion, for she had nearly begun to think him rational for a moment. Divert them, shock them, disgust them, and then gossip about it—these were the tenets of Saye, and so would ever be.

The crapulence from the champagne she drank earlier had begun to wear off, leaving a headache behind. Thoughts of her soft pillow and warm bed were increasingly appealing, and she knew she would do best to go up before she was too tired to even undergo her night-time toilette.

Rising, she said goodnight to the others, noting that Saye scarcely gave her a look, just waggled his fingers towards her as he launched off into some story about his friend Sir Frederick Moore. With a sigh, she left them, walking out into the hall and moving towards the stair.

Her progress was arrested by the sounds of a familiar voice coming from the direction of the vestibule. *No, surely not…*

Quickening her pace, she went to the front of the house, finding Lady Aurelia standing with the housekeeper and some unexpected—and from the look on Lady Aurelia's face, unwelcome—guests: Mr Balton-Sycke and his younger sister. Her footsteps slowed. "This is a surprise," she said as she approached them.

"Miss Goddard." He bowed. "So very good to see you!"

"Your friend was just telling me of some difficulty with the weather," Lady Aurelia said. "He is concerned for their travel onward, so I have, of course, insisted they must remain the night."

This appeared to be Mr Balton-Sycke's cue to babble about bridges and rain and muddy roads while Miss Balton-Sycke gawped about at the splendour of Matlock, not even bothering to disguise her awe. Lilly swallowed against a feeling of disgust that their behaviour gave her.

With Lady Aurelia occupied in instructing the housekeeper in the preparation of rooms for the two new guests, and Miss Balton-Sycke staring about, Lilly took the opportunity to greet her suitor quietly. "It is very good to see you. What a good brother you are, seeing to your sister's comfort in this way."

She forced herself to smile brightly at him, to make herself feel as glad to see him as she purported to be. He smiled back and she had, suddenly, the most wicked recollection of Saye kissing her earlier, with the taste of champagne and strawberries sweetening his lips.

"Are you well?" Balton-Sycke asked her very gravely. "You seem to have high colour."

"Perfectly well," she said. "I am only sorry you missed dinner. We had a most delightful feast of lobster, and strawberries and—"

"Strawberries? Oh no," he said as though she had just said they had eaten plague-ridden rats.

"They were delicious, I assure you."

"One should never eat berries out of season," he informed her. "Imbalances the humours. I am certain that is why you look flushed."

Saye had fed her the strawberries, paying her outrageous compliments all the while about her pretty hands and rosebud lips. Utter nonsense, all of it but...yes, it did indeed leave her flushed. *Blame it on the strawberries*, she thought with an agreeable nod at Balton-Sycke.

Of all the absolute indignity and nonsense. Aurelia is an idiot.

As if Lilly retiring early was not insult enough, Aurelia had come back into the drawing room with the unwelcome news that the Balton-Syckes were to spend the night.

Saye had scarcely a moment to rebuke his fool sister, for Ball-Sack entered the drawing room almost immediately. "Dreadful sorry to intrude," he said with a look that was not in the least apologetic. Evidently his sister had been one of a party at Longcliffe, and Ball-Sack had gone to retrieve her.

"We had only just set out—"

"At night?" Saye interrupted, not bothering to disguise his peevishness. "Peculiar business to set out at night."

"We intended only to make Derby," the scourge said with an apologetic grin. "But this deuced rain began to come down like nothing I have ever seen. The bridge is washed out near Starkholmes, so we had either to return to Long-cliffe...or come here. I hope it is no trouble?"

In truth, Saye thought it might have done well if Ball-Sack had simply slid his landau off into a muddy ravine some-where. Then again, that might have harmed his horses, and Saye could not abide reckless endangerment of good horse-flesh. Grudgingly, Saye said, "Of course you must stay the night. We would not have it otherwise."

An Unexpected Sticking Point

Sarah & Fitzwilliam

appily, Sarah was the first to reach the breakfast parlour the morning after the madcap dinner party. She loved the early mornings, and the time alone with her thoughts was much needed.

Her inclination was to try for Mr Withers. It would be a practical decision. A younger son, he had need of her money, whilst she had need of his name and his ability to give her children. *If only his laughter did not so closely resemble the snorting of those horses he dotes upon!* But surely, once she knew his true character, his various inelegant noises would pale in importance to her wish for his happiness, however it sounded. After all, her own laughter was hardly refined. Lost in these contemplations, she was startled when a bewhiskered gentleman seated himself directly across from her.

"Oh, I apologise, I was—" She broke off, suddenly realising the identity of said gentleman. It was Colonel Fitzwilliam. She coloured and was silent.

He nodded shortly to the footmen supervising the covered dishes on the buffet, and they beat a hasty retreat.

"Ahem. Miss Bentley, I owe you an apology, I believe," he said stiffly.

Well, this was unexpected! But little as she liked to admit it, he had managed to dent her usually iron-clad self-confidence. He was a handsome and arrogant nobleman who had, no doubt, broken his own code of honour in his belittling treatment of her. What she ought to do was accept his apology and follow the footmen out of the door. Instead, she smiled sunnily at him.

"Do you? Believe it, I mean. Truly, do not feel you must apologise for the sake of your gentleman's conscience. I daresay the evening was tiresome for you—what with being toppled upon, although since you were rather late joining me for dinner, it is no wonder I found my own entertainments, and I have fallen from many a taller tree and doubtlessly would have survived this time, had you not volunteered as a cushion, so to speak. And I am certain all my friends would share your aversion to dining with beetles. Still, one could presume that the creature was more entitled to a seat at the table than ourselves. We were in his orangery, after all. Although, 'tis also true that he was the intruder, as his presence could result in harm to the trees, whose chief rights to the orangery are undisputed, as is your claim to being the injured party, and thus no apologies are owed. So, save your breath to cool your porridge, as Mrs Figg would say."

The colonel blinked, furrowed his brow, and slowly smiled back. "Correct me if I am wrong, but did you just tell me to stubble it?"

It was Sarah's turn to be surprised, and she met his gaze with a mischievous look. "Surely not," she demurred.

He nodded ruefully, and she reflected how unfortunate it was that he should be so broad of shoulder, firm of chin, and, apparently, keen of wit.

"Do you know, I feel rather proud of myself," he said. "I

followed those convolutions all the way through, except for not knowing who Mrs Figg might be. And for some reason, I do not think you believed I could."

"It was more a matter of not caring whether you could or not, actually," she said, smiling again. "I have come here to find a husband, you see, and as you are already far too cognisant of my many—hmm, shall we say, imperfections?— to be in the running, I need not stifle myself around you."

"A husband? Well, that was blunt," he said, plainly taken aback.

She arched her brow. "Oh, are you here for different reasons? Your brother the viscount forced you, perhaps, to attend? You do look like the sort who enjoys the heat of battle far more than a wintry afternoon in the gardens with marriageable misses."

"I am not searching for a wife!" he protested hotly. "Why should I not be at the family seat helping round out the numbers for my brother?"

"Not even taking a peek to see who is available on the marriage mart, assuming you might someday take an interest? And why should you be embarrassed if you are? And why should I?" She sighed. "My friends have oft explained the need for less, er, frankness in company. I am not stupid. I simply have little patience for prevarication. I am unashamed of my wish to marry. It seems neither wrong, nor a particularly great secret. Does it seem inappropriate to you, that you might like to foster a connexion with one of the ladies here?"

"No...that is...one would not wish to be thought looking at my brother's guests as if one were shopping for an adequate winter overcoat. Nor would any gentleman enjoy feeling they were playing the role of fox in this hunt."

She nodded thoughtfully. "And yet, my aunt, Lady Hampton, warned me not to set my heart on external appearances, good conversation, or any of the more personal reasons why close friendships often form. She advised that all those things must come after the marriage. Specifically, she gave me a list of characteristics—all having to do with respectability, family, appeal, and the absence of certain vices—and swore that a good marriage could be built after the ceremony. There seems not much room for subtlety. You do not agree?"

"What of love?" he asked. "Does the heart have no say in this most important of all decisions?"

"I have questions about the nature of love," she admitted.

His eyes gleamed, as if this were a topic upon which he had expended much thought. "It is that certain something in the air when she walks into the room. Every word she utters is more clever, every look has added meaning—the body grows alert and life itself becomes more interesting, more vital, more necessary."

"Ah. You are speaking of sexual attraction," she nodded.

He opened his mouth, gaping at her.

"I have studied it in scientific journals of my father's, and of course, appeal is on my aunt's list. She would not recommend a man who repulses me. It seems to me a rather flimsy quality, however."

He only blinked, speechless.

"Consider my young brother, Percy. When he was born, he was the ugliest creature I had ever seen. His head was too large, besides being rather flattish, squinty-eyed, and with a slick of hair down the middle of it like a zebra stripe, while the rest of him was quite red and stick-like. What with the very unattractive squalling, he was really rather hideous. But our mama had died in giving birth to him, you see, and he had no one but the nurserymaid we hired, who was no good at all and let him cry, mostly. I finally picked him up, with experimentation discovering just the ways to rock him and hold him that brought comfort. Some months passed in this fashion, until as I entered the nursery one day and he simply lit with joy to see me, I realised I would do anything for him, really. Jump in front of a speeding carriage to push him out of its way, or sit up all night with him when his teeth began to appear. I loved him, completely, when I had not even wished to like him—I was feeling so down-spirited about Mama, you understand." She nodded to herself. "Attraction, of any sort, had naught to do with it. You will probably say it is because he was an infant or a brother, not a spouse, but love is love at the end of it all, is it not?"

The colonel cleared his throat. "I shall not argue your point," he replied gruffly, after a moment of silence. "Except to say that your brother is rather a fortunate young man."

She grinned and stood. "I tell him so often. Which reminds me that I must finish my letter to him. He is nine years old now, and I have the great secret of Lord Saye's cravat to hint about, which will drive him mad in that special way all the best elder sisters have."

Before he could respond, she hurried away, but at the door she paused and looked at him from over her shoulder. "For all her reasonable suggestions, I did not wish my aunt to pick out a spouse for me. I do think there is something in what you are saying—it would help tremendously if there were a predisposition towards affection in every newly married couple, I think. What I do not understand, I suppose, is the difference between animal spirits and real feeling, and how the one might encourage the other. Perhaps Mr Withers will agree to an experiment or two, so I might discover it."

With that remark, Miss Bentley sailed out of the door, and Fitzwilliam found himself alone in the breakfast room. He shook his head as if to clear it. *Why, she is as mad as a hatter!* Except, he knew, she was not.

After an uneasy sleep last night, he had arisen early and gone for a brisk morning walk and, unsurprisingly, found himself within the orangery, the scene of his worst behaviour the evening before. He had never said such unkind words to a lady in all his life; Miss Bentley had the peculiar power of goading him! But no; he must not blame her. He knew the importance in life of governing his tongue and temper. He was fortunate to *have* a life, as his scars attested. Allowing his jealousy of Darcy to embitter him was unacceptable. Darcy, Saye, and the like were able to have what they wanted in a way that second sons could not; so it was and so it had always been.

And then, just as if fate was determined to remind him of his foolishness, he nearly tripped over Phipps, Matlock's head gardener, who knelt near a certain set of trees—the ones Miss Bentley had been too-closely examining the night before.

"Excuse me, Phipps," he apologised immediately. "I was wool-gathering, and did not see you."

"Nawt to worry, sir," Phipps said, still intent upon the soil. "'Tis lucky we are. One of the guests discovered an infestation of cockchafers. Never would've believed it meself, nawt this time o' year. But proof is proof, an' she brought me one, bigger 'n life. We'll get it cleared."

Miss Bentley had been correct, on all points. And though it had been extremely unladylike of her to chase after beetles, he could not help but admit a thread of admiration. His life experiences had taught him to respect courage wherever it was found.

He had decided to give her an apology at the first opportunity, which had occurred far sooner than expected—fate again?—only to have her expertly deflect it.

She was an anomaly. He was accustomed to being a sought-after partner, and though he was not so handsome nor rich as Darcy, he knew his way around a charming conversation. There were degrees of beauty and desirability having nothing to do with wealth and gender, and in those arenas, he was firmly established in a higher circle than Miss Sarah Bentley.

I expected her to be flattered by my condescension.

What followed had been the most unique, thought-provoking—or perhaps, simply provoking—discussion on courtship and marriage he had ever had with anyone. Her straightforward views were refreshing, but heavens, she was a menace to herself! Amongst the *ton*, which lived for scandal and twisted words for sport, such opinions could ruin her! What were Hampton and her father thinking, not to have safely arranged her into a union at the earliest opportunity?

Though she would be devilish difficult to dictate to, he thought wryly. *Too intelligent by half. Likely smarter than both of them together.*

The story of her infant brother, although he thought it proved nothing of her point, had touched him. How old had she been? Younger than Georgiana was now, surely, and though he adored her, he could never imagine Miss Darcy of Pemberley taking charge of a nursery, or spending untold hours comforting a colicky infant.

And now...she intended to...what had she said? Experiment with animal spirits? *With Reggie Withers?*

This was his fault. She had misunderstood him and was too innocent to realise her danger. While there was nothing wrong with Withers, Fitzwilliam would certainly not leave a naïve young maiden's reputation within his clumsy hands. His true apology, his atonement for his bad behaviour, would be to keep her safe from herself. It was the least he could do.

After the previous day's rain, Sarah enjoyed her walk to the archery field with Miss Bennet. Having a few moments alone with her was a fortunate chance, as Mr Darcy was usually to be found nearby whenever she was.

"I am so happy to have the opportunity to speak to you," Sarah began eagerly. "I wonder if you would mind answering a question or two?"

If Miss Bennet was taken aback by such interrogation, she was too polite to show it, murmuring her agreement.

"Oh, thank you! You see, Mr Darcy claimed that he made an awful first impression upon you, but that eventually, he managed to overcome it. Somehow you managed to see through his worst self and into his better one. How did you know he was not merely a handsome face? Though I must say, his face is exceptional, and no one would blame you for making a fortunate guess and hoping to make the best of it after."

Miss Bennet shook her head in a little bewilderment at this onslaught, but quickly burst into laughter. "First of all, you must call me Elizabeth, as all of my friends do. You would fit right in with my sisters, who seldom hesitate to voice any questions they might have."

Sarah sighed. "Georgette reminded me only today that I must do better at fitting my curiosity into conversations in a less frantic manner. But I am certain Mr Darcy will join us at any moment, and I am so anxious to know how to tell whether a man is a worthy investment or a bad bargain. Do, please, call me Sarah."

"A worthy investment?" Elizabeth asked, still smiling.

"Well, I am depending upon my fortune rather than my looks to secure a husband," Sarah admitted honestly. "Which

of course brings me a selection of men who might unchari-
tably be called fortune hunters. Not that I would call them
any such thing—a man who wishes to improve his lot in life
is only prudent—but I would like to see beyond it. Mr Darcy
says you cared nothing for his wealth, which says a great deal
about your character, and makes me even more anxious to
know—how did he earn your good opinion?"

"I am afraid I cannot answer your question in a satisfactory manner, Sarah. It was too long ago, and I suppose I was
in the middle before I knew I had begun. I am sorry."

Sarah sighed. "I knew it was unlikely that anything about
your romance would relate to any potential one of mine."

Elizabeth patted her shoulder. "I can tell you this—never
assume that what you absolutely know is absolutely true."

"But...how can I be sure of anything at all, if I do not?"

"I suppose one must do one's best," Elizabeth answered,
laughing a little. "Long before there was a betrothal, my
aunt, uncle and I toured Mr Darcy's very grand home with
his housekeeper. Had I known he was in residence, I would
never have done it. But I did, and he was, and...I think every
once in a while, there is no harm in taking a little risk to
discover if what you know to be true...really is."

"Take risks. Discover what you do not know," Sarah
repeated, nodding thoughtfully. "I thank you. You have
confirmed my own intuition."

"Oh, I did not quite mean—" Elizabeth began, but at that
moment Mr Darcy joined them, Sarah excused herself to join
the archers, and the opportunity for sharing further confidences was lost.

Sarah approached the archery range in high spirits. For one thing, Mr Withers had specifically asked earlier whether she was going to join the archers. For another, she genuinely enjoyed the sport, was rather good at it, and expected to impress him with her prowess.

Miss Hilgrove and Miss Barlowe already tittered together at the edge of the field. And there was Mr Withers, standing with the gentlemen—including Colonel Fitzwilliam. If her heart accelerated a bit at the sight of the colonel as well, so handsome and hale in comparison, well...she looked away.

To her surprise, Mr Balton-Sycke appeared with Lady Aurelia on one arm and Lilly on the other. *What is he still doing here?*

She could not help but support Lord Saye's pursuit of Lilly, and not simply because of his title and looks. While Mr Balton-Sycke was well enough in appearance, one could just see how he would be twenty years from now, complaining of his gout and draughts and calling for the maids to build up the fires. *No wonder he wishes to marry young.*

A stand of bows was positioned to the right of the field, while two servants holding leather pouches of arrows stood beside an older gentleman, Lord Mickels—a noted toxophilite—who would officiate. Sarah walked directly to the bows and stood in contemplation of them. At the same time, she noticed the field abutted a pretty little wilderness. *It would not take much of a walk if, after the practice, Mr Withers and I were to stroll therein? And, perhaps, I could take the small risk of allowing him a kiss?* Assuming, of course, he wished for such an opportunity.

The men approached, Mr Withers pulling one of the bows from the stand, saying, "Miss Bentley, allow me to string your bow for you."

Sarah glanced at his choice, but selected a different one from the rack. "Actually, I believe this one is more suitable for me." Placing her foot on its lower limb and bending its frame, she expertly looped the bowstring into the appropriate groove. "I am quite able to string it myself, as you see."

Miss Barlowe tittered. "Mr Withers, I would be so grateful if you would string mine."

As he hurried to do her bidding, Sarah realised her mistake. And yet, the bow she had selected was clearly superior to the warped thing he had chosen, and did he truly wish for such studied helplessness? When Mr Withers walked away with Miss Barlowe, she sighed and glanced at Colonel Fitzwilliam, expecting to see a smirk at this proof of her ineptitude at flirtation.

To her surprise, he had already strung his bow, procured two pouches of arrows, and said only, "Shall we?"

He must be trying to establish his good conduct, after last night's débâcle, she thought. Still, she took his proffered arm and strolled with him towards the shooting lines, only to have him abandon her to Mr Darcy. *No matter,* she thought.

There were four bullrush targets set up, with concentric rings upon their fabric faces—one looked to be very near, a distance of perhaps only twenty yards, the second at thirty, the third at thirty-five, the fourth at forty. Since Sarah regularly shot at fifty yards, she thought that showing her proficiency here ought to be an easy business.

To her surprise, the colonel re-joined her just as Lord Mickels began fussing about rules, and the science of it, and demonstrating his scoring cards. Sarah released a little breath of impatience, even as she tried to appear attentive.

"Come, now, Pickles, let us begin," Colonel Fitzwilliam interrupted. "We planned an informal practice, not a tournament."

Mickels gave him a withering glare, but called, "Ladies and gentlemen, take your places," and the couples each chose a target—with Miss Barlowe making haste for the nearest one.

The ladies took their shots.

"The wind, no doubt," Colonel Fitzwilliam murmured in her ear as Miss Barlowe missed the target completely. It was all Sarah could do to keep her expression even, as the day was cold and clear, with nary a breeze. She had hit the nine-point gold from thirty yards.

The gentlemen nocked their arrows and took their shots. They all performed respectably, with the colonel's and Mr Withers's shots tying at nine points each.

"Mr Withers did well," she commented, and he rolled his eyes.

"Twenty yards," the colonel muttered. "A child could toss it that far."

Arrows were collected, and then it was their turn at the thirty-five-yard target. Sarah aimed and stuck exactly the mid-point of the golden centre.

"Oh, good show!" cried Mr Withers, and Sarah smiled at him.

"He was speaking to Miss Barlowe," the colonel whispered. "She almost managed almost to nick the target this time."

Sarah elbowed him.

His arrow then thudded into the centre, neatly splicing hers with a curious intimacy that made her blush. To cover her uneasiness, she turned her attention to Mr Balton-Sycke, who had yet to cease chattering away with Lady Aurelia. Beside them, Lilly looked bored, staring absently at the nearby field. She noticed Colonel Fitzwilliam's gaze followed them as well. "He is attempting an encroachment of our party. I will see that he fails," the colonel said, glaring at his sister.

"You dislike Mr Balton-Sycke?" she asked curiously, as they collected their arrows.

"I have nothing against the man," he said, "except that he is an insinuating worm."

But he refused to add any details with which she might enlighten Lilly as to the man's character. Was this brotherly loyalty? It was not unadmirable, if so.

It was their turn at the forty-yard target. Ever after, she would never quite be certain what had happened. Sarah nocked her arrow and drew, aiming well above the farthest target, beginning her calculations for its flight.

At that moment, Georgette and Mr Anderson entered the field, diverting her attention. Georgette wore a stunning archeress's dress in jade green, white silk slashing its skirt in a medieval pattern, the whole conforming to her slender, perfect figure with elegant simplicity. Mr Anderson could barely keep his eyes from her. His admiration was so obvious, so...blatant, when she had thought him the most dispassionate creature alive, that Sarah thought with some surprise, *Why...he adores her!*

This is why he is always in her company! But then, Georgette's appeal to Mr Anderson could really be no mystery. Every gentleman at the party who was not related to her or betrothed to another had made some effort to inveigle their way into her notice.

Still, why does she tolerate him? Sarah wondered. His presence was undoubtedly, at least at times, keeping more acceptable suitors at bay.

Why, if I were so beautiful, I should have a dozen hangers-on! Sarah thought. Abruptly, however, she knew the thought for the lie it was. There was only one man she had begun to desire as yet, a man so wholly her opposite, and so far from her reach, the very notion appalled her.

Completely bewildered by this sudden blaze of attraction

for her partner, Sarah stood motionless, arrow drawn, while Lady Aurelia, to her left, nocked her arrow and shot. However, possibly due to the distracting entrance of the other couple, her arrow sputtered rather than soared, feebly bouncing hardly a ten-yard distance. A rather unladylike curse flew along with it.

And between Lady Aurelia's cursing and her surprise at the discovery of her own secret passion for Colonel Fitzwilliam, Sarah somehow released her arrow, whilst still pointing at the sky.

It should not have mattered, except to her score. But the idiotic Mr Balton-Sycke shouted—"Your shot did not count, my dear Lady Aurelia! A mere accident. I shall retrieve it!"—and matching word to action, bounded the few yards to her ladyship's fallen arrow. Sarah's arrow began its descent, and she watched in horror as it slowly, leisurely glided downwards towards the oblivious Mr Balton-Sycke. The others began shouting, including the colonel—who called him by an extremely disrespectful nickname—but to no avail. Balton-Sycke only halted, looking around ineffectually as the arrow dropped unluckily, mercilessly, and directly into his buckskin-clad hindquarters.

The arrow tip was not a broadhead, but a blunt thing designed to do as little damage as possible to the targets. Still, it was hardly gentle, particularly given the gravity-fuelled trajectory. Sarah winced as her shot landed, but her victim gave a soprano-edged scream.

Colonel Fitzwilliam clapped her on the shoulder. "Extra points for you, Miss Bentley. Extra points for you."

SLINGS AND ARROWS

Darcy & Elizabeth

"Have you an archery range at Pemberley?"

Darcy steered Elizabeth around a mud puddle and away from the shooting line. "We have the equipment should we wish for it, but I prefer such activities in drier fields."

"A house party where all the ladies' skirts are six inches deep in mud sounds ideal to me."

Their shared laughter attracted more than one of Darcy's relations to come alongside them.

"Darcy, are you averse to carpets?" Saye gestured at the rugs scattered about the field. "Even a love-sick stag knows better than to lead his beloved into the muck."

Fitzwilliam leant his head towards Elizabeth. "But would the stag not be just as stupid for leading his mate onto an archery range?"

It was bad enough Elizabeth bit her lip in that way that always anticipated an amusing riposte; such an expression usually compelled Darcy to kiss her. Worse still was that he had finally wrangled her away from Miss Bentley, only to have his cousins quickly appear. If only they had their own romantic attachments rather than constantly hovering over his! At least Saye was pursuing his lady, curiously inept at it though he was. Fitzwilliam was surrounded by a surfeit of unattached, wealthy, and generally handsome young ladies; he would do well to send his teasing quips towards them, and not at ladies firmly attached to others. The audacious and self-assured manner in which Fitzwilliam had seated himself next to Elizabeth last night in the drawing room—the very moment Darcy had risen from the spot—ground at him. He was not jealous—he had her, and she loved him, after all—but he could not like his cousin's presumption.

Before the arrow he gripped could snap in two, he turned to Saye. "I heard the squeals this morning as your men sacrificed a pig for this pagan feast you have planned. Are we to play savages all week, spending our days scampering about with bows and arrows and our evenings squatting on the ground and tearing at meat with our teeth and hands?"

"I have forbidden tiresome people here." Saye peered closely at Darcy. "Your trousers are cut generously enough to allow 'squatting', but who am I to judge in what direction a man dresses, let alone the worthiness of his tailor?"

Saye tossed a smug smile at Elizabeth. "Pillows and cushions will be provided for those with delicate bottoms."

"Elizabeth, you will enjoy my brother's bacchanal," asserted Fitzwilliam, "for unlike Darcy, you have a lively, playful disposition that delights in anything ridiculous."

Fortunately for Darcy's temper, Fitzwilliam excused himself to join the shooting line and sauntered towards Miss Bentley.

Elizabeth, who had seemed alternately taken aback and amused by Saye the previous evening, now was undaunted as she spoke to him. "Surely your cousin has regaled you with tales of my boldness in walking through the wilds of Hertfordshire. I fear neither mud nor censure for such diversions."

"An admirable sort of courage, I suppose." Saye nodded in the direction of Balton-Sycke and affected a stage whisper. "Far less an outrage than audaciously scheming to impose oneself and one's simpering sister on my party. The lobcock is playing on my sister's sympathies. Washed out bridges, wretched stomachs, fears of highwaymen and forest trolls... bah!"

Darcy tried not to laugh. Saye was seriously displeased at the arrival of Balton-Sycke and his sister, a wilful girl with a pretty voice, two Seasons, and no serious suitors. Saye might think his rival had only one aim in mind when crashing their party, but Darcy suspected Miss Imogen Balton-Sycke was equally invested in the scheme. Searching briefly, he saw Balton-Sycke hovering around Lady Aurelia, loudly effusing on her inspired choice of archery for a winter house party. Miss Goddard stood on a thick carpet with a few ladies, watching the first group of archers take their places.

His eyes returned to Saye, who appeared more intent on petulance than on taking any action of his own and joining the lady who was his true target. Rather than offering advice to a man uninterested in listening, Darcy busied himself examining the selection of bows, looking for one as small, fine, and strong as the lady who would shoot with it.

Elizabeth had other ideas and continued speaking to Saye. "You must play the host and hero, and then send them on their way, no matter what forest creatures lie in wait. Escort them if you must—"

"Leave my own party? Miss Bennet," Saye gave her a look of thinly veiled impatience. "I consider it *comme il faut* that the host of the party should be the one having the most fun. Is that not the point of it all? I have gathered my nearest and dearest here to divert me. Trotting off into the forest with an idiot like Balton-Sycke would quite defeat the purpose." With a roll of his eyes, he was off to stew in what Darcy presumed to be even greater depths of irritability.

"I meant he should send a footman," Elizabeth said quietly. "I am not sure your cousin thinks I am intelligent."

"Not even a man as silly in love as Saye could think you anything but clever. I should not be amused by his inelegance at wooing the first woman to truly touch his heart." Darcy looked down, surprised by Elizabeth's sudden grip on his wrist. "What is wrong? That is my shooting hand."

"Miss Goddard is the first, truly?" she whispered. "He has never been in love?"

"Until her, love was sport and a means of amusement. Nothing to take seriously." He bent his head closer and whispered softly, "He is an even bigger fool than I am."

"A ridiculous thought, sir." She blushed and glanced off at the ladies and nodded to Sir Phineas and Mr Emerson, who stood nearby watching Mr Withers instruct Miss Barlowe in her stance.

Darcy handed Elizabeth a beautifully polished oak bow. His body tightened and flushed as he watched her stroke it and compliment the smoothness of the wood, and he was forced to look away a moment and get himself under regulation.

With cheerful innocence, she remarked, "It is rather like holding a catapult in one's hands. If you close one eye, breathe in deeply and pull back, all come together in a perfect shot."

Sir Phineas coughed loudly, and after a long moment watching the first round of shooting, Darcy managed to enquire whether she had experience as an archer.

"I know little of it beyond the aiming and breathing," Elizabeth replied, explaining she had spent one summer as a girl fascinated by a small catapult built by the neighbouring

Lucas and Goulding boys. "After they shot down most of the leaves on a small oak tree and beheaded all of the roses in Mrs Grant's garden, they began to aim at birds' nests and rabbits. It fell to Charlotte and me to hide all the rocks and pebbles they used for ammunition in order to forestall a rampage."

Others had drawn nearer now, and amid murmurs of disapproval from their audience, Darcy bit back a chuckle at his intrepid country girl.

Sir Phineas snorted. "Do you liken shooting an arrow to shooting off a catapult? Both might be used within the act of war, but only archery is an art."

They all turned to watch the second round of arrows fly to their targets.

"Yes, the archer is a romantic character," Darcy said drolly. "The muddy marksman who mans a catapult would never be compared to Cupid."

"Cupid, indeed!" roared Sir Phineas. "Saye, where are our feathery wings?"

Suddenly shouts and shrieks rang out, followed by awkward laughter. Exchanging looks with Elizabeth, Darcy was uncertain whether to be more alarmed by the sight of the injured man leaping about and swatting at his bottom, or by the peculiar expression on Saye's face.

"Cupid's arrow has gone awry," Saye observed with a smirk.

The cosiness of Matlock's smallest saloon was welcomed after a morning outside spent playing bows and arrows; Elizabeth was amused by the ornate décor and the ladies sitting within it promised equal diversion. As desperately as she had missed Darcy's ardent looks and company these past weeks, she had equally yearned for his rational and intelligent conversation. While such talk was rarely found at Long-bourn, she was finding the company at Matlock had clever-ness and wit in abundance. It was encouraging to her; she had long-feared a chilly reception among London ladies who were all of a piece with the likes of Miss Bingley. Instead, she found a group of likeable, sensible young ladies whom she might one day call real friends. It delighted her, and she found herself drawing nearer to the group of them, that she might take part in their conversation. She quickly received a warm welcome from the ladies and the offer of a cup of tea.

"Mr Darcy stares at you quite often, Miss Bennet," observed the lady to her left. Miss Hawkridge; Elizabeth had had few moments to speak to her thus far but suspected she might be the cleverest of the bunch. She was beautiful, too, with lustrous blonde hair, lips that seemed to be perma-nently curved into a pretty but dangerous smile, and eyes the most startling shade of green Elizabeth had ever seen, but she did not seem to count it her chief attribute.

Elizabeth smiled at her. "He does. He always has."

"It does not trouble you then?"

"Indeed not. I find it flattering."

Miss Hawkridge inclined her head. "He is evidently quite taken with you. I daresay you could not escape his affection even if you wished to."

"'Tis a good thing I do not wish it," she replied, laughing.

And she did not, for the most part. Darcy would prefer to monopolise her time at Matlock; she had felt his intent gaze the previous evening in the drawing room, as well as his impatience to steal away with her. She would not tell him that she was enjoying some time apart to converse with ladies she would come to know better when she became Mrs Darcy. Currently nine of them, save Lady Aurelia and Miss

Balton-Sycke, were settled into chairs in the blue sitting room, enjoying the afternoon sun and restoring themselves for the evening's festivities.

"I ate too much marzipan. My stays are poking me," whispered the tallest and most well-endowed of the ladies near her. Elizabeth paused, running names through her head. Miss Barlowe?

Miss Parker lowered her voice. "We shan't need stays tomorrow if we are truly to be savages. Lord Saye says island ladies do not wear gowns, only grass skirts on their bottoms!"

When Elizabeth's eyes met Miss Goddard's equally mirthful ones, she started to giggle. Mortified, she clapped her hand over her mouth.

"Hush, ladies. You will only give Saye more ideas for creating misery." Miss Goddard patted Elizabeth's hand. "Enough about the gentlemen. I believe most of us are acquainted in some manner, Miss Bennet. It is nice to have time for us all to get to know you without the men swirling about."

Elizabeth was overcome by such kindness. "Please, call me Elizabeth. I am in need of new friends and confidantes, and Mr Darcy has told me you are a kind-hearted lady."

Miss Goddard laughed, a dimple appearing in her cheek. "Has he? I am honoured. Mr Darcy is not a gentleman known for sharing his opinion of any particular young lady."

"Oh yes, the poor hunted man," Elizabeth replied. "I understand he has been challenged for years in society to politely ignore the attention of ladies."

"Until you, Elizabeth—and I understand you made little effort to attract his attention, but caught it nevertheless. An enviable achievement," said Miss Hawkridge, smiling kindly at her.

Elizabeth blushed, having wondered how, exactly, the

scorned and ignored ladies of the *ton* would view her fortunate situation.

"Miss Bennet. As the only lady here who is betrothed, and to a man many of our mothers wished for us—" Miss Hilgrove, a thin girl with impressively arched eyebrows, blushed before forging ahead. "As a result of your success, would you have some insight as to how gentlemen think? After all, you were disinclined towards Mr Darcy, and he nonetheless pursued you. It paints such a romantic picture in our minds, the spurned lover winning over the hand of the lady he admires."

Miss Bentley looked doubtful. "Do you suppose a lady's success in winning a proposal is best achieved by spurning interested gentlemen? Rejecting the addresses of the man whom they secretly mean to accept?"

"Perhaps," Miss Fisher replied thoughtfully. "It is not the first such tale I have heard."

"Breaking a man's heart as a means to win him as a husband is dishonest, if not cruel," Miss Hawkridge opined.

Elizabeth frowned, recalling her earlier conversation with Miss Bentley. She wondered whether the lady had herself once been spurned.

"The gentlemen are sharing their own confidences downstairs, boasting of their acumen in sport, more likely," offered Miss Hilgrove. "That is what my brothers do."

"Your brothers are only sixteen. *These* are gentlemen." Miss Hawkridge rolled her eyes before adding, a touch of mischief in her voice, "Perhaps they are choosing their favourites."

At least two ladies spoke as one. "Shall we choose ours?"

Elizabeth could not hide a smile at their eagerness, nor at their similarity to her sisters.

Miss Goddard cleared her throat. "There are many eligible gentlemen gathered here. Each has something to recommend him, quite aside from being a friend of Lord Saye."

"The viscount is said to be quite the rake." Miss Morgan's pronouncement drew its intended response from the ladies; even Miss Goddard looked down at her hands before nodding slightly.

"A rake?" Elizabeth asked carefully, "Surely not! I know him the least of all of you, I daresay, but he seems to be a lively gentleman who holds his friends and family dear, and wishes for all of us gathered here to enjoy ourselves."

"Lord Saye is the opposite of your betrothed," said Miss Hilgrove firmly.

Miss Hilgrove's intemperate declaration prompted a reproof from Miss Hawkridge. "You believe Mr Darcy does not hold his friends and family dear or wish joy on them?"

"No, no! I mean Mr Darcy is not lively, or was never seen as such until, well, he became betrothed to Miss Bennet. He is altered."

Miss Fisher nodded with all the accumulated wisdom of her eighteen years. "I have seen Mr Darcy smile on three occasions today, and laugh at least once!"

"Only once less than Lord Saye," murmured Miss Goddard.

Elizabeth was diverted. "Love alters both parties. Would you believe I was an impertinent girl who preferred proverbs to puddings and cats to dogs before I met Mr Darcy?"

"No, we would not!" cried her new champions.

"I hope I was not. But we did not appear well-matched until I better understood his character." Elizabeth turned to Miss Goddard. "I learnt that the person who most easily provoked my discomposure was the person with whom I truly shared a common interest and disposition."

A blush appeared on Miss Goddard's cheeks. "There is something to admire in a gentleman who is sure enough of himself to be quiet where others are in a constant need to prove themselves and entertain."

"Indeed!" Miss Hilgrove eagerly offered a ready example of such self-confidence. "I admire how masterful Mr Balton-Sycke was in determining that he must spare his sister the fright and danger of pressing onwards to Derby. He will take good care of his wife." She smiled meaningfully at Miss Goddard who, Elizabeth noticed, appeared less than enthusiastic in reception of the look.

"He had best take care. An arrow can do only a little damage, but I expect spears shall follow." Miss Hawkridge smiled slyly at Miss Bentley, who gracefully laughed along with the ladies not shocked by her comment.

The following day, as he watched Elizabeth delight the room with her warmth and wit, Darcy was struck anew with how great his fortune had been to visit Bingley in Hertfordshire. He and his friend had each found their hearts' desires there. Yes, Bingley had the good fortune to be wed to his, but Darcy had met Elizabeth. Her eyes sparkled with gaiety and humour as she conversed with the ladies and gentlemen. He had grown accustomed to her eyes shining only for him, but here she appeared amused and pleased by nearly everyone and everything she encountered.

Darcy's thoughts shifted abruptly when Sir Phineas's broad, silk-clad figure intruded on his pleasing view of Elizabeth. Inexplicably balancing a spyglass in one hand and a biscuit in the other, the older man leant towards Darcy and chuckled. "A long engagement for you? Your Miss Bennet is a peach. Pray keep her from the *ton*. There are enough gentlemen here who seem delighted by her."

It was a long engagement. Far too long. What gave Mr Bennet any standing to doubt his wisest daughter or to distrust him? Elizabeth had not pushed at her father's strictures as he would have wished. She had not shown him any uncertainty in her feelings, but did she in fact need time that he did not? Was it only her father who doubted their attachment?

"What is this, you are back to standing by the walls and admiring the draperies?" Darcy looked up to find Fitzwilliam standing next to him, garrulous and vexatious as he had been as a boy envying Darcy's new pony. "Is Elizabeth finding the company of others preferable to yours?"

Darcy shifted his gaze from his darling lady, surrounded by new friends on the drawing room sofa, and glowered at his cousin. "Tell me, is it difficult to be the most annoying man in the room?"

"Ha! You have forgotten Ball-Sack is present."

Before Darcy could reply or escape, he heard a hushed female voice from the window seat behind the heavy curtains.

"I like her very much. There is something engaging in her air—see how readily she laughs?"

"Very readily," came the hushed reply. "Yet something of the country lingers in her manner."

"Now, now, we could do with a little more laughter, Miss Barlowe."

Skirts rustled and then Miss Fisher emerged, pausing to smile briefly before moving across the room to join Elizabeth, Miss Goddard, and others near the fireplace. A moment later, a red-faced Miss Barlowe glided past them.

Fitzwilliam cocked an eyebrow. "It appears Elizabeth's army of admirers grows larger."

The sentiments of the ungainly third daughter of a malcontent baronet eager to marry her off meant nothing to

Darcy, but he could admire any of Elizabeth's defenders. "I am well-pleased with Miss Fisher."

"You are well-pleased with the world since you discovered Elizabeth here in the library."

Darcy ignored the sullen tone in his cousin's voice. "You must make your own discovery. Please your mother and go and talk to a lady—please me and choose one who is unattached to me."

Fitzwilliam let out an ungentlemanly snort. "I shall not talk to, let alone wed a lady simply to please my mother or ensure a best friend for your dear lady."

"Shall you even try to know one who meets every requirement you have ever stated, and, in fact, exceeds many of them?"

"I am not here to make this a matchmaking party. I am here to support my brother in his curiously clumsy romantic pursuits." Fitzwilliam took a swallow of brandy and used the glass to gesture at the assemblage of ladies. "See how his target, Miss Goddard, sits with Elizabeth, laughing and smiling? She does none of that with Saye. She seems to want nothing to do with him."

Darcy could not disagree. Saye's desire for Miss Goddard seemed to have sapped him of his overgenerous charms. The ongoing saga of the Balton-Syckes had turned Saye's blithe geniality into barest civility. The injured man refused to repair to his rooms, claiming all was well as he held court, squirming and fretting on his host's finest sofa. His sister and Miss Bentley attended him, both apparently more out of guilt than pleasure. Darcy was interested to find that Fitzwilliam appeared unduly irritated by the displays of concern Balton-Sycke merited; his cousin kept shooting dark looks at the trio when he was not staring at Elizabeth and Miss Goddard.

Not even the appearance of Saye, swathed in gold satin

robes with the hard helmet of King Kamehameha, amused him. Saye's spirits had been brightened by the memory of Ball-Sack's screams, and now he appeared to be back in good humour as he orchestrated the evening ahead. Darcy fought the urge to reply further and instead gazed at his beloved Elizabeth. He wished to be alone with her but had had only a few minutes in her exclusive company since lunch.

Saye made an undignified noise. "Will that *fundus horribilis* require a sedan chair to remove himself from my house? He already has got himself the largest pillow in Matlock. Does he presume to think he will reign over this evening's feast?"

"We have room for only one king, thankfully," observed Darcy. "You look ridiculous, but I am pleased to see you are properly attired under your robes."

"Envy is a poor colour for you." Saye's attention shifted. "Fitzwilliam, your eyes will dry out if you do not blink between your glares at Ball-Sack. Miss Bentley's poor aim and guilty spirit is a fortuitous turn. He and his sore arse will enjoy her attentions and spare my Lilly from his. Miss Bentley is a good match for him. Plump, rich, eccentric, and in need of a husband."

"Ah, is that it?" Fitzwilliam moved his glare to his brother. "Moving around ladies as if they are chess pawns?"

"An amusing game for one player only," said Darcy.

"I am in need of lively company, and no one is better suited to provide it than your dearest, loveliest Elizabeth." Fitzwilliam, rather meanly in Darcy's view, then did as he had the night before, and strolled over to the sofa to sit beside the engaged lady.

"The tragedy of a younger son is that neither money nor charm is left over for him." Saye's helmet hit Darcy's ear as he leant closer. "Elizabeth has established a friendship with Lilly. This will be useful."

"My intended is happy to befriend anyone, and is kind to

even those who may not merit it," Darcy said in low tones. Saye was too vain to understand Elizabeth's excellent advice on pleasing a lady; swathing himself in gold satin and eating a meal as if they were savages would hardly impress Miss Goddard. Saye's love life was of small consequence to Darcy; as always, all would be well for Saye, and he would likely have his way in the end.

Fitzwilliam's behaviour was more troubling. Why was he deliberately hovering around Elizabeth and neglecting the other ladies in the room? All had generous dowries and some, such as Miss Fisher and Miss Bentley, even had charm. Was he intent on provoking their jealousy...or his? If it was the former, then he could use some other lady to serve his object. If it was the latter...Darcy felt his jaw tighten and his eyes narrow.

His anxiety eased as Elizabeth caught his eye and, after raising her eyebrow in concern, gave him that smile that was his alone. *Mine. She is mine.*

"Miss Bennet is charming in spades, but do try not to devour the poor girl. This may be Saye's party, but none of these ladies will be despoiled under my watch."

Darcy spun around, shaking off his oblivion and wondering how many more ladies were destined to surprise him from behind draperies. Lady Aurelia gazed at him slyly. Lord, but he was tired of Fitzwilliams and their pointed wit.

"Cousin, I am a gentleman. I have no intention of besmirching—"

"Of course, of course, but muttering and staring is no way to exhibit your charms." She patted his arm as if he were a child and gave him a fond look. "Gird yourself and your lady. It is time for whatever pagan rituals Saye has planned for this evening. Pray he does not ruin more of Mother's rugs."

She handed him a blindfold and strolled over to her husband.

"Drop your bindings!"

Elizabeth released her hold on Darcy's arm and pulled the cloth strip from her eyes. Once her vision adjusted, and stunned by the festive exhibition before her, she joined in the communal gasp.

"This is wonderful," she murmured.

Indeed, the dining room was unlike anything she had seen. Most of the light came from a roaring fire. Low tables, lit only with thin tapers, teemed with bowls of fruits and leafy vines. Cushions and pillows taken from sofas and chairs were arranged in haphazard stacks on rugs pulled from other rooms. Giant ferns and potted trees loomed behind tall candelabras placed in various parts of the room.

"This is interesting," Darcy replied doubtfully.

"What is this? Where are the chairs?" Sir Phineas growled.

After a muttered oath or two, Fitzwilliam stalked over to Saye. "What have you done to Mother's table? Did you saw off the legs?"

"You are an idiot, little brother. It is there." Saye gestured at a long table laden with covered dishes. "These are low tables. I would not have the smell of wood dust at my party."

"The plants." Miss Bentley's eyes were wide with awe.

Saye shrugged. "I emptied the orangery of its greenery, of course. We are in the tropics. Blindfolds, coats, slippers, boots, and stays are no longer necessary."

He turned to his guests with a severe expression as a few ventured in to take their places on the pillows. "Do not trip on the rugs. The archery incident was enough. I will not have my party known about town for its endless bloodshed."

"Good lord, the bloodshed will only continue when my

aunt sees what he has done," murmured Darcy. He captured Elizabeth's hand in his and she leant her head against his shoulder, laughing quietly in delight.

"My father enjoys the ridiculous. How he would love such a spectacle."

"If Mrs Bennet is not keen on wedding planning, let Saye plan your soiree," said Fitzwilliam. "But do roll up the rugs before he arrives."

Elizabeth nodded, unable to form a response as she watched a pair of footmen enter the room, struggling under the unwieldy weight of a long board with a steaming, roasted pig atop it. So intent was her gaze, she scarcely felt it when Miss Hawkridge swooned to the floor behind her.

COCKTAILS AND COCKCHAFERS

Georgette & Anderson

Several things happened as Georgette fell: the sound of a dozen people scrabbling to their feet filled the room, something shattered loudly, and several people—not all of them women—shrieked. She bit her tongue when she hit the floor, and the metallic taste of blood filled her mouth.

"Miss Hawkridge!"

"Mind the pig!"

"Georgette!"

"Andrew, fetch help, quickly."

"Zounds, what the devil is that?"

"Be not alarmed, sir. I think it is only a—"

"Look lively! 'Tis crawling up your arm, man!"

Another frantic shuffle and a muted grunt.

"Be careful of its antennae, they are extremely delicate!"

"Georgette, can you hear me?"

"Gads! Get it off him!"

"There is no need to use your shoe, sir!"

Another wild bellow and several hearty guffaws of laughter preceded a second smash as something else was knocked over. Georgette was somewhat mollified to know she was not the only casualty. Still, the plan had not been that she would get as far as the floor.

"Georgette?" someone, perhaps Elizabeth, whispered urgently over the chaos.

Georgette kept her eyes closed and feigned shallow breaths. If one was going to be theatrical, it was always best to commit to the performance. Though, her bloodied mouth gave rather more verisimilitude to the act than she had intended.

Arms slid beneath her—solid, warm arms, but not the right ones. She would know Anderson's embrace anywhere, and whilst his hold would be strong, firm, and unapologetic, these arms were hesitant, careful.

"Can you hear me, madam?"

Mr Darcy. Drat! She owed Elizabeth an apology. Only a small one though—the woman married to these arms would have little need for the sympathy of others. Mr Darcy lifted her off the floor, and she allowed her head to loll sideways, drawing a gasp from someone.

"Georgette? Can you hear me?"

Lilly. She felt a flicker of guilt, but it passed quickly, replaced by vexation that almost every person in the room had now come to her aid but the one person who had been meant to catch her.

"Oh Lord! She has blood in her mouth!"

"Heaven's sake! Put her here, Darcy." She was placed gently on a sofa and somebody took her hand. "Georgette?" said a deep voice, soft with concern. "What is this? You are not afraid of a crusty old pig, are you? Come now, wake up, and I shall forgive you for upstaging me at my own feast."

Dear, sweet Saye! He would be furious with her for compelling him into such a public display of compassion, though Georgette did hope Lilly was watching. She could not be satisfied, however, for as considerate as her cousin may be, he was still Saye and not Anderson.

"My dear Miss Goddard. Pray, come and sit over here, away from all the gore," said Mr Balton-Sycke condescendingly, putting an end to whatever view of Saye's heroics Lilly might have had.

There was a scrape of furniture, a shout of alarm, another crash, then, in the midst of increasingly raucous laughter, a rattled plea from Sarah.

"Do try not to crush it!"

Another grunt; another clang; more hilarity.

"I thought you said you had decided against hiring dancers, Saye!"

Her cousin sighed quietly and stood up. "Keep an eye on her, will you, Darcy?" Then, his voice returning to its usual jaunty tone, he said more loudly, "Steady on, man, you'll set the place alight if you keep prancing about like that."

"Is she well?" Elizabeth asked nearby.

"Come away, Lizzy. You need not see this either."

Georgette sneaked one eye open a crack in surprise, for that had been Fitzwilliam's voice, not Darcy's. And, indeed, her cousin had put his arm around Elizabeth's shoulders and was guiding her away to the other side of the room with as much overprotective pomp as Hairy Ball-Sack had shown Lilly. Darcy, sticking dutifully to his assigned post at Georgette's side, veritably writhed with displeasure, his jaw set angrily and his eyes ablaze as he watched them go.

Oh, Fitzwilliam, you are playing a dangerous game, Georgette thought to herself. *You will get yourself run through if you are not awfully careful.* She closed her eye again and began to consider how best to extricate herself from her little predicament when the pandemonium was shattered by another, rather angry exclamation from Sarah.

"It will not hurt you! Pray, sir, do not bat at it so! There is nothing alarming about a common cockchafer!"

It was all Georgette could do not to give herself away by snorting with laughter. After a brief but palpably incredulous pause, the rest of the room obliged her by roaring its amusement to the rafters. She sucked on her throbbing tongue to prevent herself from joining in. Only Sarah could utter such a thing in complete innocence. Indeed, the poor dear evidently did not understand the hilarity, for her pleas grew ever more distressed.

"It must have come in from the orangery on one of the plants."

"Here, turn around," said Mr Withers through gleeful chuckling. "Cease flailing your arms and I might be able to swat the deuced thing!"

"There is no need!" Sarah insisted. "If you could only hold still, sir, I might be able to—oh! Oh my!"

"Hell's bells, it's gone inside my shirt!"

Georgette opened her eyes in alarm. There was no mistaking Anderson's voice, and she had never heard him sound so panicked. He was so steady, so calm, usually. She sat up and swivelled to look at him. He was standing, divested of both dinner jacket and waistcoat, in the midst of half a dozen toppled plants, pedestals, and pillows, a look of absolute horror etched upon his countenance, hitting himself repeatedly on the chest. Sarah was standing before him with her hands poised as though she meant to delve beneath his shirt at any moment.

"Mr Darcy, could you tell me what is wrong with Mr Anderson?"

His head whipped around. "Miss Hawkridge! Are you well?"

She touched her lip with the back of her finger; it came away bloodied. "Perfectly well, I thank you." Mr Darcy raised a sceptical eyebrow, which provoked her to wink at him and whisper, "It is my cousin's fault for banning stays this evening. I am used to being more restricted. I must have been overcome by the abundance of air." To her vast amusement, his eyes flicked downwards as though to verify her ridiculous claim, then his expression hardened with displeasure and he averted his gaze to the wall.

"It has gone down my leg!" Anderson shouted, hopping in a circle and hitting himself on the thigh.

"Be careful, sir!" Sarah urged.

"If you are so concerned about saving the damned thing," Anderson replied through gritted teeth, "Why do you not rescue it?"

"Hey, hey!" growled Fitzwilliam. "I shall ask you not to speak to Miss Bentley in that tone."

Georgette swung her legs off the sofa and peered around Mr Darcy to look at her cousin. Fitzwilliam was glaring at Anderson with a curiously venomous look. Elizabeth, it seemed, had been forgotten. *Interesting.*

"Have a heart, little brother," Saye said with a grin. "The poor chap has a cockchafer chafing his—"

"Have you any suggestions, Miss Bentley?" Lady Aurelia interrupted, waving her wine glass vaguely in Anderson's direction.

Sarah blanched, and though Georgette doubted Lady Aurelia had meant for her to personally intervene, she nodded and stepped towards Anderson with her hands tentatively outstretched towards him. Fitzwilliam, Georgette noticed, took a step in the same direction, his scowl darkening further still.

She stood up and moved to stand beside Saye. "What do you think she is planning to do? Tickle him?"

Saye twisted to look at her, all surprise, until his face softened into a sly smile. He passed her his handkerchief. "Welcome back."

"Thank you." She wiped the blood off her lips. "What have I missed?"

"A blasted great beetle has crawled into Blanderson's unmentionables. Liveliest I have ever seen him."

Georgette smiled broadly. Not at Anderson's misfortune, but at the discovery of his eminently reasonable excuse for bungling their plan to escape Saye's preposterous dinner plans. She watched with vast amusement as Sarah frowned at Anderson's trousers, and he recoiled in alarm. More than one person raised their voice in objection when she abruptly lunged forward. Georgette was almost disappointed when she only reached for Anderson's neck, for she rather thought her friend's insatiable curiosity might benefit from a quick rummage in a gentleman's trousers.

"It was in the folds of your cravat, sir," Sarah said with a relieved little laugh, clutching her prize proudly in her hands.

"What the devil is on the loose in his breeches then?" enquired Sir Phineas, returning the room to unrestrained merriment.

Georgette was distracted from the hullabaloo by her maid, who appeared at her side in the uncannily silent way she had. "Are you well, Miss?" she whispered. "Andrew said you had taken a turn."

"Yes, thank you, Prinny. It was a trifling episode."

"Like the one you suffered at Lord Faulkner's ball?"

"Uncommonly similar," she replied with as straight a face as Prinny herself was maintaining, for Saye was watching the exchange like a hawk.

"You won't be needing to retire then?"

"No, I believe I shall last the evening, thank you."

Prinny curtseyed and left, and Georgette, choosing to ignore her cousin's satirical glare, said to him, "I am surprised at your indifference to Lilly's present company. Are you not worried she might decide she prefers an idiotically possessive gentleman?"

Saye glanced at the sofa upon which Balton-Sycke had entrapped Lilly and scoffed. "No indeed. The more I see of the imbecile, the more I am of a mind to leave him to woo his own way out of Miss Goddard's affections. I have never known anyone so deficient in refinement. One can tell by her expression that she is repulsed by his servility."

Georgette agreed, but Lilly was one of the most well-bred ladies of her acquaintance and was as unlikely to slight a person with an unkind look as with an unkind word. It was notable, therefore, that Saye was able to so easily discern her impatience. "As long as you are sure she will not be equally repulsed by your willingness to abandon her to it."

Saye blinked at her twice, then turned on his heel and crossed the room, barking orders for the guests to take their places and the feast to begin.

"I am heartily sorry, my love."

Georgette smiled at the warmth of Anderson so close behind her and his deep voice in her ear.

"You ought to be," she replied under her breath. "We shall both have to stay and eat on the floor now."

"What can I say? Other than to confess an embarrassing dread of anything with more than four legs."

"How about things with no tongues? I almost bit mine off, thanks to you."

He pressed more heavily against her. "I am excessively relieved you did not." Then he was gone, walking away across the room to seat himself next to Miss Hilgrove.

Georgette breathed deeply, savouring the thrill he always instilled in her, before she turned to reassure her friends that she was recovered and search out her allocated patch of floor.

"Are you sure you are well?" Elizabeth enquired, finding her seat next to Georgette's. "You look rather flushed still."

Georgette arranged herself as elegantly as possible, which was not very, on the scant cushions provided, and wished she *had* foregone the hindrance of stays, for in this attitude, it would not be long before hers cut off the circulation to something vital. "I have a confession to make. It was not a genuine swoon. I availed myself of your future husband's arms quite without necessity."

Elizabeth observably wavered between disbelief and disapproval. "I see. But...you were bleeding."

"Yes, that was unfortunate. I had intended to be caught, you see, only not by your Mr Darcy. I do apologise." Seeing her new friend glance around the room, she added, "I shall not admit who was meant to catch me, even if you guess correctly."

"Oh, I would never presume to—"

"Yes you would, and I do not blame you. I would be eaten up with curiosity too, if such a delicious secret were dangled before me. Suffice it to say it seemed a preferable arrangement to squatting here, attempting not to drip pig's blood into my lap."

"Lord Saye certainly has some unusual ideas about entertaining," Elizabeth replied with a laugh, though she looked rather more alarmed than amused.

"My cousin likes to shock people, but done too often, the outrageous quickly becomes tedious."

"Count me as very much still shocked."

"It will wear off."

Mr Withers abruptly startled the gathering with a loud cry and leant sideways, pulling a shard of shattered earthenware from beneath his cushion. "Piffling thing! Almost caused me a mischief!"

"Apologies, Withers," Saye called to him. "The servants

must have missed that piece when they were cleaning up after the pre-dinner ruckus."

Anderson paused briefly in his conversation to nod apologetically at both men, but otherwise allowed the moment to pass by without further fuss. Always he knew how best to avoid a scene. *Provided there are no bugs involved,* Georgette reflected wryly.

"Poor Mr Anderson. That was a most unfortunate encounter earlier," Elizabeth said.

"Indeed, it was," Georgette agreed. "Thank goodness Sarah was here to save the day. Who knows how many more urns he would have smashed trying to squash the horrid thing otherwise?"

"True, though I thought he took it in remarkably good spirits, considering. He seems an agreeable gentleman. Admirable, too, for he runs a charitable home for poorly children out of his own pocket."

Georgette looked at her sharply. "How do you know that?"

"Why, he—he told me," Elizabeth replied, all agitation until her expression hardened into disapproval. "But perhaps I ought not to have mentioned it. I understand such activities are not palatable to everyone."

Georgette almost laughed to find herself being scolded in Anderson's defence. She was liking Elizabeth better by the moment and noted with some amusement how much more alluring she was rendered by the glint of challenge in her eyes. *I should wager this is the woman Mr Darcy truly admires!*

"I am only surprised he told you," she said calmly. "I have been acquainted with Mr Anderson for some years, and I have not often heard him speak of it."

The tension dissipated from Elizabeth's frame, and she smiled placatingly. "He was attempting to put me at ease on my first night here, for which I was exceedingly grateful. But what a shame he feels he cannot speak openly about such a worthy endeavour."

Georgette considered carefully how to answer, but in the end judged that the truth would likely persuade Elizabeth to keep silent on the matter better than anything else. She turned and made a show of plumping her cushions so she could speak discreetly. "His older brother, Matthew, suffered a childhood illness that left him severely crippled. It was widely believed his intellectual faculties had been damaged as well because his speech was affected by facial paralysis. That was untrue, but society is cruel and unforgiving."

She ran out of cushions to plump so began on Elizabeth's. "His parents felt compelled to keep Matthew hidden away to allow people to forget, which they did, until he died ten years later, and Mrs Anderson lost her wits to grief. She was committed to Bedlam and did not come out alive. Her husband never recovered from the shame, which was heaped upon them in spades by all their connexions."

Georgette gave one last, violent thump to the pillows and sat straight to meet Elizabeth's eyes. "Upon his father's death, Mr Anderson opened his institution in his brother's memory, but you will comprehend why he does not advertise his involvement."

Elizabeth nodded, visibly affected. "I value his telling me about it even more now I know the significance."

"He is a kind soul."

"He is. How are you acquainted with him?"

"Our fathers were friends—once upon a time." Beginning to feel she had said too much on the subject, Georgette leant to pluck a fig from a nearby tray and said with forced ebullience, "Mr Darcy is staring at you again."

Elizabeth dipped her head bashfully. "I know."

"He is not very subtle, is he? I suppose he does not have to be. Men such as he may admire whomever they choose, once they make their minds up to do so. They do not know how fortunate they are. Why on earth does your father not approve?"

"I cannot say that I know. He speaks of inconstancy and caprice, which he attributes to Mr Darcy having left Hertford-shire for a while before coming back to propose, but in truth, I think Papa simply does not wish to let me go. His quibbles are ridiculous. Mr Darcy and I have suffered the scrutiny of most of Hertfordshire and London, and he has not tired of me yet."

Georgette picked up her glass and gestured with it to her cousins. "Well, you never know, society may have one or two new pairings to amaze them soon, and you will be old news."

"That would please me very well. I should like to return to anonymity."

Georgette smiled broadly. "I hear it has many perquisites." Glancing again at the pained manner in which Mr Darcy was staring at Elizabeth—as though he wished to throw aside his plate and lunge across the floor to take her there and then—she added, "Perhaps you ought to try some of them—before Mr Darcy begins to crack."

She left Elizabeth puzzling over her meaning and turned to engage Lord Mickels, who had slid, still possessively clutching his wine glass, down his pile of cushions till he was almost fully recumbent and appeared to be struggling to remain conscious.

Anderson slipped away from the gathering easily enough. Going unnoticed in public was a skill he had perfected long ago, and he doubted he would be missed. Georgette would struggle more, for she was always the focus of a good deal of attention, but he did not doubt she would manage it. She was an exceedingly resourceful woman.

He made his way through mostly darkened rooms, half convinced he was going in the wrong direction; Matlock was confusing enough in daylight, never mind the gloom of late evening. Nevertheless, the noise of revelry gradually faded behind him, and the occasional shaft of moonlight through a window guided him, at length, to the library.

To his surprise, the dim glow of candlelight leached from within when he opened the door. He tentatively stepped inside, then laughed with relief. Somehow, though she had been surrounded by at least half a dozen people when he left her in the drawing room, Georgette had beaten him here. Her face lit when she saw him, and she flew into his embrace as though it were the first time they had been in company since Michaelmas. He wrapped his arms around the slender waist he loved so well and pulled her tightly to him.

"How did you manage to get here first?" he asked once he had kissed her enough to assuage the most insistent of the desires he had been suppressing all evening.

"Secret passages." She grinned wickedly. "Should you like me to show you one?"

Anderson groaned; the woman would be the death of him. He kissed her neck, speaking between touches. "And there I was expecting a set down for not catching you."

She did not reply and only held him more tightly, her head pressed heavily against his shoulder and her arms squeezing his ribs.

He ceased his caresses and leant sideways in an attempt to see her countenance better. "Is anything the matter?"

She shook her head but said nothing.

"Georgette, has something happened?"

"Only that I have found the most wonderful man in all the world to love me."

"Who?" he demanded in a deliberately urgent tone, even as warmth suffused his chest. "Tell me where to find the blackguard, and I shall call him out this instant."

Georgette let out a magnificent, deep throated giggle, and it had the same effect on him as it always did. Clutching his lapels, she lifted her face to his. "'Tis you, and you know it. I love everything you do, everything you stand for, and I love, most of all, the way you love me."

"I am heartened to hear it, but what has you in such a sentimental humour?"

"I think it is being surrounded by all these other gentlemen." His opinion of that admission must have shown on his face, for she laughed aloud and added, "Not in that way. It is seeing you in comparison to them. All their posturing and indecision has made me grateful for your conviction. You did not make me wait around, guessing and hoping. You did not leave me to wonder whether or not you loved me. And you certainly did not insult me instead of proposing."

"Are you feeling deprived of all the fuss?" he teased. "Should you really prefer me to insult you?"

"No, thank you."

"How about your family? I could start with your father." He returned his attention to her neck. "He is an enormous cockchafer."

"Stop being silly," she said, laughing. "I only mean that I appreciate how decided you were in your affections. You never doubted my worth, or your feelings for me."

He leant back and regarded her incredulously. "Georgette, there has never been room in my heart for doubt. You owned me from the very first moment of our acquaintance. You are magnificent."

"Yes, I know. But you are good. Truly good. What you have done for those children is deserving of the highest praise. It breaks my heart that you should be vilified for caring."

"I do not do it for praise."

"Precisely. You are everything that is noble. The perfect gentleman."

He huffed a soft laugh. "I was not particularly gentleman-like to your friend Miss Bentley earlier. I must apologise for speaking to her so uncivilly. She and I did not share the same apprehension for the damned beetle."

"Do not be anxious for Sarah—she is made of tough stuff. Besides, I doubt she would have flinched had she actually been required to shove her hands beneath your shirt."

"I do not believe that for a moment! She is the most innocent woman I have ever met."

"That is the problem. Her naivety makes her dangerously inquisitive. I tell you, if she wonders one more time what it must be like to be kissed by someone, I shall do it myself just to stop her asking."

He smirked, stirred by the fact that he was not quite sure whether she was joking. "Well, she does have a singularly attractive way of frowning when she is concentrating."

Georgette's eyes flashed, and her wicked smile returned. "I am glad you have been able to enjoy your company so well, sir. You certainly took a shine to Miss Bennet, telling her all about your children."

He pulled her closer. "Hmm, I like her very well. She has beautiful eyes, have you noticed?"

"I have, as it happens. She will make an excellent wife for Mr Darcy, who, by the by, has exceptionally pleasing arms."

Anderson did not answer. Instead, he kissed her, as hard as he had wished to since she had come down to dinner in her heart-stopping gown, and he reeled at the passion with which she responded. She pressed herself so firmly against him that he staggered back a step. Then he took her face in both his hands and walked her backwards across the library, never breaking his caress, until they reached the large sofa in the corner beneath the balcony ladder. He would have pulled her down onto it to continue in more comfort had not the sound of voices cut short their pleasure.

She stared at him, her lips parted, her breaths short, and devilry dancing in her eyes, as whomever it was passed by.

"Well, well, Miss Hawkridge," he murmured once the voices had gone. "I do believe you are enjoying all this skulking around."

"Had you not better make haste, Mr Anderson?" she replied breathlessly. "You would not like to be caught in the act of ruining me."

He did then lower them to the sofa, where he lavished her with attentions enough to be certain she was thinking of nobody's arms but his.

IN SICKNESS
AND IN HEALTH

Saye & Lillian

Pigs, in Lilly's estimation, were the least desirable of all creatures. She did not eat ham, bacon, or pork roast, and the smell of such was enough to send her running. For years—since an unfortunate incident in front of her father and elder sisters when she was thirteen—she had taken breakfast on a tray in her bedchamber to avoid the smell of bacon and eggs in the breakfast room.

So why she had sampled the peculiar offerings from Saye's banquet, she could not say. Not a morsel of it had appealed to her, and the manner in which they ate had only made it less palatable.

But she did not wish to be—how had Saye himself said it? —*le rabat-joie.* She had heard him teasing Sir Phineas, calling him *le rabat-joie* for the crime of refusing a drink. Her French was lacking, but she believed it meant a killer of joy, and she could not bear to have Saye think it of her. So she ate.

And now you pay the price for your silly pride.

The pains began shortly after her maid left her. They bent her double, and made it impossible to lie, sit, or stand comfortably. She remained in her bed, twisting and turning amid the fine bed linens which grew warm and unpleasantly damp beneath her, and prayed for relief. For a little while, she might have dozed fitfully, for suddenly it had gone two in the morning and her stomach had become a boiling cauldron of agony which threatened to upend itself at any moment.

If I vomit, I shall feel better. Except, she could not abide the notion of vomiting. Did not everyone? Such a miserable state for any human, huddled unhappily over a chamber pot to cast up their accounts. She prayed the chamber pot was empty at least, for if she could not refrain from vomiting, she would like to be spared that indignity at least.

When at last she felt it could no longer be avoided, she slid from between the sheets down onto the plush rug, landing on her hands and knees. Her vision swam a moment from the movement, but as the need for the pot was growing more urgent, she spared herself the briefest moment to recover. She reached beneath the bed, finding the pot—a very pretty Minton porcelain in green and gold that coordinated with her bedchamber—and pulling it towards her. She crouched in front of it, her elbows against the rug and her head in her hands and for a few blessed seconds she thought she might have escaped it.

When it came, it came with a fury. She felt she emptied herself not only of that evening's indulgence but indeed of everything she had eaten since her come-out, at least. When she sat back on her haunches, tears leaking from her eyes, panting and sweaty, it was disappointing to find that her stomach, in fact, did not feel improved. Indeed, she might have been worse.

Twice more it happened, and by then, she was weak, far too weak to rise. In fact, she was too afraid even to move, feeling that any extra motion might bring on worse. She longed for her maid, but Marleigh deserved to be in her bed and, in any case, Lilly had not the strength to get to the bell pull which seemed, at the time, miles away.

A second later, she heard a door opening. "Oh, Marleigh," she moaned thankfully. "How good you are to look in on me, for I find myself in a wretched way!"

Two shoes appeared in her line of vision—men's naval-blue slippers with gold tassels on them, very fine, attached to snow-white silk stockings and... She raised her head, seeing a positively humiliating sight above her. Saye had entered her chamber.

"Good lord, what happened here?" he asked, kneeling down beside her.

"Get out of here," she protested weakly. "You cannot be in here."

"I daresay somebody must be here, for you, madam, have yourself in quite a predicament." He sat down on the floor beside her. "A disgusting predicament. How much pig did you eat?"

"Please, Saye," she moaned. "I have no strength to escape you, but I beg you to leave me. Summon my maid for me and go."

"If I summon your maid, she will want to know how I came upon you," he said very reasonably. "And she might mention it to others."

"Tell them you heard a sound which led to your summons."

"I did hear a sound, like a horse in its death throes. Come, let me help you."

Even in the state that she was, the notion of Saye helping her made her nearly laugh. With a little grunt, she pushed herself into a more seated position, using her foot to slide the chamber pot farther from them. "My stomach is sick."

"I am drunk, to be sure, but not stupid," he replied wryly.

"Should my nose have failed to alert me to the problem, that steaming heap of salmagundi beside you would have."

"Sorry." Lilly sniffled. "If you would just go and tell Marleigh you heard a noise from my bedchamber and—

To her horror, Lilly felt her gorge rise again into her throat. One hand flew to cover her mouth, which had suddenly filled with sour salivation, while the other she placed on Saye's arm, ineffectively trying to push him away. "Go," she gasped. He did not move. "P-pray leave me, S-saye, I...I—"

She scrambled over to the chamber pot, barely making it in time for another round of painful retching and heaving. Deep in her agony, she still felt it, and registered some shock, when Saye came behind her and took hold of her plait, keeping it out of the heinous melange until she was finished. She sat back again, panting for a moment when she had finished, and he, very sweetly, rubbed her back and then proffered his handkerchief for her mouth.

When she was well enough, she sat up, gingerly moving to lean back against the side of the bed. She closed her eyes for a moment and heard Saye rise to his feet. *He will leave now*. She believed she was relieved more than she actually was, even as some dim part of her mind recognised the impropriety of him being here, him witnessing her in such a state—surely even husband and wife did not watch one another in such straits! This was what maids and valets were commissioned to do.

She opened her eyes to see him off, only to find fresh sources of astonishment. "Wait! What are you doing?"

To her absolute horror and humiliation, Saye had picked up the pot. "I shall empty it for you."

"What? No, oh no! Please, will you just leave?"

He waggled the fingers of one hand over his shoulder while he exited the room, going she knew not where. Did

Matlock have water closets? Earth rooms? Did Saye himself even know? She could not imagine he had ever given much thought to the less genteel aspects of his kingdom.

As soon as she thought it, he returned, quietly closing the door behind him. In his hand was a different pot, another Minton, but one painted in yellow and pink roses. He placed it down beside her before going to the fire. She watched him stir up the coals while reporting cheerfully, "James was all too obliging."

"James?"

"One of the night footmen. He is the one who is like a less handsome version of me." Saye had finished with the fire and now returned to her, sinking down into a seated position beside her. "Fellow needs very little sleep, it seems, and is always on hand to manage the unmanageable. I quite like the boy."

"Oh! But surely you did not tell him you were with me?" Her voice rose and she felt a clench in her gut. "Saye please, you have to go...if anyone finds out you were in here, I will be ruined."

"Ruined." He said it with no little derision. "You would not be ruined, and in any case, this is my house and they are my servants. Who would discover us?"

"Our friends, your sister, the colonel...to name but a few."

"Everyone sober is asleep, and everyone awake is too drunk to stand, much less burst in here." Saye rubbed at some spot on his breeches that Lilly suddenly realised might have been expelled from her gut. She winced.

"Forgive me, I think...I might have done that."

"Likely not. Phin vomited earlier, might have been him." He shrugged. "I can tell you what you *did* do—you have cost me a great deal of money. I was down a fair sum but feeding them all brandy by the bucket so I could regain my losses. Instead I am here with you."

"I am feeling a little better. You should go." It was true, she realised gratefully—marginally improved but, nevertheless, improved.

He turned to look at her then, his countenance marked by an uncommon earnestness, and said, "Lilly, 'tis well worth any sum to be able to be here with you."

She did not know what to say to that, but her heart and her gut gave a peculiar flutter. "Pray do not make me flutter inside," she said lightly. "Things are just beginning to settle."

Delight spread across his face, and insouciance was back. "At last she admits that I make her flutter inside. I knew it had to be so!" He rubbed his hands together, not bothering to disguise his glee.

She gave him a little shove. "Making ladies flutter has never been difficult for you, has it?"

"Making you flutter is." Saye shifted his position to be slightly nearer to her. "Your flutters are rare, and therefore more worth earning."

"Oh, Saye. You, and your compliments, and your excessive lovemaking. Are you ever in earnest?"

"I am always in earnest. But pray tell me one thing."

"What?"

"How is it that I make you flutter, yet you still tolerate the attention of that gollumpus Balton-Sycke? Can you imagine—he brought four pillows for his bruised rump just to play cards!"

"He is injured," she protested.

Saye rolled his eyes. "The man is an idiot. Who simply arrives at someone else's party? It is not done, not in my circle, it is not. I daresay his rump deserved whatever flogging it received."

This Lilly could not dispute. She thought it was rather

badly done, and the purpose of it quite transparent. Balton-Sycke did not wish her to be here alone, and that knowledge rankled as much as it pleased her. He had no claim over her —not yet—and should not presume to act the part of a betrothed or a husband.

Her stomach spasmed painfully, and for a moment she was on alert. But no—it was merely the after-effects, the tremors which remain as the storm reluctantly relinquishes its grip.

"Must we argue about Balton-Sycke again?" Lilly asked. "Yes, I know—you will never speak to me again if I marry him and as I do intend to accept his offer, our friendship appears to be on its deathbed."

"I shall still speak to you," Saye replied. "I shall have to, if I am to make good on my promises."

She immediately knew what he spoke of. Those promises, those scandalous, almost-frightening, certainly titillating acts he had murmured in her ear at a party at Rumbridge House last month. "I do not know what you are speaking of," she replied in as dignified a voice as possible.

He turned his head, meeting her gaze squarely as a lazy smile spread across his face. "Oh I think you do, but if you need me to refresh your memory…"

His words from that night rushed into her mind. No, her memory needed no refreshing, for well did she recall the whispers of such scandalous desires. He had grinned, just as he did now, while telling her of things which were surely not decent: the many places he intended to kiss her—not just on her lips!—and touch her and…and… Good lord, why had he stirred the fire as he had! It was a veritable oven in here now!

"Your face looks strange," he said. "Are you going to spew again?"

"No."

"You are certain?" He reached for the chamber pot.

"Because if it is not your stomach, I shall have to presume it is the memory itself which so unsettles you."

"I ought to have slapped your face," she told him.

"Probably," he said amiably. "But I am, above all, an honest man."

"Oh, you are not."

"Well, sometimes I am, when it suits me. And I was being completely honest when I told you of my plans."

Another lazy smile nearly melted her, but she remained outwardly unaffected, or so she hoped.

"I have great plans for you and me someday. A man could die for a figure like yours, Lilly," he told her. "Die happy, that is. *La petit mort.*"

"A little death?"

"Precisely," he replied. "Do not be looking to Mr Sore Arse down there for any of that, to be sure. Has he spoken yet?"

She was still trying to puzzle out his meaning. Saye did tend to speak rather cryptically at times, and she could not understand the connexion of *petit mort* and Balton-Sycke, if that was what he intended. Thus did it take her a moment before she said, "No, he has not. But I expect he will when we are all back in town."

"If the gollumpus thinks I shan't poach on his marriage bed, he has another think coming," Saye replied blithely. "My gift to you, so instead of lying there thinking of England, you can lie there and think of me."

"You are terrible," she told him but the words lacked conviction and she knew it.

They left the subject of Balton-Sycke then, moving on to other conversations. Saye loved to gossip and had no scruple in tearing apart the characters of his guests. Darcy, he told her, was being led about on a string by these accursed Bennet folk who were no doubt perverted and strange. Miss Elizabeth Bennet intrigued him, most notably because she had affixed Darcy so firmly to her apron. Georgette was one of his favourite cousins, but he could not comprehend her friendship with Mr Anderson. His idiot of a brother needed to stop reaching for women above his pay grade. "He has nothing, so he needs to comprehend that the beauties of the *ton* are likely beyond him," he told her. "This Miss Bentley would do well for him, despite her unfortunate fascination with the repugnant."

But it was not only gossip that passed the hours before dawn. In a most unanticipated moment, Lilly found herself listening as Saye told her, with genuine candour, how much he feared his father's death. "I saw what Darcy went through," he told her. "I could not have borne it as he did."

"But you will be older than he was," she said gently. "Wiser, no doubt with a wife and family. In any case, there are certainly far stupider people than you who manage it, and I have no doubt you will too."

And he smiled at her, his eyes warm and his face a bit slackened (for they were both exhausted by then) and looking much less like the arrogant pleasure-seeker she had always known; and it struck her that she was seeing the serious side of Saye, the side that she doubted anyone else knew in the world. Did his own brother even see this side of him? Did Mr Darcy?

It put her off-balance, to state it mildly. All of her defence against falling in love with him was based on two things: he would not marry, not soon in any case, and his character lacked gravity. If both of those things proved wrong...

"I need to go to bed," she said abruptly. "You should too, if there is to be any hope of us escaping this night unscathed."

"Let me help you." He rose and dusted himself off, then bent. He took her hand and tugged her to her feet, and they stood a moment, very close together, not touching, scarcely breathing. She was exquisitely aware of him, his faded cologne and the faint whiff of spirits commingling with his natural maleness to entice her quite neatly. She wondered if he might try to kiss her, but then remembered how the night had begun and shuddered. *He smells lovely, and I smell of vomit.*

He took a step back from her, keeping her hand in his as he bent low over it, respecting her as if they had merely been dancing at Almack's and not engaged in a clandestine and highly improper nocturnal visit.

He then bid her good night and was gone.

"I have a note for you," Sarah said eagerly as she entered the room. With a flourish, she deposited it on Lilly's blanket-covered lap.

Though Lilly had not made all the details of her night known, she did tell her maid that she had been sick in the night. While she felt perfectly well now, Marleigh was immediately in deep distress for her young mistress, declared her pale and hollow-eyed, and insisted on tucking her into her bed for the day. The effects on her countenance, Lilly thought, were very likely due to sleeplessness; but, she did not correct Marleigh and allowed herself to be put to bed.

The ladies were almost immediately upon her. She felt a little guilty, receiving all the fuss and dismayed clucks of her friends, but so it was. Georgette came in first, rolling her eyes and asking why on earth she had eaten pig, and several of the other ladies came to give her a book, or offer her tea, or fluff her pillows. Miss Balton-Sycke had been the least interested in Lilly's ailment. She had poked her head into the room and offered the hasty explanation that her brother believed van Leeuwenhoek's theory of animalcules as carriers of disease, and thus had forbidden her from entering sickrooms.

"Of course," Lilly said with a smile and a nod, but in truth, she did not agree at all. The pig had upset her humours and now she was well. What danger could that be to either Balton-Sycke? And what would they do for her once she was a member of the family?

And now Sarah had handed her a note from Balton-Sycke himself. She opened it while Sarah watched with open curiosity, no doubt anticipating flowery words of romance and despair for a lover's poor health. In fact, there were neither.

"Balton-Sycke says they will depart today," she told her. "He wishes me improved health and promises to call once we are in town."

"Oh." Sarah seemed to struggle to find some encouragement. "Dare I suppose that once in London...?"

"Likely," said Lilly with a sigh.

"How exciting!" Sarah's sweet face was bright with enthusiasm. "When will you marry, do you think? The timing is strange with the Season upon us, but surely you will not wish for a long engagement? Or perhaps you will marry in London?"

Lilly sighed again and turned her head towards the window. The weather was not promising, steel grey clouds hung over all, the sort that portended snow. She wondered whether Saye had insisted on Balton-Sycke's departure and smiled at the notion. "I have been thinking that perhaps I ought to take my chances on another Season."

"Pray, do not speak so! Not when you have a fine prospect like Mr Balton-Sycke! He is ever so kind, and I find him quite handsome and hear that his house is very modern and pretty and—"

"He is a gollumpus who got shot in the rump," Lilly said flatly. Then she said, "Oh Sarah, forgive me. I am just in a peculiar temper this morning."

"Because you are unwell," Sarah said immediately, the concern that had creased her countenance smoothing away. No doubt Lilly had alarmed her greatly. "And I shall leave you so you can get your rest."

She leant in then, giving her friend a kiss on the cheek. "No fever!" she reported happily before she left.

Lilly snuggled beneath the coverlet, permitting herself a frown. The opinions were always that she should marry Balton-Sycke. Her mother thought it, her sisters thought it, Sarah certainly thought it...indeed, Lilly herself was the only one who thought the bird in her hand was not at all worth the two—or rather the one—in the bush. And in truth, she knew not if she could fairly even imagine that Lord Saye was in the bush. He was, perhaps, circling overhead, but not lounging about in a bush, to be sure. She giggled at her own fancy.

She slept then, waking when Elizabeth knocked gently on her door. She bade her enter.

"I have not woken you, I hope?" Elizabeth's face was all smiles as she came in. "I would not like to disturb you."

"No, no, do come in." Lilly pushed herself upright and straightened the coverlet around her.

"I see you are well supplied with diversion," Elizabeth said, taking in the litter of books, half-drunk teas, and needlework around her. "I have brought sustenance. We have a particular receipt at Longbourn for a biscuit that is most soothing to an enraged gut. The cook was good enough to conjure them up for us here."

She held out a plate on which was a very nice-looking biscuit which smelt faintly of ginger. Just seeing it made

Lilly's stomach grumble with hunger. "Oh, lovely," she said. "That looks like just the thing."

Elizabeth perched on the side of Lilly's bed while Lilly took the biscuit and began, hesitantly, to nibble. "I cannot help but imagine the vagaries of dinner might be responsible for your malady."

"I suspect so. My usual diet is nowhere near so adventurous."

"I have, myself, always preferred a plain dish to a ragout...or whatever that was last evening."

The two ladies laughed lightly, and Lilly thought she might really find Elizabeth a friend someday. Not wishing her to leave, Lilly began to ask her questions about herself, her family, and her home, chief among the queries. What she heard made her pensive, and her new friend noticed at once.

"No doubt you comprehend how different I am from what sort of wife Mr Darcy had been supposed to take."

"Oh! No, do not think at all that I sit in any sort of judgment of you, or your home. I am only thinking of what a complicated business it is, finding a marriage partner. If I think that you are not what I should expect for Mr Darcy, it is only because you are so lively and—forgive me for saying so—I had always believed him so...so...dull. Stern, even."

"I daresay you are not the only one to think so," Elizabeth agreed.

"Falling in love has made him more agreeable in company."

"His manners might have been softened, it is true, although I have long believed that the easier, more lively Mr Darcy was there all along, and just hidden from the view of most."

Elizabeth's words made Lilly recall last night's observations of Saye. Whereas Mr Darcy had hidden liveliness to reveal, Saye must have hidden depths of solemnity to be shown.

"Everything is so hidden all the time," Lilly said. "It makes it all the more difficult to know—shall I be happy with this man? Or is that one better suited to me?"

Elizabeth tilted her head, seeming to study Lilly. She glanced back over her shoulder, as if wishing to ascertain they remained alone, before asking, "You are expecting an offer from Mr Balton-Sycke, I think?"

Lilly nodded. "Soon, I daresay."

Elizabeth continued in her pensive evaluation of Lilly. "I am perhaps impertinent to suggest it, as we are scarcely acquainted, but as I am rather outside your circle, I might have a unique and impartial perspective—should you need it."

"He is a very good man as you have seen, no doubt." Lilly paused to consider a moment before continuing to say, "I am simply not in love with him...and in truth, I do not think I ever would be. I would grow to care for him, I am sure. But love? I cannot imagine it."

"Well..." Elizabeth smiled. "I may know more of what you feel than you know. I turned down a good marriage prospect some time before Mr Darcy proposed. Mr Collins is my cousin, heir to my father's estate, so there was some hue and cry raised when I refused him. My mother certainly thought spinsterhood was inevitable."

"Did you do that because you were in love with Mr Darcy?"

"No!" Elizabeth laughed. "Quite the opposite, in fact. No, I had no other prospects and nothing else in mind but the fact that I simply could not do it. And I daresay it would have been much to his disadvantage, as well as mine, if I had accepted him."

"Yes, I suppose that is true."

"But you see, if I had not taken that—oh, I imagine you could call it a leap of faith?—I would not have come to fall in love with Darcy. At the time, nearly everyone thought I was being a fool, but I was prepared to live with whatever consequence came of it." Elizabeth smiled again and patted Lilly's hand. "And indeed, the consequences could have been dire. I have nothing of my own, as you might have heard said, and accepting Mr Collins was the most reasonable course. But I should have been miserable and eventually made him miserable too."

She paused then and, with great delicacy, added, "I would expect the misery would be still greater if I had been in love with someone else. I think if there is someone else in your heart...then to accept another should be quite out of the question indeed."

Their eyes met, and Lilly thought that Elizabeth, for not knowing much of her, had cut neatly to the home truth.

"But I must leave you to rest." Elizabeth rose from Lilly's bed, offering a final warm smile before asking if there was anything else required for her comfort. She departed then, and Lilly was left alone with her thoughts.

A Racing Heart, A Racing Horse

Sarah & Fitzwilliam

S arah left her friend to rest, troubled—although not for the reasons Lilly believed. It was ludicrous to think any longer that Lilly ought to marry Balton-Sycke, and only a fool would wish him on her. She had changed her mind about the man utterly—having once believed he was *Maniola jurtina*, sturdy and adaptable, instead finding him to be *Mayetiola destructor*, a serious nuisance who infested places he was unwelcome, quickly making a pest of himself. Besides, she liked Saye. He was interesting and unpredictable, and studying him was amusing. Lilly would never be bored; even if he was bewildering and eccentric, her friend was up to the task of taming him.

However, she had not been the surrogate mother of a young, stubborn, independent boy for nine years without learning a thing or two about dispensing advice to the young, stubborn, and independent. There were enough people here in Saye's corner; she would do better for the romance, she felt, by shoving her friend at the *Mayetiola*.

"Romance," she said aloud, sighing. Her own prospects were not particularly bright. Mr Withers had conspicuously avoided her ever since she had punctured Balton-Sycke, and most of the rest of the gentlemen treated her warily. As she had entered the library a few moments ago, Lord Mickels, who was then exiting, stepped back in an exaggerated manner, giving her a wide berth while saying, "What-ho, don't know what she has in her pockets! Cannot be too careful!" and chuckling merrily as if he were a great wit. Henceforth, she would likely be known as 'Lady Beetle' or something equally appalling.

It was too wet for out-of-door activities, and besides, after the late and boisterous evening, most of the guests seemed happy for a day of quiet pursuits. And while Sarah liked a good book as much as the next person, she could not settle on anything, instead staring out of the library's bay window and watching droplets pelt the glass. She ought to return to her room, where Evans was waiting and no doubt wondering what had become of her.

"Perhaps what I truly ought to do is return home to The Pillows," she murmured. "I have done my reputation more harm than good here, and at least Papa will be happy to see me."

To her surprise, a warm hand landed on her shoulder. "You surely do not pay heed to anything Lord Mickels says," came a low murmur directly behind her. "A mutton-headed lobcock, is our Pickles."

Sarah did not turn, but of course, she would know that rough voice anywhere. "If you have come to taunt me, please do not bother. You must be feeling quite justified in your opinions of me after last evening's misfortune with poor Mr Anderson."

He did not answer, but he had not moved—she could feel the heat from his body all along her spine, her shoulder warm under his hand.

She turned around to face him. Even though she was a

tall woman, she was nevertheless a few inches shorter than he; she was accustomed to being eye to eye with most gentlemen, and it was somewhat disconcerting to be…smaller. But she was. And though he was so large, when he moved, it was with an indefinable grace paired with military purpose. His older brother was unpredictable, but…'dangerous' was a better word for the younger. Still, instead of wishing for retreat, she wanted…to advance. To push.

"Why do you do it?" she asked.

He only raised his brows. He was every bit as arrogant as Saye; he had only earned it by different means. "Do what, madam?" he asked imperiously.

"Goad him. Challenge him. I thought, at first, you were in love with her. Elizabeth is an agreeable person, and would be quite easy to love, if it were so. But now, I do not really think so."

"I have no idea what you are talking about," he scoffed. But he would not meet her eyes. "And neither do you."

"Quite possibly, I do not. Very well, let us say you *are* in love with her. What good does it do you to provoke him? You ascribe to a code of honour which would never allow you to act upon those feelings. I think you care for him too much to try. And yet knowing how he suffers—"

"Suffers!" The colonel made an explosive sound of contempt. "He has everything a man could ever want—has had, since the day he was born."

"And so you wish to take away what he considers most priceless? Help him suffer some deprivation, as you do?"

Rather than rise to the bait, he only sounded amused. "Perhaps we should recite poetry together, Darcy and I? Matlock Court has a tower, even. We could dash ourselves off it, after bemoaning how we *suffer*."

She nodded. "I have suggestions for you. 'One fire burns out another's burning; One pain is less'ned by another's anguish; Turn giddy, and be holp by backward turning; One desperate grief cures with another's languish.'"

"Romeo and Juliet? This conversation has sunk to a new low." But his stiff posture eased. "I shall tell you why I tease my cousin, if you tell me why you stand at the library window and whine about being unloved."

She crooked her head at him. "I heard one of the young ladies describe you as 'charming'. Miss Hilgrove, I think. Perhaps you ought to find her now and flaunt a medal or two —you do have medals, I presume? I recommend displaying the shiniest ones. You might show better in a glare."

He grinned. "You were the one who said you no longer had to bother pretending with me, to act as someone you are not, to hide your faults, because I had already seen them." He looked down at her, his grin fading. "Perhaps I no longer need to act a part with you."

Sarah found herself unable to look away. Her heart seemed to be hammering most peculiarly, pounding away inside her chest as if trying to break free. "Why does it do that?" she softly wondered aloud.

"Do what?" he asked, and there was no longer derision in his words.

She took his hand—a rough, calloused hand, gloveless, a strong, large hand. Hers felt delicate within it. She put it high on her chest, where the beat of her heart felt loudest to her. He moved to within a hair's breadth. She peered up, that hand heavy upon her; he bent down. And for the first time, Sarah felt the touch of lips, his mouth firm and soft, cool and heated, all at once—true anomalies. Her hand reached to his chest; his heart pounded as fiercely as hers.

The kiss altered, growing wilder; it took control, even, of the temperature in the room, changing it from mildly chilly to overheated. She stepped still closer, wanting more of that delicious heat, and the kiss slowed, deepened. When it finally ended, he kept his hand right where it was, their faces so close, his gaze hooded, contemplating her, she thought, as if he were a starving man, and she were Mrs Figg's pigeon pie. It was, all unspoken, the most genuine compliment she had ever received.

"One cannot pretend this, can one?" she asked. "In my father's experiments, for example, he placed together *Drosophila* flies, some with rare yellow bodies and others with the typical yellowish-grey pigmentation. Females—no matter their body colour—continually preferred the common pigmentation over yellow males. In human terms, I am a yellow-bodied *Drosophila*. You seem to be exhibiting some physical signs of preference, but of course, I suppose you must be driven by far more complex reasoning than a common vinegar fly."

He blinked in sudden confusion, his brow furrowing as he drew back. "Yellow-bodied...vinegar... what? Devil take it, you are not experimenting on *me*, are you?"

It was her turn to smile. "Heavens, no. I believe when I am seeking test subjects, I shall choose someone more..." she trailed off at the look in his narrowed eyes.

"Who?" he demanded. "Someone more what?"

Sarah had been going to suggest someone more malleable, more easily governed, and definitely someone softer and less overpowering. Instead, she heard herself saying, "Someone more devoted to *my* pleasure, rather than his cousin's bride."

He dropped his hand, and she immediately missed its warmth. His expression had hardened again, and he looked angry. For some reason, she was completely unafraid. To be more accurate, she felt fear's opposite. She felt powerful.

Turning on his heel, he stalked away—but at the library door, he whirled back to face her. "Leave the rest of the men here be—they would not know what to do with you, Miss

Bentley. And if you truly wish to learn something, find me."
He left her standing there, her heart still beating hard. She
placed her own hand upon it, but it did not have the same
tantalising effect.

"Oh, my," she said aloud. It took several moments for her
heart to return to its usual pace, but during them, she made
a decision—it was time to take Saye's advice and seek out
Lady Aurelia. Saye's sister always showed her rather buxom
figure to fine advantage, and, as Saye had pointed out, they
were built upon the same lines. Yellow-bodied vinegar fly she
might be, but she was not stupid.

It was, as she had previously observed, simple enough to
attract male attention with eye-catching apparel emphasising
the bosom, and she had hitherto never been interested in
flaunting her shapeliest physical assets. But neither, she now
realised, had she made any effort to flatter them, to put her
best foot forward, so to speak. She still was unsure as to
whether the colonel could meet her standards in a mate—
and she disapproved completely of his constant baiting of the
lovely Mr Darcy. However, any man who knew his Shake-
speare so well could not be *too* far off the mark. And besides,
if she could initiate such a thrilling response from him in this
hideous orange gown, just think what she might be capable
of inspiring if he only knew what was hidden beneath its
shapeless folds. Perhaps, even, incentive enough to cease
underestimating her.

"The fact is, he would be a fortunate man, indeed, to win
my hand," she said aloud to the empty room, her usual confidence restored. "Although, I am not sure what it says about
my character that he was able to earn my approval by means
of decidedly proficient lovemaking skills. Nary a female
Drosophila would dare overlook *him*, to be certain—no matter
his colouring."

Fitzwilliam hurried out of the house, grateful for its relative quiet—which meant he was able to reach the stables without meeting Darcy or Saye. He was far too shaken to cope with either. It was wet, although not particularly chilly, and regardless, Zeus was a warrior—who would be thrilled for the exercise had it been snowing—and was accustomed to his daily run.

A snow storm would be ideal, he thought, wishing the weather could cool his ardour. How could he be attracted to a woman so opposite to his usual inclinations? He had always preferred a daintier sort, women fashioned after the lines of Miss Elizabeth Bennet. And yet, it was not Elizabeth who had haunted his dreams these last nights. How would it be to have a companion who confronted him, excited him, dared him to explain himself, and refused to allow him precedence simply because he was an earl's son? At the same time, he was unsure of those same qualities; it was not quite comfortable to be thus challenged.

Miss Bentley had asked him why he provoked his cousin so, and he was beginning to fear it had less to do with unrequited affections than he had hitherto believed. The conclusion did not paint him in a very good light.

Bah! I need only clear my head with a long ride and put Miss Bentley and her artless, wildly pounding heart from my mind!

But he had only just brought the stallion into the yard when he nearly knocked over the last person he expected to find at such a spot on such an inclement day.

"Oh—sorry Blanders...um, Anderson. Did not expect to meet you here." Fitzwilliam raised a brow when he noticed the mount Anderson led. "Botheration, it appears as though a mistake has been made—they've given you Thunder. Bad tempered beast. Let me see to getting you one of Saye's more suitable hacks. It will only take a moment."

But Anderson held up one hand. "Thank you. There is really no need."

Fitzwilliam was dubious but in no mood to argue. The man would likely see more of the muddy ground than the estate's surroundings; however, it was his own business. He shrugged. "Well then, I shall leave you to it." In one easy motion, he mounted, waving off the waiting stable boy.

"Colonel," the other man called, looking back over his shoulder from his saddle. "First to the south gate buys a round?"

It was madness to encourage him, yet perhaps it was as well to stay with the fool. If he was determined to race Thunder, it would be best to keep an eye out and, as would probably be necessary, know where to bring the litter to cart his broken body home. Besides, Zeus would love it, and the south gate was miles away, at the end of a good enough road; even Blanderson might live to tell the tale.

"On your signal," he said with a shrug.

Blanderson tipped his hat—and was off like a shot from a pistol. Surprised, it took Fitzwilliam a moment or two to urge Zeus into his fastest paces, racing through the wind and rain, the landscape speeding past until they were practically flying. As he did, he received a still greater surprise—the man was mad. Truly, ferociously, unapologetically insane. He did not take the well-travelled road—or rather, he did, but only to the extent that it matched his purpose, the straightest, shortest conceivable route to the postern. If shrubs or hedges or once, even, a bloody tree surrounded by boulders interfered with that course, he leapt, he twisted, he swivelled, he all but somersaulted over or around it. After a few more astonished seconds, Fitzwilliam no longer truly cared which of them won.

It was the thrill of it. Saye and Darcy were both expert horsemen but also cared for the style, the grace, the elegance of the thing—and neither preferred horses like Zeus, bred for brute strength as well as speed. Racing them was never a neck-or-nothing, vicious battle of endurance as well as speed —a reckless, filthy adventure. In the end, the only reason Fitzwilliam won was because Zeus was, at his heart, a warhorse. On the home stretch, racing neck and neck for the gate, Zeus managed an aggressive battle manoeuvre with his teeth; to avoid total disaster, Anderson was forced to dodge. Zeus took to the air as if he were winged, soaring over the high gate seconds before Thunder.

Fitzwilliam glanced over—the other man, covered in muck, hatless, was congratulating the steed as if he had won at Ascot. Thunder, well known in the stables for his ill temper and perverse disposition, was leaning against Anderson's shoulder as if he were a motherless puppy.

Fitzwilliam shook his head, dismounting Zeus to lead him into a walk. "I had no idea Thunder had it in him."

Anderson looked over with a wry expression. "Some animals might be misjudged and underestimated, even in the best stables."

Indeed.

"Touché," Fitzwilliam replied. "One thing is certain—I swear never to call you 'Blanderson' again, so long as I live."

Anderson grinned, his teeth showing white against his muddy face. "I don't suppose that horse of yours is for sale?"

"I would as soon sell my right arm," Fitzwilliam said, grinning back. "Saye bought him for me, a birthday gift some five years past. For that alone, I would gladly die for the man."

Anderson nodded, wiping his face with a large handkerchief. "What do you say we go on to the Pig & Feathers and let their stablemen brush these boys down before returning? I would just as soon not be expelled from Matlock's stables for abuse of Saye's horseflesh."

"I do not think that horse has ever been happier," Fitzwilliam answered sardonically, shaking his head at the way Thunder was currently nuzzling the other man. "But yes. Let us clear your debt."

He remounted Zeus, in a far better state of mind than he had been when leaving the house—and the intriguing, alluring, bewildering Miss Bentley. *Vinegar flies!* He bellowed sudden laughter. Anderson glanced over at him curiously, but he did not explain.

"What do you think of Darcy and Miss Bennet? Do you approve of the match?"

They were on the third round, seated before a comfortable fire in the Pig's finest private dining parlour. There had not been overmuch conversation, which was preferable, to Fitzwilliam's thinking—Anderson was no jaw-me-dead. So he was somewhat surprised at the question; what was more, he was feeling mellow enough to answer it.

"Not my place to approve or disapprove. My father was pleased enough that fastidious Darcy finally settled upon someone, and he gave it the family's sanction."

Anderson raised a brow.

Annoying fellow!

"*Of course* I approve. Darcy is like a brother to me, and

Miss Bennet is...well, she is as pretty as she is clever. She will make a fine mistress for Pemberley—as a matter of fact, it is the perfect setting for her."

The other man nodded. "I have noticed she is good for Darcy."

"Too good," Fitzwilliam snorted. Anderson only watched him.

He had never before noticed the shrewdness of Anderson's expression. It made him irritable. "Darcy did not even *see* her goodness until he had nearly destroyed any of her finer feelings towards him. He is too accustomed to gaining what he wants."

"It appears she has forgiven him."

"She is all that is good," Fitzwilliam said sulkily. "I have an obligation, as his elder cousin and nearly his closest relation in the world, to needle him a bit, to see that he does not grow smug."

"Ah. You have only his welfare at heart."

Sarcasm, now. It was none of Anderson's business, nor Miss Bentley's. Everyone in the world, it seemed, was eager to assist Darcy with his dearest concerns. He refused to comment, but his companion did not seem to mind, stretching out comfortably as if he had not a care in the world. Perhaps he did not; recalling Georgette's prevarication at dinner on the first night, a suspicion took root in his mind that, perhaps, his cousin and Anderson were not merely friends. Perhaps Georgette had made up her mind to have him. He had to admit, Anderson was a better man than he had first appeared. Anyone who rode that well could not fail to handle his mother's cousin, Hawkridge. If so, it would make Anderson yet another man more fortunate in love than he. He could not resist saying so, for even if Georgette's feelings were not engaged, his companion seemed entirely too complacent.

"Easy enough for those who are unacquainted with unrequited affections to judge." He snapped his mouth shut, having said too much.

But Anderson, unlike his brother and cousin, did not pounce on the opportunity to mock. He only smiled sympathetically. "However, I predict that time, in your case, will remove the thorn from your side."

Fitzwilliam grunted. "Fail to see how you can know a thing."

"Yet it is quite obvious. No one could like, or even accustom themselves to watching the love of one's life marry another. Especially to so close a relative, so near in age, and, except for his purse, no more worthy than yourself of the prize."

"No one could," Fitzwilliam agreed reluctantly, for his thoughts on love were increasingly confused.

"Naturally. Of course, the resentment will become obvious to your cousin, and, eventually, to his bride. They will soon grow uncomfortable in your presence, and, as tactfully as possible, distance themselves, so as to avoid antagonising the family peace. Before you know it, you will only have to put up with them for an annual visit, Easter or some such." He waved his hand, as if his little solution—losing Darcy's respect and friendship—answered everything.

"I do not say she is the love of my life—only that she never had the *opportunity* to become such. I never had *the opportunity, the means* to court her, to discover whether she might be."

"Bloody unfair," Anderson agreed. "Bad enough to be the younger brother, without being forced to watch your cousin's victories as well."

"I do not begrudge either of them," Fitzwilliam protested. But he knew, even as he said it, that he did. That he had. Not

Saye—he had found his peace years ago with that. Evidently, however, he had never done the same with Darcy.

Anderson said nothing—a talent of his. The silence stretched.

"When I returned from Spain," Fitzwilliam said at last, haltingly, "I was...not in a good way. There were things I witnessed there that—well, never mind it. I could not, at first, confide in Saye. Felt him too far removed, and too refined, I supposed, to ever understand it. Thought the same of Darcy, but he took me to his hunting lodge, to the peace and the quiet. Never even loaded his gun or so much as looked at a bird. We fished a little, and he just...waited. Asked a few questions, was never shocked by my answers, only...waited for more. I hated sleeping, avoided going to bed—the dreams, you know. So he waited up too. Just sat and dozed by the fire in the hearth-chair opposite, for weeks, I think. Never left me alone with it. Listened. Encouraged me to speak to Saye, too—good advice, that—Saye is not nearly so fastidious as he appears." He cleared his throat. "A good man, is Darcy. The best of men, really."

Anderson nodded again, his eyes kind. "Almost makes it worse, does it not?"

Fitzwilliam burst out laughing. "Indeed," he agreed.

There was no more conversation; for the first time in months, it seemed, there was nothing except peace in the room. He might even have dozed. But at last, sighing, he heaved himself up. "I suppose Zeus is ready for his own stable. I should be going back."

"Besides, who knows what adventures your brother has in store for us," Anderson replied, standing as well. "We shall be thought cowardly if we hide much longer."

At the door, Fitzwilliam paused. "Did you—did you plan this? The race? Attempting to talk sense into a hard-headed soldier?"

Anderson shrugged. "Everyone knows of your daily ride, and I thought I might liven it a bit." He paused, as if debating whether to say more. "Miss Hawkridge has been concerned for you of late. I thought it might ease her mind if we spoke, man to man."

His remark vastly increased Fitzwilliam's suspicions, and he was on the verge of challenging him, but Anderson had not finished.

"And you know, good man he may be, but Darcy seems somewhat tightly wound. Perhaps a little jealous, even, of any moment Miss Bennet cannot be with him. If you ever decide to give him a bit of advice, perhaps remind him that these days, before we must devote ourselves to the business of matrimony and heirs and life and all the rest, can be precious ones. He and Miss Bennet need only look to each other's enjoyment and pleasure. The future will take care of itself and bring its own troubles. Rejoicing in every moment we are allowed is the *only* duty of today."

And then he grinned. "On the other hand, if you wish for a bit of innocent revenge, allow him to carry on as he is."

Laughing, they walked out of the inn together.

MINOR
EXPLOSIONS

Darcy & Elizabeth

T hat afternoon, with the grounds sodden after a night of steady rain, Saye unveiled his plan for indoor entertainments. There would be a series of *tableaux vivants* highlighting the joys of spring with the ladies as goddesses and the men as warriors.

"When one has achieved, as have I, and some of you," said Saye, "one's greatest spring of youthful beauty, one should pay tribute to it. We shall begin with The Feast of the Gods, and I shall be Apollo."

The men groaned and laughed; the ladies tittered in shock. Hearing Elizabeth's laugh, Darcy looked up to see her head bent towards an equally amused Miss Goddard. The two ladies appeared to be thick as thieves, each caught up and delighting in the other's company. Saye was too occupied pontificating to notice them, but Darcy was swept by a surge of pride. Elizabeth was enchanting, able to charm man and beast. She was the worthiest of women, and he was confident that his friends would quickly come to value her intelligence, humour, and kindness as he had. *As quickly as Georgiana and Fitzwilliam did*, he thought. *Far more quickly than did I.*

That grim but thankfully long-ago memory led him to look around the drawing room. A few members of their party were missing, Fitzwilliam, Anderson, and Miss Barlowe among them; a more unlikely trio of truants he could not imagine. He turned back to Saye's blatherings.

"I shall ask all of you to go through your trunks to gather the necessary costumes and accoutrements. We have no artist in residence and will have to create our own canvases, but much remains unscathed from our Polynesian festivities and will supply us some decoration for the ballroom."

Sir Phineas leant back in his chair, a foul expression creasing his brow. "It is too blessed cold for such frolics. Could we not simply play cards?"

"Or charades," suggested Withers.

"Or sardines!" cried Miss Hilgrove.

Saye cast a withering look at them. "Let us not sink to the pedestrian, hm? We shall be artistes, dilettantes... We shall delve into the wellspring of our souls' delight and drink deeply of the sweet marrow of the sublime!" With his haughtiest sniff, he said, "Or we can play children's games."

Properly chastened, Withers asked, "Um, what is the meaning of the marrow? A punch of some sort?"

"Sounds lovely," Miss Hilgrove hastened to say. "I believe I have some scarves that may be put to good use."

"Good girl. Send someone to fetch them and bring them to the library."

Half an hour later, they adjourned to Matlock's library, a room Darcy judged more generously outfitted with comfortable napping couches than with books. Saye unrolled some drawings he had done on his grand tour—sketches of paintings and sculpture Darcy felt certain were uncommonly salacious and offering an abundance of nubile flesh and dead bodies. Small groups were staring at the drawings and murmuring their shock or excitement in equal measure. Darcy, standing close to Elizabeth, felt her swallow a gasp; although it was as likely to be a giggle, his indignation rose along with his need to steal her away from company. She was far too compelling in her dark green gown and the memories it provoked of stolen moments at Longbourn and Netherfield. He took a step closer to her as Lady Aurelia expressed her own displeasure with the drawings.

She clearly was familiar with the painting her brother had chosen, and Darcy felt vindicated by her outrage until she avowed her real point of contention. "Saye, you are not bringing a cow into Mother's ballroom."

"That is a horse. If your eyes are failing, your husband can lend you his spectacles," said Saye before turning to address a footman. "We require a few beards. Do go and shear a sheep."

A rumble of voices had expressed displeasure. "It is not yet spring. Far too cold to shear the poor things."

Darcy slipped his hand into Elizabeth's and bent to whisper in her ear. "I feel a desperate need to kiss you." Encouraged by her response—a squeeze of her hand and a quiet laugh—he drew her into the hall and through the door to a well-remembered back staircase leading to the family wing.

"The servants may hear us!"
"Then I shall kiss you more quietly."
Elizabeth laughed, scarcely able to catch her breath before Darcy's lips again captured hers. Her heart was racing, and she pressed closer against him, relishing his hard warmth beneath the soft fabric of his shirt. After a long moment, she

pulled away, near breathless. "I suppose we need chaperons after all."

"I wish we did not have any. Indeed it would suit me well if there was no one here but the two of us."

She smiled at that but then said, "We really ought to stop."

"Why?" His voice was soft, his lips tickling her ear. "We have been apart for weeks and weeks, and now we are at a house party filled with unmarried men and ladies, all with the same designs in mind." He moved his face away to gaze at her. "And unlike the others, we are engaged, and engaged couples have more freedom to—"

"—to provide an example to others still seeking their love match." Elizabeth shifted off his lap, and heard him groan as she began straightening her hair.

"We are not their elders, nor are any of them in need of our noble sufferance as an example. Do you not hear the doors opening and closing at night, the footfalls treading so lightly from one room to another?"

A noise echoed down the other side of the hall and footsteps came near. Elizabeth froze, turning wide-eyed towards Darcy as the sound grew louder before beginning to fade into the distance. "Who is that?" she whispered. "A servant? Or one of your cousins sneaking about?"

"It hardly matters." He stood, giving her an endearing half-smile as he leant his forehead against her hair. "Did you not tell me of your nocturnal visit to Miss Goddard the other night? Fairy sprites in nightgowns, discussing love and desperate to know how you captured the proud, rich, and decidedly unpleasant Mr Darcy?"

Delighted laughter bubbled up within her. This was the man she loved, the sweet, dry-humoured man who had learnt to tease her and mock himself. She turned, lifting her hand to brush his hair off his forehead and smooth it back into some semblance of order before reaching up to give him a tender kiss. He replied to it by clasping his arms around her and pulling her tightly against his body.

All her protestations notwithstanding, she did thoroughly enjoy kissing him. She had never swooned over handsome men or wondered overmuch about wedding nights; she preferred poetic allusions to bawdy novels.

But all of that had changed three months ago, in the moments between saying yes and gaining her first kiss from her husband-to-be. Then, the passion that imbued their every conversation became equally alive in the physical sense, in the touches and kisses they shared. Kisses she would gladly bestow upon him in quantity, if only she could be certain they were secure from discovery.

Elizabeth had known that they would make every effort for private moments during this sojourn. For the most part, she and Darcy had acted politely and carefully, though they had been able, once or twice, to steal away to empty rooms or take advantage of darkened corners to share intimate kisses and endearments.

But she had not expected to find herself in his chambers, nearly astride his lap, or held within his embrace, and allowing—eagerly enjoying—his tender attentions until his quiet ardour had shifted into something more. She began to see what Georgette might have meant when she advised taking steps to prevent Darcy from 'cracking', for he was wound tightly with the obvious desire for still-greater intimacy. She pulled her lips from his, took a breath, and as gently as she could, pushed him away, taking a step back to remove herself from his embrace.

"Elizabeth—"

"We simply *must* stop."

"I know that, dearest." Darcy took a step back and smiled, his eyes glinting mischievously. "I apologise for my fervour, but you must apologise for your endlessly enticing being."

Elizabeth would have returned his smile but for a loud crash in the corridor. Mortification and self-awareness arrived as one, and she gasped even as her heart rose into her throat.

"They were housemaids," Darcy assured her.

"It does not matter whether it was a scullery maid or your cousin, we—" She let out a breath, trying to calm herself. "I cannot act the country hoyden here. I want to be well regarded, to make you proud, and to disprove whatever your aunt may say of me."

"Lady Catherine's opinion is meaningless, to me and to anyone in society. You will be—you *are*—respected and admired by all who meet you. Have you not seen how accepted and liked you are by everyone here? You have enchanted everyone, even Sir Phineas."

"It has been a start, to be sure, but that is all the more reason not to turn their opinions of me by being caught out in your bedchamber." She smiled to soften the severe tone of her words. "But I am glad you think they accept me. I do like nearly everyone I have met."

Darcy chuckled. "Only *nearly* everyone? Saye is having some effect on you."

Elizabeth peered into the mirror, moving her head this way and that and adjusting the pins in her hair. "Miss Barlowe has a bit of vinegar in her, which is a shame, as she will be one of the only ladies to leave here without a future groom."

"A *bit* of vinegar? From the little I have observed of her, Miss Barlowe is never so happy as when she is miserable, and were she the only one left unattached, I do not doubt her greatest solace would be in extolling the unfairness of it all."

Diverted by such a droll study of the unfortunate lady, Elizabeth turned away from the mirror to face him. "Congratulations," she said, grinning. "You have matched my own sentiments perfectly."

Darcy pushed away from the dresser and approached her, tucking a curl behind her ear and tipping his head close to hers once again. "My observational capabilities are at least equal to yours. I have observed that you are lovely, and that nobody here will care if I kiss you again."

He looked so handsome that she allowed one chaste kiss before giving him a mockingly reproving smile and placing a hand on his chest to forestall another tight clasp. "And what else, pray, have you observed?"

"I have noticed that Miss Barlowe will most certainly not be the only lady to leave here unattached," he replied distractedly, his attention all on the curls above her ear. "We are the only people present with a whit of understanding between us."

"You are very severe on your acquaintances."

He shrugged. "Emerson and Clarke are notoriously dismissive of any attachment. Anderson is as likely to attract a statue as a spouse. Saye has made scarcely any progress with Miss Goddard, despite Balton-Sycke finally leaving. Fitzwilliam is hopeless, and in any case, most of the ladies are too young for him, and the more eligible ones seem mutually indifferent."

"Richard is not hopeless," Elizabeth said, frowning. "He only has a heart hardened by too many years living in both war and society. Miss Fisher, Miss Hilgrove, and Miss Morgan may be young, but they are all kind-hearted, and they are not overawed by his uniform like some young ladies we know. However, you may be right. If none of the ladies present may be the right match for him, more's the pity."

She saw him stiffen at her casual use of his cousin's given name. The amorous look of moments earlier was gone; his expression was blank as he looked past her to examine the folds of his cravat in the mirror. With studied calm, he said, "You take an eager interest in the romantic inclinations of my cousin."

"And you have taken note of everyone and nothing all at once," she replied soothingly, tugging on his lapels and smiling up at him. "You and I are proof that not every conversation is in a public room, and not every attraction is displayed for others to observe. We are also proof that a gentleman can fall in love with a lady and assume she feels the same while no one else in a town of four-and-twenty families has a hint of it."

"One day that story will amuse me, but as yet it does not," Darcy said.

"You were—you *are*—an object of fascination in Meryton, but you were allowed to fall in love without a Greek chorus standing about and mocking you—"

"You have forgotten your father."

She could scarcely forget her father or her current displeasure with him, but Elizabeth would not allow him to intrude upon them here, not with Darcy seeming dangerously close to true pique. "It would do us well to allow the furtive romances and pining amidst us to continue in peace."

Darcy gave her an incredulous look, but Elizabeth took no notice of it as she went on. "Leave your cousins be, and let them enjoy discovering their own course of true love."

"My cousins can both take their romantic affairs as far away from me as they please. I want nothing to do with them. And neither should you."

She grinned, though she made no attempt to keep the challenge from the look she gave him. "But I am the most fortunate of all the ladies here, dearest, for I have the privilege of being already engaged. I promise not to arrange anything, but I must lend an ear to any questions."

Darcy began to smile, but it was quickly replaced by a frown. "Who has been asking you questions?"

"You were there when Lord Saye asked my advice about Miss Goddard."

"Indeed I was." Darcy nodded curtly in acknowledgment, and her heart sank. Could he not take pride that her opinion was esteemed even by the notoriously disdainful Saye? How had they moved so rapidly from such sweet amity and accord to misunderstanding and suspicion?

For a moment, Elizabeth considered mentioning that to him. She was, in some regards, quitting her sphere for his. His friends and relations would become her own, and inasmuch as she had been thrilled by the opportunity to come to this party and see him, her desire to form her own connexions amongst his circle had been equally enticing. Did Darcy not recognise the importance of that?

This was not the time to remind him, she realised. Certainly not when the taste of her kisses remained on his lips and the frustration of a healthy young man weighed on his... She was not so much a maiden as to be insensible to that.

A gong clanged loudly from somewhere outside the door, saving them. "We must join everyone," she whispered, taking two steps away from him. "Your cousin—"

"My cousins demand too much of our time."

She gave him an astonished look. "We are here, brought together because your cousins are hosting a house party! It is a blessing for us!"

"Yet our every moment alone together is as furtive as in your father's house."

Clang!

The gong sounded again, its thunderous clang startling them both back into the urgency of the moment. Darcy, mired in frustration, heard Elizabeth gathering her skirts and her flustered whisper. "We must go. Your cousin's ridiculous artistic endeavour awaits us."

He could not like that she was leaving before he had rectified the impasse occasioned by his harshly spoken words, yet it was probably for the best that she did go. He was not yet recovered from what had briefly seemed Elizabeth's admission to sharing romantic secrets with Fitzwilliam and was still far too aroused by her sweet caresses to give a better account of himself at the present moment.

"Yes, after he deafens half the servants with that blasted gong," Darcy growled, stepping to the door and opening it. Finding the hall empty, he gestured to Elizabeth. She met his eyes briefly, both clearly uncertain what to say as they parted, and then turned left and moved quickly down the corridor.

Darcy closed the door and leant his head against it. A week more in her company here, and everyone would disperse to London or their family estates. She would go home to Longbourn, far from his reach, for six more weeks. And he had ruined the last moments of this sublime assignation with his witless grievances. Groaning, he threw open the door and stormed out in the other direction, scowling when he turned the corner and saw the two men he least wished to encounter, sauntering down the hall towards him. *The dastard and the dullard. Perfect.*

"Devil take it, you look positively fearsome, Darcy. Even your hair looks angry." Fitzwilliam stared at him curiously. "I had thought to propose some fencing matches after Saye has finished posing us in wigs and togas, but you look altogether too enraged. Mother would be unhappy with even more blood spilt on her floors."

His cousin's relentless insouciance could only amplify Darcy's resentment, and before he could temper himself, he snapped, "Especially the blood of her own son."

"What?" Fitzwilliam asked.

Anderson looked between the cousins and excused himself in a low voice.

Still grinning easily, Fitzwilliam asked, "Is that scowl blistering me because I dared to rub shoulders with Anderson? Or has Lizzy thrown you over for me?"

Pure white rage burned through Darcy's chest at Fitzwilliam's comfortable use of her nickname. "Elizabeth. Miss Bennet, even. You are not yet her relation nor a close friend to claim such a privilege with her name."

"On the contrary, I daresay I am her close friend, as I believe has been demonstrated very well this week."

Darcy clenched his hand and took a step nearer to his cousin. "You would do far better to have less concern for your friendship with my betrothed and more for your own romantic prospects. Is there not another pretty girl here to exercise your charms upon?"

Fitzwilliam snorted. "You and Miss Bentley should enjoy a conversation. You both persist in the idea that I ought to be searching through my brother's houseguests with an eye to matrimony."

"Of course you should." The sooner his cousin focused his attentions somewhere other than his betrothed, the better.

"Why should it matter to you? You are not so interested in anyone else's romantic affairs. I do not hear you suggesting that Emerson ought to offer for Miss Morgan or that my cousin ought to be saved from Anderson."

Relieved by the shift in topic, Darcy shook his head. "Do

you not think most of the women in this house would wish for a man with a livelier disposition than Anderson?"

"I imagine Lizzy's sisters may have put the same question to her." Fitzwilliam laughed again, leaning on one shoulder against the near wall. "Anderson is not a bad fellow, Darcy, and is certainly a good horseman and a decent wit to boot."

Darcy could not deny that those words stung. A livelier disposition—yes, it was something he worried over, the disparity between his and Elizabeth's temperaments. It was a particular cruelty that his cousin should hit at that home truth with such ease.

Darcy was silent for a moment. "You are as bad as Bingley, making friends with everyone that you meet."

"You ought to try it, Darcy. I am sure *Elizabeth* would appreciate it if you made the effort. Like her, I make the effort to charm those I meet. You do not, and the result is your jealousy."

"Jealous? Of you?" Darcy gave a dark chuckle, then stepped close to Fitzwilliam, seething as he glared down upon him.

"I cannot think of any other reason for your ill humour! You are stomping about gloomily at a house party, where your lady has surprised you! I should think you would be ecstatic Elizabeth has sought your society."

"I am not stomping about," Darcy replied icily. "And I am, in fact, ecstatic."

Fitzwilliam straightened. "I find it rather ridiculous that you have not forced Bennet's hand and simply married her! Instead, you brood and grumble at those of us who have yet to achieve such a blessed state and enjoy her company."

"Forced her father? Forced Elizabeth? You are too accustomed to ordering others on the battlefield but know nothing about affairs of the heart."

Fitzwilliam rolled his eyes. "So says the man who goes

here and there, arranging things to please himself, yet cannot manage it with his own lady love."

"You must stop pleasing yourself with the company of a lady you cannot have, would never have had," Darcy said in a low voice.

Fitzwilliam's eyes narrowed, and his jaw tightened; it was, to Darcy, a great improvement over his prior impudence. "Cannot have? When did I have the opportunity? Last spring, you fancied yourself in love and I ceded the field—"

"Ceded the field! You flatter yourself to imagine you were even on the field!"

"Yet here it is, nearly a year later, and still you are uncertain of your hold on her heart and accuse me of dallying with her? You are the dallying one, old man. Had another man your fortune, what is to say she might, even now, have a different bridegroom?"

"A different bridegroom?" The burning rage Darcy had felt pulsing through him stilled. They were at a tipping point now, he and his cousin, and he was acutely aware that the next question could be one whose answer would destroy their friendship. *It is best not to know his heart; all that matters is Elizabeth's.*

"Elizabeth has made her choice. I am hers and she is mine," he said carefully after a long moment spent retreating from the abyss. "My duties, my responsibilities are to my future wife and her happiness—no matter that it requires my own short-lived unhappiness. I shall wait as long as required to make her my wife."

Darcy's calm reply earned him a nod and another devilish smirk from Fitzwilliam. "Since you seem content to pass the time disdaining and misunderstanding the desires and intentions of others, perhaps I shall continue to warm my cold heart upon the flame of her conviviality."

His tenuously held composure fled. "You are the last man in the world Elizabeth would ever marry."

"Ha, let us see whether you ever become the first!" Fitzwilliam smiled meanly as he began to move past Darcy.

Anger rising, Darcy caught his cousin's arm.

Fitzwilliam shook him off roughly and pushed Darcy against the wall. "You will be a grey beard before you understand what you have lost."

With a loss of control he had not felt since he was a boy witnessing Wickham's petty cruelty to a lame dog, Darcy pushed back.

Saye was red-faced and nearly unable to speak when Elizabeth encountered him at the top of the stairs.

"Saye? Are you well?"

"Where is Darcy? Where is my brother?" He stopped in front of her and affected a cooler countenance. "Where is he?"

"He—Darcy, I mean—should be along shortly. I saw him but a few min—"

"He must come now. He is the only one of any use."

Saye began to stalk towards the corridor where Darcy's rooms were located. Elizabeth followed, picking up her hem to more quickly cover the distance between them.

"What is it? Has something happened to Georgiana? Has someone taken ill? Is it Lilly?"

Saye slowed and gave her an odd look before pressing his fingers to the bridge of his nose. "My wretched sister has schemed to destroy our *tableaux*. She has burnt my drawings. All hope is lost until I find Darcy, for only he shares my knowledge of the paintings."

Elizabeth nearly laughed at him, relief and hilarity flooding through her, before hearing voices—speaking her name amongst a flood of angry words—and then a commotion of curses and punches. Saye left her in a trice, taking off at a run and disappearing around the corner; seconds later she heard him shout, "Enough!"

For a moment, she was frozen in horrified comprehension, thinking surely she had not heard what she thought she had. Then, Elizabeth quickly followed Saye, rounding into the next corridor to find Darcy and Fitzwilliam, with Saye between them, their chests heaving and faces angry; a trickle of blood was on the lips she had kissed not ten minutes earlier.

Saye pushed the two men farther apart. If she had not known of the colonel's gentleness with Georgiana, Elizabeth might have been afraid of the blistering scowl he shot at his brother. Darcy's expression was little different, sullen, and—as he avoided her eyes—at least somewhat contrite.

"My dreams are *en feu* in the library, and the two of you are fighting over Elizabeth's charms in a common corridor."

Fitzwilliam shrugged at his brother's angry glare. "The library is on fire?"

Saye's charge of 'fighting over Elizabeth's charms' prompted an embarrassed look from Darcy. Her own face was aflame with similar sentiment, but her vexation was paramount. The phrase 'you are the last man in the world Elizabeth would ever marry' seemed to linger between them, making her less sympathetic to Darcy's split lip than she might have been otherwise.

"I heard only a little of the argument, but I shall remind you both I am not an object to be fought over," Elizabeth said and watched as the anger drained from their faces, both of them shifting uneasily on their feet. "The first man I marry will also be the last, and he will be a gentleman who respects not just his wife, but all in his family and household. He, like *all* in his family, will be kind and generous, and will not tease or mock anyone meanly."

She looked directly at each of the brawlers. "And he certainly will not tolerate insults and throw punches in the corridor of his uncle's house."

Saye chuckled. "Or his aunt's. Hardly fair to exclude Lady Catherine from these strictures."

"Lizzy," Fitzwilliam began but she interrupted him in a cool voice.

"Colonel Fitzwilliam, we soon shall be cousins. I gladly anticipate your future wife becoming one of my closest friends."

Elizabeth stepped towards Darcy, pulled his handkerchief from his pocket, and dabbed his lips. She tried to ignore the look of remorse and embarrassment in his eyes. "We shall speak later."

Elizabeth turned and walked off, towards the staircase and, undoubtedly, the smoky ruins of Saye's *tableaux vivants*. As he watched her move away, Darcy strove to understand the fierce stupidity of the last five minutes. He could take some solace in hearing Elizabeth refer to his cousin so formally; Fitzwilliam had looked properly abashed. It was a small and petty reward for his own foolish behaviour, but Darcy took some satisfaction in it nonetheless.

"Now, being that I must do everything for everyone," Saye announced, "I am going to recommend you both go and make some music with the whore's pipe, because I daresay it is confounding—"

Fitzwilliam growled something vulgar under his breath

and walked off in the direction opposite from where Elizabeth had gone.

"Well!" Saye huffed. "See what you get for trying to be helpful!" He pointed at Darcy, "You, at least, have a ship on the horizon, but if he does not get a woman soon, I cannot say what will happen."

Darcy stared down the corridor before closing his eyes and sighing deeply. "Somehow, I am the only man here who is engaged, yet I am still fighting other men to get my bride to the altar."

An Aversion
to Gossip

Georgette & Anderson

Anderson heard his man tut quietly and turned to face him, wash cloth in hand. McLeod was folding his discarded, muddy clothes, a look of weary disgust on his face.

"Sorry about all that. I had a small dash across the countryside on a rather impressive brute of a horse."

"Just so, sir."

McLeod disappeared into an antechamber and came back without the pile of clothes but with a letter, which he placed on the dresser next to the washbasin.

"This arrived while you were out, sir."

Anderson glanced down. The seal was Randalph's. He was sorely tempted to tell McLeod to burn it, but he refrained. He dried his face and, steeling himself for whatever outrageous demands his little brother had made this time, opened the letter.

Samuel,

Mrs Thornbury has sent word. Grandmother is ailing again. I am in Southampton; I shall never reach her in time. You will have to go.

Randalph

He threw the letter on the fire, wishing he had not read it first. Matlock was as far from their Somerset estate as Southampton, and his brother knew it. What Randalph evidently meant was that he would not trouble himself to go. Anderson sighed heavily. Thus ended his heavenly interlude with Georgette.

"Be a good fellow and pack our trunks, McLeod. We must leave for Gilchester Hall as soon as may be."

His man complied without question, and Anderson went in search of Georgette, not anticipating breaking the news one bit.

The house was unusually quiet. It was a vast, sprawling mansion with more rooms than could ever be necessary, and whilst that provided many convenient places for clandestine assignations, it made locating anyone absurdly difficult. Every saloon or parlour into which he looked was deserted. Supposing the exotic *tableaux vivantes* Saye had planned might require a grand setting, he wandered through the gallery, the grand entrance hall, and the ballroom. All three were empty. He was so turned about that he considered going outside and walking the exterior of the house to regain his bearings, but a faint noise arrested him, and since it sounded somewhat human, he followed that instead.

In a chiefly bare room at the rear of the house, he discovered Darcy, conducting a furious and decidedly one-sided fencing match with a straw-stuffed mannequin in the centre of the floor. Anderson could guess whom Darcy was thinking of as he jabbed at it. His and Colonel Fitzwilliam's horns had been well and truly locked when Anderson left them half an hour ago. It had not surprised him overmuch. It was evident from their talk in the alehouse the colonel had some deep-rooted misgivings to overcome before he would let his cousin slink off care-free into connubial felicity.

"You thought to go straight to the fencing and miss the *tableaux*, Darcy?"

Darcy drew himself up and turned to face him, revealing a split lip he had not possessed half an hour earlier. "The *tableaux* have been postponed. Have you time for a couple of rounds?"

Anderson sighed inwardly. Darcy was a man in obvious pursuit of relief, and he was not sure he had the fortitude to play nursemaid to two grown men in one day. He had only tackled the colonel because the man was Georgette's cousin, and she had been exceedingly persuasive in her arguments as to why he should. But she did not give two figs about this man; thus, he was not sure he did either. He supposed, however, if he could in some way reassure Darcy, then Fitzwilliam might vicariously be induced to get himself under better regulation. It would be nice to present Georgette with something to soften the disappointment of his departure.

"Very well," he answered. "Though I should warn you, I am far from proficient. I should be grateful if you would refrain from skewering me."

He stripped off his coats and took the foil Darcy handed him. Five bouts were enough to confirm Anderson's suspicions that Darcy was a master swordsman, and he was no match for him. He watched with wry amusement when his blade was knocked from his hand and sent skittering across the floor to the far corner.

"I yield, sir. You had much better find a more skilled opponent."

Darcy did not reply, and when Anderson glanced back at him, he was surprised to discover that he looked vaguely appalled.

"I apologise, Anderson. That was ill done on my part. You told me fencing was not your forte, and I played to my best form regardless. I was angry, but that was no excuse to take it out on you. I hope you will forgive me."

Anderson shrugged. "I shall take it as a compliment to my skill that I managed not to come off any worse than I did, in that case."

Darcy accepted his forbearance with a firm nod but gave no false platitudes. Indeed, he said nothing more as they both put their swords away and donned their coats. Anderson had a strong suspicion that maintaining a silence would never induce Darcy to fill it as it had with the colonel. He was also certain a direct question about what had angered him would be seen as an impertinence. In that instant, he gave up the notion of talking to Darcy about anything. The man was far too private to draw out. He held out his hand for him to shake.

"I must leave Matlock today, Darcy, so I shall say good-bye. I wish you luck with your wedding. Miss Bennet seems a wonderful young lady. Well worth the wait. I wish you every joy together."

"Are you mocking me?" Darcy said angrily. "I warn you, Anderson, I am in no humour to be ridiculed."

Anderson withdrew his hand. He resisted backing away, though he remained wary in the face of Darcy's greater strength and unprecedented outburst. "Certainly not. I apologise if it seemed I was."

Darcy ran a hand over his face. "No, I apologise. That was ill done as well. My cousin made a similar remark earlier about me waiting to marry, and his meaning was less ingenuous than yours, but that is hardly your fault. I beg your pardon."

"No harm done."

It would have been the perfect time to end the conversation, with no hard feelings between them and nothing said to make either feel awkward. *I must be a glutton for punishment,* he thought with a sigh as he held the door open for Darcy and said to him as he went through it, "I apologise if your cousin was in an agitated state before. I may have encouraged him to have one too many ales at the Pig & Feathers."

Darcy grunted but did not immediately make any other reply. They fell into step together and walked a short way in silence before he spoke.

"I ought to have known he was well oiled. His tongue was unusually loose for the time of day."

That it most certainly was, Anderson reflected. He had not expected Fitzwilliam to say half as much as he had, but then, the man was so brimming with resentment and self-pity, it had taken very little to encourage it to spill over. Something of these thoughts must have shown on his face, for Darcy fixed him with a penetrating stare.

"If my cousin has said something to you of this, I trust you will forget it. I mean no disrespect, but it is a private matter. I do not appreciate my engagement being discussed in public houses."

"A sentiment with which I can quite sympathise. I have a profound aversion to gossip."

Darcy narrowed his eyes, obviously unimpressed with the equivocation. *"Did* you discuss it?"

"I cannot deny that we discussed *you.*"

Anderson had to admit that Darcy glowered well. He had never possessed the talent himself—he had not the brow for it. Thus, it was with a disarming smile that he added, "Your cousin spoke briefly about the time you spent with him after he returned from the war."

His companion's surprise was obvious and pronounced.

"It was a fine thing you did for him. I am not surprised he esteems you so highly."

Darcy gave a small bark of derision that required no answer; therefore, Anderson gave none. The matter was dropped, and they passed through the ballroom and a series of smaller chambers before either spoke again.

"What calls you away?" Darcy enquired.

"My grandmother is unwell."

"I am sorry to hear that."

"It is not a new illness, but she is not sound of mind, and when she has a turn, it is usually only my brother or I who seem able to recall her to the present. We think probably because we both look so much like our late grandfather."

"Cannot your brother go, then?"

Anderson grimaced tightly. "Not on this occasion."

"That is a shame. You will miss the masquerade."

"Regrettably, I have no choice. My grandmother will not eat when she is in this state, so one or other of us must always go when it happens. If you had met my brother, you would not need me to explain that it is usually I who does."

"A heavy burden indeed."

"I might consider it so, were it not such a starkly finite problem. Besides, it is easy not to begrudge those parts of my life over which I have no control when there are so few of them. I am, like you, my own master and therefore largely free to do as I please. It might be different had I more limitations placed upon me. A man without any opportunity to do as he chooses might have more reason to be resentful."

Darcy cast him a dubious glance, undoubtedly not fooled into thinking they were talking about his grandmother anymore. "Are you suggesting that, had you generally less liberty, it would justify resenting your grandmother more?"

Anderson shook his head, smiling fondly. "I could never resent such a kind-hearted woman. But I could easily take exception to the circumstances that gave me this countenance, or my grandmother her failing mind, or my grandfather such a devoted wife that his face would be the only one she recalled after the rest of her memories had faded. Resentment is not confined to people, Darcy. Circumstances—or the want of them—are often equally deserving."

"You need not convince me of that. I resent the circumstance of not yet being married equally as much as I resent the man responsible for it."

Anderson said nothing. Resentful natures were evidently a family trait, and the way to make Darcy talk was clearly to poke at his. It was not something he took any pleasure in doing.

"I see that you wish me to make the comparison to you and your grandmother," Darcy said, looking and sounding exceedingly cross about it. "That the timing of my marriage is one of very few matters not of my choosing, and therefore I ought to resent the delay less."

"It would be futile for anyone to tell you what you ought and ought not to resent. But, perhaps knowing you have been free to make the choices that please you best in so many other respects will make the teasing of those with less opportunity to do so more tolerable."

Darcy made another small noise of contempt. "You have observed my cousin's provocations, I take it?" He banged open a door onto the passageway that led to the library. "He only succeeds in vexing me about it because he is right. I *ought* to have been able to marry by now."

"I am afraid I must disagree with your cousin on that score. In my opinion, you are doing the only right thing by waiting. It would be inadvisable to force Miss Bennet to oppose her father. She would not thank you for it. And, for what it is worth, I would think better of any man who did not impose his will on the woman he purported to love. As must she."

Darcy gave him a shrewd look. "Are you still speaking of my situation?"

Anderson grinned. "There are simply some women in this

world worth waiting for, Darcy. I am a patient man, with little cause to repine."

The sound of raised voices interrupted them. They frowned at each other and followed the sound to the library.

Georgette gave up attempting to cajole her cousins into accord when Lady Aurelia set fire to the drawings. Up to that point, she had found the entire argument vastly entertaining, but Lady Aurelia was evidently in her cups again, and no matter what her objection to Saye's plans, it did not excuse the destruction of what had been beautifully wrought sketches. She retired to the large leather sofa in front of the fire and watched as two footmen swept up the ashes. The rest of the guests all stood about whispering to each other, some visibly shocked, a few appalled, most amused. Sir Phineas was fuming.

"Good God, Aurelia, you have scorched the table! You might at least have put them in the hearth. What possessed you to set them alight here? What the devil am I to tell your father?"

"My brother charged me with safeguarding the innocence of all these young ladies, and that is what I intend to do. Those pictures were a corrupting influence."

"I hope you do not feel the need to set fire to every threat of corruption, else half the men in this room will be ablaze," said Saye, coming into the library behind his sister.

He had shed his pique, Georgette noticed. That was the thing about Saye; his temper burnt hot, but it cooled just as rapidly, and he never held a grudge. Lady Aurelia did not deserve his clemency, in her opinion.

"You have not found Darcy, I see?" said Mr Emerson.

"Oh, I found him. He was not inclined to help, ungrateful wretch. But I have the next best thing." He stepped sideways, revealing Mr Darcy's betrothed. "Elizabeth tells me she has discovered a section in here that contains copies of a number of these paintings. Would you show us where, Elizabeth?"

Elizabeth walked to the dark corner of the library beneath the balcony ladder, with which Georgette was well acquainted, and not because she had been admiring the books there.

"What is that face for?" said Saye, dropping heavily onto the sofa next to her.

"I heard some whispers in that corner recently. I was just reflecting that I hope it is not haunted."

Her cousin gave her an assessing look. "What have you been up to?"

"It is odd you should ask me that. I meant to ask you the same thing."

"Oh?"

Georgette glanced around to ensure nobody was within earshot, then spoke in a low voice. "My maid tells me there was a bit of confusion below stairs yesterday. Somehow—and I cannot *imagine* how—the chamber pot from your apartments was discovered by one of the charwomen in Lilly's bedchamber."

Saye gasped theatrically. "The minx stole my Minton? I shall summon the magistrate directly."

Georgette cast him a sidelong glance that she hoped conveyed all the doubt, censure, and amusement she felt for such a pointless demurral. "I shudder to think what manner of diversion resulted in the swapping of your chamber pots, but you will be pleased to know that your dalliance has not been discovered. My maid informed them all that I did it as a dare to get you into trouble."

"You are all that is noble, fair cousin, but there was no need."

"There was every need," Georgette replied, her voice still quiet but her tone firm. "Lilly is a dear friend. When I agreed to come here, it was on the condition that you would not toy with her."

"I am not."

"You quite clearly are, and I insist you stop."

Saye adjusted himself to face away from her and crossed his arms petulantly. "I cannot stop until I have changed her mind. She is determined to have Ball-Sack, and it is the biggest mistake she will ever make."

"If you will not step up to the mark, then you must put up with whatever decision she makes, whether or not it is a mistake. I would not have you ruin her reputation. And I *will* not have you play fast and loose with her heart."

"It is not her heart I wish to play with but the lovely hillocks situated directly—blazes, that hurt!" He stared balefully at Georgette, rubbing at the spot where she had pinched him hard.

"I am in earnest, Saye! This is not a game."

A flash of irritation showed on his countenance before he covered it with insouciance. "You are one to talk. I need not ask why it is that Blanderson follows you around the place like a puppy."

She raised an eyebrow. "I do hope you are not about to tell me women may not enjoy the same diversions as men."

That she did not deny it clearly surprised him, which she enjoyed, and then so did he.

"We always did take pleasure in the same things," he said with a smirk.

"Indeed, but notwithstanding our similarities, there is one very important difference. I have made no promises that I am not willing to keep."

"Tosh! You cannot possibly mean to tell me that you have promised yourself to that starched prig." He affected a mocking voice. "*Samuel David Anderson.* Heaven's sake, even his *name* is dull!"

"David Anderson?" said Lord Mickels from alarmingly close behind them. "Was that not the gent whose wife went mad and tried to jump off the roof of their house in town?"

Georgette twisted to see him pass behind their sofa on his way to another part of the room. Following Anderson's example, she did not answer, but the conversation, instead of petering into nothing, ricocheted around the room, swelling in volume and folly alike.

"Good Lord!" Mr Clarke exclaimed. "Are you telling me Blanderson's mother was *that* Mrs Anderson?"

"Which Mrs Anderson?" enquired Miss Parker. "I never heard of her."

"And you have not suffered for it, so there can be no need to hear of her now," remarked Lilly, sending an expressive, questioning glance at Georgette.

"I heard about it from my mother," Miss Barlowe said in an absurdly proud voice. "Mrs Anderson lost her wits when her son died. It was said she pulled out all her hair in grief and was completely bald when they took her to Bedlam."

A soft gasp drew everyone's notice to the doorway, where Sarah had just arrived. Had she heard the disagreeable origins of the discussion, she would likely have held her tongue. Instead, she directed a pitying look at Georgette, and exclaimed, "Mr Anderson's brother died?"

Then, of course, the idiotic Miss Parker wished to know what it was that had killed him.

"He was born addled in the head," Miss Barlowe replied.

Georgette's jaw ached from being clenched, and her chest was full to bursting with the set down she could not deliver. She could feel Saye looking at her, but she continued to stare directly ahead, her chin held high as the nastiness flowed around her.

"Nay, he was left enfeebled after a childhood illness," Mr Clarke corrected her. "Almost died and was rendered simple thereafter. Nasty business."

"Just so," agreed Mr Withers. "I daresay it would make any mother a lunatic to see her child thus afflicted."

Georgette sent Saye a plaintive look, and he spoke up, giving everyone a frown. "There now, that is enough. Surely there are pleasanter things we might speak of."

"Pleasanter than what?" enquired Mr Emerson, emerging from the corner of the library where he had been inspecting books with Elizabeth.

Miss Morgan, who had been wafting her assets under Mr Emerson's nose all week, leapt out of her chair and thrust her breasts at him along with the answer. "Than talking about Mr Anderson's crippled brother."

Several of the girls closest to her admonished her use of such callous language, and Mr Emerson frowned at her in distaste, but Mr Wigsby was not quite as averse to the topic.

"Anderson has a crippled brother? I say, he is not the same Anderson who owns that institute for freaks and unwanteds in Golders Green, is he?"

Georgette let out a small noise of disbelief. *Freaks and unwanteds!* Anderson was right—the bleaker side of life truly did weed out those lacking a heart.

"If it is, then he is a braver man than I—or as mad as his mother," muttered Mr Clarke.

Saye stood. "Come on then, you lazy fools. What have you found over in that corner? Anything of use?"

Georgette scarcely heard him. She did not often feel anger; she enjoyed life too well to wallow in its vexations. She was particularly inured to attacks on Anderson's perceived dreariness, secure in the knowledge that everybody was grossly mistaken about that. Yet, this attack on his family, on his mother and his beloved brother Matthew, and on his beautiful home for children, made her blood boil.

"Who would have credited that a man so dull should come from such a colourful family?" Lord Mickels said, laughing as though it were funny. "It is always the quiet ones you have to watch."

Mr Wigsby shook his head. "I should keep quiet, too, if I had so many damning secrets to—"

"That is enough, you *beasts!*" Georgette cried, surging to her feet. Her breath was coming so fast that speaking was difficult. It made her sound hysterical. Perhaps she was. "Mr Anderson is a better man than any of you could ever hope to be. While you all sit about gorging on burnt pigs, torching each other's prized possessions, and arguing over who loves whom best, he is making a real difference in the world. He is saving lives—*actually* saving the lives of people who do not have the privilege of family or fortune. Children whose own mothers turned them out at birth because they were not pretty enough to love. If that is *dull* to you, then I choose dull over all your specious elegance. I choose *heart*. And I shall never be ashamed to call such a man my husband!"

A collective gasp went up, followed by an unearthly silence.

Georgette held her breath. She had not meant to say that. She looked around the room in dismay. Everybody was staring at her, their expressions varying from disbelief to revulsion. Lady Aurelia, whose gaze was suddenly horribly sober, looked livid, as did her husband. Lilly and Sarah were staring at her as though she were a stranger, and she felt all the guilt of having concealed the truth from them.

"*Merde*, Georgette," said Saye under his breath.

"Husband?" cried Miss Barlowe. "You are going to marry him?"

Saye then exclaimed, his voice dripping with false jollity, "Ho, Darcy! How nice of you to join us."

Georgette turned to see Mr Darcy in the doorway, and then her stomach turned over, for there at his side was Anderson. He was staring directly at her, unblinking, his countenance devoid of any emotion.

"Samuel!" she mouthed silently.

He did not answer her. Instead, he turned to Saye. "My lord, I have been called away on urgent business and must leave Matlock immediately. Pray forgive my early departure." He gave a perfunctory bow, then turned and stalked away.

His departure created a vacuum that tugged a sound of dismay from the pit of Georgette's stomach up into her throat. They had never had a cross word between them in all the time they had known each other. She did not know what to do. Her heart would not stop pounding its alarm against her ribs, and she felt dangerously close to tears.

"Darcy, I have found copies of some of the drawings in Saye's sketches in the books on these shelves over here. Will you help me pick out the right ones?" Elizabeth said loudly into the silence.

Mr Darcy agreed and called on several of the other gentlemen to assist, and with their perseverance, a general milling of chatter gradually returned to the room.

"Husband?" Lady Aurelia approached Georgette and Saye, and spoke so only they could hear. "That cannot happen, Georgette. You must know that. It is an entirely unsuitable alliance, and your father will never agree to it."

Georgette shook her head, unable to fix upon her cousin's words.

"Saye? Tell her, for you know as well as I do that our father will not permit this any more than hers will."

"I shall not need either's permission when I come of age. I shall marry him then," Georgette objected. She tried to sound defiant, but she could not hear whether she was successful over the ringing in her ears.

"Not if your father marries you to someone else before then, which he will when he finds out," Lady Aurelia snapped.

"He will not find out if you do not tell him," Saye replied impatiently.

"I shall not tell a soul. I do not need to. Half the people in this house just heard it, and at least two footmen. And Phin. He plays cards with your father, for heaven's sake, Georgette. He will find out."

Saye pulled a face of disgust. "Aurelia, you are acting like a twatwaffle. What is it to you whom Georgette marries, hm?"

"Saye, you need to grow up and realise there are more important things in this world than pranks and debauchery."

"Such as?" Saye retorted. "Superiority and cruelty?"

"I think I am going to be sick," Georgette said breathlessly.

"I believe you have my chamber pot somewhere. Use that." Saye turned on his heel and walked to join the others in looking at the books. He had not liked his sister's set down, it would seem. He never had cared for other people's anger.

Georgette stared after him for a moment, then as gracefully as she could, she walked out of the library. She kept walking all through the house until she reached the attic where they had used to play as children. She curled up on the dusty old chest on which Fitzwilliam had always stood to issue the rules of whatever game they were to play. And there she remained, not knowing what to do, for a very, very long time.

NEVER SAYE NEVER

Saye & Lillian

L illy had what she had long considered one of the most dreadful habits in the world. In the face of any sort of difficulty, strain, or strife, she wept. No matter that it was not her own difficulty, it made her cry. It did not even need to be a real difficulty; some hapless heroine in a novel or in the life of a friend of a friend, even some ancestor long dead, and she would weep for their plight. "A gentleman despises a weeping woman, Lilly," her mother often admonished, but she could not help herself. Efforts at restraint would often result in an unladylike hiccough or snort, sometimes an inelegant spurt of mucus from her nose, and then the weeping would come. Best to just let it proceed apace.

Strangely, however, in the face of these astonishing events —Georgette engaged? Truly? And without a word said to anyone!—Lilly was beset by a most peculiar sensation. She wanted to scream, and perhaps kick or punch something. She raised a finger to the corner of her eye and confirmed that it was quite dry. A good thing that, for here came Saye, and the last thing she wished to do was to weep on his shoulder.

He was blithe and mildly disdainful, and rolled his eyes when he arrived. "Lord, what a scene, and from Little Georgette no less! I had always thought her the least insane of all my relations, yet there she went, rattling away like some operatic diva on the stage. I daresay—"

"Saye!" Lilly gasped at his rudeness. "She was upset!"

"Upset," he scoffed. "'Tis her own fault for falling in with such a—"

And that was it. It was too much atop all the shock and dismay of moments earlier, to have him be so...so...*Saye* about it all. Before she could stop herself, she blurted out, "Must you... Must you be so...so ridiculous all the time?"

Her words obviously shocked but did not discompose him. Indeed, she hardly thought discomposure was possible for him; he drew up and, if anything, seemed amused. Rage flooded her, making her itchy and hot.

He raised one perfect brow. "Ridiculous?"

His insouciance further stoked her ire. "Yes! This whole party—the absurd, makeshift dining rooms, silly pigs, and ridiculous *tableaux*—they are designed to do nothing but hint at scandal and amuse you."

Infuriatingly, Saye only raised his hand and began examining his fingernails. "To be fair, Aurelia ruined my plans for the *tableaux*. I am quite put out."

Lilly could only gape at him. She was aware, vaguely, of Sarah placing a hand on her arm, but she shook her off. She could not have answered for the justice of it, but every bit of upset she had experienced over the whole of this absurd week was presently focused on Saye.

"This! This is why a woman would much prefer to marry a 'Blanderson' or a 'Ball-Sack'—because...because a woman needs stability and sureness of purpose, someone who will always be there for her, by her side. Not...not some absurd *bon vivant* whose first object is forever and always his own amusement!"

Saye levelled her with a look she could not interpret. Her own anger was so great, she could not imagine he felt anything but the same, yet his tone, when he spoke, was maddeningly dismissive.

"Firstly, women who settle for the likes of those two are stupid. And secondly, I might observe that Ball-Sack, despite his stability, was too busy coddling his own smacked arse to concern himself with you."

Lilly flushed hot and opened her mouth to make a scathing retort, but found her mental faculties had deserted her. In any case, there was not time. Scarcely had the words fallen from his lips than Saye turned and walked away.

She did weep then, and Sarah, who had been silent and wide-eyed throughout her entire speech, grabbed her arm.

"We must go and find Georgette."

"Yes, we must," Lilly said, her anger still at a boil. "And once we do, I am ordering my carriage and taking myself away from this place!"

Saye exited the drawing room, taking great care to walk with all the dignity of his station. He permitted himself one outward display of his exaltation—a single, decisive clap of both hands as soon as the door closed behind him.

Hard on his heels came Darcy, all frowny-faced and anxious. "Saye, what on earth was that?"

"Darcy!" Saye said warmly. "My dearest cousin. How grateful I am to you!"

"Grateful? What do you mean?"

Saye gave him a firm clap on the back, then slung one arm

around his shoulder as they walked through the great hall. Darcy shrugged his shoulders to try and dislodge his clasp, but Saye did not allow it. "Did you see that in there?"

"Did I see your cousin announce her engagement to the most ineligible man under this roof?"

"What? No, not that bit."

"Oh, then you mean did I see the woman you love dressing you down? Yes, I did. It was not pretty."

"I know," Saye replied with a smirk. "She loves me."

Darcy stopped, and for a moment only stared, brow furrowed. "What are you talking about?"

"She loves me," Saye repeated, unable to contain his grin. "Quite out of her stockings for me, poor dear. So now I shall go and fix everything with Blanderson, come back here, say my piece, and done! Better step lively, Cuz, or Lilly and I shall be married before you."

He set off again, and Darcy followed. "Saye, Miss Goddard just lambasted you for being ridiculous and insincere. I am struggling to comprehend your confidence."

"Delicious, was it not? And were it not for your fine example, I might become distraught over it. But now..." He shook his head gleefully. "Now I know the truth."

"I do not see—"

"Come! How many women in your life have ever given you a proper set down?"

Darcy took a deep breath before admitting, "One."

"One!" Saye laughed.

"But she despised me when she did it!"

"I doubt that. If she despised you, she would have simply ignored you."

"I was standing before her, proposing. What was she to do, throw herself out of the window?"

"Now you are being ridiculous. Elizabeth might have hated you," Saye conceded, "but she possessed amorous inclination enough to wish to aid you in reforming your character."

"I do not think you understand—"

Lord but Darcy could be tedious at times, forever wanting to discuss how once upon a time Elizabeth disliked him. *Get past it, man! She's nearly frothing at the mouth for you now, so who cares how it got there!*

"What you have helped me realise," Saye interrupted, "is that a man's worst enemy is indifference. And Lilly just ejaculated an enormous helping of non-indifference all over me. So, will you come with me to retrieve him?"

Darcy shook his head as if to clear water from his ears. "Retrieve who?"

Saye rolled his eyes and spoke slowly, so his less adventurous cousin could keep up. "Anderson! I suppose I must cease calling him Blanderson, since he will soon be family, and Blandy will not do, of course. I shall bring him back here, and then I shall propose to Lilly."

"I do not think Anderson can be brought back. He has urgent business in Somerset." Darcy hastily explained the situation with Anderson's grandmother, the sum total of which equated to nothing Saye cared two straws about. Anderson needed to be absent for a time—enough said, and onto happier thoughts of himself, and Lilly, and the night ahead which he imagined would bring the delighted acceptance of his proposal...followed by a bit of *faire des papouilles*.

"Very well, I shall simply persuade him to come back afterwards. I cannot take my carriage—it will make me too dull. To horse! And let us hope Dunbar is ready for a good gallop." With a renewal of his delight and an amazed shake of his head, he grinned at his cousin once more. "After all this, the happiest, wisest, most reasonable end—she loves me! I knew I could not be so beautiful for nothing."

Saye was several miles along the road before he realised he ought to have changed into proper riding clothes. It was not the ruination of his trousers that troubled him—someone had to keep the tailors' pockets full—but rather the uncomfortable chafing on his arse. *Silk and saddle do not mix,* he mused, *particularly when one is in heated pursuit of a lovelorn cousin's particular friend.*

Fortunately, it was not long before he espied what must be Anderson's carriage. It bore no discernible markings, but it was on the road from Matlock, and the time was about right—he reasoned that Anderson could not have gone much farther. With a few heels to his horse's flanks and a wince for his poor hindquarters, he soon drew near.

The coachman looked at him with some concern, and he enjoyed the fleeting but immensely diverting notion of pretending to be a highwayman. *No! No reason to terrify the wretched sod, not when he has already been roughed over in the drawing room.* Instead, he politely gestured at the men to stop.

"This Anderson's?"

"Lord Saye?" Anderson was himself already half out of the window. "What are you doing?"

"Buying you a drink," Saye replied cheerily. "Pig & Feathers is less than a mile ahead. See you there!" With not a syllable more, he nudged his horse to a gallop. He was seated with two tankards of the best ale when Anderson entered, looking inordinately wary. Saye grinned genially and gestured at the seat across from his own.

Anderson did as he was bid, but other than nodding his thanks for the ale, gave no other reply.

"You know, I have a raging sore arse thanks to my heroic dash to catch up with you," Saye said. "A little conversation would help distract me from the discomfort. You could begin by asking me why I have come."

"I am not sure I wish to know."

"You think I mean to call you out for having the audacity to absent yourself from my *tableaux vivant*? No mind, Aurelia has dashed every hope in that quarter already. Have you any sisters? They are, in my opinion, a far greater arse-chafe than even the one I have just endured."

Anderson gave the unutterably dreary reply that no, he did not have sisters. Then he once again closed his lips and said no more.

Saye was saved from death by tedium when the innkeeper arrived with a platter of bread and cheese. Truly, it was good to be lord of the manor in one's home county. He gestured that Anderson should help himself and then looked on in disgust as the man took a chunk of cheese and nibbled at it. *Like a rat!—but no!* Saye would not think of him in such disparaging terms. He had always been exceedingly mindful of how eating appeared repulsive and had spent considerable time in front of his own mirror, learning to eat charmingly. He had to recall, however, that too many others had never done likewise. Thus did men nibble like mice and never know how unmanly it appeared while thus engaged.

The display ceased mercifully quickly. Having evidently rallied sufficient courage to speak, Anderson set the cheese aside.

"I rather thought your lordship might have come to insist that I absent myself from a different sort of engagement."

"I should never presume to tell Georgette whom she ought to wed, though others might."

Anderson sighed heavily. "It was always a possibility. It is inevitable after that little scene in your library."

"I confess I have never heard her speak so passionately

about anything, and I have known her a good deal longer than you have."

"Do not think I blame her—she is an extraordinary woman, and her defence of me was magnificent. I still wish she had not done it. There was no need. I am well used to society's scorn, and her speaking for me in that way has only jeopardised her reputation."

"Bah! If you were worried about reputation, you would not be marrying her." Saye enjoyed Anderson's shock, but then, he enjoyed most things that proved he was right. "In any case, Georgette is no fool. She knows precisely what risk an alliance with you poses to her reputation, and she has accepted you nevertheless. Her good name is not why you were in such high dudgeon."

Anderson regarded him searchingly for a moment or two, then gave in to a wry smile. "You are quite astute, sir. It has been the study of my life to be unremarkable. Notice brings ruin when you have a reputation like mine. And I have more people than myself, or even Georgette, relying upon me to remain inconspicuous."

"So, you ran away."

Anderson inhaled deeply but then nodded.

"How exceedingly gallant of you."

"I cannot defend myself, except to say that every person in that room was staring at me, and every one of them knew what I was, where I came from, and what I would do to their friend and cousin once I took the selfish step of making her my wife. It was a bloody uncomfortable situation for a man as unused to attention as I. Yes, I confess, I ran away." He exhaled forcefully and spoke with startling emotion, almost snarling as he added, "You do not need to tell me that I ought to have gone to Georgette. Instead, I left her to fend for herself. It was poorly done."

"You did not cover yourself in glory, it is true. But that is why I am here. To help you redeem yourself."

Anderson said nothing, but he looked intrigued.

"Truth be told, I was not entirely blameless in the matter. Had I not teased Georgette about her entanglement with you, we would never have been overheard talking about you, and the whole thing might have been avoided. Now my cousin has been hurt, and I am in the devil of a bind with Miss Goddard over it. We shall put things to rights, I assure you."

Anderson's impassive countenance reflected none of the gratitude or excitement Saye had anticipated. He looked disappointed, resigned almost.

"I cannot change who or what I am. Even were I willing, which I am not, the memories of neither my mother nor my brother can be erased. And the stain of my work in Golders Green cannot be removed, as you well know. Society's memory is long, and its compassion in short supply."

"It is not compassion you need, but influence, and that I have in abundance. I can fix you, Anderson. You need only to concern yourself with Georgette."

"Fix me?" Anderson gave him an odd look. "How do you propose to do that?"

Saye leant back in his chair. "Do you know the best part of being handsome, titled, and outrageously wealthy?"

"Forcing large groups of people to come to your house and submit themselves to your strange perversions?"

Saye laughed heartily. "Well done! Quite funny, in fact. That is amusing, I admit, but even more so, I happen to enjoy taking things that are unpopular and making them popular. You know that absolutely no one wore lace at their wrists until I did? Many thought it quite pinkish, in fact, but now? *De rigueur.*"

"Is that so?"

"And blue velvet coats. I was first, at the theatre back in '04."

"Indeed? Polite society is quite in your debt."

Saye nodded. "Anyone can fashion themselves after the plates. A certain few can even set a fashion, like Brummell, so proud of his accursed cravats and really, what is it but tying knots in different ways? But it takes someone truly magnificent, a man of exceedingly great influence and power to take the unfashionable and make it fashion." With a modest nod, he added, "I am that man."

Anderson looked supremely and irritatingly unimpressed. "You are saying you would make me fashionable?"

Saye eyed Anderson's coat. "That may be beyond even my powers." Then he smirked. "I am saying I can remove your stain. We Matlocks give so much to the penitent prostitutes and beggars—why not help a few wretched children besides? I shall make it my personal philanthropy, perhaps even get my mother to throw in with her friends. A salon or something. She will know just how to do it."

Anderson cleared his throat. "I comprehend that your intentions are noble, and I am grateful for it—"

Saye forced himself to keep grinning, despite his incredulity. The ingrate was going to refuse his help!

"—but I am not another of your madcap adventures, and neither are any of the children under my care. My endeavours are not entertaining or even pleasurable much of the time. But these children rely on me to put food in their mouths and a roof above their heads. I cannot afford to be made the current fascination of your set, for when they lose interest— and they *will* lose interest—I shall be worse off than I was before. Tainted *and* outmoded. My life is not a game for you to pick up and toy with on a whim. If it is all the same to you, I should prefer to continue as I am."

"That was quite a speech," Saye said once he was satisfied

Anderson had—*finally*—finished. His ire had evaporated, and he made a note to thank Darcy again—that was twice in one day his cousin had saved him by his miserable example. Eight-and-twenty years triumphing over Darcy's stupendous pride was more than enough practice to inure him to Anderson's posturing. "I should have little claim to greatness if my schemes went out of favour as quickly as you imply. The very best fashions are timeless. Thus, I shall make you enduringly fascinating. But we must walk before we can run."

He pointed a crust of bread at Anderson. "Just you see if by the end of the Season, you are not the talk of the *ton.*"

"It must be difficult for a man like you to comprehend that I do not enjoy scrutiny." A ghost of a smile flitted across Anderson's face, belying his despondent tone. "Yet, my discomfort notwithstanding, I cannot deny you would make Georgette exceedingly happy if you were to succeed."

If I were to succeed? Lord, who does this man think I am? "Consider it done." Saye gave the table three staccato beats with his hand, as he often did when satisfied. "So, we know what I shall do to fix you, and you will have the whole of your travels to contemplate what grand gesture you might bestow upon Georgette."

"I beg your pardon?"

Try to keep apace, Blandy. "You have just acknowledged that my cousin enjoys attention, and that you did her a disservice when you ran away this afternoon. What better way to regain her favour than with a grand gesture?"

"We have also just established that I do not care for making a spectacle of myself."

Saye fixed Anderson with a look he did not often employ, but which he knew to be effective. "I daresay Georgette would not have chosen a life on the periphery of society, but such she was willing to submit to—for you." He waited until Anderson gave a brief, chastened nod, then returned to grinning amiably. "Besides, your secrets are all out now. You have nothing to hide, at least from my house guests. Send me an express when you have settled on an idea. I shall undertake to make whatever preparations are necessary in time for your return."

He rose, popping one last bite of cheese in his mouth and chewing it with proficient elegance as he prepared to leave. He wondered whether it would be impertinent to ask Anderson for a spare pair of buckskins, for he knew not how much more punishment his tender hindquarters might endure. But no, it was too much. Almost-cousins they might be, but Saye did not wear small clothes, and the imposition of his own ballocks in another man's breeches was likely too dear. With a short bow, he bade Anderson a good journey and went to his horse.

Perhaps, if I propose very nicely, Lilly might be prevailed upon to aid me later in soothing whatever has been made sore, he thought with a grin.

Georgette was not to be found anywhere they sought her. They first went to her bedchamber, of course, where their knocks elicited confusion from Prinny, who had been within, tending to her mistress's frocks, and had not seen her for above an hour.

"Shall I ask them below stairs if any have seen her?" she said with concern.

"No, let us not raise a hue and cry just yet," Sarah said while Lilly snivelled uselessly beside her. "Is her pelisse here? All her bonnets?"

As Prinny nodded, Lilly looked at Sarah questioningly, and Sarah added, "So we can assume she is still indoors."

"Of course." Lilly sighed. It was so helpful to have a clever friend like Sarah, who considered all the possibilities.

Then they were off, tearing all about Matlock in search of their friend who was stubbornly impossible to find, not in the drawing rooms, nor the library, nor even the billiards room. At length, Elizabeth joined them, but when Miss Barlowe offered her assistance, they refused. As the ladies walked away, Elizabeth said, under her breath, "The sight of her would likely send Georgette running in the opposite direction." That made Lilly laugh, just a little, through her dismay.

When nearly three-quarters of an hour had passed with no luck, Lady Aurelia interrupted their search. "You might wish to check the attics. There is a particular tower window with a trunk beneath it. Georgette always did like to hide up there."

"To hide?" Sarah enquired disbelievingly. "The Georgette I know has no need of a hiding place. She is far too brave."

"I must agree," Elizabeth replied. "I was surprised to see her so affected just now. I had formed the impression she is not easily discomposed."

Lady Aurelia gave a short huff of displeasure. "Well, she does not usually make such a prodigious exhibition of herself. Perhaps when you find her, you will succeed in talking her out of this preposterous alliance. The attics are your best hope."

"That might have been useful information some while ago," Sarah muttered as the three ladies went off at a quick pace.

"Why, Sarah! That was positively snappish of you. Well done, darling," Lilly said.

Indeed, the attic was where they found their friend, her knees tucked up and her head resting on the glass.

"Georgette?"

When there was no reply to Lilly's call, Sarah asked, "Georgette? Dearest, are you well?"

From her unmarred countenance, it seemed Georgette had not cried, and Lilly admired her for that. She just sat there, silent and still, her gaze fixed at some point only her mind's eye could see.

"Shall I leave you?" Elizabeth asked in a whisper.

"No," Georgette replied finally with a sigh, straightening herself. "I daresay, Elizabeth, you might be the only one without reason to despise me."

"What nonsense!" Sarah cried.

"Why ever would you think so?" Lilly asked.

"Because I have been hiding this from you," Georgette acknowledged. "Hiding and sneaking and lying—unpardonably dishonourable, and I knew it was no good but..." With a little shrug, she said, "The heart wants what it wants, even when your own friends might revile and scorn you."

"Revile and scorn? If you speak of those ninnies in the drawing room, they are no friends of mine." Lilly pushed herself in on the seat beside her friend. Not a seat, as it turned out, but a trunk as Lady Aurelia had mentioned. There was an uncomfortable lock that pressed into Lilly's hindquarters, but for Georgette, it would be tolerated.

"Mr Emerson is going to be terribly disappointed, you know. He has been ogling you since he arrived."

Georgette smiled sadly. "The three of you must surely wonder what I am about. I am sure the whole of it seems absurd to you. Everyone is so determined to think Anderson the dullest, most uninspiring man, and with these untenable predispositions towards the outcasts of society."

"I think it exceedingly noble," Elizabeth offered.

"As do I," Lilly said.

"And as fond as I am of things that rather disgust most others, I can hardly dislike him for helping some unfortunate children," Sarah added. "Besides, I have begun to think much better of him since I have seen how well you both get along."

Georgette smiled weakly. "He thinks you are lovely, too, Sarah. He told me you have a pretty frown."

Lilly grinned to see Sarah flounder in the face of this compliment. "There is no reason to suspect it is not true, darling, for Mr Anderson is evidently an expert in beauty, else he would not be marrying our dear Georgette." To her, she said, "But why on earth did you feel you could not confide in us?"

"It was not just you. It was everyone. You know I had an offer—in a manner of speaking—from one of the de Borchgraves."

"Oh yes," Lilly said. "I had forgotten about that."

"Anderson and I were already...well, we were not yet in love—although perhaps we were, for I could not even contemplate marrying another, even then, so I refused. I am sure you can imagine how the family thought me mad for not considering such an offer. Shortly after that, Anderson asked Father for my hand, and he was—well, in short, he threatened to force me to marry the viscount unless I promised never to see Anderson again. The taint of such a name was more than my father could countenance, whereas a Belgian viscountess for a daughter would have been just the thing, evidently."

"That is horrid!" Lilly exclaimed.

"More than passably vexing, yes. Thus, we have grown accustomed to being discreet. It was easiest not to tell anyone than to expect any of you to keep it a secret. We planned to marry when I came of age, but now...Oh lord, now I do not know *what* will happen! Anderson has left, my father is bound to find out about our plans, and I *refuse* to marry a de Borchgrave, for I have no wish to live in Belgium!"

Elizabeth laughed and they all turned to look at her. "Forgive me," she said. "I was only thinking of my own first offer, from the cousin who is heir to my father's estate. Hardly a Belgian viscount, to be sure, but the family was not best pleased with me either, when I refused him, particularly as I had no other prospects to content them with."

"But they must surely be delighted now?" Sarah asked.

Elizabeth made a little wry smile. "They are, but not nearly as much as I am. All I mean to say is that practicality and pleasure are often at odds in the marriage mart."

The ladies all laughed.

"If only the rest of the world were not so scandalised by Anderson's charity. 'Tis an admirable endeavour in my opinion, and I love him all the more for it," Georgette lamented. "But so it is, and I shall not be moved from my decision, even if everyone who is anyone condemns me for it." She quieted a little, and gave a rueful grin. "It is nevertheless pleasant to hear you say, Elizabeth, that you would advise me to follow my heart."

"I make it a practice to avoid advice," she replied. "All I can say is that I acted very foolishly once, to refuse an eligible man when I had nothing of my own and no other prospects. But I am certainly heartily glad I did, for I shudder to imagine what I might have missed out on, had I settled for what, in the eyes of society, seemed best."

"I daresay *my* prospects just disappeared." Lilly said so unthinkingly, and at once the other ladies were all looking at her." She offered a weak smile. "I just gave your cousin quite a set-down, Georgette."

Her friend winced. "You did? He could not have received that well."

"I think it fair to say he despises me now," she admitted. "Yet, Ball-Sack seems an equally unlikely match, though for different reasons. So I think I shall be forced to distress my mother and tell her I am not to marry, not this Season and perhaps not the one after that either."

"Mr Balton-Sycke would not make you happy," Sarah said. "He is *Phyllaphis fagi*, a pesky, destructive nuisance, while you are the lovely *Coccinella magnifica*. You would eat him for breakfast. It would not do."

"I have no idea what you mean by that, but I do appreciate your seeing my side of things." Lilly smiled at her friend. "So you can upset your father by telling him of your engagement, Georgette, and I shall upset my mother by telling her my news, and we shall endure the whispers together."

Georgette at last rose, kissing Lilly on the cheek and extending her arms towards the others. "That sounds perfectly wonderful."

"And so have a cheer," Sarah offered. "William Buckland —the palaeontologist, you know—served an entire salver of *Calliphoridae* to the Regent—bluebottle flies, that is. Father said he is destined to be elected a fellow of the Royal Society, even so. There is always some newer scandal to come along and make the rest of them less interesting."

An Inspired Intervention

Sarah & Fitzwilliam

All things considered, Sarah had enjoyed a delightful morning with Phipps, Matlock's head gardener, as he showed her his experimental plantings. Really, the man was a genius with *Euonymus vulgaris* and other decorative varieties. These pleasant thoughts were interrupted by the appearance in the garden of two of her dearest friends, and one of her newest ones. Avoiding temptation, she stood her ground, instead of immediately making a run for the maze and hoping to lose them within it.

"I have been speaking with Lady Aurelia," Georgette said agreeably.

Sarah was not fooled by her genial tone. "You are cousins," she replied, with equal amiability. "And very near in age. I suppose such conversations are unremarkable."

"She said you cancelled your engagement to go with her to her dressmaker today. Oh, Sarah, why?" Lilly asked, her blue eyes full of sorrowful accusation.

"You seemed so excited to go," Elizabeth agreed. "You said you have always used your aunt's dressmaker, and you decided it time for a different opinion."

Sarah made herself shrug in what she hoped was an insouciant manner. "I shall, most likely, change dressmakers. But truthfully, you believe yours are so talented, yet, what effort have they to expend? They could put the lot of you into grain sacks, and suddenly grain sacks would become high fashion."

"Do not attempt distraction, Sarah," Georgette said severely. "Why will you not go with Lady Aurelia?"

Sarah gave up her attempts at dissembling. "What would be the point?" she asked quietly. "You all know I was here for one purpose, and it had nothing to do with exotic *tableaux* or pagan feasts. I wished to find someone. A mate of my own. There is no sense in acquiring a dressmaker so far from town to impress a man who is not here."

Elizabeth's eyes widened, and Sarah realised she had said too much. Her friends were too accustomed to her frankness to pay heed to her peculiarities, but Elizabeth's response made clear why the colonel had noticed.

"I heard Mr Withers specifically request to partner with you at last night's card party," Lilly reminded. "You are not without your own little conquests here."

"Mr Withers devoted just enough time in Saye's library to learn the coarser English nicknames of several insects, and spent the entire evening quizzing me in order to make Miss Morgan and Miss Barlowe giggle."

Lilly's big blue eyes filled with tears. "You ought to have told me! It only goes to show what crude, undisciplined friends Lord Saye permits to—"

"I was too busy ignoring Miss Morgan and Miss Barlowe's whispers that Anderson has jilted me to listen to anything else," Georgette interrupted furiously. "I would have enjoyed giving those dreadful chits a proper set down."

"I ought to have noticed and nipped such idiocy in the

bud," Elizabeth offered. "I was unforgivably distracted last evening and lost every hand I played. I am sorry."

Sarah frowned. Why should Elizabeth be downcast? She had been too distracted herself to notice it at the time, but now that she considered, Mr Darcy and Elizabeth had not paired with each other for a single hand in the entire interminable evening.

She examined the three miserable faces before her. Her own travails were not the worst of it; if she had not garnered any admirers, well that was nothing new, was it? "We are, none of us, having any luck with this house party mating ritual. Can we not simply make our excuses and leave? My coachman is here as well as yours, Lilly."

Georgette shook her head. "Lady Aurelia would never forgive me, and she is family. I cannot ruin her party with a dramatic exit. I must make the best of things."

"As must I," sniffed Lilly. "If I returned home early, my mama would immediately be suspicious, and she has the nose of a bloodhound."

"Thank goodness you cannot go, for I certainly must stay," Elizabeth said. "It was difficult enough to arrange my visit, much less an early departure. My father has no idea I am here, with my betrothed, and would be furious should he discover it."

Sarah could not imagine a father in the kingdom who would not drive Mr Darcy directly to the church should he pay court to a daughter. Mr Bennet was a mystery.

"Discontent is only to be expected," Lilly added with her own little bitterness. "Maniacal moving meals and disorderly dinners! Now that Lady Aurelia has announced her intention of taking charge of all future entertainments, surely the atmosphere will grow more conducive to a spirit of genteel romance."

Sarah cocked her head. "If her card party last evening was an example, I find your conclusion dubious. I shall not discover my future here."

But Georgette protested. "It is like riding a horse. One does not become an expert rider on one's first time in the saddle. You expect everything to happen too quickly. Give it a bit more time."

An arctic breeze blew through the denuded garden, chilling Sarah through her very warm, very practical, very ugly clothing. These ladies must be freezing, even in their coats. But they were no hothouse flowers, for all their elegant, innate beauty. Although they looked nothing alike, they were each suffering in some way—even though Sarah did not know the details of Elizabeth's suffering—and in one way they were identical. They each were determined to help her, to encourage her, or to stay out here and freeze with her if they could not. It touched her deeply.

She plopped down upon a nearby stone bench, smiling weakly at her friends. "Oh, but I climbed on that horse immediately, it seems. I have already been thrown." She explained, then, about the colonel's kisses in the library, including her own determination to see where they led. She did not explain about the intense feelings, the wildness of emotion those kisses encouraged. These women would already know.

"I shall be having a conversation with my cousin, after which he will be sporting his dress sword in a wholly new scabbard," Georgette seethed.

"Please, do not, if you care about me at all. I *wanted* it to happen. I am not sorry."

Lilly appeared thoughtful. "But Sarah…this is positively wonderful. It would be an ideal match for both of you. Why did I not think of it before?"

Sarah thought about trying to explain the differences between yellow and grey *Drosophila* flies, but sadly, no one ever made much effort to understand her deeper meanings in such comparisons; equally unfortunate was her own inexperience in communicating in a less scientific manner. Perhaps it was why the colonel could not love her.

"Do not think of it now. I do not mind that he did not fall instantly in love with me, I promise. I did not instantly fall in love with him! But I *could* have rapidly made the leap from respect and admiration to love, given any more encouragement. I have withdrawn my mind from the notion, but I find my feelings are still...leaping."

"Simply because he has not fallen in love yet—" Georgette began.

"He has!" Sarah blurted. "But...but not with me."

Lilly and Georgette, in unison, turned to look at Elizabeth; apparently Sarah was not the only one who had observed the colonel's frequent attentions to Mr Darcy's bride-to-be.

Elizabeth flushed and immediately demurred. "Colonel Fitzwilliam is *not* in love with *me!*"

Sarah met her gaze. "He believes he is. I heard him shouting it. 'I ceded the field,' he said. 'Had another man your fortune, what is to say she might, even now, have a different bridegroom?' were the very words he used."

"It was a stupid brawl between two grown men who ought to have known better," Elizabeth declared. "Have you no brother or sister? I speak from experience—families bicker. It had *nothing* to do with me."

"I do not mean to imply you encouraged him," Sarah sighed. "But neither am I interested in a man who is jealous of his cousin's bright, shiny new *acquisition*. As if you were a sporting curricle!"

"I do not think it precisely that," Georgette protested. "Consider that Fitzwilliam is not even a year younger than Saye. A mere accident of birth, or health, or luck, and all of this could have been his. Some jealousy must be understandable, even expected. But he has never betrayed even the smallest hint, and on the contrary, is extraordinarily loyal. My mother once said that when they were young and mischievous, every scrape those boys got into, they both had to be punished equally—even when their parents *knew* one of them was not guilty. Neither would ever betray the other. It has never changed."

Sarah smiled sadly. "And so he had to resort to violence against a man he supposedly loves like a brother? Here is what *I* believe. You touched his heart, Elizabeth. And whether he is too loyal to those feelings to love another, or whether it was an impossible dream in the first place, I am unable to replace you in it."

Her friends protested, but Sarah could still laugh at herself, interrupting their objections.

"Very well, you are correct. My little speech sounds plucked from a bad novel. There are much better volumes in the magnificent Matlock library, and I would be remiss if I wasted what little time remains of the party without exploring it. If you will excuse me?"

And that is that, she thought as she escaped at last, hoping she had finished with the subject of Colonel Richard Fitzwilliam forever.

The last four-and-twenty hours had been his worst in recent memory. Fitzwilliam's entire body ached—Darcy did not strike often, but he hit *hard*. He had submitted to a dressing down from his younger sister, endured the dullest card party ever hosted, and had been unable to plant Reggie Withers a facer because he had already thrown one too many punches that day. Rationally, he knew that Darcy had been only responding to his own goading; he was already aware that he had been paying too much attention to his cousin's bride-to-be. Had he not been determined to apologise to him directly after leaving the Pig & Feathers with Anderson?

How had it come to this? He was not usually a fractious fellow. Though a man of war, he understood only too well how seldom violence resolved anything. Darcy had thus far managed to avoid Fitzwilliam's every attempt to seek him out, and now he had disappeared with Saye—no one knew quite where—leaving Fitzwilliam, alone, to carry out all of Aurelia's demands for a cavalcade of carriages to parade through the countryside for the benefit of their guests. Unfortunately, the reward of descending upon a tea shop some ten miles from Matlock had not enticed every gentleman to participate, and he was required to beg, bribe, and threaten to ensure Aurelia had enough partners to accompany those ladies eager to take part.

Drat Saye for escaping—and drat him for taking Darcy!

The one woman whose company he might very easily tolerate had sent her excuses. He could not blame Sarah Bentley; the outing sounded very dull indeed. To make matters worse, somehow Aurelia had managed to arrange that his carriage be occupied by Miss Bennet—it might be years before he dared address her less formally—Miss Goddard, and Georgette. Since the very awkward, very uncomfortable apology he had made that morning to Darcy's betrothed, he would much rather be on the battlefield than facing her again so soon.

The three of them stared across the carriage at him with eyes so cool he was almost unsurprised when Miss Goddard commanded him to stop the vehicle after barely starting on their way. "Let the rest go on," she ordered. "It is too cold a drive for me, after all. I shall be a block of ice within minutes."

"For me as well, I find," Miss Bennet said, suddenly shivering. "If you would be so kind as to stop at once."

"As you wish." Fitzwilliam banged on the roof, alerting Saye's coachman. Georgette, he noticed, appeared completely unsurprised by these sudden attacks of the chills. "Ah, then," she said. "I shall collect my maid and return shortly. Wait here. Do not move," she ordered him.

And so he waited, whilst mind and body ached.

Sarah had claimed a megrim—an ailment she had certainly never before endured—to avoid the torture of a carriage ride with whichever gentlemen could not escape the duty of escorting her. Once she thought everyone gone, she made her way to the library—Evans moping beside her because the other lady's maids were all sewing and gossiping together in the absence of their mistresses. Sarah, of course, could not care less if she were accompanied, but Evans was pretending to be a much better chaperon than was usual for her, in imitation of some of the other maids.

The library door burst open.

"Here you are!" Lilly exclaimed. "What are you doing? The carriages are about to leave!"

"Oh! I sent word—"

"I heard, and your claim to a megrim is, of course, nonsense, as we both know. The numbers have not worked, and I shall be forced to spend an afternoon sitting between

Miss Morgan and Miss Barlowe! If you love me at all, you will come at once!"

There was no time to change, but Evans hastily procured a wrap, and Sarah followed Lilly, who was racing down the steps to where a carriage was waiting. A footman opened its door, and Lilly waved Sarah in—but then slammed it behind her. Before she had even settled herself, the carriage was off, throwing her back into the seat with a sharp jerk.

It took a moment for her eyes to grow accustomed to the dim interior, but the solitary person seated across from her was neither Miss Barlowe nor Miss Morgan.

"You!" she cried. "How could she?"

Fitzwilliam peered out of the window when the carriage started forward without his expected occupants. Georgette stood on the step, arms folded, giving him what could only be described as a warning glare. He glanced back at Miss Bentley. After her initial, dismayed comment, she spoke not a word, only gazing out of the window.

Had her friends tricked her into accompanying him? Did she hate him, too? She might; had she not warned him he was taking his teasing of Darcy too far? Why could he not have listened to her? Yet, the situation had been, somehow, like a wood sliver—a constant, gnawing irritant he had been unable to let go—until blood was shed and words exchanged, requiring far longer to heal than any bruises.

"You are the last man in the world Elizabeth would ever marry," Darcy had accused.

It was only now, after much miserable contemplation, that he could admit the truth of what his heart had actually heard: *"You are the last man in the world any truly worthy woman would ever marry."*

Were he Elizabeth's father, he would do all in his power to see the marriage accomplished quickly, and Darcy's cautious approach had annoyed him—but why? What business had it been of his? He had believed himself jealous of Darcy's wealth, resentful of his ability to marry where he chose, and perhaps he was. But it was not *only* that. In addition to owning thousands of acres and untold riches, Darcy possessed a heart bigger than England. Certainly, Elizabeth had captured the better man.

What did Miss Bentley see when *she* looked at him— something she was plainly loath to do? She had allowed him to kiss her; was he so repulsive to her now? He immediately recalled, however, the feeling that she might have been merely 'practising' on him, using him to prepare for a life with another man. It had inexplicably fired his temper—he had not wanted her kissing anyone at all. *Anyone else*, that was. She had not spoken to him since. And then she had accepted beef-witted Withers as her partner last evening, having not heard his own invitation—or at least pretending she had not. Maybe she had wanted to avoid him, as she obviously did now?

Well, then. He had better find out how badly he had mucked things up with her, too.

"Are you angry with me?"

She looked at him with that clear, direct gaze so many found disconcerting. Perhaps he had once, as well, but now he rather liked it. She did not simper and hide behind a fan or a twirling parasol. She did not see the 'earl's son'. She saw *him*.

"No," she answered, finally, turning back to the window.

A wave of fatigue washed over him. For all his practised charm with females, he was no good at this—*real* feelings, honest expressions, as certainly Miss Bennet could attest. He ought to say nothing further and allow the day to proceed to its tedious conclusion. But was that not how his foolish anger with Darcy had grown into a foolish row? Because he *allowed* it to?

He rapped on the roof, stopping the carriage, exited, had a few words with the coachman, and returned to his seat. They proceeded onward.

After several moments, she turned back to him. It was another of the things he liked about her; when she had questions, she asked them.

"Did you change our destination?"

"Yes. Just over the dale is a pleasure garden, not far from the River Derwent. There is a walk that is truly lovely. It will not be crowded at this time of year."

Her brow furrowed. "Why did Lady Aurelia not choose this locale, instead of a tea shop?"

"It is not the weather for it. It will likely be cold." He frowned. "Perhaps too cold. You are not dressed for it."

She shrugged. "I shall walk faster then, until I am warm. My shoes are practical." She lifted the hem of her skirt an inch to reveal sturdy half-boots in a bright red leather, and he struggled not to smile.

"There is a path—it is very steep, you may not like it—which leads directly up the edge of High Tor. One can see the entire village of Matlock Bath, which is known for its spa waters."

For the remaining distance, he talked about the sights of the pleasure park, with its river walks and pretty paths. Gradually, she unbent a bit. By the time the carriage stopped, she had even laughed at a little story he told about punting—and capsizing—on the river.

But while he had managed to set her at ease with his 'tried and true' charm, once they were strolling side by side on the river walk, he attempted, again, to set the conversation upon a less familiar, less comfortable path.

"I suppose you heard that Darcy and I fought."

She stiffened immediately. "Yes."

"It was my fault, of course."

"Of course."

Well, no attempt at softening his self-accusations here. Not that he had expected her to.

"I am not even sure how it happened—" he began, but she interrupted.

"Are you not? Well, then, allow me to enlighten you." Her tone was dry. "Rather than choosing to regulate your feelings and moderate your behaviour, you dwelt upon your resentment and fed upon your annoyance. It happened because you gave yourself *permission* for it to happen. That is how self-pity and entitlement work together to cause grief and pain in others."

His jaw clenched, the more familiar anger flooding him. He turned to look at her, but she was not looking at him.

To his surprise, although she had sounded composed, a tear tracked down her cheek, and then another, as she stared, all unseeing, at the path ahead.

"Do not cry," he whispered. "I am not worth any of your tears."

"I know," she said, still calm. "I am crying over Mr Darcy's split lip. Such an awful blemish to a perfect face."

He grinned at that, stopping, stepping in front of her. He took her face in his hands, marvelling at the delicacy of her skin. Her eyes were blue, but so dark at their edges as to almost be navy. Unique. Like she was. Another tear escaped.

"Why are you crying?" he asked gently.

"Because..." she took a deep breath, gazing at him, those unique eyes filled with sorrow. "Because...I wanted you to be a better man."

He had disappointed her. Not just himself, and not just Darcy, and not just Miss Bennet. And the feeling of it...the feeling of bearing her disappointment was...excruciating. He wanted to run from it, not wallow in it by standing here, facing her.

Instead, he dropped his forehead to hers. "I am sorry," he said.

They stayed that way for a long while. When she moved away at last, he felt bereft.

"I have always prided myself on my rational mind," Sarah said—panting a little. The trail was steep and rough, and the last place a gentleman would take a lady. She liked that he had brought her up it. "But you confuse me."

"I confuse myself," the colonel replied. "Why not you too?"

"Are you in love with Elizabeth?"

He stopped mid-step to look at her, and she wondered if he would be angry with her bold question. But he only shook his head.

"As I recall, you were the first to tell me I was not. Have you ever been stupid, Sarah? Utterly, wrongly, stupid?" It was his first use of her given name, and she was so surprised he even knew it that when he quickly began tramping up the hillside again, he outpaced her and then had to wait for her to catch up. When she did, he was staring over the valley floor. "Many women, usually the least appropriate ones, desire a connexion to my family. I am accustomed to being pursued, and not because I am an interesting, handsome fellow. I have grown adept at making it known that they ought to hunt elsewhere. I did so immediately when I met Miss Bennet."

"I cannot imagine her as a huntress."

"She was not pursuing me, I soon realised. Just...seeing me, as I was unaccustomed to being seen."

"You 'ceded the field' too soon, then. And gave Mr Darcy the advantage."

To her surprise, he laughed. "Of course you heard my blustering, since I was determined to make a fool of myself. No, I gave nothing. The story of Darcy's courtship is his own, and Miss Bennet's. I was jealous, horribly so. But I have since realised Miss Bennet had little or nothing to do with it."

Sarah raised a brow. "Jealous of your cousin, then? His wealth, his power?"

"No." He looked at her directly. "Jealous of deserving a love so precious. He saw her too, you know. I never did. Never truly even looked. When *you* look at *me*, what do you see?"

She did not hesitate. "*Cantharis fulva.* A handsome species, prevalent in warmer months, often found on the prettiest summer flowers. Remarkable pollinators. More commonly known as red soldier beetles."

He grinned, and she grinned back. He really was unfairly intelligent. What was more, he understood her, and her sly, eccentric sense of humour.

"You do not yet trust me, and with good reason. But I shall earn your trust, Sarah. You are *Chrysoperla rufilabris.*"

She gasped, her mouth opening in utter shock. He lightly traced her lips with a single finger; she felt it all the way to her toes. "A lacewing? But...why?"

"Lacewings are capable of coping with a wide variety of conditions, have a high tolerance for the unusual, and are one of the loveliest insects on earth. Like you, Sarah. I see you now."

Slowly, cautiously, her shock gave way to a secret smile. She took his hand, his rough, calloused hand, and placed it, once again, over her pounding heart. "It only does this for you, you know," she confided.

And because he understood, he joined his mouth to hers.

ONLY A
FLESH WOUND

Darcy & Elizabeth

Elizabeth stood in silence with Lilly and Georgette, watching Sarah's determined steps as she hurried away from the garden. Mired as she was in her own unhappiness this morning, missing Darcy and regretting the pain she had given him, Elizabeth was shocked that the three ladies she liked best might also believe she enjoyed the colonel's attentions and the drama and jealousy that resulted.

"Colonel Fitzwilliam does not love me," she finally said. "I am in love. I have watched true love take shape, grow, and deepen. This was nothing like it."

Georgette sighed. "Elizabeth is correct. Fitzwilliam probably did it for sport, to goad Mr Darcy. My cousins tease each other incessantly—always have, for as long as I have known them. There is every reason to suspect Mr Darcy is just as bad."

"It does not matter what it was," Lilly said. "It only matters what Sarah thinks it was—or was not. I have never known her to be theatrical. She really must care for her colonel."

There was a long silence as the ladies considered Sarah's plight. Elizabeth regretted that she may have contributed to her new friend's confusion; while she had not encouraged the colonel's attention and conversation, neither had she ignored him. Darcy had reacted as any man long separated from his lady would. He was furious and jealous, and now seemingly too mortified—or too angry—to speak to her. She had been careless with the heart of a man who had done all she could have hoped for in proving himself the best man she knew.

Swallowing her own heartache, and determined to mend what had been fractured between them, she looked meaningfully at her downcast friends.

"Ladies, Sarah is correct. This whole, um, 'mating ritual' has gone badly. I must address my own mistakes, but first we must help our friends." She smiled at her two companions with what could only be described as a martial gleam. "I was not formed for unhappiness. None of us were."

Despite nursing their melancholy, Lilly and Georgette were delighted with the plan she unveiled. Elizabeth retreated to her room to spend the hour before they had planned to meet again at her writing desk. She was determined to do all she was able to ensure happiness for herself and her beloved Darcy. She missed him, and was angry with herself for the distance now between them. Enough of intransigence and sulking; that was the bane of her father—and he was at fault for their situation. Darcy had been patient enough.

Once she put pen to paper, Elizabeth required less time than anticipated to write the long overdue words. When her letters were sealed, sanded, and ready for the post, she donned her coat and bonnet, anticipating that after her short interval with Lilly and Georgette in the carriage, she would go in search of Darcy. Clasping the letters in her gloved hand, she moved swiftly down the staircase and nearly walked headlong into the man she least wished to meet.

"Eliz-er, Miss Bennet," Fitzwilliam stuttered.

Before he bowed, she noticed a blaze of heat upon his cheeks.

"Colonel Fitzwilliam," she said, inclining her head.

"I owe you an apology," he blurted.

"I believe the greatest apology is owed to Darcy." Elizabeth pursed her lips and watched as his eyes closed briefly. He looked as if in pain, and she was a little glad of it as recompense for Darcy's bruised lip.

"Yes. Yes, him as well. But you see, Darcy will eventually forgive me whether I say it or not. It is his way—to look for ways to put things right, whenever they go wrong. He has ever put my feelings ahead of his own. But if you required it, he would cut me from his life—if it would put things right with you."

"Perhaps that is why he chose me as his bride—I would never require the removal from his life of anyone he loves, no matter how great a jingle-brain."

"I deserve that."

"Yes, you do. Is that why you have been provoking him, using me to tease and upset him? Because you fear he no longer loves you best?"

She rarely was this angry; she wanted him to feel her anger, for he certainly deserved it.

"I-I did not think it all out, I suppose, until very recently. It was very ill-mannered of me, ma'am, to be so inconsiderate of his feelings."

"Yet, you have been raised a gentleman, undoubtedly knowing better, and 'ill-mannered' is the least of it! He is dear. He should never have been hurt, especially by one of his own family! What is wrong with you?"

Her eyes filled with tears.

"I have no excuse for it, ma'am," he replied.

"And before you *hit* him, before you threatened to see if he could indeed be the first man I marry, I heard you bark—for all to hear—that you 'ceded the field' to him. As if there ever *was* a field, and you and I had played upon it! As if there was ever *anything* between us! In, as I recall, our very first private conversation, you most politely made it clear that I was ineligible. Do you think yours was the first 'hint' of that nature I had ever received? Do you think I am so stupid as to entertain the slightest romantic feeling for any man who declares himself out of bounds? Do you imagine I would enjoy demeaning myself in that way?"

She waited, watching as the man whose easy camaraderie she had once appreciated turned pale, seemingly at a loss for words. After a long moment, a torrent of them flew from his lips.

"Never, ma'am. It has been most mortifying, the realisation that, had Darcy been in my own circumstances and met and loved you, he would never have withdrawn. He would have worked, and wooed, and tried to find a way. And if he could not make the match, if you would not have him, he would...he would still have tried...something. Anything. Anything to make your life better, in any way he could, if he could. It is what he does. And he would never—ever—have simply stood aside whilst hoping that a richer version of you would wondrously, effortlessly appear in his life."

He bowed again, clearly hoping for her benediction. Elizabeth let him wait. And then at last she nodded.

"I will, of course, accept your apology—but only to the extent that you put yourself forward in attempting to make it up to him. And of course, I shall expect that all future behaviour towards myself be above reproach."

"Yes, ma'am. Thank you, ma'am."

She nodded and turned away. But she had only taken a

few steps when she looked back. "Whilst you are 'thinking things out' and coming to 'realisations', you might glance around and try to see if your 'richer version'—a lady who is, to my way of thinking, far more suited to you than I ever would have been—might still have you. That is, unless you truly are a jingle-brain."

Elizabeth strode away to meet Georgette and Lilly, happy to put the whole incident behind her. Now if only Darcy could!

"She is meant to be a figurehead of feminine responsibility, not to be in charge of anything! She has no experience managing the particulars of a house party of this importance." Saye kicked at a tree branch that refused to move from his intended path.

Mired as he was in his own self-loathing, Darcy had little patience for Saye whinging on about his sister, not when he had finally come up with the words to say—and the courage to say them—to Elizabeth. He had spent a sleepless night trying to forget the look of shock and disappointment on her beautiful face, and risen early to take a furious hours-long ride. Now, as the clock ticked away on an afternoon wasted without her company, he glared at his cousin, standing a few feet away looking over the sodden field he had wished to use for a croquet tournament. "You forget she is no longer your little sister, crying for her lost dolly."

"She is justly famed for her tantrums."

"And yet years past such outbursts, here she is acting as hostess for the house party you wished to hold—and a good thing she is, else none of the ladies would be present. She is three years married to a baronet. She has greater experience in hosting society than any one present."

"She is—"

"Older than Miss Goddard, or any of the ladies here."

"You are no help, Darcy. My guests expect fine entertainment and pleasures, not a carriage promenade to a bloody teahouse."

"I did not see a mutiny among your guests. Perhaps some of them are eager for more, shall we say, straightforward entertainments." He glanced at Saye, who despite his pique appeared distracted by other matters. Darcy had enough of his own troubles to think over; he had little interest in territorial squabbles between the two cousins with whom he remained civil. "Why waste your time complaining to me about your sister? Write to your mother and tell her how Aurelia has ruined your fun. Be certain to mention how she prevented any further damage to your family home."

As the two men turned away from the field and began to walk back towards the manor house, Darcy watched Saye step stiffly across an icy puddle. "I understand you wished to avoid the stables while the carriages were being readied, but why could you not call horses for us? You have never been one to walk across a muddy field."

"It is a matter of some delicacy. A dreadful case of satin versus saddle."

Darcy looked askance at him.

"I may have been a tad precipitate leaving to chase after Blandy without changing my trousers first."

Darcy chuckled. "Resulting in that extra cushion on your chair last evening. Ironic, is it not, given your censure of Balton-Sycke?"

Saye ignored his bit of sly remonstrance. "That few inches of plump pillow allowed me a better view of my future wife's delights as she awaits my proposal...or rather, my next proposal."

"You have proposed to her?"

Saye shrugged and then, indifference cast aside, cursed. "Are not women the strangest things! All I meant to do was speak to her of some of the challenges facing our union and all the reply I received for the compliment of my candour was a—"

Darcy immediately stopped walking. "Saye, pray tell me you did not insult her."

Saye rolled his eyes. "Insult her? Of course not. What sort of idiot— Oh, wait." He then cast Darcy a smirk that made Darcy realise the entire conversation had been managed to deliver a rather inconsequential insult to him.

Now it was Darcy's turn to roll his eyes. "Very well, haha. Yes, I made a dreadful first offer. But Elizabeth is here, and she is engaged to me, which is more than you can say for Miss Goddard."

"Darcy, no one sinks a battleship with the first cannon-ball," Saye replied.

"Actually, if they hit the—"

"In any case, I merely spoke to her of the difficulties inherent in being a future earl."

"Such as?"

"Such as my mother is called Lady Matlock. And, not a decade ago, was herself Lady Saye. So, I was merely observing that to call Lilly 'Lady Saye' might...well I am just not certain how the captain down there will fare, knowing her as my own Lady Saye and yet clearly recollecting the days when Lady Saye referred to my mother. You must see how difficult that is."

"Not really, no. What man does not call his wife by a name his mother once held?"

"Well," Saye pondered a moment. "You, for example. Your mother was Lady Anne. Your wife will be Mrs Darcy."

"Regardless," Darcy said, "to me she will be Elizabeth—as she should be to you as well. I surely do not intend to refer to her as Mrs Darcy in the comforts of our own chambers. In any case, surely this was not your proposal?"

"A successful marriage proposal is like a game of chess," Saye began.

"No, not really."

"One does not simply capture the king—or queen, as the case may be—on the first move. There are manoeuvres, schemes, plans—"

"Tell her you love her and wish to marry her."

"—bishops on the diagonal and rooks going vertically—"

"Good lord, Saye. You are worse at this than I was."

Saye cast him an eye that was no doubt meant to look haughty. "You lack imagination. In any case, you and my brother have your own chess game going, do you not?"

"Your brother is a numbskull."

"As are so many when it comes to understanding their heart's desires."

"I remind you again, I am the only man here with a willing bride and a wedding date." Darcy nearly bit his tongue as he said the ill-thought words; he had laid himself open to more of Saye's mockery. Oddly, none came; only the sound of their boots hitting the ground was heard for a full minute.

"I take it that no apologies have been offered or received."

Darcy shook his head. "I am here, with you. Elizabeth is in a carriage with her new friends."

"And Aurelia had my brother racing about like a lunatic...he will apologise, you know. Possibly even grovel."

"He must, and soon, to Elizabeth. I can forgive him only when she does—if she does." Darcy let out a breath. "It was a wise thing, offering me a walk rather than a shooting foray."

"Ah, blood on the carpets would be the capstone for Aurelia's betrayals to Mother."

Darcy laughed quietly and blinked as the sun hit his eye; he squinted upwards to see soft grey clouds drifting away, and a weak but welcome winter sun emerge. Looking ahead to Matlock, he saw the last in a parade of carriages was rolling down the drive. Three small figures moved swiftly towards the house. He would recognise Elizabeth's red cloak anywhere. What had happened? Why was she not in a carriage?

Darcy turned to Saye. "Speaking of chess, I have another move or two I must make. Can you not walk any faster?"

Matlock was not so large as Pemberley, but Darcy knew it nearly as well. Still, it took him better than a quarter of an hour to find a footman who correctly directed him to a maid who knew of Elizabeth's whereabouts. He entered the orangery without assurances that she would be alone, but uncaring in his desperation to see her.

He found her sitting on Lady Matlock's overstuffed chaise-longue, her eyes closed, a book unopened on her lap. Moving closer, Darcy sank to his knees and gazed freely on the face he so loved; her lips were turned up in a small smile, dark lashes rimmed pale cheeks. He whispered her name and gently laid his hand on hers. When her eyes flew open, he smiled tenderly, and her startled expression softened.

"Darcy."

She said his name with such happy warmth, he could

have wept. "Elizabeth, are you well? You are not with the others in carriages."

She replied with a wan smile. "Nor are you. And neither did you play cards last evening."

"You had others eager to partner with you. In truth, I was not fit to partner anyone." He shrugged, glad she had missed him but hoping she had not felt abandoned; Darcy had wished her to enjoy the camaraderie of others without his own looming presence—and split lip—to distract her.

"Are you well?" Was it surprise or confusion that clouded her expression?

"No, I am heartsick, knowing you are angry with me."

She sat up, looking stricken. "I am not angry with you. I am angry with your cousin, and with my father, and with myself."

"You are blameless in all of it!" He scarcely heard her dismissal of his faults.

"Darcy, you have been subject to endless provocations from my father, as well as from your cousin. I have been—" here, she struggled for composure—"complicit by allowing one to keep us apart and the other to think himself some rival to you. I am ashamed of what I have become, comfortable and secure in your love, and yet allowing others to create strife and misunderstanding."

"You are innocent in the games they have played!" Darcy moved quickly to sit beside her, gathering her soft form in his arms. "When we first met, you provoked me as well, and those provocations and teases prompted me to fall in love with you."

Her eyes glistened with tears. "I am a fortunate woman."

Darcy smiled wryly. "No more than I am a fortunate man, my love, but in this, I am at fault. We have been apart for weeks, and this house party is but a respite before we again will part. I have little interest in the company of friends and relations, nor making conversation with those new to me. I have wanted only your company, your conversation, and in that I have been selfish, failing to recognise the joy you take in making new acquaintances and the importance to you of establishing new friendships."

Elizabeth was surprised to find uncertainty in Darcy's eyes.

"I am a selfish being still in need of correcting my course. While you are doing as any proper person should, becoming familiar with those who will be part of our social circle in town, I have cared only for the moments when I can be with you, as the centre of your attentions."

"Those moments have been my favourite as well," she whispered. Needing to feel him, to touch his flesh, she stroked his cheek, wincing at the sight of his lip, evidence of what had occurred the previous day. "I shall not wish to share you once we are in greater society. You will be off with your steward or solicitor, attending to your business and visiting your club."

Elizabeth's confession earned a small smile from Darcy, followed by a gentle kiss to her forehead. "Society be damned. I shall pull the knocker off the door and allow dust to collect on my ledgers. All I require is your company."

Darcy breathed in deeply before he again spoke. "I have been thoughtless. Friendship with you is so effortless that watching you charm everyone here has made me proud of you and resentful of others."

Elizabeth's finger trailed lightly around the cut on his lower lip. "You were justified in your resentment of one man."

"I am ashamed of my response to it."

"He is your cousin, but he was too forward in his friendship with me. In truth, while he enjoyed goading you, I believe he was using me to avoid entanglement with other, more eager ladies."

"That is one interpretation for his attentions." Darcy looked at her gravely. "You did nothing to encourage him or lead to my anger. It was—is—evident you enjoyed his friendship, and only that."

"Of course—only that," Elizabeth replied with no little relief. She pulled Darcy closer and kissed the spot below his ear that she knew would please him. When he sighed, she buried her lips in his neck. "I cannot speak for your cousin. He has come to me and apologised. He grovelled in a manner that made me uncomfortable, but I am satisfied that he understands the gravity of his poor behaviour, provoking you and presuming I wished for his company over yours."

Darcy growled. "He is a fool."

"He was humiliated, realising how true your words to him were—that he could never have been my husband. Colonel Fitzwilliam"—she pronounced his name in a crisp voice— "may not admit defeat on the field of battle, but it is you who has the larger share of valour and determination." She lifted her face to his and smiled softly. "Even if you could not have had my hand, he said, you would have done anything you could to increase my happiness—'in any way he could, if he could. It is what he does.'

"Fool though he is, he spoke the truth. It is what you do, my dear man."

His expression softened. "Elizabeth..."

They leant into each other and kissed, gently at first, and then with greater passion until Darcy winced. He touched his lip and wiped away a trace of blood. "I am sorry. My cousin's words may assuage feelings, but their impact lingers on the flesh."

Elizabeth's expression fell as she watched Darcy press his handkerchief to his mouth. She reached for his other hand and held it to her heart.

"You have done all you could, for more than a year, to increase my happiness. I have brought you more distress than you deserve." Elizabeth sighed. "I am angry with my father, who has outgrown the memory of being in love and is resistant to the changes in the life he was settled into with five daughters. His eldest and youngest are gone, and he is selfish...unwilling to part with me as well."

"He doubts our felicity, and believes my love for you is fleeting...that you accepted me out of gratitude."

"You know this is untrue, and he knows it as well. My father claims he does not want me to suffer in a marriage lacking harmony and happiness, yet he ignores our mutual ardour and affection."

"Aye, he thinks it is your gratitude and my lust." Darcy shook his head. "Your father is a fool about love. He mocks the calm felicity of Bingley and Jane, yet doubts the more fevered amity between us. He wishes for you to prove yourself truly in love with me rather than grateful for my assistance—"

"And for you to prove that your love outweighs your desire? That you will care for me when I am fat and silver-haired?" She laughed at Darcy's amused and emphatic nod. "Does he think I shall be my mother and destroy your affection for me?"

Darcy brushed a hair from her cheek and looked at her intently. "Are the doubts only your father's, or do you have them as well?"

"I have no doubts, none at all," cried Elizabeth. "We are not as Georgette and Mr Anderson are—her family and society would oppose their union, and he appears prepared to give her up. Her heart is broken, but her reputation is left intact. Where is the worth in that?"

His voice deepened as he replied. "I should not give up on Anderson just yet, Elizabeth, but never mind them. Are we not perfectly aligned in our interests and intents? Our hearts are engaged, our desire alit, and we are kept apart only because your father wishes to test our love."

She was quiet, holding his hand and gently caressing his fingers.

"It is not fair. It is you who brought Jane and Bingley back together. It is you who saved my sister, *and* my family's name, and wished I would not tell my father. I am grateful to you for all you have done, but even had those events not come to pass, still I would love you."

Though he received her words with a smile, its warmth did not extend to his eyes; instead, he looked more troubled than he had moments earlier.

"I have been in love with you for well over a year now, and certain of my feelings for nearly as long—however ineptly I first spoke them to you. We would be married now but that I thought to respect your father's edict and please you by earning favour with him and the neighbourhood. But for the past day or so, I lost some favour with you, and with myself. I have been my own man for many years. I am unhappy with this waiting, feeling as though we are as unsettled as those around us hoping for a match. I wish our life together to begin."

Elizabeth sat up fully and turned to face Darcy, grasping his shoulders as she settled on his lap. "I share your desire. You, the master of Pemberley, acceded to my father's request because you wished to please me. You may please me now by marrying me with all due haste."

His eyes darkened. "All due haste? What do you mean?"

"I hope you do not mind my arranging our affairs, but I would prefer to return to Longbourn as a bride—"

Her next words disappeared, quickly forgotten in the force of Darcy's joyful exclamation of relief and the impassioned kisses that followed.

SOMETHING OF A SPECTACLE

Georgette & Anderson

Anderson walked to hand down the occupant of the awaiting carriage. "Thank you for coming."

"I could hardly refuse after the abominable way you treated poor George. Somebody must help you fix things." As soon as her feet touched the ground, Lady Penelope Frey dropped his hand. "That had better be the last time you ever abandon my friend, Mr Anderson."

It had never been his intention to forsake Georgette, only to absent himself from the intolerable scrutiny of Saye's guests. Yet to have departed as he did, to have occasioned such pain and humiliation to the person dearest to him in all the world, was abhorrent to him. And he knew he had hurt her, for it was not concern for *his* happiness that had brought Saye chasing after him.

He hoped matters would soon be remedied. His indolent rakehell of a brother had been dispatched to attend to their grandmother, with threats of withheld allowances if he did not comply. Lady Penelope had been lured north with the inducement of making a nuisance of herself. And Anderson had spent the last two days, against all his natural inclinations, shopping for extravagant evening attire. He would make amends with Georgette if it was the last thing he did.

"Your ladyship has my word."

Lady Penelope gave a curt nod and set off towards the house. "Come, then. Let us get you an audience with Hawkridge."

It was a while since Anderson had been to Georgette's family home, a well-proportioned and imposing house designed to loom over approaching visitors. On his previous visit, Georgette had met him at the front door when he arrived—and waved him goodbye from her bedroom window as he was escorted off the premises by her eldest brother. He sincerely hoped this audience would end differently.

"I can see why George likes you," Lady Penelope said abruptly.

Anderson was disconcerted to discover her unashamedly appraising his person.

"Do not look so astonished. I can appreciate a thing without wishing to play with it. You do not advertise it as most other young fops your age do, but on close inspection, you are agreeably well formed."

Anderson hoped that was as close as she would ever attempt to inspect him but would put nothing past the woman about whom he had heard such outrageous tales from Georgette. He was relieved when the door opened, and she ceased staring at him.

The footman recognised him instantly, and it looked as though he would close the door again directly until Lady Penelope barged past him into the lobby. Anderson followed, the servant too busy tripping after her to notice him.

"I beg your pardon, ma'am—"

"Why, what have you done?" she interrupted as she nonchalantly reached past him to lay her bonnet on the hall table.

"Nothing, ma'am, I—"

"Then why did you apologise?"

"I did not—"

"You most certainly did, and now you are arguing with me as well. Are you the master of this house?"

"No, I—"

"Then you will cease addressing me in this scandalous manner and inform Mr Hawkridge he has visitors." She began removing her gloves, making plain her intention to remain in the house.

"I am afraid—"

"Of what?"

"Pardon?"

"You said you were afraid. What has frightened you?"

"I—I am not afraid."

"Then why did you say you were?"

"I beg your pardon—"

"Why, what have you done now?"

"Nothing, ma'am! If you would—"

"I cannot fathom why Mr Hawkridge has such an impertinent upstart in his employ, but unless you would like me to give you something of which to *be* afraid, you will run along, *tout de suite*, and inform your master that Lady Penelope Frey wishes to see him. Make haste, I have somewhere to be."

He evidently recognised the name, for his eyes widened. "I am certain Mr Hawkridge would be happy to receive you, Lady Penelope, but he is not at home to that gentleman." The servant glanced at Anderson.

Her ladyship whipped her gloves across the palm of one hand, making the footman jump. "Where is Mr Hawkridge?"

After a brief pause to own his defeat, the man admitted, "In his study, ma'am."

"Then inform him I have arrived."

The footman left.

"That was unpleasant," Anderson remarked.

Lady Penelope made a noise of contempt. "You asked me to get you in front of Hawkridge. You did not say I had to mollycoddle his servants while I was at it."

Neither had he suggested she ought to abuse them, but he refrained from commenting further. Lady Penelope could be a fearsome creature, and he needed her on his side if he was to have any hope of getting close enough to make his application. Better to allow her to have her fun.

"You have a nerve, Anderson!" boomed Georgette's father as he appeared at the head of the stairs, red faced and scowling.

Anderson bowed in a manner he hoped appeared respectful and prayed his antipathy was not obvious.

"There you are, Grammaticus!" said Lady Penelope, already making her way up the stairs. "I began to wonder whether your dimwit of a footman would ever pass on my message."

"Lady Penelope, what a pleasure," replied Hawkridge in a tone that made clear it was anything but. "Have you forgotten that my sister is married now and no longer lives here?"

"Of course not. I saw her only last week, in fact. Her husband is away again, and she came to me for some company. Such a delightful time we had!" She reached the top step and stood to her full height with a flourish. "And unless you would like me to detail all the specifics of our time together for your entire household to hear, I suggest you take Mr Anderson and me somewhere we can speak more privately."

"I should have you thrown out," he said darkly.

"Absolutely, but you won't, so let us get on with it."

He turned on his heel and stalked away along the landing. Lady Penelope gestured for Anderson to follow, and he took the stairs two at a time in his haste to catch up before Hawkridge changed his mind and had them both ejected from the house.

"You have three minutes, and then I shall have you removed again."

Anderson inclined his head and kept his expression neutral. There were very few people in the world he overtly disliked, but here sat one of them, in all his corpulent glory. "I would like your consent to marry your daughter."

"And I shall not give it. I thought I had made that clear the last time you asked."

"Abundantly, sir."

"Did you think I might have changed my mind?"

"I hoped I might change it for you."

"Have you severed all connexion with your blasted institution?"

"I have not."

"Then you are wasting my time and your own."

"Those children would die if I did not provide for them, sir. I shall never step away from my responsibilities there."

"Are you wholly without compassion, Grammaticus?" enquired Lady Penelope.

He turned to her. "We both know I have more compassion in my little finger than your ladyship possesses in her entire body. Besides, I thought you despised children."

"I despise you, too, but that does not mean I wish you to die. Although that would resolve Mr Anderson's problem rather neatly."

"I do not suggest that Mr Anderson's undertaking is not commendable. That has never been my concern." He pointed a finger at Anderson, though he continued talking to Lady Penelope as though he could not bring himself to look at the source of his disgust. "I will not have Georgette scorned, reviled, and harried into madness in the same way his mother was."

"You discredit your daughter more with this underestimation of her character than if the whole world were to ridicule her for marrying me," Anderson retorted. "Yes, my mother lost her wits, God rest her soul, but she was never a strong woman. She found life difficult, even before it became so.

"Your daughter *laughs* in the face of difficulty. I have never met any person so unafraid of living, and I do not mean because she has the fortune to buy her way out of any unpleasantness, but because she loves life—*all* life. Whether it is the children at my institution, her friends and family, the fools who make sport of her affection for me, or a darned stray cat—she takes pleasure in all of it. If you think the censure of a few bitter ladies with pretensions to consequence is enough to send her distracted, then you do not know her at all. Furthermore, if you force her to marry someone who does not value her beautiful *joie de vivre*, you will condemn her to a life of abject misery."

"Well said!" Lady Penelope exclaimed.

"Thank you for explaining my own daughter's character to me, Mr Anderson," Hawkridge said coldly. "I am sure I thought her a sweet, tractable creature until this moment. But it changes nothing. My answer is still no."

Anderson sighed aloud. "I thought you might say that. If my avowals and Miss Hawkridge's wishes are not sufficient to persuade you, then perhaps this will." He vastly enjoyed the flash of alarm on Hawkridge's face and Lady Penelope's eager interest as he reached into his inside pocket.

Georgette closed her bedchamber door behind her and leant against it, exhaling heavily. Her face ached from the smile she had kept on it throughout every interminable activity her cousins had foisted upon them these past two days. Lady Aurelia's poetry reading two nights prior, which her brothers had sabotaged by spiriting the men away, one at a time, for a billiards tournament. Saye's absurd game of croquet on a frozen field, which had infuriated his sister as it prevented anyone attending her tour of the winter gardens. The shambolic last-minute dance practice for which Saye had summoned an eminent and exorbitant dancing master. And Lady Aurelia's extravagant luncheon just now, which nobody had wanted, for who was hungry two hours after breakfast?

But then, Georgette was struggling to find enjoyment in anything at present. She rang for her maid, then flopped onto her bed and stared disconsolately at the canopy until Prinny bustled in with a tray.

"Coffee, Miss Hawkridge."

Georgette sat up with a grateful sigh. "You are a wonder."

"I was not sure whether you would prefer to nap before the revelries begin later, but I thought it likely not. I know how you prefer to enjoy the anticipation."

"There is not much to anticipate, Prinny, for I do not mean to do any revelling."

"What?"

Startled, Georgette whipped around to see Lilly standing in the doorway.

"I shall come back later," Prinny whispered, quitting the room.

Lilly came to Georgette, frowning. "Darling, whatever do you mean? You simply must come to the masquerade."

"No, Lilly, it is you who must go. It is in your honour, after all. I shall not be missed by anyone."

"You will be missed by me! And Sarah, and I daresay Elizabeth, and—"

"Coffee?" Georgette interrupted, leaning forward to pour herself some.

"No, thank you."

"Good. I only have one cup."

"Do not change the subject. Tell me why you do not wish to come to the ball."

Georgette felt a sudden wave of emotion that left her momentarily unable to speak.

"Because Anderson will not be there—is that it?"

Georgette turned her face away, sucking in a disconcertingly uneven breath.

Lilly dragged a chair closer and sat down, taking up Georgette's hand in her own. "If I can brave the evening in Saye's presence, then you must be able to tolerate Anderson's absence."

Georgette rapidly found her voice again. "Surely Saye has forgiven you for your dressing down by now? That was days ago. I have never known him to hold a grudge."

"Oh, he is not angry with me. I am only concerned for how I am to avoid him all evening."

"Why would you wish to avoid him?"

"So he does not propose to me again."

Georgette sat up straighter, clutching Lilly's hand in both of hers. "Saye proposed to you?"

"Twice, actually. I think twice. Maybe once and a half."

"You do not look pleased. I take it I should not begin calling you Cousin yet."

"No, for I refused him both times."

"Oh, Lilly, why? You are completely in love with him, you know. I have known it for months."

Lilly pulled her hand free of Georgette's grasp and stood up to begin pacing. "What do you think of this for a proposal? He asked if I should like to see the east wing, which has evidently been closed for some time. I said certainly, I would go, and suggested Elizabeth accompany us, but he said he 'did not wish to frighten Zabet'. Is that her nickname, by the by? She did not tell me it was."

"I think Saye has made that up."

"Ah. Nevertheless, I went with him, and he began by showing me the dining room."

"The east wing has its own dining room? I do not remember it."

Lilly nodded. "Smaller than the main one, of course, but still grand. He told me he intends to have a feast in there on our wedding day. A feast...of me."

Georgette snorted with laughter.

"You see—he laughed as well, and now you are laughing, too!"

"Forgive me. Carry on."

"Well, knowing Saye, it seemed safe to tell him I ought to slap him as hard as I could. And do you know what he said to that?"

"I am afraid to ask."

"He said 'Darling Lilly, if that should excite you, have at it'. I swear I hardly know what he means half the time. And as always, just when he had vexed me so that I could hardly see straight, he came over all lovely and sincere. We were nearly back to the drawing room, and he begged me—with utter earnestness—to promise I would not leave. He said I am the love of his life, and he cannot let me leave Matlock until he has convinced me of the sublime felicity we might have together. Then he kissed my hand and strolled off without a care, as though it had not been the most discomposing hour of my life!"

Georgette grinned broadly at her. "And was this the first or second proposal?"

"The second. The first was even more nonsensical. He rattled away about how difficult it was being a viscount because one day he would be forced to call me Lady Matlock. He said that made him feel conflicted—well, in truth he used a different phrase, but I shall not repeat it, even to you, for I should blush like a tomato if I said it aloud. In any case, he spouted gibberish about heirs deserving the right to rename their earldoms such that their wives and mothers would never need share a name, and said he intended to speak to the Prince Regent about it next time he was at Carlton House. I cannot even say whether I truly refused that one, because he neglected to ask me the question!"

Georgette shook her head, glad of her first genuine laugh in days. "Only Saye! But why not just accept him and be happy?"

Lilly sat down heavily in her chair. "Because he is only mocking me. I gave consideration to a man he finds ridiculous, and suddenly my marriage prospects are an object of hilarity to him."

Georgette regarded her friend gravely. "I do not think he is joking."

"Of course he is. Have you not always told me he is not the marrying kind?"

"I never heard him speak about any other woman in such terms—of sharing his name with her. And Lilly, if he *is* in love with you, and if he *was* serious when he said those things, then I beg you would not continue to evade him. I do not like to think how unhappy he must be that you have not said yes."

"Saye is not capable of being unhappy—he is far too delighted with himself," Lilly objected heatedly.

"No, that is not true," Georgette said quietly. "I know,

because he and I are so alike. And everybody believes I am only a little put out that Anderson has left. Whereas, in truth, I...I think I am a little bit—"

It had been so long since she last wept, Georgette did not immediately recognise the burning sensation at the back of her nose as the precursor to tears. She was taken aback when she began to cry, though once she had begun, she simply could not stop.

Lilly's arms were about her in an instant. "Oh heavens, Georgette! Why did you not say?"

"Because I thought he would come back," she mumbled between sobs. "Or write. But it has been days, and I have had no word. I begin to think he cannot forgive me."

"Forgive you! Whatever for? You were defending him!"

Georgette sat up and wiped at her tears with her sleeve. "That is precisely what for. You do not understand. His parents' ruin condemned him and his brother to a life of obscurity. Randalph's answer is to bury himself in the gambling dens of London, but Anderson does not have that luxury. He has Gilchester Hall to oversee, and his institution, and he must do it all in as unremarkable a way as possible lest anyone notice and remember who his mother was. And going unnoticed is not easy for him. You would not know it, but he is excessively sportive by nature. He takes pleasure in good company and clever wit, in cards and games. He loves to race. Yet he has had to learn to be inconspicuous, and he needs a wife who will help him do that.

"He does not need a wife who will lose her temper and shriek all his secrets to the world in a fit of pique. Defending him in that way was the very worst thing I could have done."

Lilly tucked a strand of Georgette's hair behind her ear and peered at her sympathetically. "Darling, if he is not in want of a wonderful, strong woman, who supports him in all his endeavours and is passionate about his work, then permit me to say that he ought not to have been marrying you in the first place."

"You are a dear, but I am a more selfish creature than you give me credit for, and I am less concerned about what I can give to Anderson than with what he can give me. I am in want of a man who can love me in spite of my sharp tongue and occasional thoughtlessness. A man who values my understanding and respects my opinion despite my dreadful habit of taking nothing seriously. A man who finds me beautiful. A man who feasts on me—"

"Georgette!"

She gave a teary grin and shrugged. "I am in want of *Samuel*, Lilly. I cannot bear the thought that I have lost him."

"If he loves you as well as you say, he will come back to you. Have a little faith in him."

Georgette took a deep breath and nodded. "Very well. If you will have a little faith in Saye."

Lilly nodded back. "Very well. I shall try."

Lady Aurelia knew how to throw a ball. Matlock had been transformed into a veritable wonderland of glittering whimsy, every banister and cornice draped with some sparkling ornamentation or other. The ballroom was incandescent with the light of what must be a thousand candles, whose glow was refracted in all directions by gilt-edged mirrors and crystal-draped chandeliers. A cavalcade of carriages had arrived to swell the house party's numbers into a mad crush of masked beauties, and word had it that the musicians counted three harpists and a renowned opera singer amongst their number. Georgette had to admit, she was pleased not to have missed it.

She walked on her own through the crowd, eschewing any conversation, for she did not trust herself to keep her composure were anyone to enquire about Anderson. Her mask, and her efforts to remain inconspicuous, only sharpened her thoughts of him. She wished it had been this display of discretion he had last witnessed rather than her gauche exhibition in the library. She might have grown maudlin dwelling upon it had not someone spoken her name in a startlingly familiar voice, bringing her spinning around to search for familiar features among the masks.

"Father!"

Those close enough to perceive her alarm quieted and stepped back to clear a path between them. She hurried towards him, her heart and mind both racing.

"Georgette. I trust you are well," he said gravely.

"My cousins did not tell me they had invited you."

"It was a recent decision." He nodded at someone over her shoulder, and she looked to see Saye walk past in his unmistakable ivory velvet domino. His mask was preposterous, as was to be expected, but beneath it, she could clearly see his smirk.

"Why are you here? Is something amiss?"

Her father grunted in the way he always did when he was unhappy about something. "I suspect it is about to be." He cleared his throat and in a louder voice said, "I shall come directly to the point. I have come to give you my consent—my consent and my blessing—for you to marry Mr Anderson."

A rumble of gasps and whispers rippled through the gathering crowd of onlookers, but Georgette ignored it. Caught between elation and despair, she was scarcely able to keep from weeping again. "You cannot know what that means to me, Father. But I fear it is too late. Mr Anderson has gone."

"Has he? Who is that bloody fool then?"

Georgette looked to where he pointed. The crowd had parted behind her to form a large circle around one man— unmistakably her favourite one—dressed in an exquisitely well-fitted matador's outfit with a cape about his shoulders and wearing a leather half-mask in the shape of a bull's head, complete with horns and nose ring. Someone clapped their hands twice, and a harpist began to play. Even to someone with Georgette's fondness for exhibition, this was deliciously over the top, and she laughed with sheer delight.

She walked into the centre of the circle with him, her heart over-full and her smile over-wide. "Mr Anderson, you seem to be making something of a spectacle of yourself."

"Yes. You had better take pity on me and answer my question quickly, before I incur any lasting injury from the ordeal." Without further ado, he sank down to one knee and asked her, in the uncomplicated, understated, sincere way she loved so dearly, whether she would do him the honour of becoming his wife.

She gave her laughing, joyful acceptance, and somewhere off to her left, she heard Lilly's unmistakable cry of delight. Her father announced he was off to play cards with Sir Phineas, then Saye declared loudly that Anderson had held the floor for too long and demanded that everybody join the first set.

"Thank God for that," Anderson said quietly as the circle around them collapsed, and they were once more buffeted on all sides by the crowd. "I was not sure how much longer I could withstand all that staring. My skin was crawling so, I thought it might slither off me altogether."

Georgette squeezed both his hands. "You came back!"

He tugged one of his hands free and pushed his mask away from his face. Georgette inhaled sharply. Never had she seen him so affected, nor so wholly without the faintest sliver of amusement in his gaze.

"Pray, forgive me, my love. I was an ass, but I swear I shall never run away again. I mean to spend the rest of my life running to you."

"Then I shall make sure to always walk slowly to ensure you are able to keep up."

"I shall keep up. You may count upon it."

He lifted her hand to kiss her fingers. She recognised the glint in his eye and hoped he was about to suggest they sneak away to celebrate their engagement somewhere more private, but such was not to be. A tall gentleman in a full face mask cut in, taking Georgette's hand right out of Anderson's and pulling her towards him.

"Do not forget our bargain, Mr Anderson. I said I would help you in exchange for the first set."

To Georgette's surprise, Anderson made no objection—he only smiled knowingly. She looked harder at the interloper, then gasped in astonishment. "Loppy! Whatever are you doing here?"

"Dance with me, and I shall tell you."

The gratification of dancing with such a notoriously improper woman as Lady Penelope Frey, dressed convincingly as a gentleman of the first water, almost made up for being snatched away from Anderson so precipitately. She had done an excellent job of disguising herself, but Georgette nevertheless suspected Lady Aurelia would be furious if she discovered such a disreputable personage amongst her guests. It would not be Lady Penelope's dancing that gave her away, however. Her ladyship had learnt to lead faultlessly.

"I came with your young man," she explained as they went through the first pattern. "He enlisted me to help get him an audience with your father."

"How did you manage that? My father hates you!"

Lady Penelope only shrugged enigmatically as she wove in

and out of the other dancers. "I do like Mr Anderson though, George," she said when they joined hands to go down the line.

"And so you should. He is wonderful. What did he say to my father to change his mind?"

"Oh, he said some very charming things, all of which proved how well he loves you, but it was not his pretty words that persuaded your father."

"Then what did?"

"Viscount Saye's letter. He has invested in Mr Anderson's institution and put himself forward as patron. Your cousin is on a mission to make your future husband the very paragon of fashionable charity. I think he might even have recommended him for the Corinthians based on his riding prowess, though that might have been a joke. Where are you going?"

Georgette did not hear the rest. She abandoned the dance and ran to clamber onto an empty chair, then urgently searched the room for the foot-tall mask she had seen Saye wearing before. When she spotted him, she jumped down and dashed through the crowd, elbowing people out of her way until she reached him, whereupon she threw her arms around his neck and clung to him. She felt him move them out of the dance and heard him tell everyone to carry on without him.

"Georgette, kindly unpeel yourself from my person, you are crushing my velvet!"

"No." She shook her head, all the emotion of Anderson's proposal apparently having seen fit to wait for this moment to bubble out onto her cousin instead.

"Georgette, what on earth are you doing?" asked Lilly from somewhere nearby.

Oh lord, I have interrupted their first dance together! There was nothing to be done about it now. "You are the very best of men, Saye."

"Pray do not speak so," he hissed, pushing her gently but firmly away and dusting his domino furiously. "You will ruin me. Now leave me to your friend."

"You are wonderful, and you *deserve* to be hugged."

"I do, but not by you. Besides, Darcy wrote to your father as well. Go and hug him and leave me alone."

Georgette laughed at the prospect of how little the Great Standing Stone would like that. "I most certainly shall thank him, from the bottom of my heart, but we both know it was your idea, and for that, I love you." She kissed Saye on his cheek, and whispered, "But not nearly as much as Lilly loves you—and *definitely* not in the same way."

A Masquerade Unmasked

Saye & Lillian

I t was extraordinarily vexing to Saye that Aurelia should receive the felicitations and congratulations for what promised to be an unparalleled event. The idea had been his; the dance master had agreed to come on his name; and the Yellow Escubac had been chosen by him to be the signature drink of the party. Aurelia, unimaginative bird that she was, had whinged that the guests ought to be served a more customary ratafia besides, but Saye had rejected that outright. "The moment you said customary, you lost me," he informed her.

Then there was the matter of his costume. The time he had put into thinking of it was not inconsiderable, and the fortune it had cost him not insubstantial. But worth it? Indubitably.

He had chosen Gatto as his mask, but not the cat alone; he had a *masque con gatto veneziano*, two masks in one—the first, a handsome man, the second a cat, heavily bejewelled and elegantly perched atop the face of the man. It was also twice the dose of cleverness—not only was his Gatto the match to Lilly's, but the cat wore a collar of aquamarines and diamonds that was, in truth, an engagement present. He would propose, Lilly would accept, and then she would receive her gift.

But it would be the proposal itself which would be truly outrageous. Naturally, his first inclination was to fill a room somewhere with exotic flowers, set off fireworks, have the opera singer serenade her, something with true éclat. It had been Darcy who had rather put a damper on all of that.

"I have always supposed that you hide behind your excess," he had said. "Better to stupefy and amaze than allow some proper romantic frailty to show. Have you considered that she might appreciate being acquainted with your sensibilities?"

Darcy did say the stupidest things sometimes, and Saye had not scrupled to tell him so—but dash it all if that accursed brother of his had not got in on the act, stroking his chin like some great philosopher and opining, "'Tis rather a terrifying business, to lay oneself bare before a woman."

But the *de rigueur* quip about the miniaturised flute Fitzwilliam kept in his breeches had gone unheard. Darcy was all grave and instructional, telling them all, for the thousandth iteration, "I can assure you, when Elizabeth and I went walking that October afternoon, right at the very moment I knew was my chance to offer a second—"

"Bah! Do we need to hear this again?" Saye had cried out. In truth, it had become almost physically painful to him to be subjected, once again, to the tales of Darcy's courtship of Elizabeth.

"I am saying it required a great deal of courage, because not only did I need to bare my soul, I needed to do it with the sounds of her vehement refusal yet in my ears!"

"In this we are equal. Lilly has refused me twice."

"Those were nothing to how Elizabeth refused me."

"Oh? How might you have liked it if she refused you in your very own home?" Saye retorted.

"Are we truly going to compete for who was rejected the most violently?"

"I am only saying there is no more grievous insult to a man than to be cut down on the very floors his ancestors trod."

And somehow amid various boasts, insults, dares, and exclamations over the meaning of true courage, Saye had found himself betting his cousin and brother that he would have his beloved's hand with nothing to recommend his suit but his own flawless exposition of charming vulnerability and humble entreaty. *Blast!*

He supposed he might find solace in the fact that it was sure to astonish her.

He had procured an unfair advantage for himself, of course, by making certain that she would indeed be Gatto. And so she was, a pretty little puss with a painted and twinkling mask that matched her gown and the rose-coloured domino she wore. It was a new dance, one he had commissioned especially for the affair—*Viscount Saye's Hornpipe*. "Very similar to *Parker's Hornpipe*," he told his guests with a smirk, "save for the repeated thrusts up the middle."

He was one of the few who was truly practised in the dance; only he and Fitzwilliam had known about it since the very notion occurred to him. Everyone else had learnt it the day prior, when he had commissioned the dance master to come out and teach it to everyone in the house; Saye had enjoyed it very much when the dance master had informed them all, "Gentlemen, you must be prepared to aid the ladies in the upshot during the climax."

"One must never stumble during the climax," Saye had added, to the very great mirth of his brother and, shockingly, Sir Phin. Evidently the rest of them were virgins.

Now he was here, with Lilly's undivided attention. "They say dancing is a first step towards falling in love," he remarked to her, shortly after they began.

"That seems impossible, at least for a lady," she said. "After all, we must accept any man who asks, or else risk sitting out the evening complete."

"And that is quite unfair for us all," Saye replied. "Why should I have the same chance of acceptance as say…old Jolly over there?" He gave a discreet little point towards Jolly Rawlings, an amiable fellow of good fortune who nevertheless appeared, always, to be garbed in clothing that was simultaneously too large and too small. Even now, he stamped about inelegantly, his mask askew and his domino doing nothing to disguise the unruly shock of red hair atop his head. "I have quite truthfully never seen the man well in looks."

Lilly giggled and then frowned. "Bad boy. He is your friend!"

"And an excellent fellow he is—just badly dressed." Saye smiled at her. "A hopeless case, sartorially, but I do not doubt he will make someone an excellent husband."

"Playing matchmaker? A peculiar diversion for a man most think is not the marrying kind."

"I cannot argue with them," he said. "Indeed, I have always found the notion of marriage quite unappetising."

The conversation had come just to the spot he wished it to and then, from nowhere! Blasted Georgette, all full of teary-eyed joy and hell-bent on destroying his domino and forcing them to step out of the set—his dance! "Kindly unpeel yourself from my person; you are crushing my velvet!"

"Georgette, what on earth are you doing?" asked Lilly.

Georgette had him in a half-hug, gazing up at him tenderly. "You are the very best of men, Saye."

"Pray do not speak so." There were creases, obvious wrinkles, in his velvet. He gave her his most thunderous scowl. "You will ruin me. Now leave me to your friend."

"You are wonderful, and you deserve to be hugged."

"I do, but not by you. Besides, Darcy wrote to your father as well. Go and hug him and leave me alone."

Georgette laughed and said, "I most certainly shall thank him, from the bottom of my heart, but we both know it was your idea, and for that, I love you."

But she had not done. She insisted on kissing him, whispering as she did, "But not nearly as much as Lilly loves you —and *definitely* not in the same way!" Then at last she left, nearly skipping away. At least her last words to him had made him forgive her a little.

"What was that about?" Lilly asked curiously.

"I am sure I do not have the least notion. Woman troubles?" He smiled. "Let us return to our dance. It is very nearly time for the decisive and final thrust, and we surely do not wish to miss that. No one wants to be left unsatisfied."

The intended entendre was unnoticed. Lilly's curiosity was fixed on her friend. "Obviously she is happy Anderson is returned, and happy to be engaged—but what did you have to do with it?"

"Nothing." Saye took her arm and gently prodded her back towards the dancers, joining the end of the line as they waited their turn to thrust.

Lilly turned and gave him a look, the blue of her eyes seeming somehow sharper, more unyielding. It was most peculiar—as if she already knew, but wanted to make him say it, or something like that. He heaved an enormous sigh. "Well, Hawkridge is dreadfully high in the instep, but you must have known that."

"He had always seemed perfectly amiable to me, until I

learnt this week that he forbade Georgette from marrying Mr Anderson."

Saye shrugged. "He does fancy himself as a man of fashion, or at least what passes for one among gentlemen of that age, but absolutely abhors anything unseemly."

"Like Anderson's helpless children," Lilly said with a charming little frown. So charming it was, in fact, that Saye forgot to reply for a moment. "And his family history."

"Quite right."

"You have had a hand, then, in persuading Georgette's father to overlook Anderson's peculiar fondness for the little unfortunates? But you count yourself a man of fashion too—do you not? How can you reconcile it?"

"You are quite wrong, my darling girl," he said. "I am decidedly not a man of fashion. Rather the fashions are of me."

That made her both laugh and roll her eyes, but as the pattern dictated that they move, she was unable to press for more. Relieved, he hoped she would say nothing else about it —but the way that she cast a little glance towards him told him her curiosity had not been sated.

She held it until the dance was finished. "But how could you persuade your mother's cousin to accept a man he was so thoroughly set on disliking?"

"Why must you be so fixed on this? Look." He gestured towards the windows at the side of the room, through which a nearly full moon could be seen. "Shall we take some air?"

"You are being impossible," she told him.

"Well, as that is his specialty, one can hardly expect otherwise." Aurelia had arrived, peevish and irritated, to demand her elder brother's attention. "Saye, you are needed immediately."

"Where is your mask?" Saye asked.

"Who cares!"

"I care," Saye replied, very reasonably. "I cannot have people thinking this is some half-hearted masquerade, as they will if our hostess herself is unmasked."

"If you are so worried about what people are thinking, then you should know the enthusiasm of our disguise should be the least of your worries. All of these people you invited are hearing the tales of the goings-on here, and word will get out to London!"

"So let it. Why should I care?"

Aurelia's eyes nearly popped out of her head for his blithe response and regretfully, Saye saw Lilly slip away with a little wave to him, retrieving her domino from the footman as she went. "Aurelia, I have half a mind to murder you dead," he scolded. "The *pièce de résistance* of my entire party, and you turn the whole thing into a dry bob with your nonsense."

"As murder is the only scandal this party has wanted for so far, you might as well! I have just heard it reported that Lady Penelope Frey is here. Lady Penelope! That will only confirm what people are saying—that it has been a debauchery, all of us behaving as savages and half the ladies ruined!"

"Well the maids can set everyone straight on that account," Saye replied. "The bed-linens at Matlock are yet pristine."

"We hope so," Aurelia replied darkly. "After all, where has Darcy been these last days? Where is Miss Elizabeth Bennet?"

Saye considered that for a moment. Darcy had been notably absent from the croquet and his dance lesson...had he dined with them last night? This was the trouble with the taciturn, you scarcely noted when they were not there. "If Darcy had not taken her before he got here, he surely could have restrained himself in his uncle's house."

"Well, where is he then? Because I have not seen him in at least two days complete."

"And you are choosing to seek him now? During a masquerade?" Saye shook his head. "Aurelia, go and enjoy the party. We can fuss over Miss Bennet's chastity later. I must go and find Lilly."

Feeling thoroughly discomposed, Lilly walked away from Saye. She could not say why it was so important to her, this matter of what he had done for Georgette—well, that was untrue. She knew why it mattered. Her entire opinion of Saye, her understanding of everything he did and said and thought was based on her belief that he was a selfish rake, pleasure-bent and heedless of anything that did not benefit him directly.

If he somehow persuaded his mother's cousin to accept Anderson's suit—an act which can only degrade him, no matter how much delight it brings dear Georgette—why, then I suppose he is not so selfish after all.

These ridiculous proposals he had offered...were they in earnest? *Unappetising,* she reminded herself. *He finds the notion of marriage unappetising.*

She found Georgette and Anderson moments later in the library. Anderson's mask had been laid aside, and Georgette's was down around her neck; Lilly belatedly realised she had caught them kissing. "Oh, um, apologies, I can come back. I just had a question for you."

"No, no." Georgette grinned rather roguishly and ran a hand over her skirts. "What is it?"

Anderson turned his back and made what appeared to be some adjustments to his trousers, and a hot blush assailed Lilly. Thankful for the dimness of the room, she hurriedly spoke. "I only wondered what it was Saye did to change your father's mind. You seemed so very thankful, I thought it must be something excessively grand. Does he have some gossip to hang over your father? Some debt?" She laughed, weakly, to show she meant the last in jest.

"Saye, and Darcy as well, have lent their support." Anderson turned back to face her, speaking with earnest feeling. "Not only in money, but in name. They both intend to be recognised patrons."

"So the unfashionable shall become the fashion," Georgette finished. "You know how Saye is, by Easter, everyone will know that Anderson's children are absolutely the prevailing concern, and, by Ascot, people will be in the depths of despair if they are not themselves involved in the cause."

"Of course, being Saye, he intends to have a party attached to it. A ball in town, one which people pay to attend and the proceeds go to the children." Anderson shook his head, clearly in wonderment at his good fortune. "I cannot deny that having such a man for a friend will do the institution untold good."

"What if he forgets?" Lilly asked. "Saye does tend to just rattle away, drunk half the time and always trying to scandalise or provoke people."

"That was my concern initially, Miss Goddard, but I can assure you such worries are without foundation. Lord Saye had his man of business writing letters within the hour. It is all done."

"I will say this for Saye, once he sets his mind to something…" Georgette lost interest in her own sentence, plainly having become distracted by her betrothed's warm look.

It seemed they were about to begin kissing again directly before her, and Lilly realised she should do best to leave them to it. With a little pained clearing of her throat, she quit the room, moving back towards the ballroom. Another dance was in progress, and Saye was dancing with a lady harlequin. She studied him for a moment. He was, as always, elegant and expert in his rendering of the figures. As she watched him, he saw her and, although the mask made it difficult to tell, it seemed that he gave her a little wink that made her feel fluttery inside.

She turned, walking away from the dancers, intent on getting a drink or finding a friend or something, when a conversation stopped her in her tracks. Jolly Rawlings and someone she did not know—perhaps one of Matlock's neighbours in Derbyshire.

"...just like him, is it not? Some grand expense of a house party, all to win a lady." Jolly chuckled. "I can tell you my father would not have sanctioned this."

"Surely not? There are parties aplenty in London if you want to woo a lady. Call on her, man, send some flowers, it will be far less expensive."

"I was sitting beside them at the club when they spoke of it," Jolly said. "Saye, Fitzwilliam, Darcy, all sitting there talking about it. I am not one to listen where I am not part of the conversation, but he was not very quiet. Rather overset, if I must say so. Some other fellow was about to propose or did propose and he was determined to put a stop to it."

"Well, I have known Saye many years, and if you want my opinion, 'tis likely this is but a contest between him and the other suitor."

Exactly! Lilly thought. *He does not want me. He just wants to defeat Balton-Sycke!*

"No," Jolly said, and he sounded quite certain. "Darcy and Fitzwilliam both asked that same thing, and Saye grew quite angry with them. Told them in no uncertain terms that he loved her and would die of misery without her. Of course, he did admit that besting the other fellow would be sweet, but he did not mince words. He loves her."

The other man chuckled. "I do not know Miss Goddard, although I do know her elder brother Arthur. He is a fine fellow. His sister must be uncommon indeed to have brought Saye to heel."

"Firmly on her apron strings, he is," Jolly agreed.

Lilly heard no more than that. Nearly stumbling, she went back towards the dance floor. The set had just ended, and she went to find Saye, rising on her toes to find the enormous mask he was wearing in the crowd. When she found him, she went to him directly, determined there would be plain words between them before she lost her courage.

"May I speak to you?" she asked him.

"Of course. Where?"

"Somewhere more private," she said. "Perhaps...?" She gestured towards the door that would lead them outside. He offered her his arm, and they walked out together, finding themselves on the terrace only moments later. The crisp late winter air was a relief after the heat of the ballroom, and Lilly removed her mask to thoroughly enjoy it. The moon had lent everything a spectral glow; it was all really quite enchanting, even if Lilly refused to be enchanted. Saye removed his mask, setting it on the balustrade beside him. She placed hers beside it.

"Are you well?" he asked in a concerned voice.

"Yes, it is only that I, um, I heard some people talking about this, your party."

"The ball? Or—"

"All of it."

"What about it?"

She found that her mouth had gone suddenly very dry. She turned, looking out over the lawn, unable to meet his eyes. Quietly, she said, "They said you planned this house party as a means of winning a lady's hand...to win *my* hand."

She heard him take a deep breath before admitting, "Yes."

After a short pause, he added, "It is rather an odd time of year to host a house party. Hence we are playing frozen croquet and doing archery in the mud."

Then in a softer voice, he added, "But well worth it for the privilege of having you under my roof for a fortnight."

She turned back to look at him. "So all of this was to prevent me from accepting Mr Balton-Sycke?"

He stepped closer to her and took her face in his hands, his eyes intent upon her. She closed her eyes a moment, a most inconsequential thought in her mind—when did he remove his gloves?—then opened them again to find him looking intently at her.

"Lilly, if you can tell me right now that marrying Balton-Sycke is what you truly want, what will make you happy, then I will walk away."

"And hate me forever?"

"No." He kissed her, so lightly she wondered if it even happened, on her forehead, then dropped his hands. "No, I will always love you, always be a friend to you, no matter what you decide. But I think you should pick me, for surely no other man could ever love you as much as I do."

"But-but you are not the marrying kind," she said, her voice trembling.

"Not in the general sense, no," he said. "But I am the kind who wants to marry you. You have changed my opinion on the subject simply because I find I want to be with you all the time. Is that not what marriage should be? One finds the person who one wishes to spend time with above any other, the person to whom one is unafraid to show one's real self, the person of endless fascination...and then if it turns out one would like to tup that person as well, then it is as good as done."

"Saye..."

"I suppose it is rather badly done to use the word 'tup' in

a marriage proposal, hm? Forgive me. Just know that to me, you are the person I want to be with all the time, the person whose happiness…" He ran one finger along her cheek. "The person whose happiness means more to me than my own. No, I did not ever believe I would find such a person, but now I have, and it is you."

It was shockingly frank, delivered in the most grave, un-mocking tones she had ever heard from him. He stood before her, his mask discarded in every sense of the word, and the most astonishing of all notions came into her head. *He is in my power. I can make him happy in a way no other lady could.*

"Are you truly proposing to me?"

He smiled a little then and took both of her hands in his. In excessively formal accents, he said, "Miss Goddard, pray do me the very great honour of becoming my wife?"

Pure elated giddiness came into her chest, and her eyes blurred with tears. She was breathless and weightless all at once, and could not even speak the required syllable, sure she would burst if she did. So she nodded, vigorously, and then he pulled her into his chest, putting one finger beneath her chin and one arm tightly around her waist, while he kissed her.

He pulled away eventually, telling her, "My friend Gatto here has something for you."

Taking his mask, he removed the cat's collar; Lilly was shocked to realise it was a bracelet—a beautiful bracelet of diamonds and aquamarines—and that Saye intended to put it on her wrist. "This diamond right here?" He touched one finger to the largest gem. "That was the main stone on the engagement ring given to Miss Anne Stringer-Montagu by the very first earl of Matlock, John Fitzwilliam. The aqua-marines are for you, for your eyes."

It took her breath away to have such a piece of jewellery,

a part of his family history, already on her wrist. "But how did you do this? Have this made, I mean. When did you—"

"In London, the very day I thought of having this party," he replied with a cocksure grin.

With a laugh, she said, "You were very sure of getting what you wished for then!"

"Lilly." His voice had grown serious again. "What I was sure of was that if I did not have you, I would surely die trying."

When he uses that voice, my knees weaken, she thought, just as his lips met hers and made her feel utterly insensible once again.

NOTHING BUT THE TRUTH

Sarah & Fitzwilliam

S arah entered the ballroom alone. Her friends had offered her escort, and she appreciated their support, but she had teetered between avoiding the event utterly and eager anticipation; she simply did not know which sentiment would win out, and thus chose a solo entry, if she entered at all.

It was very late, crowds shifting amidst the smells of wax, sweat, and pomade, the music swelling as the dancing had long ago begun, laughter and the excitement of anonymity surrounding her. Unfortunately, her independence meant she could not identify her friends, and she was late enough that the crush would have made it difficult, even had they not been masked and costumed.

She was not unaware of the admiring gazes from masked harlequins, kings, and magicians, and did her best not to be self-conscious. The gauzy layers of her gown, draped artistically in a classical style, showed off her figure to advantage, she knew, even while her headdress seemed to discourage any approaches.

She had come this far but hesitated to go farther; she had

not even told him...*Richard*...whether or not she would come tonight. She was competent and spirited, but never had she been so at sea. Her only real experience in *l'amour* was with a single gentleman who might or might not be in love with another woman.

He had said he was not, and she knew he believed himself to be telling the truth. She was alarmed, however, by the intensity of her desire to believe it too. Would she turn a blind eye to an obvious mismatch in order to have him? He was a passionate man, but was that passion for her? Or was she merely a convenient receptacle for his unrequited feelings for another?

"Sarah!" a voice interrupted her thoughts, and she looked around for the speaker.

The tall, willowy, blonde female was swathed in forest green velvet, her mask a sculpted array of bronzed leaves with gilded edges, a matching sparkle of gold thread shining from within the intricate embroidery of her domino—a spectacular *Salix Babylonica*, a most distinctive tree in the landscape of lesser species surrounding her.

Georgette joined her, all smiles—a completely different demeanour from the last few days.

"You are happy!" Sarah blurted. "What has changed?"

"Me. I have taken the bull by the horns, so to speak." At Sarah's look of confusion, Georgette laughed. A gentleman in a formidable bull's mask loomed behind her. She glanced over her shoulder, smiled, and took the bull's hand.

"You must have been the only one who missed the excitement, Sarah. Mr Anderson has proposed marriage before the whole company, and I have accepted."

"Oh!" Sarah cried. "Why, this is wonderful! Surely your father will—"

"My father has already given his blessing," Georgette interrupted with an appraising glance at Sarah's costume. "I must admit, I almost did not recognise you. You were right not to wear the pink domino. You look far more exotic as you are. Deliciously wild."

Behind her, the bull—could it truly be Mr Anderson?—gave a small bow and added, "You look enchanting, Miss Bentley," which reminded Sarah that he had said he thought her handsome, and caused a blush.

"Has Fitzwilliam seen you?" Georgette enquired.

"If he has, he has not acknowledged me."

"He is dressed as Zeus, complete with a thunderbolt." Georgette turned back to her masked bull. "I saw Lilly leave the ballroom with Saye. I suspect she will soon be a bride as well. Has anyone seen Elizabeth? Someone said she had the headache."

The first notes of a waltz began to play, and Mr Anderson tugged her closer in a masterful manner. He plainly could not care less about the whereabouts of their friends, and Georgette seemed to forget her questions, and everything else, as he swept her onto the dance floor.

Georgette and Anderson. Lilly and Saye. Elizabeth and Darcy. They each, somehow, overcame every obstacle encountered on their paths to happiness. Is not a determination to confront your own problems the reason you chose this costume, Sarah? For courage?

Head high, she peered around more carefully. Thanks to Georgette's description, she soon found him, surrounded by a crowd of men and women, telling some story that was making everyone laugh. Wide shoulders, narrow hips, strong forearms bared beneath his white, short-sleeved tunic, he exuded masculine strength as well as bonhomie. The tunic's trims were golden like his mask, complemented by a swath of gold satin robing, exposing his muscular calves strapped in leather. Miss Barlowe, clad in the scanty costume of a shepherdess, was practically fondling the metallic thunderbolt at his side, staring up at him adoringly.

Sarah wore no mask, but Lady Aurelia's maid had painted her face in artistic layers of gold and bronze tints, adding paste stones that glistened eerily in a multi-hued gaze. Her headdress, however, was all Sarah's own work, made up of different coloured silks, each fashioned with a startling realism. The maid had shuddered to see it.

"I don't know as how ye'll convince many to dance with ye, miss," she had warned.

All for the better, Sarah had thought. Dancing was not her greatest skill; a light and pleasing delicacy would never be her strong suit. But now, nearly facing Colonel Richard Fitzwilliam, she wondered if she had made yet another mistake. He, undoubtedly, was a brilliant dancer, a master of every social grace.

Courage, Sarah. She stepped closer to the golden circle of his admirers.

His sharp gaze captured her at once. Appreciative eyes travelled up and down her form, widening slightly in surprise; a slight grin tugged at his lips. But it was Mr Withers—dressed quite unflatteringly, she thought, in jester's threads—who spoke first.

"Ho-ho! Thought you'd show up as a creepy-crawly of some sort! I was right, was I not?" He neighed his horsey laugh, joined in immediately by the ladies nearby, with Miss Barlowe's titters the loudest of all. Ignoring them, the colonel strode directly to her, reminding her startlingly of the god he portrayed, all power and light. He reached out to touch her headdress, smoothing his hand down one of the entwined figures covering it.

"Is this a warning to me?" he asked. "Will you turn my heart to stone?"

"I cannot tell if you are laughing at me behind your mask, as do your friends, or if you truly wish me to answer," she replied.

"I will never wear a mask with you," he said, startling her by wrenching his off and tossing it behind him. It clattered to the floor, bouncing off Miss Barlowe's starched petticoats. "Will you answer my question?"

"I have always admired Medusa," she replied obliquely. "Athena, a fabled beauty, could think of nothing worse than a scourge of ugliness, and yet, great power accompanied her curse. Medusa is foreign, forthright, and fearsome. Dangerous."

"Also, I would guess, you love snakes."

She grinned up at him. "I had a pet grass snake once. He was very pretty, yellow collared and every shade of green. He would rest coiled upon my neck and shoulders, which my young brother found impressive." Her smile faded. "But I began to worry he was unhappy, caged in London, when he belonged near forest and open sky. I brought him to Hampton's estate and released him. He is there still—only last spring, he greeted me on the banks of its biggest pond. They live for many years, you know."

"I did not know, but I am unsurprised that you do." He touched again one of the entwined serpents covering her head and shoulders. "Would you dance with me, Medusa?"

"Ah. Dancing." She shook her head. "My dancing master says I have two left feet, but Lilly claims it is only that I am so distracted by the music and beauty of the dance and the dancers, I forget to mind my patterns. Either way, your sandals will be safer with Miss Barlowe."

He laughed. "Have you ever tried a waltz? This one still has some life in it. Come." He put out his hand, and she could not think what else to do but take it. At the edge of the dance floor, he stopped. "There is only one imperative to enjoying a waltz. You must allow your partner to lead. You must have confidence that he will never tread on your toes or hurl you into other dancers. He will protect you, guide you, look after your happiness with every bit of strength he possesses. Even if you make a misstep, he will not falter or fade or fumble." He stared directly into her eyes. "Can you trust me?"

A dance was not all he wanted, and she knew it. But it was a start. A beginning. She set her hand upon his broad shoulder, resting her other in his own. She did not keep him at arm's length; she could feel the heat from his body. Consciously, she forced herself to allow him...admission to some secret, private sovereignty. To have faith in him...in them.

She succeeded for a few minutes, allowing him to whirl her through the other dancers. But just as she was thinking, '*This is so much fun, perhaps I am even good at this!*' she caught sight of the stares of women and men alike, their masks not disguising open-mouthed curiosity, frowns, perhaps disbelief. Abruptly, her feet tangled, and she would have tumbled them both to the floor, except that her partner was a man of strength, control and balance, a man who could not *be* tripped up.

He slowed his step, carefully leading her through a half-speed beat until she calmed. "Look at me, Sarah," he said. "Never mind the others. They do not exist. It is only you and me. It is only us."

Us. Only us. She took a deep breath, and then another. He made some signal she could not interpret to the orchestra's leader, and the rhythm of the waltz changed, slowed, lengthened like a lover's kiss. He lifted her chin an inch, so that he was gazing into her eyes before moving into the pattern of the dance.

Everything seemed to ease. The world became his dark-eyed stare, his whispered words.

"You are so lovely," he murmured. "You must promise never to waltz with another. I could not bear it."

"An easy promise to make," she replied. "Other men do not, precisely, line up for the privilege."

"Fools and idiots. Perhaps they have not looked yet, but they will. They will when they learn I have reserved the supper dance as yours—for I have never danced with a woman twice at any ball, ever in my life. They will when I lead you onto the floor a third time, for the final dance of this night. They will when I stare daggers at any of your other partners. They will when I call upon your father as soon as we return to London."

He led her through a series of twirls, each faster, more intricate, than the one before it. It did not matter; she simply allowed his power to flow through hers, his strength directing, guiding, her faith in him in every footstep.

"I will not keep you," she said, "if we cannot be happy."

"I have discovered that my happiness requires yours."

It was magic, that dance. After a time, she even closed her eyes, knowing he would never lose his way. As he promised, they were alone in the ballroom, the music the only other guest allowed within the bubble they inhabited. It lasted longer, she was sure, than any usual waltz, whether his signal to the musicians or her pure joy extended it. But at last, the music soared, then quieted, and then, finally, ceased.

When they stopped moving, she opened her eyes. The noise of the party resumed abruptly, as if they truly had been alone in the ballroom. He bowed, but she was too bewildered to curtsey.

"The supper dance is the set after next. It is mine?"

She nodded confusedly. He bowed again, and stalked away.

Fitzwilliam reached the desperately needed cold of the terrace in record time, inhaling deep breaths of the frozen air. The feel of her! The look in her eyes! And that dress, heavens almighty! The way she had softened in his arms, allowing him...well, suffice it to say that she was much too innocent to realise just what her body promised his. How long before she would agree to marry him? And then how lengthy a betrothal would she require?

Too late, he realised he was not alone. There stood his brother in the terrace shadows, wrapped around a domino-clad female as if he would consume her whole.

"Aurelia first, and now you," Saye sighed, straightening without letting go of his companion. "A rankling redundancy of relations."

"Miss Goddard?" Fitzwilliam asked, rather disturbed by his brother's blatant absence of discretion. "You are well?"

Saye smiled with a delight unusual to him. "You may congratulate us, Richard. Miss Goddard has agreed to become my viscountess."

"Excellent!" Fitzwilliam cried. "Well done, man. Miss Goddard, my felicitations. I could not be happier that you will take the risk."

"Risk! What risk?" Saye made only a faint protest, apparently unable to summon his customary pique. "That I shall be as ham-handed a husband as I have been a beau? Never! Lilly, my sweet, pray explain to my battle-hardened brother how you led me, most meekly, into the divine decadence of monogamy."

Lilly pulled away from his embrace, obviously trying for some dignity as she brushed rather futilely at the wrinkles in her domino. Fitzwilliam moved forward, his every instinct to put her at ease, and held out his hand.

"May I be the first to welcome you to the family, Miss Goddard. I promise you a brother's protection, as well as a complete catalogue of Saye's most embarrassing boyhood blunders, for use at your discretion any time henceforth. Battle-hardened, I may be, but you shall not enter wedlock weapon-less, upon my honour."

Miss Goddard smiled gently, accepting Fitzwilliam's kiss on her hand before submitting again to Saye's embrace.

"Never mind him, darling," Saye said dismissively, keeping his arm solicitously about her. "Now, tell me, Brother—what was this ramshackle barging onto the balcony all about? You galloped out here as if your toga was afire."

"Have you seen her tonight?" Fitzwilliam exclaimed. "Saye, she is enrapturing. Fascinating. And that costume she wears! Gauzy, silky thing. I fear a snow storm could not extinguish my—" He caught the astonished look upon Miss Goddard's face and abruptly shut his mouth. But Saye did not take the opportunity to condemn his coarseness, only sounding thoughtful.

"For the benefit of my bride-to-be, perhaps you ought to explain just who has sent you into such unusual transports of beguilement."

"Why, Miss Bentley, of course. The thing is, she—"

But Saye interrupted him, sounding...relieved? "Pray, spare us the details of your ardour as we have quite enough of our own to contemplate. Well, Mama will be delighted with two sons on the verge of matrimony. Sell your commission, and she will scarcely know where to look."

"I hope so, for we shall likely be joining her at Matlock, at least until we can—"

"Oh very well, I suppose you may have the Bridgelands estate. 'Tis but thirty miles of good road from Hampton's seat, and it is mine to give." Saye shrugged. "But do not dare whelp a boy before I do, or I shall never forgive you."

Fitzwilliam opened his mouth in shocked astonishment. "What? But Saye...I...I..." He swallowed, barely able to even comprehend this unlooked for generosity. Miss Goddard, however, found words for him.

"Oh, Saye, how wonderful you are!"

He smiled down upon her. "I am, rather, am I not?" His gaze turned stern. "You are to tell no one."

He glanced up from his betrothed. "I should probably point out—although as a decorated officer of His Majesty's army, one would think you capable of reaching this conclusion yourself—that if the sight of Miss Bentley out of her usual shapeless shades of bilious green has inspired your passion, it might so inspire others."

Saye, as usual, was correct. "An excellent point," Fitzwilliam replied, suddenly as eager to re-join the masque as he had formerly been to escape it. "Congratulations. Again. If there is anything I can do, ever, to—"

"Yes, yes," Saye waved him off. "You may start by disappearing. You are decidedly *de trop*."

Grinning, Fitzwilliam hastily made for the door, but he was only just reaching for it when Saye's voice halted him.

"I say, what costume did Miss Bentley choose?"

Fitzwilliam turned back, still smiling. "She is a golden-faced Medusa, with a hundred silky serpents braided into her hair. Magnificent."

From the dark came Saye's sigh. "You *would* think so. I suppose it is marginally better than appearing in my ballroom as a giant cockchafer."

Sarah's first instinct was to flee, as her colonel had. Was he as bewildered as she was? But no, that was impossible. She did not need to be experienced herself to recognise when a man knew what he was about. Had she been at home, she would have headed for the kitchen and calmed herself with kneading and mixing and simmering and baking, but if the Matlock cook was as high in the instep as its butler, she would never be welcome there.

To her left, she saw a man in a plain black domino heading her way with determined purpose—was it Mr Wigsby, or Mr Emerson, of equivalent weak chin? Neither of whom had ever before looked at her twice? The thought of pretending to enjoy either's company was beyond her. Quickly, she slipped behind a stand of potted trees, discovering a door on the other side, and upon opening it, found some sort of utility corridor for the ease of delivering trays to the ballroom. She unhesitatingly traversed it, fortunately encountering no one. At a juncture, she listened; the noises of busy servants sounded to her left, so she took the right turning. At length, she found herself in a well-lit vestibule she had never before seen, probably a side entrance for use by the family. It should be easy enough to find her way to the front of the house again from here, but there was a low, cushioned chair and a perfect emptiness that appealed to her frayed senses.

With a deep sense of relief, she sat and simply...remembered. Remembered that first hum of attraction, the many ways she had talked herself out of it, and the many times he had returned to haunt her feelings again and again. His kisses, of course, spiked her every sense, but it was more than that. That entire carriage ride back from the pleasure gardens, they had talked, learning about and coming to know each other—she, agreeing to call him 'Richard', and he, expressing delight at hearing his name upon her lips. The drive had seemed mere moments.

If she paired with the colonel again on that dance floor, she was as much as announcing her acceptance of his suit. Should she?

She was startled from her thoughts by the opening of the heavy door, bringing with it a rush of cold air. To her surprise, Elizabeth and Mr Darcy, clothed in simple dominos, carrying their masks, entered, both laughing at some private joke, his eyes on hers, her eyes bright with mirth and love, and she with the look of a woman who has recently been thoroughly kissed.

That is what I want, Sarah thought. Neither of them noticed her, so rapt were they in each other. She stood.

"Sarah!" Elizabeth started, hand at her throat. "How you surprised me!"

"Miss Bentley," Mr Darcy said, bowing, suddenly again grave and severe as ever.

"Pardon me," Sarah said. "I think I am a bit lost—"

"Easily done in this old pile," Mr Darcy hastened to assure. "We can show you the way back to the ballroom."

"No. I mean, yes, that too, but...I have a question, and I think you are likely the only one who can answer it. Your cousin—Colonel Fitzwilliam, that is—has declared his intentions. And what I want to know...to the best one can know anything, I suppose, is...do you trust him? I mean, not do you trust Elizabeth *with* him, because of course she is eminently trustworthy, and besides, everyone can see she only has eyes for you. But him...just...Richard. Your cousin. Your friend, or he was once. I am sorry to be so bold but beg you to be honest with me, for if I turn away now, I shall still be able to find happiness. If I allow myself to love him, however, as I am capable of loving him..." she trailed off, her cheeks blazing with embarrassment beneath the gold paint, barely managing to hold Mr Darcy's gaze.

He looked at her for long moments, his eyes dark and fathomless. She could not read that look, and never would be able to. Elizabeth, she noted, quietly placed her hand upon his arm, saying nothing, allowing him his answer, whatever it might be. Sarah hardly dared breathe.

"Yes," he said at last, and paused. "With my life. With my life, and with my...with Elizabeth's. You are safe with him."

Sarah felt her smile begin at the top of her serpent-covered head and travel all the way to the tips of her toes—she had not, until this moment, known a smile *could* fill every corner of her being, every nook and cranny. Her face was far too small to contain it.

"Thank you!" she exclaimed, just as a nearby clock began to chime the hour. "Thank you so much. Oh, Elizabeth, I am very glad your megrim did not keep you away. If you will pardon me—I believe it is time for the supper dance, and...I think I can find my own way, after all."

Fitzwilliam was nearly frantic. He had been searching everywhere, and Sarah was nowhere to be found. No one had seen her, and since her costume was so very distinctive, he had the sinking feeling she had left the masque altogether. Had he scared her off? Been over-bold?

It was only that he had already wasted so much time! Never had he met a woman so unique, so interesting, so courageous—it would take him a lifetime to learn her, a life that would never be dull. Added to that, she had a softness, a womanliness he could lose himself in...it was simply not in his nature to hesitate or waver once he had made up his mind. And his mind and heart wanted Sarah Bentley.

A horrifying thought occurred to him. Had one of these masked 'fools and idiots' borne her away? If anyone had hurt her, he would find him and he would kill him, and no one would ever find the body. A home, an estate of his own—

none of it would matter if Sarah were not there to share it with him.

Until the start of the supper dance, he held out hope that she was merely biding her time until its beginning. Cursing himself for ever letting her from his sight in the first place, he had just decided he would interrogate Sarah's maid, when his lost Medusa burst into the ballroom as if she had been running. Unfortunately, it was the wrong side of the ball-room, with fifty couples impeding his path to her.

They could not stop him.

With single-eyed purpose, he stalked through patterns and upended pairings. It was also possible that in the disrup-tion he 'accidentally' tripped Reggie Withers, causing him to fall face-first onto Miss Barlowe, producing a costume malfunction of vastly embarrassing proportions. He did not stay to watch it, only moved ever closer to his goal.

Sarah held still, simply waiting for him, beaming a sunny, funny, wickedly clever, and deeply innocent ray of light and goodness—all while wearing a dress designed to bring him to his knees. At long last, he reached her, taking both her hands in his.

"I cannot go down on bended knee, for I have not yet spoken to your father," he said. "I would not insult you by failing to do the thing correctly. But I want everyone here to know that I am yours. May I shout it from the rafters?"

He followed Sarah's gaze and glanced at the havoc behind him, where dancers were struggling to re-form their circles, Withers limped off the floor covering his eye, and Miss Barlowe, flanked by Aurelia and Miss Hilgrove, was being quickly escorted from the room.

"I think you already have," Sarah replied.

"Shall we dance?" he asked. She nodded, and he gave the conductor—a good comrade whose pockets he had already lined—another signal, this one meaning, 'Forget whatever dance *was called, make it a waltz instead, and do it now'.* The musicians, with hardly a missed beat, slipped into the slower tune. Most of the dancers—barely regrouped from his previous disruption—were confused, and there was some stumbling, commotion, and a loudly voiced complaint from Miss Fisher. But he thought he heard Saye's laughter.

And then she was in his arms, still smiling, and he felt that smile reach into his scarred heart and make itself a home there.

Wherever she was, from this time forward, would always be home.

A LOSS
IS A WIN

Darcy & Elizabeth

"Mrs Darcy, you look enchanting in your hood. Must you wear anything else?"

"I believe I must, Mr Darcy. It is close to an hour's drive from Pemberley to Matlock." Elizabeth gathered the red folds of her domino and leant over to kiss his nose. "I have had enough of your covetous looks. You have what you wanted," she added warmly as she entwined their hands. "I am yours, and you are mine."

It was true, rendered formal and done. She smiled—her face should ache from so much happiness—as the memories of the past two days flitted through her mind. The nearly wild carriage ride to Pemberley, with Robbins and Darcy's manservant doing their best to ignore Darcy's visible impatience; her brief, wholly embarrassing meetings with Mrs Reynolds and the vicar; and the short, sweet ceremony that united them as man and wife. And then these precious hours spent alone exploring, mapping, and claiming one another. She would meet the servants as their mistress when they returned in June. For now, Elizabeth was a new wife, a new lover, and nothing else could be required of her.

"Red Riding Hood and the Huntsman...pray do you not prefer me to be your wolf?"

"You would give leave to everyone to tease you? I think not." Elizabeth glanced at Robbins climbing into the second, smaller carriage before she stepped into their own.

Darcy took a basket and warmed blanket from a footman then climbed in next to her. Elizabeth gave her husband an appraising look. "What is this? You cannot be the wolf to my Red Riding Hood, so you would dress as my grandmother instead? Should we ask Mrs Reynolds to find you a shawl to complete the ensemble?"

Darcy chuckled and proceeded to spread the blanket across their laps, leisurely tucking it around Elizabeth's hips and feet. "I shall dress as you command. I am certain nothing I wear will outshine Saye. Nor should it. He will be in some magnificent get-up, a turban or crown upon his head."

"Not so *outré*, as I believe he may wish to match with Lilly."

"For his sake, I hope her wish is the same. He has proposed to her as many times as I have proposed to you, and has not received the happy answer he assumed would be easy to win."

"Has he not?" Her lips quirked, repressing any comparison between memories of the tousled-haired, half-dressed man who had claimed her for a lifetime and his perfectly coiffed, impeccably natty—and titled—cousin. Every man had flaws and vulnerabilities; it was showing them, softening themselves, that could earn a lady's trust and win her heart. Darcy had greater depths and gravitas than she had yet seen in Saye, but it was not she who must see those qualities; it was Lilly who needed it. "Saye is a man of no small confidence—"

"Conceit," replied Darcy as he rapped on the carriage roof to begin their journey.

"Yes, your cousin is proud, but so is Lilly. She deserves a proposal of love, from his truest self."

"Unrequited love is difficult enough—it cannot be long hidden behind a mask." His words prompted Elizabeth to sigh and lean her head against his shoulder. "Saye knows what he is about."

"As do you," she whispered, "and thus, you have been my husband more than a full day."

"Has it been full?" He gave her a mischievous smile and slid his hand underneath the blanket. "I think we must fill up more of this day."

Elizabeth put a hand on his chest. "You may not undo Robbins's hours of work. I am to be the innocent Red Riding Hood, and not even my mask would disguise the effects of being thoroughly kissed and ravaged."

"You have only proven yourself more enticing, my dear lady of the woods."

"We must arrive looking respectable. It is enough that your servants—"

"*Our* servants."

"—must think us the madcap master and mistress of Pemberley, arriving in haste and disappearing behind closed doors for the entirety of our brief visit."

"I do not pay my servants to gossip. If we must be alliterative, they will think us markedly in love to mizzle off from Matlock and marry." Darcy's silly grin turned earnest when he asked whether it was the servants or the guests at Matlock she most considered. They planned no grand announcement of the nuptials, only a quiet whisper to their closest friends and relations there.

Elizabeth returned his smile. "Everyone there will see that I am the happiest creature in the world. Perhaps other people have said so before, but not one with such justice. My father will see I am happier even than Jane—she only smiles, while I laugh. And it is with you that I laugh, and he will have to accept your position as paramount in my heart. Whatever lessons he hoped you and I would learn through distance, while unnecessary—"

"As well as petty and cruel."

"—are ones *he* will be forced to learn now that Longbourn is no longer my home."

Darcy's nod affirmed his agreement.

"I am not the sentimental lady that Jane is, nor one who collects keepsakes of ribbons and cards like Kitty. I spent my final days at Longbourn wishing only to leave there, to be married to you. My wishes have come to happy fruition. I have left my home to join yours and will only see it again through the eyes of a wife. My former home. Forgive my slow-dawning recognition."

"Do you regret it?"

"Never."

"Of course, in my letters, I shall assure my mother, as often as needed, that Mr Darcy sends all the love in the world that he can spare from me."

"There will be none to spare! None for her nor anyone else, except, of course, Georgiana."

She held up her hand and began counting on her fingers. "And my sisters—most of them. And the Gardiners. And your horse and dogs."

"'Tis a good thing I have an enormous heart." He exhaled heavily, prompting Elizabeth to giggle. "And a very large estate," he added, smirking as her eyes widened, "into which the two of us might escape when our families descend upon us."

It was just above an hour later, the moon full in the night sky, that the Pemberley party descended from their carriages.

Darcy and Elizabeth watched their servants—sworn to secrecy about their short disappearance—move off towards the kitchens for a warm meal. The music swelled from Matlock's ballroom yet was nearly drowned out by the hum of voices and laughter. Clearly Saye and Lady Aurelia had invited everyone within thirty miles, he thought, completely uncaring about the crush of the crowd.

"With the smiles we are wearing, it will be the work of a moment until we are found out," said Elizabeth.

"I have long anticipated being found out."

"Then we had best join the party. We have been missing these past two days, and I wish to dance with my husband before supper."

"I should have carried you off that very night. Instead, I am pleased at how joyfully you have been received. Not surprised, of course," he added as he caught her bemused smile. "Only you could charm Sir Phineas, and confound Saye with your intelligent advice about pleasing a woman by being the man she believes you should be."

"Let us hope he listened to the advice you gave him."

"My cousin is a skilled actor. Like his brother, he does not wish for a constant display of his kindness and decency." Darcy sighed at her expectant expression. "I shall not walk away when Fitzwilliam approaches me. I shall accept his apologies, as well as his congratulations, when I reveal to him our news." Taking note of her pleased smile, he shrugged. "He remains my closest friend and relation, and I wish to be the one to inform him."

"I am glad, and though I prefer that you remain the happiest man in the world, he might have news to impart to you as well."

His puzzlement disappeared under the warmth of a kiss,

cut short when Elizabeth's stomach rumbled. She gave him a rueful look and laughed. "'Tis your fault! Cook's basket went unopened."

He joined in her laughter. "We were too well-occupied to eat, dear wife."

"Sarah!"

Elizabeth smiled as Miss Bentley disappeared down the corridor. "Well, we enter changed from who we were when we were last here, and I suspect we shall find our friends changed as well."

"Apparently."

She held her red silk mask to her face as Darcy tied the ribbons to hold it in place. Then he lowered his own mask, a gleaming black shield with a thick gold brow as its only orna-mentation. Elizabeth placed her arm in his as they walked through the velvet draping the grand hall, past harlequins holding feathered staffs or juggling, and potted shrubs carved to resemble cats and cherubs, and entered the cacophonous ballroom. Some sort of commotion had occurred—Darcy led Elizabeth around at least one trampled mask and what appeared to be a leopard's tail—pausing the music long enough for them to join the other dancing couples. He saw Fitzwilliam's solid frame gripping tightly to some sort of iridescent Medusa and beyond them, espied two cats, one of them clearly Saye; no mask could hide his satisfied hauteur. As he swept Elizabeth in their direction, they were found out —undoubtedly due to Darcy's height or his bride's happy glow—and commanded to join their host and the small coterie of the house party standing nearby, awaiting supper.

Saye, of course, had the first word. "There you are at

last." He flicked a cursory glance over them both. "I must say I expected you were seeking to build my anticipation and had imagined something extraordinary, but you arrive as a lovelorn crow and a redbird."

"I am not a crow," replied Darcy with no small amount of indignation. He despised masquerades, but Elizabeth was enchanted by them.

A man in a green feathered mask—Clarke, he suspected—barked a rattling laugh. "Of course you are not, but you did fly off and abandon us, Darcy. Just as Anderson did."

A radiant Miss Goddard, costumed as a cat, said quietly, "He returned and created a scene with Georgette."

Elizabeth looked delighted at the news. Darcy watched as they fell into a quiet conversation punctuated by giggles and sighs. He turned to Saye. "It was a happy scene, I trust?"

"Darcy, this party will be spoken of in London all Season, see if it is not! Aurelia has established herself as a noted hostess, all thanks to me, and everyone you see is leaving much improved over what sorry states they arrived in." Saye gave a self-satisfied smirk, but behind it, Darcy perceived an unusual contentment.

"I cannot disagree."

"Hawkridge has agreed Georgette may wed Anderson. As a connoisseur of repulsive creatures, Miss Bentley has formed an attachment to my brother, and..." He smiled, looking silly and self-conscious. "Lilly has at last succumbed to my considerable charms."

"You finally managed it. Congratulations." As he shook Saye's hand, Darcy's smile turned wry. "Fitzwilliam and Miss Bentley, eh?"

"Love is all the fashion, and my brother has at last stopped fighting it off."

"I am pleased for him. For them." Darcy's smile returned, and he quickly felt himself under Saye's scrutiny.

"And you...there is something different about you." Saye's eye roamed him and Darcy fought the urge to squirm. "You have tasted the pleasures of connubial bliss! In my mother's home!"

"I have done no such thing."

Darcy watched as Saye turned to look at Elizabeth, now halfway across the room with Miss Goddard, Lady Aurelia, Sir Phineas, and a smattering of other masked guests. She was luminous, her joyful spirit affecting even the usually sombre man, who was actually laughing aloud, in a roomful of people half his age, many of whom he likely disdained. Darcy's heart soared; if he had had his wits about him, he might have questioned the possibility that his heart could grow fuller. As the music ebbed, he caught the sound of her laugh and smiled, somehow prompting Elizabeth to turn and meet his gaze. Darcy did not need Saye to tell him he looked like a fool in love; it was a palpable, constant warmth thrumming through him.

"You are married."

He grinned. "Elizabeth insisted."

"And you are a man who knows when to lose an argument."

"Only to her."

Suddenly Sir Phineas stood before him.

"I enjoy conviviality as much as the next man, but it is an unfortunate development if a man such as you is reduced to a silly giggling ninny. I had my doubts about the leading strings your lady had attached to your trouser snake, but I must say, you have done well. I like your Mrs Darcy."

After it was evident her supper plate was filled to her satisfaction, Darcy bent his lips to Elizabeth's ear and gestured across the table to Miss Goddard and Miss Bentley, the latter smiling at Elizabeth with some urgency. "Your friends have been abandoned by their lovers and are in need of your guidance as the happiest married lady in the land."

Laughing, she replied, "You, too, have a friend eager for conversation." He followed her gaze, turning to find Fitzwilliam watching them with poorly disguised interest.

After carrying their plates over to empty seats by the ladies, Darcy sauntered over to his white-robed cousin. He dipped his head in greeting, but his eyes remained on Elizabeth, lighting up with pleasure as her new friends grasped her hands.

Fitzwilliam nodded. His eyes, too, were captured by the ladies. "You are returned."

"Indeed, only to learn I am to wish you joy." Darcy was amused by the speed of the blush that overtook his cousin's face.

"You must think me a great fool."

"No, I know you are a great fool."

"Right. And you are a great master of stealing away. I have sought you out the past two days."

"It is not my place to judge your tracking skills, but I was much occupied with Elizabeth."

Fitzwilliam cleared his throat. "To whom I *did* apologise."

"You grovelled, and rather effectively." Darcy crossed his arms. "She is satisfied with you."

"And are you? I owe you an apology as well."

Darcy sighed and finally turned to face his cousin. "Accepted, but I must protest your aim. Was it necessary to strike my face—to bruise my lip—when I am in company with Elizabeth?"

"It has been awkward, I am sure." Fitzwilliam looked more amused than chagrined.

"A bit, although we share a talent for improvisation."

Fitzwilliam snorted. "Well, then. She does seem quite pleased with the evening, and more than pleased in your company." He paused and then spoke his regrets in a torrent of words. "I was in the wrong, mean-spirited and foolhardy. She is more than content in your company, and in my own struggles to determine my path, I selfishly interfered in your courtship. From the look of things, there has been no lasting harm."

Darcy gave him a grave look. "You are mistaken if you think your jibes at me and your ridiculous efforts to monopolise her company had no effect on us."

"What do you mean? She—you—I see only happy looks exchanged between you both!"

Darcy's silence prompted Fitzwilliam to speak more forcefully.

"I am the last man in the world who should make an appeal to Miss Bennet on your behalf, but if—"

"Her name is Mrs Darcy, you dolt." Darcy broke into a broad smile. "I did as you advised. We are wed."

"Oho! You old dog! Congratulations!" Fitzwilliam clapped him on the shoulder. "You made off and made her your wife? I knew it!"

"Did you?"

"I hoped," he said, shrugging. "I did not hit you hard enough to scare you away."

Darcy held out his hand and firmly gripped the one his cousin extended in return. "A few blows knocked sense into both of us. And I am happy, albeit surprised, for you and Miss Bentley." He lowered his voice as a small group of masked revellers passed by them. "I am nearly five years younger than Saye and the first to the altar. I hope you and your lady will move with some haste so we can ruffle his fine feathers by both being first to the nursery as well."

"Miss Elizabeth Bennet? An express has come for you."

"Just this moment?"

Elizabeth's breathless response appeared to startle the young footman, whose blushing cheeks indicated he had not much experience with masquerades, debauched society, or any of Saye's eccentricities. He stood just around the corner from the ladies' retiring room, averting his eyes from the low bodices seen in nearly every direction.

"Yes, Miss. It was delivered not five minutes ago. I came as fast as I could, what with the crowds and such."

He bowed and fled as soon as Elizabeth took the letter from the salver. Seeing the handwriting, she moved down the corridor to Darcy.

"Elizabeth?"

She showed him the handwriting. Mr Bennet, known to set aside the post for days or weeks, had rallied himself to reply to Elizabeth's news.

Lizzy,

Your letter, which I hoped would bring welcome relief from dull company, has only worsened the excessive vexation I presently endure in my own home. Your mother, you see, returned from Bletchley five days ago, in quite a state of hysteria. Reading poetry to a cow has consequences—in this case, a pox of some kind on dear Aunt Boothe's person. Mrs Bennet fled, and upon her arrival at Longbourn without you, assured me of your health and safety—not amongst the pox-ridden, but at a house party in Derbyshire. How sly are the ladies of Longbourn.

Mr Darcy is in possession of a good fortune, a man whom I dared not refuse nor, it now is apparent, delay. Your expectations for felicity and understanding in marriage are higher than most; Mr Darcy is as determined in his love for you as I, and therefore I wish you joy.

I shall address you by your married name when you return to Longbourn—which you must do if only to claim your bonnets from your sisters, allow your mother the opportunity to exhibit you to the neighbours, and provide me some recompense for bearing up through these past few days of deafening joy.

Yours &c.

T Bennet

"A blessing, of sorts," she said quietly, handing the letter to Darcy. "There is a note on the back intended for you."

Darcy kissed her temple and held the paper where they both could read it.

Mr Darcy,

While Bingley will likely amuse me more, and Wickham will please me merely by his absence, do not set aside your hope of becoming my favourite son-in-law. After all, I have heard much of Pemberley's library and expect to enjoy its riches.

T Bennet

He chuckled. "Your father's disinterest in business surprises me, for he certainly understands the importance of striking a bargain agreeable to all sides."

Elizabeth placed her hand on the black domino covering her husband's chest, feeling the steady beat of his heart underneath the fine woven cloth. "There is nothing more agreeable than this, you and I, together as husband and wife, united by love of the deepest kind."

PERFECTLY
WELL-MATCHED

Georgette & Anderson

B y the time Georgette and Anderson returned to the
party, the ballroom was more than half empty. A
footman was petitioned for information, and their
attention directed to the crowded veranda.

"It must be time for the fireworks!" Georgette grabbed
Anderson's hand and tugged him towards the doors, going
not onto the teeming veranda but a smaller, less public
balcony. It was not as high up as it had seemed when she was
little, but it gave a superior view and, as she had expected, it
was not unoccupied.

"There you are!" Lilly held out her hand and pulled Georgette to the parapet.

"Georgette! Where have you been?" Sarah asked.

Fitzwilliam, on Sarah's other side, said, "I think it might
be better not to enquire, dearest."

Georgette raised an eyebrow. "Dearest, is it? My, my, we
must have been gone longer than I thought."

Whatever her cousin replied was drowned beneath the
deafening crash of the first firework and a loud chorus of
gasps from those gathered below.

Georgette did not need to hear his words to discern his happiness—or Sarah's. She spoke over her shoulder to Anderson. "They are engaged!"

Anderson grinned and turned to shake hands with Fitzwilliam, then bowed to Sarah. "Happiness looks exceedingly well on you, Miss Bentley."

Georgette rolled her eyes when her friend nervously licked her lips. "You really must practise accepting compliments, Sarah. You cannot grimace so every time someone remarks on your beauty. I am sure my cousin will oblige you with some flattery."

A succession of screeching rockets lit up the sky, commanding everybody's attention. Amid the distraction, Georgette caught Lilly's eye and mouthed, "Does Mr Darcy know?"

Lilly nodded. Leaning backwards, she pointed beyond Saye, standing on her other side, to the far end of the balcony. Georgette peered around them both, and there were Elizabeth and Mr Darcy. Elizabeth waved merrily.

"She looks extraordinarily pleased with herself," Georgette said as she waved back.

"She ought to—she has just got married!"

"Faith! How long was I gone? I thought I only missed supper."

The next several fireworks were so loud that even shouts could not be heard, but at length, Lilly was able to explain. "They stole away to Pemberley two days ago. None of us noticed because we were all too busy being miserable."

"They came back to see my fireworks, which you are both missing, thanks to your endless chatter," Saye complained, though without any hint of true vexation in his voice.

Even had Georgette not learnt of his engagement earlier, she would have guessed by the gleam of heartfelt delight in his eyes. For once, she could not tease him, not when it was the happiest she had ever seen him. When Anderson stepped close to wrap her in his arms and kiss her temple, it was the happiest she had ever felt.

The finale to the fireworks was truly spectacular. Over and again, the night sky was rendered incandescent as an endless stream of rockets shrieked into the air, every one exploding into glittering cascades of light. The final, vast explosion was accompanied by a roar of approval from below that gradually ebbed into enraptured silence. As Georgette joined everyone in watching the illuminations fade, she realised it was not the last embers raining from the sky that she could see.

"It is snowing!"

For a few magical moments, time stood still as snowflakes danced about on the frozen air before them.

Then Saye swore, and all hell broke loose.

"What is wrong?" Sarah exclaimed.

Fitzwilliam gestured to the veranda where what could only be described as an exodus was occurring. Guests were elbowing each other, masks were being crushed under foot, and the ballroom doors looked in imminent danger of being torn off their hinges as people fought their way through.

Saye gave his brother a none-too-gentle shove towards the door. "Find Aurelia before those idiots cause a stampede."

"What is happening?" Elizabeth asked.

"Everyone is leaving before they are snowed in," Darcy replied. "This is why balls are not generally held at this time of year in the peaks. I ought to help."

"Never a dull moment with your cousins, is there?" Anderson muttered to Georgette before offering to accompany Darcy.

As the two men departed, Anderson began expressing his thanks for what Darcy had done for him, and before they exited the balcony, they could be seen shaking hands. Georgette answered Elizabeth's querying gaze with an explanation of what her new husband had done to help secure their engagement.

Elizabeth gave an unsteady smile. "I had no idea, though I cannot say I am surprised. It is not the first time he has helped bring two people in love back together."

"And now it is your turn—I hear congratulations are in order."

"Thank you. And to you, too, on your engagement."

"Georgette?" Sarah interrupted. "Where *have* you been all evening?"

"I think Fitzwilliam was right—we would do better not to ask," Lilly replied with a sly glance at Georgette. "I am coming to understand that our darling friend has more secrets than any of us ever suspected."

They would have been disappointed to know the truth. It was true that Georgette and Anderson had enjoyed their share of clandestine rendezvous—they had been eluding scandal longer than the rest of her friends had been in love— but that evening, they had occupied themselves with the simple pleasure of conversation.

Having been plagued with uncertainty for the entirety of their acquaintance, they had never dared to make any serious plans. Always, they skirted around matters any other affianced couple might consider pedestrian—where they might summer, what colour they might decorate the drawing room, what they might call their children. The freedom to discuss such things without the fear that they would never come to pass felt like the most exquisite indulgence.

Georgette's felicity notwithstanding, she did not consider it imperative to disclose all her confidences in the course of one house party. With a vague smirk, she said, "And we must be allowed to keep our secrets, Lilly, otherwise I should be insisting that you explain how my cousin's chamber pot ended up in your bedchamber last week."

The snow had manners enough to allow everybody who was not staying at Matlock to depart in a timely and, with one or two exceptions, orderly fashion. After that, it blanketed the surrounding fells so that the following day, the view from every window was a glistening wintry vista. Despite the early end to proceedings the previous evening, the house was still quiet at noon.

Anderson had never much cared for lounging abed while there was daylight left of which to take advantage. Thus, after a few words in the right ears amongst the servants, and a little time directing his man to persuade Georgette's maid to rouse her mistress and dress her warmly, he arrived at the top of the slope behind Matlock with his beautiful bride-to-be and a rather ropey-looking toboggan.

"Are you certain that is safe?" Georgette enquired dubiously.

"No. I shall go first, if you like, to test its strength."

"I did not come all this way in the freezing cold to go second!" She playfully nudged him out of the way so she could take her place, then squawked when the toboggan began sliding down the hill before she had properly seated herself. "I could be tucked up in my nice warm bed like all the other sensible ladies, you know."

Anderson crouched behind the toboggan to hold it steady. "But you are not, and that is why I love you. Ready?" At her nod, he gave the toboggan a shove. It slid forwards slowly at first, then quickly gathered momentum until it was sliding away from him at an alarming pace.

When Georgette shrieked, Anderson began to run after her, but she was travelling too fast, and in the blink of an eye, the toboggan hit a rise, twisted violently to one side, and threw her off. The air was instantly filled with her laughter, and Anderson's heart, already hammering its alarm, swelled with affection as he skidded down next to her.

"Are you hurt?"

She shook her head and accepted his help getting up and patting the snow off her coat. "No, and I have discovered the toboggan is perfectly sound. It only wants for somebody who is able to steer it."

"Will you leave it to me to teach our children to drive?"

"Yes—if you leave it to me to teach them to shoot."

"We have an accord, madam."

"Come, then, sir. You had better prove yourself a worthy master." Georgette picked up the leading rope and began pulling the toboggan back up the slope.

Anderson took it from her. "Will you be disappointed if I do not fall off as well?"

"You are only saying that so that if you do, you can claim it was done for my benefit."

He did not fall off, and Georgette rewarded him richly for his success when he re-joined her at the top of the rise.

"Are there any hills near Gilchester Hall steep enough to sledge on?" she enquired.

"Plenty. And Glastonbury Tor is close by, which is always full of people whenever there is snow."

"Is Gilchester warm? I cannot abide a draught."

He smiled tenderly at her, delighted to hear her speak so eagerly about their life together. "The house shall be as warm as you wish it to be, my love. And painted whatever colour pleases you and filled with as many children as you choose. I shall be content regardless of any detail, as long as you are there with me."

She kissed him, but it did not last long before they were interrupted by shouting from farther down the slope.

"Look at that! Brazen, the pair of them!"

"Certainly not the sport I envisaged when I was told they had come up here to play in the snow!"

They broke apart and looked down the hill. A small army of people was making its way towards them, Saye and Fitzwilliam at its lead. They were closely followed by Mr and Mrs Darcy, Miss Goddard, and Miss Bentley. Behind them came several servants, pulling more toboggans, all loaded with supplies.

"What are you doing here?" Georgette called. Anderson could easily discern her delight. She wore joy like jewellery—only he had yet to see her wear a diamond that enhanced her beauty as well her own smile.

"A little bird told me you were up here, tobogganing without us," Saye replied.

"Do you mind, Georgette?" asked Miss Goddard. "I am sorry if we have interrupted, only it sounded such fun."

"Of course we do not mind," Georgette replied. "But you will have to be braver than you were when my brother took you for a ride in his curricle. 'Tis fast going down—I have already fallen off once."

Saye looked positively aghast. "Lilly, I absolutely *forbid* you from riding in my cousin's curricle ever again. Hawk is an oaf who cannot drive to save his life."

"My brother is not an oaf," Georgette objected.

It was a sentiment with which Anderson could not entirely agree. "Saye is right, though—he cannot drive for toffee. It must be a family failing."

Georgette pouted, but Fitzwilliam laughed heartily and slapped Anderson on the shoulder. "You've the measure of your new family, it seems. Welcome aboard."

A glib observation, but it provoked Anderson to ponder

the truth of it. Georgette saw her brothers but rarely, yet he could foresee that he would be spending a good deal more time in the present company.

"Come on then, Georgette," Miss Bentley announced, already gamely tugging one of the toboggans into position. "First to the bottom wins."

Georgette took a moment to glance warmly at Anderson and squeeze his arm, then she was off, teasing her friend as she took the advantage on the descent.

There were five toboggans between them, and after some hasty jostling, Georgette and Miss Bentley were followed down the hill by Mrs Darcy, her husband, and Fitzwilliam. Anderson watched in amusement for a moment, but when he turned to remark on the latter two's repeated attempts to unseat each other, he was arrested by what he saw.

Saye and Miss Goddard were quietly engaged in directing the servants, who were laying out food and mugs of steaming hot drink on a table. Anderson smiled. Saye certainly played the part of lord of the manor well. There was no doubt he played it subtly, when he thought nobody was looking, but Anderson had seen the viscount's true colours the night he chased him down to deliver his unforgettable set down at the Pig & Feathers. Veiled as a jape and couched in exhibition and foppery, Saye's intolerance for any injury to his family had nevertheless been unmistakable.

He was a deeply loyal and deceptively astute man, but above all else, his generosity in patronising the institute in Golder's Green marked him as a good one. Indeed, Anderson's previous opinion of him—a spoilt, dandified creature with little interest in anything but his own pleasure—might have shamed him, had he not been convinced it was a reputation Saye had taken pains to cultivate himself.

Miss Goddard noticed him looking then, and with a conscious smile, brought him one of the mugs of mulled wine. "This was a wonderful idea. I hope you do not mind us obtruding on your time with Georgette."

"Since your future husband has secured Georgette and me all the time together we could wish for, I am hardly likely to begrudge him—or his lovely future wife—a few hours of our company."

"Will you marry soon, do you think?"

"As soon as we are able."

"You had better not marry before me, Anderson. It is galling enough that Darcy has pipped me at the post," said Saye, coming to join them.

"We shall have our turn soon enough," Miss Goddard said, attaching herself to Saye's arm and grinning up at him.

There was something in the way she addressed him, part diverted, part placating, that persuaded Anderson she would make him the ideal wife. She appeared to have seamlessly stepped into her place at Saye's side, her demure fortitude the perfect foil for his outlandish ways.

"We plan to return to London as soon as the weather allows, and marry from there," she told Anderson.

Before he could reply, the slope was overrun as the others returned, the ladies laughing, and Darcy and Fitzwilliam complaining breathlessly. Anderson chuckled to see the pair of them had lugged all five toboggans back up the hill between them in a show of gallantry they looked very much to be regretting.

"Why have you done that?" Saye enquired.

"Manners," Fitzwilliam panted. "A foreign concept to you, I know."

"I have manners, little brother. What is more, I have foresight. Or did you think I brought John up here to titillate the ladies with his winsome smile?" He pointed at one of the footmen.

"Bah! You might have sent him down a bit sooner, then!"

Fitzwilliam tossed his fistful of leading ropes to the ground and stalked off, returning with a drink in hand.

It was Saye's turn to race Miss Goddard, and Georgette and Miss Bentley insisted on another turn, apparently having crashed into each other on their first run. Mr and Mrs Darcy went to fetch themselves drinks, leaving Anderson and the colonel alone.

Anderson raised his mug in cheers. "Miss Goddard informs me she and Saye mean to marry in town. Will you and Miss Bentley do likewise?"

"We shall stay here until my parents return. Miss Bentley means to invite her father and brother to visit so we might all become acquainted. Then I daresay we might marry from The Pillows."

Anderson raised an eyebrow. "Are you sure Miss Bentley would not prefer a more traditional order of events?"

"What—oh!" The colonel gave an abrupt bark of laughter. "The Pillows is old Wendell Bentley's house in town. Stupid name, I quite agree."

Anderson was still attempting to recall Miss Bentley's connexions when Fitzwilliam cleared his throat and spoke again. "I must thank you for your counsel that day we rode out. I may not have heeded it immediately, but it did, in the end, help direct my resentment in the proper direction. You are a decent man, Anderson. I shall be proud to call you my cousin."

"Thank you," he replied, taken aback by the colonel's forthrightness even as he appreciated it. "The sentiment is mutual, I assure you."

"Right then," Fitzwilliam said brusquely. "Are you as good on a toboggan as you are on a horse?"

"Are you hoping to beat me again?"

"Thought I might try."

They were obliged to wait briefly for another toboggan,

but it was soon discovered that neither man could claim any of the same prowess in the snow as they could in the saddle. Anderson reached the bottom first—but without his toboggan. The colonel ended up tangled in his halfway down the slope, much to Miss Bentley's amusement.

Anderson pulled his own toboggan back up the hill, his chest heaving by the time he reached the top.

"We are too old for this," Darcy complained, twisting as though to release a muscle.

"This gentleman certainly is," Georgette said with a grin as she handed Anderson a freshly poured drink.

"Too cruel, Georgette! Mr Anderson did not have a servant to pull his toboggan up the hill," Miss Bentley objected.

"At least I have secured a beautiful woman to nurse me in my dotage." Anderson brought Georgette's hand to his lips and kissed her fingers, winking at her as he did.

Miss Bentley watched with unblinking fascination, reminding him what Georgette had said of her friend's interest in love and its various forms. He scarcely dared imagine what scenes might arise when her unbridled curiosity was met by the colonel's unwavering frankness.

"Fitzwilliam tells me you are hoping to receive your relations at Matlock," he said to her. "I am sure they will be delighted when they hear your news."

"Thank you. Have you sent word to your brother yet?"

Anderson grimaced wryly. "Ah…no. Randalph is unlikely to be interested."

"That is a shame. What would your older brother have thought?"

Anderson's insides twisted sharply at the wholly unexpected mention of Matthew. Yet, Miss Bentley was regarding him earnestly, the look in her eyes one of neither pity nor meanness but simple, ingenuous interest. The knot in his stomach eased a little in the face of such unaffected kindness.

"He would have absolutely adored Georgette. I thank you for asking."

"What about you, Mr Darcy?" Georgette enquired. "Does Miss Darcy know she has a new sister yet?"

"I have written to her," he replied. "She will be delighted by the news."

He stated it artlessly—some might say disinterestedly—but then, Darcy was not an effusive man. Indeed, he had a reputation for being serious and exacting. Anderson could see why people might think so, but the past few days had shown him glimpses of a man with far deeper feelings.

After all, a dispassionate man was not likely to be caught slashing a straw dummy to pieces in a jealous pique. A man who placed no value on connubial felicity would scarcely waste his time or his money salvaging other people's doomed engagements. And a man who was all implacable solemnity would not light up, as Darcy had just done, at the mention of taking his beloved new wife home to his cherished sister. Reserved he may be, but unfeeling he was not.

"I look forward to seeing you in town soon," Anderson replied and meant it.

"You plan to return directly?"

"We shall travel to Gilchester first, to tell everyone there our news, then on to London. I have business at the institution. I hope you will visit it. It would be a shame not to see what you have invested your money in."

"We certainly shall." With a slight frown, Darcy added, "I hope you will not rely on all your patrons showing an interest."

"What are you insinuating?" Saye demanded as he crested the brow of the hill with Miss Goddard on his arm.

"He means there are not enough hours in the day for you

to look at all the things you spend money on," Fitzwilliam remarked, arriving behind his brother with Mrs Darcy. Anderson was pleased to observe no hint of hostility from Darcy at the sight. Marriage had evidently settled his qualms.

"That is only true when I spend my money on you," Saye retorted.

The colonel replied with a snowball.

"For God's sake, mind his hair, Fitzwilliam. We shall never hear the end of it if you dishevel him," Darcy quipped.

"You are very quiet."

Anderson looked at Georgette. She was regarding him with some concern.

"I was only taking the measure of my new family," he assured her.

"And what is your opinion?"

She really was the most sublimely handsome woman Anderson had ever met. When she looked at him in this way, with solicitude, with love in her gaze, he felt his good fortune in every dusty corner of his soul. Yes, his new family was filled with intricate characters, all of whom he could admire in one way or another, and all of whom he looked forward to becoming better acquainted with. But he would know none of them had it not been for Georgette.

Her faith in him was astounding. When all the rest of the world had been happy to leave him in the shadows, she had seen him, and she had loved him. She had not been ashamed to bring him here, to guide her family and friends into knowing him, investing in him, liking him. She had made him a part of her family, and he loved her more deeply for it than he had ever comprehended it was possible to love anyone.

"My opinion is that they are all exceedingly agreeable, but that you, my love, are the very best of them."

She had no answer for that, which was the greatest

response she could have given him, for he knew it meant she liked what he said too well to be facetious about it.

"Let us all have a race, then," Mrs Darcy said.

"Sorry—what was that, Elizabeth?" Georgette asked.

"Saye has declared that Lilly can beat Elizabeth in a race," Miss Bentley explained. "She suggested we girls all race each other."

Georgette was game and jumped directly onto the nearest toboggan.

"Hardly a fair contest," Saye remarked with a snort. "Georgette and Miss Bentley cannot hold a straight line for more than five yards."

"That is easily resolved," Anderson replied, squeezing onto the toboggan behind Georgette and giving her a quick kiss on the cheek as he reached around her for the leading rope.

"Aye, we must be assured of an unswerving descent," Fitzwilliam agreed, seating himself behind Miss Bentley.

Not to be outdone, Saye and Darcy hastily found space on their respective ladies' toboggans.

"On three!" Saye called, and after the count, off they went, all laughing merrily, all perfectly well-matched as they set off on their journeys to the finish.

Epilogue

A Fortnight Thereafter

The note he received was nothing short of hilarious, but laughter aside, it required an answer. Uncertain of what answer he should give, Saye thought it best to talk it over with Fitzwilliam and Darcy. He found them together in Darcy's study, having only just returned from Rotten Row.

"You should have come with us," Fitzwilliam said. "Delightful morning, perfect for a ride."

"My nights are no longer my own," Saye replied. "I need my beauty sleep."

"You seem to be in uncommonly good humour," Fitzwilliam observed as he took the missive from his brother's hands. "What is this?"

"Do read it. I daresay you will be as diverted as I." Saye helped himself to some of the coffee they were drinking and settled himself on the chair nearby.

Darcy had leant over Fitzwilliam's shoulder to read, and

straightened, more alarmed than either of his cousins. "Balton-Sycke wants to meet you on the field of honour?"

"I know," Saye said with a grin.

"I suppose I am your second, then?" Fitzwilliam asked with a chuckle.

"Only if Sarah is unavailable," Saye replied. "After all, she has already proved her worth on the archery range."

"What right has he?" Fitzwilliam asked. "They were not engaged."

"No, but he had spoken with her father." Saye took a large swallow of the coffee. "It seems he felt it sufficient to stake his claim on her."

"Her father? But not her?" Darcy asked, still studying the note. Did he think it was written in ancient Egyptian symbols?

Saye reached out, jerking the page from Darcy's hands. "He had not spoken to her. Of this I am sure," Saye said firmly. "More's the pity, I should have liked to see the lobcock jilted."

"So you will offer an apology," Darcy said. "See a peaceful end to it."

"What am I to apologise for? Being handsomer than he? Cleverer? Richer? I cannot apologise for what I am, men."

"So you intend to fight him? What if he tears your hair out? What if you bleed on Florizel?"

Saye finished the last of his coffee and set the cup down firmly on the table in front of him. "Those are the chances I shall take, and gladly."

Being engaged in London exceeded all of Lilly's dearest expectations. Congratulations and felicitations abounded, her mother was proud of her and already calling her Viscountess, and her father had told her no expense would be spared for her trousseau. It was a rarefied time, exciting and love-washed, and she intended to commit every morsel of it to her memory—even this bit, entering a party on his arm as the whispers of admiration went up around them.

She was smiling and nodding to their friends as they passed when she heard Saye mutter, "Well, this is dashed awkward."

"What is?"

"Your friend is over there." Saye gestured across the room where stood Balton-Sycke, evidently attempting to appear fearsome.

"We all got on well enough at Matlock. Why should it be awkward now?"

"Because he is hoping to kill me tomorrow," Saye replied.

Lilly halted immediately, her former delight fled. "Wants to *kill* you?"

Saye shrugged and gave her hand a little pat. "Not to worry, my darling, there is no sacrifice too great for your honour."

Shocked and more than a little horrified, Lilly tugged him into the relative privacy of a small space behind a column nearby. Her cheeks had flushed hot and panic made her shaky. She could not allow it! He could be hurt, or maimed, or sent to gaol...nothing good ever came of a duel!

"You cannot duel," she said urgently. "I forbid it in every respect."

"Forbid me?" He gave her an imperious look, one brow raised.

"Yes, forbid you," she replied anxiously. Then she whispered, "Or next time you come calling at night, you will find my window closed!"

"That is as much to your detriment as mine," he hissed back. "If we kept score—"

"I know! But I am better able to withstand the lack! I already have for above two decades!" She felt her eyes fill with tears, and her voice shook a little as she said, "But what I cannot withstand is to be without you."

Saye's eyes softened, and he ran the back of two fingers down her cheek. "He will not—"

"Saye, I beg you not to do this."

"—kill me. I can shoot a pigeon—"

Her heart now throbbed in her throat, such that she could barely utter the next, most necessary words. Indeed she was ashamed that she had been too shy to speak them previously, but if they could now stop him from some manly foolishness, time was of the essence.

"—from two miles away and—"

"Saye! Listen to me!" She swallowed to gather her courage. "I love you. I do—I love you too dearly to let you endanger yourself in this careless, stupid way."

Her words had a shocking effect; Saye stopped talking. "What did you say?"

She laughed nervously, blinking madly through a blur of tears. "You heard me. Vain creature, I shan't puff your head up with more."

"Dear girl." He pulled her into his arms and murmured into her ear, "Do you truly?"

"Would I marry you if I did not?"

"Maybe," he said, pulling back to peer into her face. "After all, I am sinfully wealthy, devilishly handsome, and titled."

She smiled at him. "If you were a shabbaroon born of a stonemason, I would still be madly in love with you."

"I cannot believe how you have ruined me," he exclaimed. "I am tied to your apron strings! I might as well be one of these insipid poets who languishes about caterwauling about love. Or worse! I have become just like Darcy!"

At this, she laughed aloud, then kissed him once again before saying, "You have won my heart, and in some few weeks will have my hand as well. Do console poor Balton-Sycke with whatever apology his pride demands, and let us all part ways in peace."

He sighed heavily. "I shall go and speak to him. For you. And then I shall take you and your mother home, pretend to leave, and sneak up the back stair."

He left her then; she followed him around the column, watching as he moved through the crowd towards a fellow he scorned, to humble himself for her. *We shall be the happiest couple in the world,* she thought.

Five Months Thereafter

Colonel Richard Fitzwilliam was the happiest of men—or he expected to be, within a very few days. He was pleased now to greet Mr and Mrs Darcy from his own home, Bridgelands Manor.

It was a jewel, and though nothing to Pemberley, he did not require grandeur. All he needed was Sarah's happiness in creating a home to be treasured by them both. The ruggedly beautiful countryside appealed to something within him, and he had already begun the improvements recommended by his brother and cousin that would increase their income and the wellbeing of all who resided here.

"A long wait is almost finished," Darcy remarked once his wife had been shown to their chambers and they were alone in Fitzwilliam's study. "I must say, I thought you would take your own advice and beat Saye to the altar—instead of delaying the ceremony so long."

"And you will never allow me to forget it, will you?" Fitzwilliam asked, without heat. He deserved Darcy's mild ribbing, and a good deal more.

"Oh, in a decade or two the joke will grow old, I suppose," Darcy said, smiling. Darcy smiled often these days. "But seriously—you did seem eager to marry at the end of Saye's party. Mrs Darcy and I both were surprised at a delay of five months."

Fitzwilliam stretched his feet out before the fire. "Sarah has always felt like an outsider looking in upon society, observing more than experiencing. Her life, while it is a life she has enjoyed, has not always been an easy one, and she was unable to spend as much time with her friends as she may have wished. Even then, she is older than they are, and…"

Darcy nodded, and Fitzwilliam knew he need not explain more. His Sarah was different, and there was no getting around it. She was also the most joyful woman he had ever known, and loving beyond his wildest dreams. He could not wait to make her his wife in all ways, and complete the love he felt for her, to wake every morning in her bed or her in his…*Stop it,* he warned himself, conscious of Darcy's knowing look. He was accustomed to bridling his passions, but it was not easy.

"I wanted her to have the rest of her Season, and dance attendance upon her with the world watching me do it. I wanted her to…to have some fun. Besides which, my mother had distinct ideas about what bringing her into the family should mean, in the way of balls, a trousseau, et cetera, et cetera."

"How does Miss Bentley do with your dear mama," Darcy said, with another hint of a smile. Everyone knew that Lady Matlock was as formal as any countess in the realm.

"It was difficult in the beginning," Fitzwilliam admitted.

"But the Easter visit to Lady Catherine's...well, let us just say that Sarah's conversations with our aunt managed something that my mother, with all her flinty politeness, never managed. She shut her up."

Darcy's brows rose. "Shut up Lady Catherine? Impossible!"

Fitzwilliam's answering smile was sly. "Indeed. It is just that Sarah was so genuinely interested in what Lady Catherine had to say, questioning her, in the most well-bred way, on her feelings about nearly every subject—and then rhapsodising about imperial three-tongued maggots or the like, with anecdotal evidence to prove *they* felt the same way. I believe our aunt grew afraid to say anything for fear of being compared to a cockchafer."

Darcy laughed aloud. "And our aunt did not attempt to put her in her place? I am astonished!"

"Well, she did, of course. But clever Sarah would only find another marvellous similarity, until Lady Catherine evidently decided silence was her only recourse. Never even suspected Sarah was putting her on, what with Father encouraging her. But what truly won Mother's heart was how she treated Anne."

Darcy's brows rose, because, as they both knew, sickly, cross Anne was not known for her affability.

"Sarah was so careful with her, quietly spending time with her, showing gentle interest...just as if Anne were some shy, reclusive woodland creature she was attempting to tame, persisting until she found subjects of interest to them both. It was not easy, by Jove—but by the end of the visit, Anne was taking her about in her phaeton, *laughing* with her."

They were both silent a few moments. "I believe you discovered a rare gem at a common house party," Darcy mused.

"Hah! There is nothing common about Saye's parties."

Darcy nodded. "I would never admit it to him, but… praise the heavens it is so."

And both men smiled.

Sarah sat before a large, mirrored dressing table in a chamber that had been her grandmother's, left as it had been in Grandmama's day—pale yellows, ivory, and soft-blooming roses. Her reflection showed a wide-eyed, radiant bride, and she tried not to feel amazed at it.

"You look lovely, Sarah," Lady Matlock said. "The royal blue silk was just the thing, after all."

"Oh, you are beautiful, Sarah," Lilly, Lady Saye, put in, her golden curls appearing like another sun in the glass.

The door opened at that moment, and Georgette poked her head inside. Her brow raised in delight at the sight before her. "Well! You are positively dashing! Lilly, you had better tell Saye to be ready to restrain Fitzwilliam when she enters the chapel. It was very naughty of you, Sarah, to keep him waiting so many months. And I completely approve."

"Oh, but I am no *periodical cicadettine*—" Sarah began, as Lady Matlock's brows drew together.

"Dear Lady Matlock," Lilly interrupted, "I shall cry and spoil my own dress if I stay to admire the bride much longer. I had better fetch another handkerchief, though I suppose Saye will bring an extra. He is always prepared for me on such occasions, though he pretends to be annoyed."

"Yes," the countess agreed, "we had all best go down. Your father will be here any moment." She patted Sarah's shoulder. "We shall see you in the chapel. I daresay your groom will behave as a gentleman ought." She cast her young relation a warning glance, but Georgette only grinned unrepentantly.

Finally alone, Sarah breathed a little sigh of relief. Thank goodness for Lilly, and her kind friendship; she had eased the way for Sarah more than once in the last months. In retrospect, she could remember that her mother-in-law would not understand the comparison between a grasshopper who mated once every ten years and her own lengthy betrothal, but she could be forgiven a few lapses on her wedding day.

There was a knock on the door. "Come in," she called, rising from her velvet stool as her papa entered—and blushing when he halted in surprise at the sight of her.

"Well then," he said, after a moment of silence. "My dear girl. My very dear girl."

She bit her lip to halt her own tears, while he fumbled for his handkerchief and loudly blew his nose.

Holding out his arm, together they made their way down towards a carriage pulled by four matching white horses and bedecked in cream-coloured roses. "It is beautiful, Papa," she breathed.

"Like you," he said, pausing, for once not showing a single sign of distraction. "I warned that pup you are marrying: I know a thousand untraceable means of killing a man. He *will* treat you well."

"Oh, Papa," she beamed up at him.

The short ride to the chapel passed in a heartbeat. And then there was young Percy, grinning, sweeping open the door with a flourish, looking very grown up as she blew him a kiss.

Finally, finally, she could see her groom, so utterly handsome in his wedding clothes. His expression as she walked to him would remain with her always.

"Dearly beloved," the vicar began at last. Richard reached for her hand, uncaring that it was not yet time.

"I love you," he mouthed.

"Always," she whispered, a vow as sacred as any they had yet to share.

Eighteen Months Thereafter

Georgette had not doubted Saye would succeed in making Anderson's institution the most fashionable charitable cause in London. She had, however, shared her husbands' scepticism for the longevity of that renown. Nevertheless, a year and a half on, its popularity had not waned. At least two dozen peeresses were still desirous of putting their names and their husband's money into the venture. Several of them were present that afternoon at the fête arranged to honour the home's newest patron and—so they had let it be rumoured—where Anderson would be reconnoitring for others.

Georgette had the less well-advertised but far more enjoyable task of weeding out the unsuitable candidates. She was presently speaking to Lady Swift, a robust woman who was seizing as possessively to Georgette's every *bon mot* as she was clutching her plate of petit fours to her bosom.

"I have always admired your husband, Mrs Anderson," she said. "One cannot help but respect such philanthropy."

"I am pleased you approve. Though it is not strictly true that you have always respected him, is it? I recall you referring to him on more than one occasion as 'Blanderson'."

Lady Swift coughed, spraying crumbs everywhere. "Well, no, I...that is, if I did, it was only because I thought that was his name. I heard it said so often amongst my acquaintances."

"Were those the same acquaintances who nicknamed me

'Forgette' and put it about that I lighten my hair with lemon juice?"

Lady Swift mumbled an incoherent demurral.

"You are a true wit, madam. Though we had better not let you loose on the children at Mr Anderson's institution. They have rather more serious afflictions than banality and blonde hair. You would be in danger of exhausting your supply of puns."

"Yes, better to keep those for your friends, Lady Swift," said somebody behind them.

Her ladyship started. Georgette did not, for she recognised the distinctive Flemish accent.

"Viscount de Borchgrave, what a surprise to see you here. Are you interested in patronising my husband's institution as well?"

He only smiled and stared pointedly at Lady Swift until she made her excuses and hastened away. Once she was gone, he turned insouciantly to Georgette. "I was curious to see how you fared. I am relieved to discover that you look as well as ever. *Remarkably* well, considering."

Georgette refused to be drawn and only inclined her head.

De Borchgrave smiled. "You could have had *me*, Georgette."

"Oh, I know, but you could never have had me."

"You think yourself better than me, do you?"

She smiled expressively. "But that is not the reason I refused you. You were simply too late. I was already in love with Mr Anderson."

"Are you still in love with him?" he asked with a pout. "For I was going to suggest you could still have me. No one need know."

Georgette pinched his chin playfully. "That is a terribly sweet offer, Borchy—you are good to think of me—but I must decline. I am afraid I am every bit as in love with my husband now as I was then, if not more. But look, here comes your new wife. Perhaps she will oblige you if you are feeling unloved."

He cast a panicked glance over his shoulder, muttered something uncharitable, and beat a hasty retreat. Georgette pitied him, but not everyone could be as blissfully happy in marriage as she. Equally undesirous of speaking to the ghastly Viscountess de Borchgrave, she went in search of her two favourite people in all the world.

Anderson was supposed to be making himself available to the good and the great of the *haut ton,* but his attention had been entirely usurped by one particularly captivating person, and the task of securing extra patrons for the institution had been wholly forgotten. Ignoring the various clusters of nobles awaiting his attention, he stepped closer to the nearest shrub and pointed out a large pink flower to the bundle in his arms.

"You never get any less strange, do you?"

Anderson turned around in surprise. "Randalph! I had no idea you were in town."

"Had to get away for a few days."

Anderson sighed heavily and pointedly declined to enquire why. "I told you I would give you no more money. That last sum ought to have been enough to set you up for life." The babe whimpered with displeasure at being ignored; he adjusted his hold and hushed it soothingly.

Randalph pulled a disgusted face. "Is it not enough that you have made your fascination with London's Undesirables known to the whole world? Must you parade them around in front of every illustrious personage in town as well?"

A slow smile overtook Anderson's frown. "It is not unheard of for me to treat the children to a day out, 'tis true, but this one is not from the institution. This one is mine."

"Yours? But…I had no idea—"

"I have not seen or heard from you since Grandmother's funeral. I knew not where to send word. He is named Matthew, after our brother. Should you like to hold him?"

Randalph shook his head violently, but after a moment, crept warily forwards, as though approaching a dangerous animal. "I suppose I could. He looks tolerably endearing."

Anderson handed his son into his brother's awkward embrace. "I have wondered more than once these past months whether you were still alive."

Randalph glanced at him ruefully. "Forgive me. I ought to have written. I have been busy attempting to make something of myself. I've not made too much of a hash of it, actually."

"Why have you left, then?"

His brother blushed and mumbled, "Small matter of a broken heart."

"Ah. Tricky things, those."

Randalph nodded.

"Will you come to dinner this evening?"

"Your wife would not object?"

Anderson chuckled. "Take the time to become acquainted with your new sister, and you will soon discover how absurd that question is." He reclaimed his son and led his brother towards the place he had last seen Georgette, daring to hope his family might at last be whole again.

Three Years Thereafter

"A penny for a posie?" sang a gentle tenor.

Smiling at the familiar voice, Elizabeth glanced up to see Darcy walking towards her across Pemberley's south lawn. Lowering her scissors from the rose bush, she placed them in the basket, her eyes never leaving the delicious sight of her husband in his waistcoat and shirtsleeves, his cravat discarded an hour earlier during a madcap game of croquet. After the festivities and demands of Georgiana's wedding and hosting a houseful of family and friends, she was happy to see the ease that had returned to him.

"None for sale, kind sir," she replied, laughing, as he came to stand beside her. "How did you find me?"

Darcy gave her a wry grin as he reached for the basket. "You may place the blame on your son, for bleating 'Mama' at full cry as the nurse led him away from your side."

"Much like his father, endlessly frustrated if left unaware of my whereabouts at all times."

"Minx." Darcy slipped his hand into hers. "The husband and children of Elizabeth Darcy will always wish to be in her presence, especially at this time." He leant over and kissed her cheek, his eyes fixed on the round swell of her midsection. "Are you well? Shall we sit?"

She shook her head and indicated walking was her preference. "I shall be improved in a month or so. It would appear we have ourselves another acrobat."

Darcy's brows furrowed. "A son who excels at cricket, or a daughter who dances, but not an acrobat, if you please."

Elizabeth laughed again as he led her along the path to where Pemberley's remaining houseguests were enjoying the fine summer weather. Young Bennet Darcy had been returned to the nursery, where he enjoyed the company of his younger—by mere months and weeks—cousins.

But at least one dawdler remained out of doors, gurgling on the knee of her father. Elizabeth smiled at the sight of Saye, lounging on the grass with Lilly and their daughter.

Florizel scampered about, exciting the little girl into fits of giggling.

Their antics prompted a chuckle from Darcy. "Saye's reputation for modesty is thrown over by his adoration of Annabella. A being more perfect than himself?"

"She is an angel."

"He is enamoured," replied Darcy. "He does not even begrudge his brother for begetting a son before him."

Elizabeth stifled a giggle. "Saye may even refrain from arranging an engagement in the cradle to her Darcy cousin, as is the Fitzwilliam family tradition."

Her husband managed not to growl, so she continued. "Do you know, I have spent untold hours with your cousins these past two years, but it was not until this week that I recognised the full likeness you share with them."

"In looks?" Darcy scoffed. "Saye would be appalled. He believes himself far prettier than Fitzwilliam. And though he never would say it in her presence, comelier than Aurelia."

Elizabeth bit her lip, amused that Darcy ignored any comparison to his own appearance. "I refer to the wonderful lack of dignity all of you display with your children. It is a true mark of parental love when the presence of a man's first child can render him so eminently silly. Saye and Fitzwilliam behave with their children much as you do with Bennet. You, however, have no equal in delighting me as husband and father."

Such a compliment merited his gratitude, and after expressing it as discreetly as one could on one's own estate, where a gardener, small escapee from the nursery, or overly inquisitive relation might suddenly appear, Darcy asked about her original statement. "Is the similarity also seen in the distaff side of the family?"

"Georgette has the mischief in her eyes, Georgiana is more heartfelt, but she is not yet a mother." Elizabeth felt her husband sigh. His sister had been wed only a few days, after an engagement he took pains not to prolong to a more favourable length. Then, in Pemberley's chapel, when Darcy had looked his most vulnerable, she had seen his cousins—Saye, Fitzwilliam, and Aurelia—with similarly pensive expressions as they stood with their spouses.

Now all of them could be seen on the lawn. Anderson and Georgette strolled arm in arm towards Sarah, who was gazing through a spyglass at something in the branches of a tall oak while Fitzwilliam stood watching her.

Darcy wondered at his wife's wistful expression, prompting him to reflect back on the festivities that had brought the family together at Pemberley, and in the past. "Georgiana made a lovely bride."

He felt Elizabeth sigh. "I regret I could not dance with you, but you cut an elegant figure with her."

"You were a beautiful queen, reigning over your subjects." Darcy looked at her thoughtfully. "We have attended countless balls, before our marriage and since, but you did not have the wedding or many celebrations you deserved. My aunt would have given you a ball, had she not been distracted with her sons' engagements."

"And our own distraction to 'just get on with it', as you said?"

"Forgive me," he said ruefully. "But do tell me, do you regret our lack of ceremony? Without even Jane to bear witness for you?"

"I had been without her since her marriage. I was eager for my own, to you." Elizabeth nudged him lightly. "There was much to be eager for, as I recall."

His face flushed. "Every minute of every day. My fervour has yet to wane. I proposed to you poorly the first time, and properly the second. Even though we were already betrothed, it was the last proposal—made by you—that was the most perfect."

"You were an obedient suitor, and you have become a forgiving son-in-law. You have become my father's favourite, and I have become your aunt's favourite..." She trailed off, laughing merrily at his vexed expression.

How she can soothe me, provoke me, and amuse me, all in one moment!

Darcy squeezed her hand and guided her carefully around Florizel and the large chunk of cheese he was devouring. "Forgiving Lady Catherine for her slights and insults is more easily done since she has moved her ire towards Saye and Lady Aurelia for the house party that brought wives to the Fitzwilliam brothers."

"And yet one Fitzwilliam cousin remains unwed—Anne," said Elizabeth as she settled onto the lawn blanket. She greeted Saye and Lilly, then grinned mischievously at Darcy.

"All of us are so content," she said, "I wonder if perhaps it is time for another house party? After all the matches made at Matlock, who knows what could happen at Rosings?"

The End

FROM THE PUBLISHER

The favour of your rating or review would be greatly appreciated.

Subscribers to the Quills & Quartos mailing list receive advance notice of sales, bonus content, and giveaways. You can join our mailing list at www.QuillsandQuartos.com where you will also find excerpts from recent releases.

QuillsandQuartos.com